ALIEN BOOTLEGGER
and Other Stories

Tor Books by Rebecca Ore

Alien Bootlegger
Becoming Alien
Being Alien
Declaration Rules
Human To Human
The Illegal Rebirth of Billy the Kid

ALIEN BOOTLEGGER and Other Stories

Rebecca Ore

A TOM DOHERTY ASSOCIATES BOOK
NEW YORK

This is a work of fiction. All the characters and events portrayed in this book are fictitious, and any resemblance to real people or events is purely coincidental.

ALIEN BOOTLEGGER AND OTHER STORIES

This book is printed on acid-free paper.

A Tor Book
Published by Tom Doherty Associates, Inc.
175 Fifth Avenue
New York, N.Y. 10010

Library of Congress Cataloging-in-Publication Data

Ore, Rebecca.
Alien bootlegger and other stories / Rebecca Ore.
p. cm.
"A Tom Doherty Associates book."
ISBN 0-312-85549-4
1. Science fiction, American. I. Title.
PS3565.R385A45 1993
813'.54—dc20 93-19381
CIP

First edition: August 1993

Printed in the United States of America

0 9 8 7 6 5 4 3 2 1

Contents

Alien Bootlegger

1

Lilly Nelson at the Hardware Store

When I first saw the alien was the first warm day after a terrible winter of layoffs. Years like these, men stare at the seed packs, the catalogues for fertilizer spreaders, and wonder if they've got enough land for a distiller's corn crop. Or would the mills hire back soon enough as to make farming superfluous? Rocky Mount was full that day of men speculating about turning back to what their ancestors did back when southwestern Virginia was the frontier. Sort of like what didn't starve out the great-grandparents won't starve out us. But few had kept their tractors. No one had draft animals. The ancestors had hated farming like crazy, and the descendants really wanted the factories to start hiring again. But meantime, let's get some equipment clerk to distract us or go out and gossip about the alien.

My own business wasn't off—none of my Driving Under the Influence clients had written me a bad check yet—but I'd still gone to the hardware store, even knowing how crowded it would be. I needed my own distraction. Fibroids waited in my uterus for a sonogram on Tuesday, so today I hefted plastic mesh bags full of spring bulbs, comparing the lies on the package flap to the real flowers I'd seen the last summer I'd planted them.

Just my luck, I'd have to have surgery. Odd, I'd never wanted children, and it would have been absurd to have a child to take care of when I was forty-three and had my aunt Berenice to worry about, but to have it come to this. Then while I was drinking a Dr Pepper for the caffeine to soothe my addiction headache and waiting for a clerk to sell me some dahlias, the alien walked in and I was finally distracted.

Nobody wanted to acted like a gawking hick. We watched each other to time one quick stare apiece, aiming our eyes when nobody else was looking. The hardware store itself looked weird after I looked away. The alien jolted my eyes into seeing more detail than I'd ever noticed before—dead flies on a fly strip, the little bumps in the plastic weave under my fingers, a cracked front tooth in the clerk's face as he came around the counter.

"Welding equipment," the alien said as a nervous man in a business suit tugged on one of his long bony arms. "Stainless steel welding equipment, stainless-steel pipe, stainless sheets, stainless-steel milk tank."

The clerk looked at me. I nodded, meaning *okay, deal with that first.*

As the clerk came to him, the alien adjusted the flow on an acetylene torch. He looked like a man crossed with a praying mantis, something a farmer watched for crop-damaging tendencies. In the chitinous head, the eyes looked more jelly-like than decent, though I suspect my own eyes in that head would look just as bad. Actually, the eyes were more or less like human eyes; it was the ears that were faceted like stereo speakers. Big enough. Little indentations inside the facets. I bet it could tell you precisely where a noise was coming from.

So here the alien is, one of the ones about which we've been reading all the reassurances the government chose to give us, I thought. One was hiking the Japanese central mountain crest trail. That was the one the media went crazy over, but others were living in Africa working on tilapia and other food-fish recombinant DNA projects and weaving handicrafts or in Europe taking sailing lessons or studying automotive mechanics. They'd all arrived in a faster-than-light ship and said they were tourists. Yeah, sure, but they had that FTL ship and we didn't.

"Lilly, told you I been seeing saucers since 1990 down in Wytheville off I-77 junction," a bootlegger's driver said to me quietly. I looked at the man and wondered if he was driving for one of the DeSpain cousins now. Berenice was always curious about the DeSpains, as though they were a natural phenomenon, not criminals at all. She accused me of resenting criminals who made more money than I did.

"Look at its ears," I said, meaning *let's not talk until it's out of the building at least.*

He considered them and looked back at me with tighter lips.

I shrugged and visualized the fibroids down inside me, flattened sea cucumbers squirming around. Maybe the alien would bring us better medicine? He bought his equipment and said, "Pickup truck with diplomatic plates."

"Bring it around to the side," the clerk said, trying to sound normal, almost making it.

After the alien left, the bootlegger's driver said, "What is he planning to weld stainless for?"

We all knew one of the options—still-making, no lead salts in stainless-steel boys' product, and the metal was cheaper than copper. Or maybe he was setting up a dairy? "Maybe he's a romantic." I paused. "You ever consider working for Coors?" I said before walking back to the office. I knew his answer before he could have replied—

driving legal was a boring-ass job; driving illegal was an adventure.

Tomorrow was Legal Aid, so I wanted to get the partnership papers filed on the Witherspoon Craft Factory before five. I dreaded Legal Aid. When times were bad, the men screamed at their wives and children, and the women wanted divorces. If he beats you, I'd always say, I'll help you, but just for yelling at you, come on, honey, you can't support kids on seven dollars an hour. Better to dust off the old copper pot and get a gristmill, clean the coil, fill a propane tank, and cook some local color in the basement that tax evaders and tourists pay good money for.

When we heard the aliens were just tourists, the first joke everyone in Franklin County seemed to have heard or simultaneously invented was if having one around was going to drive up real estate taxes again.

When I got into the office, the answering machine was blinking. My aunt Berenice spoke off the disc: "I remembered hearing where Patty Hearst was hiding, but I think it was just some fire-mouthing. Even then, I was getting too old for simple rhetoric. Bring me something . . . I forget now . . . when you come home. And, Lilly, your message makes you sound impossibly country."

It wasn't that she was that senile, Berenice was simply righteously paranoid from a long radical life. I made a note to pick up some single scotch malt from Bobby. He was making fine liquor for now. An independent, but maybe everyone would leave him alone because he made such classic liquor. And he had hospital bills to pay. Pre-existing condition in his child.

Then I wondered why I wasn't more excited about the alien. Maybe because I had so much to worry about myself, like who was going to take care of Berenice when I went under the knife?

I filled the partnership papers at the courthouse and drove by Bobby's to pick up the single malt. When I pulled up at his house, he was sitting on the porch, twitching a straw in his hand.

"Bobby," I said. He had to know what I was here for.

"Yo, Luce. I had a visitor today."

"Um," meaning *are you going to be a client of mine anytime soon*?

"One of the DeSpains."

"You been aging it for five years—"

He interrupted, "More."

"So didn't you just slip it to friends like I suggested? It's not like you do it for a living."

"I do need the money. But I wanted to make really good liquor. Seemed less desperate that way."

"It's fine liquor," I said.

"It was fine liquor," Bobby said. "DeSpain isn't going to make me his man."

"Well, Bobby," I said, watching the straw still rolling between his hands, "be careful." What could I tell him? Dennis DeSpain wasn't the roughest cousin, and nothing in the liquor business was as rough as the drug business. "You don't have any liquor now?" Bobby shook his head, the straw pausing a second. Now I had to stop by the ABC store before I went home. Daddy always said legal liquor had artificial dyes and synthetic odors in it.

When I got up to go, Bobby said, "I guess my wife will have to start waiting tables over at the Lake. I'm just lucky I'm on first shift. In the dye house." We both knew why the dye house never laid anyone off—the heat drove close to a hundred percent turnovers there.

"When I was younger," I said as I got my car keys back out of my purse, "I was going to reform the world. Then, Franklin County. Now . . ."

"Yeah, now," Bobby said.

"Well, I won't have you as a client, then."

He jerked his shoulders. "I don't know what I thought I was doing."

"Liquor-making the old way is a fine craft."

"Oh, shut the fuck up, Lilly. I thought if I did it fine, it wouldn't be so desperate. Man with bad debts turns to making liquor."

So, bad times and no simple solutions. I sighed and got in the car, then remembered the alien buying stainless-steel welding equipment, his fingers longer than a man's but fiddling with the valve with the same bent-head attention as a skilled human.

I drove back to the ABC store. The alien was leaning against the wall of the ABC store, eating Fig Newtons. At his feet was an ABC store brown bag full of what looked like sampler bottles. The man with him looked even more nervous than the two of them in the hardware store, furtive like. When the alien opened his mouth to bite, I saw his teeth were either crusted with tartar or very weird. They were also rounded, like a child draws teeth, not squared. He stopped to watch me go in. When I came out with the legal malt whiskey, I nodded to him.

"Lawyer," he said. "Ex-radical. Wanted to meet you, but not so much by accident that you'd be suspicious." I went zero to the bone. The voice seemed synthetic, the intonation off even though the accent was utter broadcast journalism.

"He's very interested in Franklin County," his human guide said. "And liquor." Poor guy sounded like he knew precisely why the alien had bought all the stainless-steel welding equipment and the liquor samples.

"Really?" I said, not quite asking, remembering quite well the year when most of the distillers went to stainless steel—thank God, no more of the car-radiator stills that killed drinkers.

The man said, "I'm Henry Allen, with the State Department. He's Turkemaw of Svarti, a guest of our government."

"And a vegetarian," I said, having recovered enough to pass by them and get back in my car. A farmer would try

Sevrin dust or even an illegal brew of DDT if he saw the alien in a stand of corn.

I don't know why I think farmer—I've never farmed day one in my life and I lived in New York for years. Berenice complains I sound like I'm trying to pass for redneck, but the sound's inside my head, too. Back at home, a chill intensifying with the dark, Berenice and a young black woman were sitting on the porch talking. They didn't have the porch light on, so I knew they'd been sitting there awhile, Berenice in the swing, the black woman stiff on the teak bench, both so absorbed in each other they were oblivious to the cold and dark. I tried to remember her name . . . Mary . . . no, Marie, a chemical engineering student who'd grow up to be one of those black women who'd gone to college and become plant chemical control officers, rather ferocious about their rise up. Berenice loved anyone who had ears to listen and hadn't heard all her stories yet.

As I got out of the car, I felt a bit ashamed of myself for thinking that. She'd told me enough about Marie that I should have realized Berenice listened to her, too.

When Berenice said, "And the Howe women I knew from Boston said that Emily Dickinson was a senator's daughter and that she tried like a motherfucker to get published," the girl threw her head back and laughed. Laughed without holding back, genuinely fond of my aunt, genuinely amused, so I thought better of her.

Marie said, "They didn't teach me that at Tech."

"No, professors all want to believe they're more than schoolteachers, but they don't know what real poets are like." Berenice could be fierce about this. One of her husbands or lovers wrote poetry books that sold in the forties of thousands. "Always remember you're more than a chemical engineering student, Marie. Everyone is always more than the labels other people want to put on them."

"Of course I'm more than a chemical engineer," Marie said, tightening the dignity muscles again. I reminded myself of what I'd been like at eighteen and felt more compassionate to us all.

"Terrella—" Berenice began. I remembered hearing about Terrella, the black woman bootlegger in the forties who killed a man.

"Terrella," Marie said. "That kind of kin threatens me."

I set the bottle down by Berenice. She sniffed and opened it, sniffed again. "Argh, fake esters. What happened to Bobby's?"

"DeSpain."

Marie stiffened. Yeah, I remembered too late that I'd named a lover she'd just broken with. Berenice had heard quite a bit about it, as Berenice, when she was in her best mind, could get people to talk. I'd hear more later. Berenice said, "Lilly, get three glasses."

"I don't want to talk about Terrella," Marie said again. As I got the little glasses we used for straight liquor, I wondered if two denials made a positive. Terrella wore long black skirts way into the fifties, with a pistol and a knife hidden in the folds. Her hair had grown into dreadlocks before we ever knew the style was a style and had a name. She left $25,000 and a house to her daughter when she died, which was remarkable for a black woman in those days, however she got the money. Berenice admired people who could work around the system and not lose, even when they were criminals. To Berenice, one should never resign oneself to any status other people thought appropriate.

"So you're kin to Terrella," I said, putting all the glasses on the table that went with the bench and pouring us each about an inch of the Scotch.

"I'm even kin to Hugous, the man who runs The Door 18."

"Smart man," Berenice said. "Terrella was smart, too."

"She was a hoodlum," Marie said. "Hugous—"

"Hugous puts money aside, no matter how he makes it," Berenice said. "That's always useful in a capitalist state.

Considering that sloppy capitalism's all we have to work with." Berenice freed her long gray hair to dangle radical-hippie style and grinned at me. So she'd always been looser and more tolerant than I. I had enough rigidity to get a law degree so that I could support her. Retirement homes, even ones better than she could have afforded, terrified her.

Not that we weren't more two of a kind than anyone else in the county, but I always wanted to organize the poor while she thought the poor ought to kick liberal ass as well as boss ass.

"I saw the alien today after I made the appointment for the sonogram," I said.

"Fibroids. Mother had them," Berenice said. "They thought they were cancer and sent her womb to Wake Forest."

"Jesus, Berenice," Marie said. "That's like hearing Dennis talk about jail rape."

So, I wondered, what was the context? Did Dennis rape or get raped? Berenice picked up her scotch and drank it all down in one swallow, the crepey skin jerking on her scrawny neck, the long gray hair flying. "Well, Marie, you like your life?"

"It's fine," the girls said tonelessly. "I like Montgomery County better than here."

Meaning gossip in Rocky Mount about Dennis DeSpain was a problem, I thought, and none of the Tech students knew yet that she had outlaw kin. I looked at Berenice. Marie got up to go, her hypercorrect suit wrinkled anyway around her rump. I watched as she got in her little Honda.

"Berenice, I saw the alien buying welding equipment."

Berenice said in a conspiratorial whisper, "Marie can weld, too."

"DeSpain won't like that."

"Dennis taught Marie about bootlegging. She left him because he tempted her."

"Tempted her? I mean, it isn't like half of Rocky Mount

didn't see them having breakfast and smelling of come last fall."

"Tempted her to become a bootlegger. I suspect it's become like any other supervisory job to Dennis and he needs to have someone new see him as glamorous and dangerous."

"Jesus, I thought he was about half in the Klan, certainly able to fuck blacks, but not able to admit they've got brains as good as a white boy's."

"Marie's definitely smarter than most white boys." Berenice looked for the clip she'd pulled out of her hair and tucked all her hair in the clip behind her neck again. "She's specializing in alcohols and esters. State's going to legalize liquor-making one of these days to get some of the taxes."

"Why would a Tech student want to make liquor?" I said, angry that she'd risk a college degree for something that trivial. Not so trivial, perhaps, if one was Bobby sweating in a polyester dye house for two dollars an hour over minimum wage, but for a chemical engineering student—stupid.

"I didn't say she was making liquor now," Berenice said. She looked down at her hands, then rubbed a large brown patch between her index finger knuckle and her thumb. "First sign I had I was getting old were wrinkles going up and down my fingers on the palm side. Nobody ever warned me about them. I like Marie, but the youth doesn't rub off, does it?"

"Berenice, there's an alien in Franklin County."

"So the government put it here. We never have any real say, do we? Alien? No different than a foreigner in most folks' minds." *Foreigner* means from outside our home county. The Welsh brought the concept with them, which is only fitting, as *welsh* means foreigner in Anglo-Saxon. Berenice continued, "You think Marie's sad, don't you? Like self–cultural genocide? Maybe she'd be happier if she were more like Terrella?"

"Cultural genocide is a stupid term. It trivializes things like really murdered people."

"Well, then I'll just say she's awful divided against herself then."

"Are we supposed to judge blacks?"

"It's racist not to," Berenice said, and I realized she'd been teasing me. Berenice could be such a yo-yo, but she'd ceased to take herself seriously without giving up what had been good about her ideals. Taking her in, I had to watch her mind wobble, but right now Berenice seemed fine, not bitterly ironic, not lapsing into the past because the present jammed in short-term memory, three-minute chunks throwing each past three minutes into oblivion. "Lilly, you're sure you're going to have to have surgery?" She asked sharply as though needing surgery were my fault.

If I did have cancer, Berenice would be extremely pissed. She'd have to go to a nursing home. The jittery insistance I tolerated for the delight she was on good days would get drugged out of her. I nodded, then said yes because she wasn't looking at me directly.

Berenice poured herself another whiskey, drained it, and said, "I've lived fully, interestingly. I'd rather lose my present than my past. At least senility won't suck that away. Did I tell you about the time I hitchhiked down to Big Sur and met Henry Miller?"

Not that she hadn't had senile moments already, I thought in pity. Then I realized I had not heard about Henry Miller and said, "Tell me."

DeSpain in Tailwater

DeSpain cast out with his Orvis rod, the Hardy Princess reel waiting for a big brown trout to inhale his Martin's

Crook rigged behind the gold-plated spinner. He was missing Marie, wanted her back and wanted to kill her, but he'd do a sixteen-inch-plus trout instead.

Or break the law and kill a little one. But DeSpain had principles. He broke the law only for serious money. One of his nephews who'd gone to Johns Hopkins said that DeSpain was trying to work sympathetic magic with the law.

The Smith River fell with the sun as the Danville and Martinsville offices and factories turned out their lights. *All but poachers out of the water in half an hour.* DeSpain remembered what the guide told him about trying on a stonefly nymph, but he hated strike indicators and fishing something he couldn't see upstream.

Intending this to be the last cast of the day, DeSpain pulled up the sink tip and cast the big wet fly and the spinner across the river, shooting out line, then reeling it in. Then he saw the alien standing in bare legs in the cold Smith River, casting with the guide, coming along the opposite bank. DeSpain realized that the alien was two feet longer in the legs than the guide, who was up to his hips in the river, closer to the bank than the alien.

DeSpain yelled, "I knew the Smith was famous nationally, but this is ridiculous."

The alien said, "DeSpain. Liquor distributor. Still maker."

The Smith wasn't chilly enough to suit DeSpain right then, and his waders were much too warm. He'd heard the alien was rude. Correct—rude or very alien. DeSpain remembered gossip about the alien and said, "Turkemaw, Svarti resident extraterrestrial, mate went back home after two weeks here." He felt better.

"Dennis, you fishing a stonefly nymph?" the guide asked.

DeSpain pretended not to hear and left his line in the water, no orange foam strike indicator on the leader, obviously either real cocky about his skill with upwater nymphs or not fishing one.

The alien pushed a button on a small box hanging like a locket around his neck. The box laughed.

DeSpain remembered hearing last week from one of his drivers that the alien had bought stainless-steel welding rods and that its farm had corn acreage. Everyone wondered if so conspicuous a creature was going to be so very more flagrantly making liquor. Or maybe the creature was making spaceships in its basement? "Be careful," he said to both of them. After they waded on, DeSpain caught the spinner and fly in his hand, then switched to the stonefly nymph.

A trout took it. As he played it, then reeled it in, it came jaws out of the water, eyeballs rolled to see the hook in its mouth. He netted it, then measured it: fifteen inches three-quarters. *We can fix that,* DeSpain thought as he broke the fish's spine and stretched. *Bingo, sixteen and one-tenth. The hell I work sympathetic magic with the law.*

Satisfied with the dead trout, DeSpain left the river, his eidetic memory reviewing his investments, both legal and illegal. *I have to be so mean with the illegal ones.* Fourteen trucks out with piggyback stills, $200,000 in a Uzbek metallurgical firm, $50,000 in Central Asian cotton mills, and maybe $500,000 in various inventories, legal and illegal.

His brain began to run more detail, like a self-programming and overeager computer. No spreadsheets, he thought as he began to wonder again if he'd bought into the global equivalent of just another Franklin County. He had first wondered if the Armenians were cheating him, but then he considered he was damn apt at bullying other men into working for him. Let other people run their butts off when the law came to blow a still.

The true reality of the world wasn't Tokyo's glitter, DeSpain had long since decided after one trip to Tokyo, but the harsh little deals driven in places like Rocky Mount and Uralsk. Tokyo and New York could evaporate and the small traders would still be off making deals, machine oil under their nails, doing the world's real business.

But that nigger bitch got away from him like no man had ever been able to. Goddamn great body and smart, too. He had a lust like a pain for women like her and his wife, Orris. Yeah, Orris, she wanted him to have only simple women on the side.

He pulled the rod apart and wound down the line to keep the two sections together and the fly hook in the keeper. The trunk security chimed as he opened it. He pushed the code buttons and put the rod and vest in it before he stripped off his waders and boots and put them in a bag, then laid the trout carefully on ice, making sure it stayed stretched out.

Remembering that he paid $400 to get a ten percent casting improvement over the cheaper generic rod, DeSpain thought, *Wouldn't do that in business, but . . .*

"If you just want to kill trout, may I suggest a spinning rod," the clerk had said in tones that condemned meat fishing and people too cheap or insensitive to the nuances of a $400 rod.

Liquor. A man needs the illegal to bankroll him for the legal. "It's not romantic with me," he said out loud, thinking about the folklorist who'd come from Ferrum to tape his father about his grandfather's suicide after the feds broke his ring in the thirties.

DeSpain felt a touch of guilt that he was sending bootleg money out of the country, but no more than when he yanked an extra fraction of an inch out of a Smith River brown so that it would go over sixteen inches. He turned the key in the Volvo's ignition and drove home.

His wife came out when she heard the garage door open. When she wore her red silk dress like she was, she expected to go out to eat. Her hair was blowing, but instead of reaching to smooth it, she folded her arms across her breasts. DeSpain pulled on into the garage and turned off the electric eye. "Orris," DeSpain said in the garage, "what did you fix for dinner?"

"Steven's at Mother's. You owe me, Dennis. The bitch is a college student. You've even taken her out for breakfast."

"Why does that make it different? She's just another one of my dancing girlfriends. I'm tired."

"I can drive myself to Roanoke if you're that tired. I know what it means when a man wants to talk to a woman in the morning. And you were telling her about still workings. At breakfast."

DeSpain knew if he stayed home Orris would harangue his ass off about that bitch Marie. When a particular black woman was seducing him out of moonshine technology and college tuition, then he should have known Orris would see the woman as a real rival. "Okay, let's go. You don't have to drive." He wouldn't tell her that Marie had left him.

"To the Japanese place."

The Japanese place made Dennis nervous. Orris had picked up more about Japan than he had. "I need to log some items on the bulletin board." He watched Orris carefully for a loosening of those arms before he went inside. He got his Toshiba out of the safe, unfolded it, and plugged in the phone line. His bat file brought up all his bulletin boards: Posse Commitatus, the Junk Market, Technology Today, and Loose Trade. He pushed for the Loose Trade bulletin board and scanned through the messages. All his messages were coded:

TO RICHARD CROOK: BOONE MILLS LOST HUBCAP, FOUND, NO PROBLEM. GOT GAS AT THE USUAL. SPINNER.

TO MR. MAX: COLLEAGUES REALLY APPRECIATED THE LOBSTER. WOULD LIKE TO ORDER DOZEN MORE CHICKEN-SIZED.

TO RICHARD CROOK: HOPE CAN BUY ANOTHER FIVE LAMB'S FLEECES, WASHABLE TANNED.

TO BUD G. R. HARESEAR: NEED SOME SENSE OF PROGRESS REPORT.

One of his trucks had almost been busted at the Cave Spring I-81 exit Exxon station. Three of his suppliers needed deliveries. DeSpain made code notes and purged the messages. Then he noticed that the alien was asking in plain text if anyone wanted to sell it an old tractor. *Why is he on this bulletin board?* DeSpain swore he'd bring in the feds if the alien was going to be able to distill openly when people had to be discreet about it. *Fool, the feds brought the alien here to begin with.*

After DeSpain exited Loose Trade, he took his accounting disks out of his safe. He needed to ship out twenty-seven gallons to the small bars and then collect on some of the larger accounts. Follett's salary came due again. DeSpain paid his men full rate when they were in jail and half rate when they were on probation and not working a full schedule, but Follett would be off probation next week. Damn Follett, DeSpain thought, he just sits there when he's raided. Most of his still men had never been busted. He wrote a check on his hardware store account.

An image of the researcher listening to his grandmother came to mind, all romantic-ass about the business, and believing the guff that no one ever died at a still raid, that both sides of the game had an understanding. Yeah, and the mountain counties averaged a murder a week in the twenties and thirties.

His grandfather wouldn't have hanged himself over a game.

Orris came in and said, as though she hadn't been bitching at him minutes earlier, "I hope your foreign investments do well."

DeSpain rubbed his eyes and said, "I've got to go back over there in September."

"I'd like to go with you this time."

"Babe, it's just like Detroit over there. Really."

"If you went to Detroit for a month, I'd want to come along."

He wasn't sure if she were implying anything further, so he decided to just stomp change the subject. "You think I should wear a suit?" Wrong, that sounded hick asking his more sophisticated wife what to wear in the larger sense. DeSpain learned how to dress at Emory & Henry before they threw him out for getting arrested.

She said, "It's not Sunday."

"Man who looks like he was just in the river they know is rich enough not to care what a waiter thinks. Mud equals real estate."

Orris said, "Not on a nigger or a neck, mud doesn't."

DeSpain wondered if she thought her red dress would look like polyester if he didn't dress to match. He said, "I'll change," and she stepped her skinny body out on her high heels without indicating whether she was pleased or not. *Orris, an iris root.* DeSpain had looked it up once and wondered who in her family knew such an arcane thing.

He folded his computer and put all his records and it back in the safe, then found a blue suit to wear with a string tie. String ties made Orris nervous.

On the drive to Roanoke, she said, "Don't do that to me again."

"What, with a college student?" Dennis realized she knew the affair was over, but did she know the how and why?

"Right, Dennis."

"And if I did it with some poor-ass good old girl, I'd probably be fucking your family."

"So crude, but then what was I to expect, marrying a bootlegger."

"Not that I'm not employing half your cousins. The bitch left me, if that's any damn consolation."

She laughed, then said, "One of my friends said at least recently you'd been more considerate."

Stomp change again. "Did I tell you I saw the alien when I was fishing?"

"Dennis, you are so obvious when you don't want to talk about something. I heard he was rich."

"I suppose. He had a guide with him."

"And I've heard he's rude. Is he?"

"He told me to my face I was a still maker and a liquor investor."

"Maybe he's just alien, doesn't know not to think out loud. At least he didn't tell you about he knew about Marie."

"Gee, Orris, you can find the good side of anyone, can't you?"

"Not everyone," Orris said. They pulled up to the restaurant and walked in. "I need sashimi tonight," she said as if eating raw fish took guts.

Marie

Sometimes I play black and tough, but not at Tech. It'd be too easy to slide from a Dennis DeSpain to a drunk rich frat boy who knows his daddy's lawyer will get him off if he leaves a woman to strangle in ropes, or to a cracker trucker with a knife.

I hate my colorful ancestors, the liquor queens, the Jesus priestesses. Times were I suspected they just renamed a Dahomey god Jesus so they could keep on writhing to him.

But here I was, home for the weekend in a brick house in a compound that reminded me unpleasantly of anthropology class, the whole lineage spread kraal-style from broke-down trailers to $100,000 brick ranch houses with $20,000 in landscaping.

We were at least in one of the nice houses; Momma was waiting for me. "You broke with DeSpain like I told you. I'm satisfied."

"Yes, ma'am."

"I saw what you were taking at Tech when your grades came. We're not paying for you to learn bootlegging."

"Chemical engineering, Mamma."

She sat down on the piano bench and closed her eyes. I sat down on one of the red velvet armchairs and leaned my head back against the antimacassar. "I know they can use you at DuPont or in a dye house. Find a place that will pay you to take a master's in business. Daddy's been knowing a white boy all his life that's now doing that."

I wondered if we'd moved away from the trailer kin what my life would have been like. I could have grown up in Charlotte, North Carolina—black, white, and mulatto all doing airy things like architecture and graphics design. Momma saw the look on my face and said, "Do you think you collected all the white blood in the family?"

"No, Mamma."

"You white granddaddies better than that DeSpain."

Lapsing out of proper English again, Mamma? I rolled my eyes at her and said, "I need be studying." Yeah, yeah, I know Black English grammar has its own formal structure and I was hashing it.

"You need the computer?"

"Maybe I shouldn't have come home for the weekend. It's so depressing around here."

"You are an example to your kin."

I thought about Grannie crocheting billions of antimacassars like giant mutant snowflakes, rabidly industrious while her sisters slid by on their asses. "Do you think they really appreciate it?"

Momma asked, half interested and half to abruptly change the subject, "Is there really an alien down near Endicott?"

"He was walking around Rocky Mount, trying to pass for a good old boy. Yeah, let me get on the computer." Momma grew up associating computers with school as they didn't have node numbers and nets and gossip by the megabyte when she was coming along. I could access all sorts of trash while she thought I was studying.

Orris had left me a message on Loose Trade: DENNIS'S DANCING GIRLFRIEND: SORRY, BETTER LUCK/CHOICE NEXT TIME. I felt my tongue begin to throb; I'd pushed against my teeth so hard.

But before I sniped back at her, I noticed messages about the alien: ALIEN IS A BASTARD. HEARD WHEN PEOPLE CLAIM THEY WERE KIDNAPPED BY HIM, HE SAYS HE DOESN'T REMEMBER THEM IN A WAY THAT MAKES EVEN CRAZY PEOPLE FEEL REAL TRIVIAL.

I wondered if he had really kidnapped people, if his people had.

Another message about the alien: HE'S OFF BACK ABOUT A MILE AND A HALF FROM THE HARDTOP. WON'T LET THE HIGHWAY DEPARTMENT SELL HIM THE SURFACE TREATMENT EITHER.

I left a message to Dennis: MRS. DESPAIN CALLED. TERRELLA IF YOU WANT TO THINK OF ME THAT WAY. I knew he wanted me to be more like her than I could ever wish to be.

Then the alien came on the board in real time: PLEASE, I HOPE TO DO BUSINESS HERE. MY WIFE LEFT ME. I WISH ONLY TO LIVE QUIETLY. YOUR RESIDENT ALIEN.

Someone quickly typed back: ARE YOU FOR REAL?

I DON'T REMEMBER KIDNAPPING ANYONE FROM THIS COUNTY.

I wondered why an alien would be doing business on a semi-honest bulletin board and remembered Lilly saw him buying welding equipment. I typed, THIS BULLETIN BOARD ISN'T AS SECURE AS THE SYSTEMS OPERATOR MAY HAVE TOLD YOU WHEN YOU SIGNED ON.

The alien replied: IF I NEEDED SECURITY, I WOULDN'T BE ON THIS PLANET.

2

Lilly: As Alien as It Gets

The next Saturday, as I helped Berenice with her bath, I told her how startled I'd been when the alien told me my name and occupation.

"Lilly, you afraid of the alien?" she asked me, sitting in the tub covered with bubbles. I turned on the sprayer and began rinsing her hair.

"I was startled."

"Do you hate being startled at your age? I hate limping."

"Well, if you'd let me help you with the bath yesterday, you . . ." Nope, I needed to help her in and out of the tub all the time.

Berenice bent forward and pulled the drain lever down. "The alien wants to see you. He called here."

"Why?"

"He's on that bulletin board everyone uses for selling liquor."

"Everyone doesn't use it for selling liquor."

"DeSpain's on it. Bobby's on it." She leaned on me as

she stood up, all baggy skin over what seemed to have been fairly decent muscles. I rinsed her free of soap and wrapped a towel around her. "I said I was your aunt and that I'd like to talk to him even if you couldn't come. I faxed him my Freedom of Information file."

"Does he have a name?"

"He's calling himself Turk. Can we go over this afternoon? He said it would be acceptable. You don't have any appointments."

I shrugged and walked her into her bedroom. She sat down on the bed to dry off while I got together her panties, bra, slacks, socks, and top. L.L. Bean shipped just this week the thirtieth or so pair of a shoe she'd been wearing for over five decades. She watched me pull the paper out of the toes. "I don't wear them out often these days," she said as she wiggled into the slacks and top. I put the socks on her feet, smoothing them, then slipped the shoes on, tying the knots tightly so the laces wouldn't come undone and trip her. "So I've lived to see an alien in Franklin County."

And Berenice was going to make the most of it even if he wasn't the sort of client I wanted. I held her elbow as we walked to the car.

"Why did you fax him your Freedom of Information file?" I asked while the car ran diagnostics on the pollution control devices.

"Well, I thought an alien who came to Franklin County might be weird." She didn't want to see him unless he found the file unobjectionable.

I don't tell people about my past, but Berenice lets anyone she meets know what a bit part player she was in the events of '68. And I'm being cynical because bit player is all I've been, too. But Berenice refuses to admit that anyone has more than a bit part. I said, "I hope Turk was impressed."

The car diagnostics showed that the catalytic converter would need to be replaced soon. Thanks to the reprogramming I'd done to prolong the active-with-warning phase, that probably meant the converter was gone completely by now, as I'd been getting a REPLACE SOON reading for about four months now.

"There is a reason to keep the car burning clean."

"I guess, Berenice," I said as I pulled out of our driveway, "but I've got to replace the air conditioner at the office first."

"Your lungs aren't as fragile as mine."

"Don't play Earth Firster with me this afternoon, okay."

"No, that's not appropriate, considering who we're going to see."

I asked, "And where does this Turk live?"

"Shooting Creek section. Patrick and Franklin. On the line. He's renting from Delacort heirs."

I could visualize the place, three miles of mud roads, oil pan gashing rocks, then the house, some three-story family place slowly twisting to the ground, riddled with powder-post beetles. The grandchildren would own and neglect it and rent it to summer people. Or aliens, why not? Maybe the Turk liked leaking roofs?

We drove down to Ferrum and took the road toward Shooting Creek. The road was exactly as I'd imagined it, but the house looked like several military freight helicopters had to have dropped it in last week. It was a replica of a ranch house. No, just because an alien lived there didn't mean it wasn't actually a ranch house.

Berenice looked a long while, then said, "I wonder if he got the design from TV real estate channels."

The alien came up to us, his machine laughing for him. "Ladies, lawyer, radical social worker. Berenice's file fascinates."

"Where did you get the house?" I asked.

Turk said, "Restored it."

Berenice looked slightly disappointed. I tried to remember what I could about the Delacourt family, but they were as mixed a bunch as anyone in the area, from jewel thieves to corporate executives.

We followed Turk around to the kitchen entrance. The backyard looked freshly bulldozed, raw soil faintly hazed with grass seedlings. I heard an exhaust fan running and couldn't make out where the sound was, exactly. Exhaust fans in strange places trigger my sniffing reflex—but no mash odor here, or alcohol smell either.

Turk moved a few magazines—one in some alien script that could have been just another Earth language—and we sat down.

"Do you want to meet people or do you prefer to be left alone?" I asked.

His ear facets glinted as he shifted his head. "Some people," he answered. His tongue flicked out, bristled at the tip. Like a lory, I thought, a nectar-feeding parrot. He asked, "Would you like a drink?" That was the most complete sentence I'd heard him speak.

"Yes," Berenice said quickly.

The alien made the kitchen look bizarre. His hands made the brushed nickel sink fixtures look like spacecraft gizmos that would regulate fuel mixes or the temperature of water, just as he was doing here, filling a glass teakettle that looked like laboratory equipment. The light mix—I thought—he's got weird-spectrum tubes in the fixtures. Then my mind redid some parameters and the kitchen looked like a kitchen with an alien in it, setting a glass teakettle on a burner. Berenice tightened the muscles around her mouth. She didn't consider tea a drink.

"Why did you come to Franklin County?" I asked.

"I heard about Franklin County from time-aged analogues," Turk said as he reached up in his cupboard for glasses and a teacup. Berenice watched the teacup as though hoping it wasn't for her. "But isn't here Franklin County?" He stuck his hand back into the cupboard and came back with a bottled and bonded vodka. Berenice smiled, but sat down when her legs began to quiver.

The Turk poured vodka, then tonic into two glasses for us, then put some dried green leaves in a strainer, balanced the strainer over his own cup, and filled it from the teakettle. He narrowed his eyes, but his face seemed bizarre even with that expression. I realized he'd made it with eyelids alone, without shifting a face muscle. His face skin was too rigid for muscle gestures to penetrate.

I moved to take the drink the Turk offered me and realized I was stiff. He came closer to Berenice with hers, recognizing her feebleness, perhaps.

It was alcohol but not vodka. Berenice said, "I understand you're on Loose Trade."

An iridescent flush washed over the Turk's face. He lifted his strainer and put it in the sink. The herb he'd used in his brew wasn't tea, but wasn't anything I knew to be illegal. He added white grains, about a quarter cup, of what was either sugar or salt. A sugar or a salt, I reminded myself, or protein crystals, not necessarily dextrose or sodium chloride.

I smelled my drink again and caught an echo of that herb smell as though he'd put a sprig of the herb in the liquor bottle.

Berenice said, "Can you drink alcohol yourself?"

"No." The alien put his tongue down close to his tea and rolled it into a tube. He dangled the fringed end in the tea for a few seconds before drawing the tea up. His eyes widened as if the tea startled him. Definitely a drug, I thought.

Berenice sipped her drink, but she kept her face carefully in neutral. She said, "You know this isn't vodka?"

"Yes," the alien said. "I would like to put Lilly on retainer." He spoke as though he'd memorized the phrase.

"I'm not a bootlegger lawyer," I said.

"Don't be so stuffy," Berenice said. "They're social outlaws."

"They all become mill owners in the end."

The alien said, "I will never become a mill owner in the end."

I stopped mentally cursing all the liquor makers and investors and looked more closely at the alien. "What is your civic standing here?"

"Resident alien," he said. "I am legally human."

"What kind of retainer?" I said, thinking about replacing the old air conditioner with one more compatible with the ozone layer.

"Ten thousand for the year. I can pay you now." He went to one of the cabinets and began laying hands on it, then pushing it. The door opened as if it were quite dense. Turk pulled out a contract and then counted out ten stacks of bills, Crestar bank wrappers still on them.

I asked, "Do you expect to get busted?"

He looked at me, flushed rainbow again, then said, "I plan to have fun."

I hated him for a second. "It's not a game for the people around here. People get killed."

"Killed is an option. Bored, not."

"Glad you feel that way. You're risking it." I looked over his contract. I'd have to defend him in any criminal or civil suit during the year of retainer for my usual fee less twenty-five percent. I sighed and signed it, then said, "You really need a checking account."

Berenice said, "Or DeSpain's broker."

Turk said, "I had most invested in a money market."

I wondered how long the aliens had been dealing with the government, and what these aliens were to a ACLU part-time radical lawyer like me. "Why me?"

The alien studied me three seconds, then said, "You're odd."

"I don't know why I'm agreeing to this."

Berenice said, "Because you get bored in Rocky Mount, too."

Turk blinked slowly at me, then nodded as if translating

blinks to nods with his cross-species semiotic dictionary. I blinked at him and he triggered his laugh machine. I thought I'd gotten too old for illegal thrills, but then Berenice proved that was impossible for those of my lineage.

Bobby Wasn't Working

MR. B. CORN WON'T DO IT, DeSpain read on the computer screen. *Damn Bobby, I'm going to get the boys to beat him.*

He went in to the bathroom and saw Orris washing her feet, rubbing them under the running tap in the tub. It reminded him of broke mountain people living in waterless shacks, hauling jugs of water up from neighbors. Her mother had grown up like that, washing bony dirty feet with water from milk cartons, in a thirty-dollar-a-month house wired for enough electricity to take care of the stove and the rented TV. Seeing Orris washing her feet made DeSpain's stomach lurch. "You need a bath, Orris, take a whole one."

"I just got my feet dirty when I was working in the garden." She looked up at him with her pale eyes. He suspected she washed her feet this way to tell him that he was only a bit further from the shacks than she.

"Bobby won't work for me."

"You do what you need to," Orris said. She got out of the way of the toilet so he could piss, which he always needed to do when he got angry. Her dress rode up her thighs as she toweled her feet dry.

"I'm glad you understand that."

"Why does washing my feet bother you so?"

"It reminds me of welfare bitches too broke to have tubs."

"I was doing it in one of our *three* tubs. You do what you need to do, Dennis, and I trust the tubs won't evaporate."

DeSpain thought, *don't keep leaving Steve with your mother to let him pick up hick ways, too,* but said, "I really won't trust the money until I've got a good income coming from something safe."

"Safe? Then maybe I do need to keep in practice for water conservation if you think we might end up back having to haul it from a well." Orris smiled and went out of the bathroom in her bare feet, heels chapped as though shoes were new to her.

DeSpain had kin, distant kin, living on roads so rough Social Service made visits in four-wheel-drive vehicles. "Safe. Like a marina on the lake. The Russian stuff isn't safe enough."

Orris, from her bedroom, said, "You'd be bored shitless smiling at rich foreigners and gassing their idiot two-bedroom yachts in a lake too small for an overnight cruise."

"You want one of those yachts."

"Not here. Maybe in Russia, on the Black Sea." He could tell from her voice that she was smiling.

"I guess I should call the nephews and cousins."

"Is he making liquor behind your back, Dennis?"

"He won't make it. I thought it would be great for the lake people—good liquor, fine made, aged. Run them some bull about our Scottish heritage and Bobby's old family equipment passed on for twelve generations. Look, I already do the same thing as gassing tourists' boats."

"If he quit . . . I don't know, Dennis. I know you can't afford to get soft-headed."

"You want to go with the boys and lay in a few licks, too?"

"Might take you up on that, Dennis."

The notion of Orris in jeans and a pillowcase hood beating a man appalled Dennis. She was strong enough, he knew. He said, "Let us men take care of it."

"Okay, Dennis, but I'll go if you need me. Maybe if I beat up his wife . . ."

"Well, I appreciate that, Orris." Dennis went back in his room, turned off the computer, and put the 9-millimeter Beretta Orris gave him for Christmas in his briefcase. Pausing in front of the dresser, he stared at his collection of car keys and decided to take the pickup he'd gotten at the government auction. Let them take it and resell it again. He wondered if they could seize the Volvo, just because it might have come from liquor money. He pulled off his white shirt and pulled on a Japanese T-shirt he'd picked up in the Urals. Then dark glasses with the enhancer circuit in case he got caught by the dark. He grimaced at himself and added a Ford Motor Company baseball cap. Maybe some chewing tobacco? he wondered.

Orris's reflection appeared in the dresser mirror. "Wear that cap in Uralsk where nobody knows what it means," she said, "not here."

"We both hoed up our roots, haven't we?"

"It's tacky, considering what you're going out to do. Or are you stalling?"

He threw the cap on the bed and left, feeling pretty obvious in the truck that had been auctioned after seizures four times now.

His nephews and cousins were at one of their houses with a pool, barbecuing a split pig over half an oil drum full of charcoal, drinking beer and swimming naked while their women sat around in bathing suits looking embarrassed. "Ken," DeSpain said to the cousin whose house it was, "I need a little help with Bobby." Ken had built forty houses on the lake, run drugs, and retired at thirty-four after investing in detox centers. DeSpain's broker said detox centers could lose you money if the Feds stopped the Medicaid subsidy.

Ken pulled himself out of the pool and said, "Is he undercutting you?"

"No, he just not working. Your brothers want to help me?"

"Gee, Dennis, we've got this pig on." Ken padded over to the oil drum and brushed on a mix of vinegar and red pepper, then turned the crank of the spit. He'd geared the crank so one man could roll a whole pig. "You want us to deal with it without you. Say while you're off on a lunch boat cruising the lake?"

"I'm going, too. Be nice."

"Thanks, Dennis, but I don't think so. You ought to get out of that stupid-ass liquor business anyhow."

"Feds don't bother a man these days."

"Feds don't bother much since when their budgets got cut. You just do what they're not specializing in busting."

DeSpain felt like he'd gobbled down half a pound of hot pork already. "We don't have to go tonight, but I don't like someone sneaking out on me."

"You plan to beat on him, too?" Ken used a long fork to twist off some barbecue. He held the fork out to DeSpain, who pinched the meat away and tasted it. "Done?" Ken asked.

"Done," DeSpain said.

"You know, we put my daughter in that Montessori school, but I made Helen go out and work to pay for it."

"Maybe I should put Steve in it, too."

"Don't know. Helen plans to have Ann go to law school, medical school, something a woman can make money on around here. Stevie, I don't know if he needs more than public school."

"Stevie will get all he needs," DeSpain said.

Ken said, "We starting to sound like women in the mommy wars. Get naked. Swim."

"I'm ready to talk to Bobby tonight." DeSpain noticed two teenaged nephews pulled up to the poolside, arms folded across the rim. "You boys want to go?"

"Beat someone up?" The one who spoke looked at the other.

DeSpain couldn't even remember their names. The family

was drifting apart. But maybe tonight that was just was well. "Can we use one of the other cars?"

Ken said, "Nope. We can't afford to lose any of them."

The boys toweled off and pulled on jeans and cutoff T-shirts. DeSpain grimaced. Six-packs in hand, they climbed up into the truck bed.

As DeSpain drove the truck toward Bobby's, he looked up at the rearview mirror and saw the bigger nephew poke the littler one in the ribs below the shirt. They both laughed and the little one threw up a leg as the truck turned.

Nobody's a professional anymore, DeSpain thought. He thought about taking them back to Ken's, but kept going and pulled up to Bobby's house.

Bobby came up to the door with a shotgun in his hand. "Leave me alone, DeSpain."

"Bobby, all I want is to protect you, find you good sales." DeSpain stayed in the cab of the truck.

"I won't make liquor for you."

The two nephews in the back of the truck stood up. The bigger one smiled. DeSpain looked back at them, then at Bobby and said, "I didn't come here to beat on you. But I do have a market for what you're making and can help you out with any cash-flow problems."

The bigger nephew said, "We didn't bring guns this time."

"Damn and a half," the little one said, "why didn't I bring my old AK-47? We'll have to remember that next time."

"Think a little plastique in the basement might help his attitude, Dennis," the bigger one said.

Dennis opened his briefcase and slid his hand inside, felt the Beretta, then sighed. "Bobby, I don't know what you're trying to do to me."

"I've got three shells in this, DeSpain. I can kill all you."

"Well, tonight, I guess you could, Bobby. If that's what you want to do. But I don't think it would be lawful, seeing as how I'm sitting in my truck and the boys aren't armed. You do something like that and you'll have both law and the DeSpains against you."

The boys in the back made DeSpain more nervous than Bobby himself, but they had sense enough to shut up. The little one popped open another beer. Bobby did swing the gun up slightly, DeSpain noticed. He also noticed that Bobby was trembling. When the shotgun went down again, DeSpain looked around the yard and saw a car motor dangling from a hoist, a car sitting on blocks, leads from a diagnostic computer running out one window. "Cash-flow problems?" DeSpain suggested.

"Damn you, Dennis DeSpain," Bobby said.

"You don't want to kill anyone, Bobby," DeSpain said. He eased the safety off on the Beretta. Sometimes a man would shoot you when you said such a thing just to prove you wrong. Bobby's wife came out then and he gave her the shotgun and spoke to her too softly for DeSpain to make out.

The little cousin whistled. Bobby's wife looked back as if she wanted to give the gun back to her husband, but finally went into the house.

"I hope you didn't ask her to call the sheriff, Bobby. We're here to work this out like businessmen."

"Dennis, I don't want to make liquor."

"Well, you did make the liquor and you were looking for customers. I'm not asking you to make white liquor. That aged barley malt of yours would be real good to have around Smith Mountain Lake. Hey, Bobby, let me loan you something to get that car back together. No, let me give you something." DeSpain arched his back to get at his wallet and pulled out four hundred dollars. He stuck his arm out of the cab and said, "Won't that help?"

"You know that it would." Bobby wouldn't come take it.

Then, in the house, Bobby's sick baby cried. Bobby closed his eyes one long moment and came up and took the money. "It takes years to age. I dumped all I made, all that was aging."

"Don't worry, Bobby. We're both young men, you especially. I've got someone working accelerating the aging process. I've thought about counterfeiting bottled-in-bond liquors, to diversify, so to speak."

"Can I quit when I get out from under?" Bobby asked.

Oh, Bobby, you'll never get out from under, DeSpain thought, but he said, "Sure, Bobby. The main thing was, I didn't want you calling attention to the business. Amateurs often aren't discreet enough, and if anyone gets real obvious, then the state's going to come in serious in the county."

"You made it sound like I was competing with you and you were going to beat my butt if I didn't work for you regardless."

"Well, yeah, I'd be less than honest if I said I welcomed competition, but the real concern was for the business as a whole. And you were hardly serious competition, just making fine liquor I happen to have a personal fondness for."

Bobby looked like he knew he was being lied to, but he'd settle since DeSpain fed him lies that let him keep some face. DeSpain watched him, amazed that someone could think to get into liquor-making with a face so connected to his thoughts. They both settled into an agreeable silence.

"Aw, shit, Dennis, you not going to need us to beat him up?" the bigger nephew finally said.

"Not tonight," Dennis said. "Bobby here understands my concerns. I'll take you for a treat." He drove them up to Roanoke, where he called Maudie from a phone booth to see if the girl the bigger nephew liked was available.

She was. Dennis got back in the truck and drove them to the little house behind the brick fence up near Hollins—very clean women, Miss Maudie had.

"Hi, Dennis, what can I do for you?" Maudie asked as she got them beyond the door. She was a skinny woman with long thick dark-blond hair, gray in it, who wore gold bangles from wristbone to elbow on her left arm to be used as brass knuckles in a fight.

"I'll just listen to music. The boys want to have fun." Patsy, the girl his nephew thought was so neat, came out with a girl DeSpain hadn't seen before. She was a deep mountain girl, or an imitation of one, barefoot and in gingham shorts and tube top for the tourists, DeSpain thought. He grimaced at Maudie, who took his arm and led him to the parlor where a couple of high-school-looking boys sat drinking and listening to jazz piano played by a half-black, half-Chinese girl. She wore a thin blue negligee but was playing her piano so earnestly it wasn't sexy.

"She's a student at Hollins," Maudie said as she slid a iced whiskey into Dennis's hand. "She's from Mississippi."

"Aren't they all college girls?"

"Want to talk?"

Dennis sipped his drink, listening to the nephews babbling about how they'd just whipped the shit out of one of his competitors and didn't even get bloody. "No, I'm tired. Will you be needing supplies, now that I'm here?"

"Send me in more apple brandy, if you can get some. I'm tired, too. Some of these girls are absolute cunts."

"I'll let you know how the Russian deals go."

"That apartment house you told me to buy is doing reasonable, but it's too much like this to be what I'd like to do."

"What would you like to do?"

Maudie shrugged like whatever it was she was way too old and wise to try. "You know how it is, Dennis. We have to work out our own retirement plans."

The half-breed girl paused in her playing, stared at the keyboard as if pushing the keys with brain waves, then put her hands back and began playing something classical that reminded Dennis of a time he and Orris had been to the Roanoke Symphony with Orris's college roommate. He'd felt considerably uncomfortable then, but was somewhat relieved now that he could recognize the music as classical, that a half-breed whore wasn't impossibly different from him. Dennis asked Maudie, "Do you ever feel like you were leading a whole bunch of different lives, here, the other investments?"

"Aren't we all?"

The half-breed girl stared at Dennis then, playing on as if her fingers knew the keyboard better than her eyes. She sighed and looked as if she was going to cry.

"Does she fuck, too?" Dennis asked.

"She's having a bad night. Let's see about someone else."

"No, I'll come back for her."

"The alien tried last night."

"Damn. He's on one of my bulletin boards, too. Just one of them in this area, isn't there?"

"Yes."

"If he's making liquor here, I'm gonna collide with the bastard."

"Here here, or here on Earth?"

"Franklin County, Patrick, wherever the hell he's living now."

"Didn't say. Seemed sleazy, but I don't know how his kind's supposed to be."

"And he wanted to fuck her?" The half-breed girl's fingers jerked discords on the keyboard and her shoulders rounded. Dennis felt sorry for her; then for an instant he wondered what Orris would say if he fucked a Hollins girl, even one in a whorehouse. "Tell the boys I didn't buy them all night," Dennis said to Maudie. He went up to the girl and put a twenty on top of the piano, then went outside to stand by his truck until the boys finished.

3

Marie Sees Something Unusual

After my spring semester exams, I took what I learned from Tech and from Dennis DeSpain and set up a mechanically cooled still. One advantage of being a black woman engineering student is that you can get your hands on such wonderful things as a twelve-volt hydro heat pump and no one suspects you'll be making liquor with it. Run it with a transformer or solar and your electric bill won't jump like it would running equipment with regular house current. State ABC officers and the local narcs cruise Appalachian power bills looking for bills that are just too big.

The only house I could rent cheap enough was an old Giles County A-frame made of weird stiff foam-over-metal ribs, an early Tech architectural school folly. When I rented it, there was a big hole where a tree'd come down on it, so I had to patch it with new foam. Earlier owners and renters had done the same, so the house was mottled grays, browns, and creams, and lumpy inside and out along the corrugated foam ribs. Whatever, I liked it because it didn't look like a still house.

When I brought in the heat pump, I put it on the floor and sat in the gloom half ironic about the thrill. Me, bootlegging.

Actually, my body missed Dennis's body. So I was reverting to Terrella with her big skirts, her dreadlocks, and her pistol because I really wanted to call Dennis up and say, "It's okay. I don't really need you all the time."

Brain, tell the body no, I thought as I ran the heat exchanger coils into the basement water tank and then used a plumber's bit on my drill to bring them upstairs to the bedroom.

Reasonable enough to heat people with wood, but I'd cook my mash over precisely controlled electric heat.

Down under the house on the other side from the water tank, the mash, in five-gallon drums, fermented buried in compost, rigged to a meter that told me the sugar was now done. I'd used a wheat malt, since I remembered a white man friend of my grandfather's saying wheat made the best liquor he'd run. Sprout it just a little, dry it, grind it coarse, wet it down and add molasses and yeast, then some chicken shit. I left out the chicken shit, added nitrates and some urea instead. The mash was ready.

The still was upstairs in the bedroom, where a steady run of electricity wouldn't be suspicious. I took the heat pump and the transformer upstairs.

About halfway upstairs, I felt utterly foolish, but so? All I'd get if I was busted would be a suspended sentence. Tech wouldn't kick me out.

I opened the door to my still room and began building a marine plywood box for the cooler and coil. The wires from the coil thermocouple controlled the fan motor. I sat back on my heels wondering if I should insulate the box, then decided it was better to disperse the heat, even with the cooking element being also thermostatically controlled. The jigsaw cut the vents for the cold air and the exhaust; then I soldered the box and fitted it around the worm.

For the cooking thermostats, I'd taken old fishtank heaters and broken the override high points, then recalibrated them so I could keep the mash around 205. The cooking pot was insulated at the sides. I went downstairs for five gallons of mash.

Rather than lift a five-gallon wooden barrel, I drained the mash into a plastic water carrier. *Don't breathe it,* I'd heard all my life. It was more vomit-provoking than peyote. I needed an activated carbon filter face mask. Shit, I might have to make some money on liquor to pay for all this stuff, I thought as I lugged the mash upstairs. The mash gurgled into the pot like rotten oatmeal and I capped it quickly and began cooking.

The first couple of tablespoons I threw away. That's poisonous low-temperature fusels and esters. Then I began running the distillate into glass bottles, not quite having the equipment for another doubling still. I probed through my valved probe hole—temperature at the cap holding steady at 190, so I shouldn't be getting too much water boiling off, mostly alcohol.

Next, I'd automate, so I wouldn't have to be on site. I kept my eye on the distillate stream, and when it slowed down slightly, I ran the rest off and threw it away. Just save the middles.

As I waited for the cooker to cool, I fantasized rigging an automated still, computer-controlled, just like one of DeSpain's better operators had, hogs getting the spent mash augered up to them.

I love work with electronics and machines. I forget I'm black and a woman, which is very restful some days.

I lifted the top and went back to town to pick up a Spraypro respirator. The clerk looked at me funny and I realized I smelled of alcohol and mash. My hair'd frizzed half a foot beyond my head. Bad as picking up a man's odor from sex, I thought as I blushed. The clerk smiled and handed me the respirator. "Honey, I'd recommend a full-face airline respirator myself. What you got ain't good against mash fumes," he said and handed me an extra box of gas filter canisters.

"Thanks," I said. I hate being called honey. Colorwise, molasses would be more appropriate. Now, was he going to call a distributor and report me? Fool, I told myself, you didn't show him ID.

Back at the house, I put the liquor I'd stilled off in the refrigerator and began packing the mash up in a plastic heat-seal bag, snorting through the respirator the whole time. Then I hauled the cooking vessel into the bathroom and scrubbed it out before putting the first run through. First wine, the old people called the first run.

I used an old iron to heat-seal the mash bag. I should have rigged a centrifuge to whirl out the remaining liquor. Next time, I thought as I lugged the bag downstairs, I'd find out how to process the spent mash in a ecologically correct way. Freeze-dry it and get some pigs to eat it.

The alcohol, when I doubled it, tested out at 190 proof. It tasted like straight grain alcohol, which was, after all, what it was. I wondered what chemicals made scotch scotch and not vodka. DeSpain once asked me if I could counterfeit aged liquors. I swirled the liquor in its glass jar, watching the fine fine bubbles bead up. Surely it could be done. But this batch I poured in a small oak cask that I'd charred inside with a propane torch. I took the cask to the basement and put it in the compost bin.

Leaving the house with the bagged mash in a plastic trash can to dump in someone's field, I thought that distilling could get to be rather boring if that's all one did. Obviously, Dennis had sense enough to hire poor boys to tend still for him.

As I dumped the mash in a pig pasture, I considered I might sell the liquor at The Door 18, a juke joint near

Fairystone Park made with a real hotel door in front. Hugous, a third cousin some removed, ran it and sold liquor and marijuana to his friends. A big, even more distant kinsman played jazz bass there on weekends. I knew of the place through trailer cousins who'd taken me there a couple of times before Mamma heard about it. Back in my dorm room, I changed into something red velvetine.

It's a long drive and I took a disk of some white guy reading a piece for next year's English as I go. The guy narrating finds someone floating in a swimming pool over a woman name Daisy when I turn off 57 to the road leading to the place. Couple miles further, there's a big dirt parking lot and two Dobermans wandering around looking for white people to bite. I sort of nod to them and push through The Door 18 and see Hugous sitting wiping glasses and smiling. The big cousin is booming out jazz chords to a hymn playing tinny from a little Taiwanese tape deck.

"Hi, Hugous, you know Albert?"

"Been knowing him since he was a baby."

"I'm his second cousin once removed. We all live on Tiggman Adams Boulevard."

"One them Crowley people."

"Yeah. You might have heard of Tirrella."

"Midwife. She catched my daddy."

I wondered how long I ought to reckon kin with Luther, but decided to get down to business, slant-wise. "You have something a woman could drink."

The cousin playing with the bass stopped. Hugous shrugged and said, "Woman shouldn't, but a woman could." He fetched a bottle from under the counter and poured me a tiny shot.

It wasn't just liquor. The alcohol wheeled the other chemicals into the bloodstream faster. I felt buzzy and the dust motes seemed to be stars. Deep laugh, then bass chords. I managed to say, "I bet it's a hit."

Hugous nodded. We stared at each other, then I had a

vision—Dennis DeSpain riding a still barrel, guiding it through the stars by the coil. Then back to The Door 18. Then a vision: a long pink car with women in it squealing. Then I saw Hugous had moved. "How long does it last?" The ocean swept me away to a steel gull-winged car where an Arab-looking man sat counting money. He looked like the photo Dennis had shown me of his partner.

"Oh, tiny time."

"I was going to ask you if I could sell you some liquor." I waited for another vision, but the special effects seemed to be over.

"No more illegal than untaxed liquor, this stuff. Quick change stuff."

I asked, "Can I have a sample? Maybe I can duplicate it?"

"Sure and a half." Hugous put some in a grapefruit juice bottle. "It been to Tech already, though. Nice, not so much effect you got to have it, mellow, not going to attract lots of attention. Some folks confuse it with having a daydream, like the drug wasn't putting in more than they could do themselves musing."

The alcohol part wasn't missing either. I felt very nice now. "Well, if you need any straight liquor, then I could help you. Where did you get this?"

"Alien up in Franklin County. He cra-zy." Hugous's nephew hit a low bass chord on *crazy* and boinged the strings as though he and Hugous'd rehearsed hitting the emphasis. Or else the drug wasn't completely metabolized out.

"Stupid. Everyone can identify him."

"Maybe he got kin working for him," the nephew said.

Hugous said, not really asking, "Maybe he worse to cross than the law. Uglier than the law."

"Maybe it's like if a dog could take up stilling," I said. "Like he isn't human."

"Or they don't have no idea an alien do the unlawful like us," Hugous's nephew said. I was about to tell him I wasn't an us when I caught sight of myself in my velveteen dress in the bar mirror.

DeSpain, you turned me into this velveteen fool.

I was starting to move my stuff out to the A-frame when Berenice called me at the dorm. "Marie, what are you doing for the summer?"

Stilling, I thought but didn't say. "I rented a house off in Giles. I have to be out of the dorm by next week."

"I don't want to make this sound like I was looking for a maid, but Lilly's going in to have a hysterectomy. Marie, I don't want to have to go to a nursing home, not even for a month."

If it had been Lilly, I'd have taken offense, but Berenice sounded desperate, which is pitiful in a seventy-six-year-old radical woman. Did I really want to get into stilling? Berenice couldn't wait out my pause and said, "We can help pay next year's tuition."

"I've got a full scholarship."

"Can't you get out of the house in Giles County?"

"Not easy. I'd lose my deposit." And I'd have to move this illegal equipment.

"We can pay for it."

"Let me think about it." Shit, why not? I wouldn't have to distill to pay the summer rent then, or go back to Momma's surrounded by all those various kin, some who wanted me to be starchy like them, the others waiting for me to fall. "Would you want me to clean?"

"No, really, I can manage that. Just help with the groceries, carrying them, not buying them. I've got a power vacuum system in the walls."

"*Je ne suis pas une* maid."

"Of course not. *Vous être* companion. Lilly told me it wasn't cancer. Do you think she's lying? If she still wants me to go to the Institute, then I'm going to be paranoid."

I felt like I'd just tottered back from the edge of a cliff, a criminal career, Dennis DeSpain's black mistress and business partner. "Why would Lilly lie to you about that?" I could keep the house in Giles and sneak off from time to time when Berenice visited old radical friends.

"I just realized she could die before me. It isn't likely, but she could. To spite me. I want her around to rub my feet when I'm dying."

"Oh, Berenice."

"And you'll have to go back to school in the fall."

"Yes, regardless of whatever else happens."

"Good for young people to be tough. You're not headed for the grave, so what concern of yours is it?"

Momma doesn't want me to ever work as a maid, I thought. "I could get paralyzed by a car and then you and Lilly would both have to take care of me."

Berenice laughed. I might as well have something more legal to do this summer. And Berenice and Lilly would discourage me from going back to DeSpain and making liquor both. I said, "I think you're being a bit fussy, Berenice." My belly was going, *DeSpain, DeSpain.*

"Sorry. Will you help us out?" She sounded much younger then, more like a regular person instead of whizzy Berenice.

"Sure. And you tell me I'm being a fool if I start talking to Dennis DeSpain again."

"Well, we don't want you to do that. Lilly's representing the alien."

"He'll need her soon," I said.

"Explain."

"I shouldn't have said that," I said, remembering their paranoia that their phones were tapped.

"I agree with you, twice," Berenice said.

"I'll bring my stuff over now if you've got a spare room."

"Then it's a done deal." Berenice sounded so relived. We hung up.

I went downstairs with my computer and saw Dennis waiting by my car. He didn't look angry, so I hoped he hadn't found out about my own still.

"Marie."

"Dennis, I'm going to be taking care of Berenice Nelson while Lilly's in the hospital having surgery."

"Orris thought we were getting too serious. That's when I realized how much I . . ." Dennis couldn't quite say *wanted*, but he knew *lusted* would be a bit too crude. Seeing him cooled me off a little. I guess. "Would Berenice . . . yeah, she'd mind, wouldn't she? How come you're doing maid's work for her?"

"Companion, not maid. Because otherwise I have to stay at home with all my loser relatives."

"Not all of them are losers, Marie."

"No, but the ones who aren't tell me how stupid it is to have an affair with a cracker bootlegger. No offense, Dennis."

"Orris was threatened because you're at Tech."

"Like if I'd been at New River or cleaning up rooms, Orris would have approved? Jesus, Dennis, how can even a bootlegger stand to be married to such a bitch?"

He twitched his face muscles and froze them. I feared I'd protested too much or that he'd caught some vocal cord corrosion from my breathing in over mash. "Orris made herself into a lady."

Well, I *was* just insulting his wife. "I'm honored that she considers me a threat, but, Dennis, I quit you. Not the other way around."

"I thought of you when I saw a Chinese Negro Hollins student."

"Go after her then, Dennis."

"She was a whore."

"Dennis, if it takes slutting to get rid of you, I'll take out a license."

"You're not like that."

"Not before I met you, I wasn't. I'm still an honors chemical engineering student. I'm not sleazing around with a poly sci degree just to say I'm not a mill hand."

"You think you're better than us?"

"I will be."

"Christ, Marie. I want to see you again." Then he said, "Lilly's that alien's lawyer, isn't she?" Dennis is so sneaky. Maybe he had my phone tapped to see where I'd be next?

"I don't know."

"When she going in for surgery, Marie?" He started to come closer, but moved back when I stiffened.

"I don't know that, either."

"Well, I can ask around. Probably call her office. Have someone else call. She refused to represent me."

"Well, she has better sense than some people."

"Marie, I just want to talk to you." He ought to have known *talking to* in Black English meant *seeing*, meant *going out with*, all those euphemisms. He smiled slightly as if he'd realized what he'd have said if he'd been talking Black.

"Dennis, what you thinking about that alien?"

"I been seeing sign of its dealing on Loose Trade. And someone got Hugous's account away from me."

"You been following him?"

He shuddered ever so slightly. "I dunno."

I didn't want to provoke Dennis by asking if he feared the alien.

DeSpain Identifies a Trade Rival at Least Once

DeSpain decided the alien seemed to be in the liquor business without anyone's permission—no legal license, even if a man could get one in Southwest Virginia, no agreements with the present illegal distributors. But the only thing wrong was that alien seemed too open about what he was doing. DeSpain sat in front of his computer for an hour as Loose Trade deals popped on and off the screen. He wondered what arcane connections this alien could have.

Orris came in and leaned her breasts against his back. The nipples felt accusing. "How's Steve doing in school?" DeSpain asked.

"I have no idea. You signed his report card last week. I told you I wanted to see it." Her voice rumbled through his body.

"I've got a rival. He hired that Lilly Nelson woman to represent him."

"I've heard that she never represents liquor makers."

"He's that fucking alien. I guess minority something or other played a part, manipulated her sympathies. How is he getting away with it? Who is he paying off?"

"Is he really that much of a threat?"

"Somebody's taken half my nigger accounts."

Orris pulled her breasts out of his back so her voice wasn't vibrating through his spine and ribs but hit him straight in the ears. "You don't need a female black to be helping. What about bringing in a male?"

"I've got to find out what I'm up against." DeSpain sat thinking in front of the keyboard, then exited the system and said, "I'll go pay him a visit. No threats, just sniff around a little."

"Take me out to lunch first."

They drove to the Shogun, where Orris ordered miso soup and a cold noodle dish. DeSpain stared at the octopus legs with their organic suction cups and said, "I'll order in a minute."

Orris said, "Europeans think Americans work too much." She and the Japanese chef always slightly mocked every other living being who wasn't Japanese or Orris.

The Japanese chef giggled. DeSpain felt his face turn red. Orris whispered, "Ask him what Japanese eat for lunch."

DeSpain knew what he felt about the businessmen who ordered various sushi cuts set up on plastic slabs, talking about Citicorp, Mitsubishi, and the Orvis catalogue center. "Knowing you, it's miso soup and noodles."

"Precisely."

"Well, bad enough dealing with them all so superior in Tokyo. Now they moving to Roanoke." DeSpain heard the old accent grip his voice and saw the business guys at the table wince. Well, if they were so stupid as to eat sushi for lunch when real Japanese ate miso soup and noddles, DeSpain wasn't going to cringe.

"You couldn't deal with an Osaka bean tractor factory. What makes you think you can cut an alien out of your territory?"

"Shit, Orris. If I'd known you were in this mood, I'd have brung you an Elastrator and you could snag my balls with the rubber rings." DeSpain scowled at the businessmen too dumb to know what to order from a Japanese for lunch.

The chef muttered, "Europeans think Americans work too hard. Europeans must not work at all."

DeSpain said to Orris, "You made his day." He ordered miso soup himself and ate it even if it did seem made from fermented leaves and slightly rotten soybeans. He asked the chef, "Is it hot in Japan?"

"Not all over," the chef said.

When they finished eating, DeSpain said, "Orris, would you want to go with me to see the alien?"

Orris looked as if she wanted to remind him that on their wedding day he'd promised to handle all the illegalities without bothering her. Then she sighed and said, "Why not? If I'm with you, it's just a social call, right."

"Right."

"What about Steve?"

Dennis said, "Go call your mother and see if she can pick him up at the bus stop."

DeSpain waited. Orris came back from the phone booth and nodded. He helped her in the car and asked, "Scenic route or 220?"

"Let's just get there okay. I don't want to be too late coming home or Mother will worry."

They took 220 to Rocky Mount and picked up 40. Orris said, "I sometimes wish we lived in Roanoke."

"Man once told me Roanoke had the worse vice for a city that size he'd ever seen."

Orris laughed. "I'm not being hypocritical," DeSpain said. "Liquor's not like drugs. People can afford liquor without stealing."

"I said when I married you that I understood what you did. Are you getting too soft, perhaps?"

Shit on Orris when she had these Elastrator moods. They passed out of the rest of Rocky Mount in silence. Then, as they passed Ferrum College and began the mountain part of the ride, Orris said, "I have a tremendous nostalgia for the present."

"What do you mean by that?" DeSpain said, sure that Orris had deliberately made a confusing statement.

"Whatever happens at the alien's house will be the future. I love everything in my life up to that moment."

"Even me?"

"I do love you, Dennis. You make my life dramatic, but you're not so brutal that you make me nervous. Even if that reduces your efficiency."

"You think this alien's going to gobble us up."

A semi was laboring up the road, having ignored the warnings back in Woolwine. Orris watched it, Dennis watched it, both wondering if it would collapse on them and make all Orris's fears of the alien moot. It tottered on the turn but didn't fall.

"I saw one once crush a Volkswagen on Route 8," Orris

said. "Mother beat me for coming home late. I had to go back and cut across to 58. We'd gone to the beach music festival and we were going to take the parkway home."

"You want to go to the beach music festival? It's next week."

"I really am worried about what we're going to be doing in the next hour."

"And you still remember your mamma whipping you for coming home late, even worry about it at twenty-seven years old. God, Orris, she won't whip Steve because we're late."

"This alien, I hear that he spies on us. He memorizes what people do."

"He knew what I did."

"Did you tell me that?"

"I can't remember."

They shut up again. Dennis looked over at Orris and saw her lips move as if she was worrying them with her teeth, without letting the teeth show. Discreetly scared.

Another truck passed them, on straight enough road that they didn't have to worry. Then Dennis saw a glimpse of faceted ears under a baseball cap, the alien driving a deluxe Oldsmobile van. "That's him," he said to Orris. "In the cruiser van." He found a driveway and turned around.

Orris said, "Maybe the trucks are his, too. It's a bit unusual to see two tractor-trailer rigs trying to make it up Route 40 in the same hour."

"Well, at least he didn't know we were coming," Dennis said, noting the license plate on the cruiser: TURK. It reminded him that he had to fly over to Uralsk the first of July.

The Oldsmobile pulled over. Dennis pulled over behind him. The alien came out of the car and handed Dennis house keys and said, "You can wait for me at my house." His English was better than it had been when DeSpain was fishing on the Smith.

Orris took the alien's house keys from Dennis and said, "Thanks."

Dennis wondered if she'd gone nuts. He asked the alien, "You want us to wait for you at your house. Why?"

"You were looking for me, weren't you?"

"Yes." Dennis wondered for a second how the alien knew, then remembered that he'd turned around to follow the Oldsmobile.

"We should talk, you and I," the alien said. "And you must know where my house is if you were driving this way."

"People gossip," Orris said to the alien as he turned to go back to the Oldsmobile cruiser. The alien shrugged his shoulders before he got back in the car.

DeSpain started his car again. For an instant he thought about following the alien, now disappearing around a curve. *Those were his trucks. He's really operating at scale.* "What do you think?" he said to Orris.

"It's your business. Is it better to be friendly at first or hostile?"

"I don't know in this case. He's traveling awful conspicuous." He turned toward Patrick County. Orris looked at the alien's house keys. DeSpain glanced over briefly and saw a cylinder key and two computer card keys on the chain.

Yes, those were his trucks, DeSpain thought as they pulled in the dirt road full of double tire tracks just beyond the Patrick County line that would wind back into Franklin. "I know someone's in on this," he said.

"Do you bribe law enforcement officers?" Orris asked almost as if it had never occurred to her.

"You're supposed to be discreet." DeSpain tried to sort out the tracks—at least two tractor-trailer rigs, the cruiser, and one motorcycle. "This is crazy."

"Unless he has alien weapons." Orris said that as if she'd discarded the thought really, but just wanted to mention it in case.

The Volvo motor cut dead, the car rolling uphill on its own momentum as though the timing belt broke. But it wasn't the kind of car that broke its timing belt. DeSpain threw on the brakes to keep from rolling backward and tried the lights—no electrical system. "You know, if he'd been human," DeSpain said to Orris, "I wouldn't have been so stupid as to take his goddamn keys."

Orris said, "We'll have to wait for him now."

"If he's got a phone, I'm calling a tow truck. Of course he'd got a phone line out."

"Maybe it's dedicated to computers?"

"Orris, I'll get someone to get me a tow truck. I think a motorcycle went in and not out."

Orris sighed and opened the car door. "Shouldn't we push it off the road?"

"Shit." DeSpain saw that he could roll the Volvo backwards downhill. Once he did that, he tried to start it again. It started. Something a few yards away killed electrical systems. He was glad he didn't have a pacemaker. "We can mail him his keys."

Just then they heard the motorcycle in the distance. Its sound shifted, dopplering in on them. They saw the helmeted motorcyclist dressed in unstudded leathers, a skid scuff along one arm. He stopped, went to a tree, then said, "You can bring the car through now." The voice was broadcast outside the helmet, which was too opaque to see though. The face screen looked newer than the rest of the helmet, which seemed to have been abraded in the same accident that scarred the leather jacket.

DeSpain followed the motorcyclist back to the house, stopping twice when the man got off and fiddled with various trees. The motorcyclist asked, "Do you have the keys? Turk locked me out."

Before DeSpain could decided whether to admit he did, Orris said, "Yes."

The motorcyclist took off his helmet. He had short dark

hair and a perfect nose with a matching jawline that DeSpain had priced once at a plastic surgeon's at $25,000. DeSpain wondered what was this clown. He said to the man, "I'm Dennis DeSpain. Turk is the alien, right?" When the man nodded, he kept on, "He sent out a load of liquor."

"We're not sure what to make of this, Mr. DeSpain, but then you're a liquor distributor, too, aren't you?"

"I don't know a man who's proved it in nine years. We've got a hardware store in town, health-food store by the lake, motel, overseas investments."

"Mr. DeSpain, neither the Department of Defense nor the State Department cares about Franklin County illegalities except that an alien is here, modeling his behavior after you people, giving keys to his house to local moonshiners."

"I'm not a moonshiner," DeSpain said. He always associated the terms *moonshine* and *moonshiner* with people from Greensboro who wanted to play folkloristic. "I wanted to meet the alien."

"Why? Don't explain. I know why."

"And why haven't you federal people done anything?"

Orris said, "Why don't we go inside? I'm Orris DeSpain. And what shall we call you?"

"Henry Allen," the man said. Orris gave the keys to DeSpain, who found the hole for the round key and the slots for the two cards. Allen said, "Put the two cards in first, then turn the key. Otherwise, you release the Dobermans."

DeSpain put the cards in carefully, then turned the key. He listened for dogs before he opened the door. "Do you know he's hired a lawyer?"

"We need to know more about Turk and his relationships to the other aliens before we do anything."

"He must know what he'd doing is illegal, so why don't you bust him?" DeSpain looked around the entranceway and saw nothing alien about it—chrome chandelier, flocked white wallpaper, terrazzo tile.

"This way's the living room," Allen said.

They went to the left through an archway. The men sat down on suede chairs, leaving the couch to Orris. She took off one shoe and dragged her nylon-covered toes through the deep pile. DeSpain knew she could feel if the carpet was wool or synthetic, even through her stockings.

"I think he thought I'd go home after we finished talking," Allen said. "So he locked me out. But he knows what I'm doing."

Orris said, "Maybe he has our house bugged? And he didn't want you to meet us."

"Orris," DeSpain said, thinking she'd gone a bit paranoid with that.

"He could easily," Allen said.

"And you letting him bug U.S. citizens?"

"We're trying to see what's going on. We . . ." The man stopped talking as if realizing that the alien could be listening in now.

A wheeled robot turtle came in and triangulated each of them with its servomotor neck. Allen said, "If you remember anything after it sprays us, call State."

DeSpain had only a vague recollection of it later. He and Orris were driving home when the radio programs told them that five hours had elapsed.

Orris looked at her watch and said, "Mother will be furious."

4

The Game of the Name

I hate it when I can't remember, Despain thought as he shaved himself in the morning. Vague images of a wheeled turtle named Henry Allen floated through his mind. He decided he'd gotten drunk with a human cohort of the alien's. Nothing had been resolved. The alien never came back.

Orris watched him from the bathroom door. She looked haggard without the polish makeup gave her.

"I'm going to see Hugous at The Door 18. He's buying from the alien."

"Dennis, I think our memories were tampered with. Maybe you should let this one alone."

"Orris, maybe that alien is just checking out the territory before whole bunches of alien bootleggers come in."

"And maybe his kind is going to push us out of the business. You've got other investments."

"Orris, now you want me to quit." DeSpain wondered if Marie would have dared him on and decided that she would have. He finished shaving and combed his hair, then put on a suit to show respect to Hugous.

Orris didn't volunteer to come this time. She found the Volvo keys for him and looked down and to the side as she dangled the keys out to him on her straight-out arm and index finger, as rigid as an admonishing statue.

Be that way, DeSpain thought. Her mother had yelled at them when they picked up Steve, tucking him in the backseat of the Volvo still half asleep.

Hugous was out on a tractor plowing corn land behind The Door 18. DeSpain wondered how, even with income from The Door, the man could afford a balloon-tired air-conditioned cab item like the yellow machine now folding the ends of its giant harrows and turning in the field. The harrows unfolded and the steel spikes bounced against the clay, then impaled the clods.

DeSpain went through the hanging open old hotel door and sat down at the bar, watching the dust motes in the sun coming in through the back window. He figured this'd get some communication from Hugous faster than going out to the field and yelling through the machine noise.

A small camera over the bar swiveled. DeSpain crouched, uneasy. Turtles with mobile steel necks. He reached over the bar and brought out a bottle and glass. Let's see what the alien's making, he thought. He poured a taste in a glass and drank.

Scuffed leather . . . call the State Department and ask for Henry Allen . . . motorcycles . . . stalled engines.

Damn stuff is drugged. And I was drugged with something the opposite earlier. We didn't get blind drunk.

Hugous came in with just the sweat he'd built up walking away from the air-conditioned tractor cab. He said, "DeSpain. You go on now after you pay me for my liquor."

DeSpain had never heard the man sound so full of menace. He had to call the State Department, ask for Henry Allen before this alien's man did something worse to his memory. "How much I owe you?"

Hugous's chest rumbled something too nasty to be a chuckle. "About five hundred dollars from all the time you cheat me," he said, "but five dollars will cover what you just drank."

DeSpain pulled out a twenty and looked up at the camera. It nodded at him, but then he saw the remote controller in the black man's fist. Hugous nodded, too.

Why doesn't someone stop the alien? What the alien could do to a man's memory was a national security threat. He wasn't just a business rival; he had tricks beyond human nature. DeSpain went to a public phone at a country store out Route 57 near Philpott and used his phone credit card to call the State Department. "I'm looking for a man named Henry Allen," he said to the first human-sounding interactive voice that picked up after the touch-tone connection messages had played.

Another voice, male, replied, "Henry Allen is on vacation."

"I saw him in Franklin County." DeSpain wondered if the alien sent out a bug from The Door 18 to follow him, but continued, "He was observing the alien."

"My information is that he's on vacation. Could you leave a number where he can call you back?"

DeSpain left the number of the motel he co-owned with a third cousin down near the Henry County line, a man who often took messages for him. Then he said, "Look, the alien is selling drugs disguised in bootleg liquor. I think you ought to look into it. He has another drug that destroys more than short-term memory."

"Alcohol does that," the man said.

"It isn't alcohol," DeSpain said. "I seriously advise someone to look into it. Someone else. Henry's too cozy with the alien."

"Mr. DeSpain, our voice-print records show that you

served a month of a two-year suspended sentence for liquor distribution when you were nineteen. And your driver's license was suspended. What are you trying to pull?"

"Okay, okay, I used to sell liquor. The alien is doing it now and he's mixed drugs in it. Memory-flash drugs."

"Mr. DeSpain, I advise you to mind your own business."

I am, DeSpain thought. "Henry asked me to call him at the State Department if I got any memories back. I'm doing precisely that now."

"Henry Allen is on vacation."

DeSpain hung up and wondered if Henry Allen would be reprimanded for speaking to a felon. Then he wondered if that bitch Marie knew enough biochemistry to make an antidote to the alien's drugs.

He thought about calling her, remembered how nasty Marie's mother was. Instead, he called up the Virginia Alcohol Beverage Control Board—this is how people at the stills went from being independent to employees of distributors in the first place.

"ABC," the voice answered.

"I'd like to report a still." DeSpain hoped the ABC office didn't have a voice analyzer. "The alien who's living below Ferrum."

"You want to give a name?"

"No."

"Sounds dubious to me. Why should this alien be making liquor?"

"Send one of your people to The Door 18 on Route 666 in Patrick County." DeSpain heard a helicopter flying over, toward the phone booth. He hung up the phone. The helicopter swung around overhead. He pulled out his Beretta and wished he'd thought to bring a gas mask. The gun felt hot in his hand. DeSpain hoped he wasn't being bombarded with microwaves.

The phone rang. *Should I shoot or answer it?*

He picked up the phone and breathed into it, just to let

whoever know someone was listening. "DeSpain? This is Henry Allen."

"Are you in the helicopter?"

"I can hear it. I'm sorry, DeSpain."

DeSpain stepped outside, checked the helicopter's belly for police insignia, and raised his gun, fired, missed the gas tanks. The helicopter swung out of range and hovered.

Allen yelled into the phone. DeSpain went to pick up the receiver and said, "Fortunately, the helicopter didn't seem to have an effective drug delivery system on board. So what can you do for me?"

"I need help evaluating the situation."

"Your alien's drugging the liquor supplies. Is that your helicopter out there? State Department? CIA?"

"Go in the grocery and wait."

DeSpain wondered if the clerks had called the deputies already, but crouched down and ran to the store. A young man behind the cash register had a twelve-gauge pointing at DeSpain's belly. DeSpain smiled and tried to put his automatic up. Outside, the helicopter had grappled his car's front bumper and was half dragging, half lifting it away.

"Dennis DeSpain, who are you messing with these days?" the man with the twelve-gauge said.

DeSpain remembered the man now: as a teenager, he'd driven liquor to Roanoke for DeSpain when his daddy was in jail. DeSpain finally got his automatic back in its holster. "Jack, sorry, Jack. I don't know who's out there, but it's not ABC or local law."

"Aliens abducted a couple from around here," one of the other men in the store said. "They used a helicopter just like that." The machine he pointed to had finally wenched DeSpain's Volvo under its belly and was flying away.

DeSpain wondered if all the hillbilly paranoia about aliens was accurate, a real war was going on while most Americans watched television. The helicopter came back and landed outside the phone booth. The alien, wearing body armor and a helmet, got out and spoke into the phone.

"Son of a bitch," DeSpain said. "I'm going to call the fucking State Department back and tell them they lied."

One of the guys said. "Government always lies. DeSpain, you especially ought to know that."

The alien moved slowly toward the store. Half the guys in the store pulled out boot knives or handguns. A Yankee woman began screaming when the man next to her pulled an Uzi out of his attaché case. DeSpain nodded to the man with the Uzi, Jones, a competitor who occasionally tried to set up shop around the 122 bridge. Jones said to the woman, who'd shut it down to gasping, "You go outside and make peace, you think guns so bad."

The woman was going toward the door when the phone rang. The store manager swung his twelve-gauge around across his shoulder and answered the phone, "Kirtland General Store." He handed the phone to DeSpain and said, "Guy named Allen."

DeSpain said into the phone, "The son of a bitch stole my car, he tinkered with my memory, he's coming in now."

Allen said, "Tell him he needs to talk to Droymaruse."

DeSpain said, "Tell him to talk to Droymaruse? Who the fuck is Droymaruse, and what the fuck good will that do?"

"It's another one of his people," Allen said.

At the same time, the woman said, "I'll give him the message." She was pretty brave for a pacifist, DeSpain thought as she went to the door, opened it, and said, "You need to talk to Droymaruse."

The alien stopped and turned around. DeSpain asked Allen, "What the fuck was that all about?"

"Droymaruse claims he doesn't know what he's doing, either."

The helicopter blades began turning. DeSpain wondered whether he could drive his car away, if he dared. He said to the world at large, "I need a beer."

Allen's voice from the receiver seemed remote. He seemed to be saying, "I'll come pick you up." DeSpain wondered if they'd all been drugged anyway. He couldn't remember feeling this buzzed since the night the ABC and state drug people snagged his car. Almost like the helicopter had done today, but it had been a big road hook adapted from gear used to land planes on carriers. Popped up out of the highway and bang-go. They'd torn his car to large metal shreds looking for cocaine even after they found the liquor.

"Here's your beer. We won't charge you for the army," the manager said. He fitted his shotgun back under the counter, then took DeSpain's money. "You've got to drink it off premises," he said when DeSpain popped the top.

"Oh, give me a fucking break," DeSpain said. The other customers stared him down, so DeSpain decided to go out front anyway. He wrapped the can in a brown paper bag and walked through the parking lot to the weeds near a power line, drained the can in two breaths.

Allen came up on his stupid motorcycle. "I don't think your car is drivable. Can you ride on the back of this?"

DeSpain decided to chance it. "But let me drive," he said, aware of his competition watching from inside.

"You have to wear the helmet, then. I don't have a spare." Allen handed the helmet to DeSpain, who grunted as he forced the thing on. Allen's braincase was a tad too little.

DeSpain gunned the engine and felt Allen's fingers tighten around his waist, then tap—*be careful with my machine*. Sumbitch pantywaist cookie pusher, DeSpain thought, twisting his wrist and stomping on the pedals to get the Honda moving. He headed up toward Franklin County waiting for a helicopter to pounce, but made it home okay.

Orris and Steve came out when they heard the unfamiliar machine. DeSpain wanted to curse them out for not being more careful, but instead introduced Henry Allen: "Mr. Allen is with the State Department. He's helping figure out the alien."

"Glad to meet you. I'm Orris DeSpain and this is our son, Steve. Would you like to come in?"

"Your husband and I need to talk. Thanks."

"Tea or coffee?" Orris asked. "I've got fruit compote or a cheesecake."

"Coffee, that's enough," Allen said.

Orris nodded and went to the kitchen. The men sat down, DeSpain and Henry on the couch. DeSpain looked at his son and said, "You know you're not supposed to go outside if you don't recognize the car."

"Sorry," Steve said.

"We're going to be in the basement talking after we have our coffee."

"Is this man investigating you? Kids at school say you're a bootlegger."

Allen's lip on one side went back, so fast that if DeSpain wasn't looking at him, he would have missed the expression. Allen said, "We're asking your daddy's advice on how to deal with someone who's making drugged liquor."

Damn, DeSpain thought, you have the dialect almost right, Mr. Diplomatic Corps, except that I never wanted my son to know where half the money comes from. Steve looked at his father and sighed like a little old man. He said, "It's okay, Daddy, the teacher says liquor-making should be legal, without taxes."

DeSpain said, "Steve, we're not talking about me. Why don't you go find your mother?"

"But, Daddy, we've been talking about this in school."

"Go. I'll tell you about moonshine later."

Steve went out, his feet dragging his sock toes under.

Allen said, "I thought a moonshine area would be more rugged."

"Never could grow corn on a 45-degree slope," DeSpain said. "Also, how you going to get enough sugar in? In the old days, we used about a ton a week. Took trains to deliver."

"Now there's not much market for moonshine, I suppose," Allen said, "other than the blind pigs."

"As long the price doubles from federal tax, you gonna have a market for it," DeSpain said. "But I've personally gotten out of it."

Allen looked like he was going to contradict DeSpain, but instead asked, "Do you know the alien has a lawyer on retainer? Lilly Nelson."

DeSpain said, "She'd never take human liquor makers as clients unless they were black and she thought they were innocent."

Orris brought in the coffee. Steve, with a little smile on his face, carried in the cups and saucers. Mr. Allen stood, but DeSpain didn't. Orris served them quietly and then said to Steve, "Let's leave the men alone, sweetheart. Dennis, he was in the hall, listening."

"Daddy's talking to a federal man."

Allen said, "I'm not here to bust moonshiners. I'm here to find out what the alien is doing and why."

"Steve, the alien wrecked my memory Wednesday and then tried to attack me today. He isn't one of us just because he makes liquor."

Orris was smiling as if thinking *since when does a new liquor distributor not have to hack a place for himself*? She said, "Steve, now, or we can't go swimming before the pool closes."

"Oh, goody, a bribe. I want to know what's going on."

DeSpain said, "Don't act like such a jerk in front of company."

"Okay, but we can swim all night at my uncle's."

Orris said, "Those people are a bit rough."

Allen said, "Look, if you don't listen to your parents, I'm going to have to swat you."

"Daddy won't let you."

"Come on, Steve, go with your mother, now. Orris, call back before you leave, okay?"

After Orris and Steve had left, Allen said, "Droymaruse will keep Turkemaw busy for a few hours. I don't believe they're all tourists, but that's what they claim. Somebody's got to be crew. At least, Droymaruse."

DeSpain needed to check his bulletin boards. Pending deals from Roanoke to the Urals needed his attention soon. His real business could slump while the government used him to fight the alien. Maybe he could make a deal with the alien himself. Lilly Nelson did. Sentimentality for minorities quite overcame her prejudice against distillers. DeSpain said, "Since Reagan, the feds have been out of the still-busting business. Why are you here?"

"We've got information enough to say the business continues, which did surprise me when I was assigned to Turkemaw, but we're more concerned that his people get a good impression of us."

"Like Americans in Russia who were real rollovers. You know how much I had to be fighting that."

"Yes, we're beginning to understand Turkemaw might be probing us in some way, with plausible deniability by the others. It seems a shame to start interplanetary relations on a paranoid basis, though."

"Knew a paranoid once. He had great ideas if you could put them together. I used him for a while in security," DeSpain said. He remembered how the man didn't work out in the end, rather spectacularly, but DeSpain himself had a good working knowledge of plausible deniability.

"I get your meaning," Allen said. "Maybe there were kidnappings."

"Especially of folks who wander about of a night." DeSpain decided he'd drift dialect toward the folksy, keep Allen slightly to way off guard, depending on how bigoted he was. "Folks coming back from something they shouldn't outta gone to might like to be kidnapped." Nope, that comment was a little too perceptive. "So what do you want to do? I ain't had no experience with stereo-speaker-eared creatures."

"Give it a break, DeSpain. I also know you went to Emory and Henry."

"God, you're smarter than I thought you was. Man, you must have gone to Harvard."

"Princeton."

"Even better."

"We know Turk's lawyer is going in for surgery in a few days. She'll be pretty inactive for a month. If he put a lawyer on retainer, he must feel vulnerable in a way we haven't spotted yet."

"He's making illegal liquor. He's drugging people."

"State doesn't get involved in disputes between businessmen, even illegal businessmen. That's Department of Justice."

"I resent you implying that I'm in illegal businesses." DeSpain didn't want any competitors, human or alien, to hear what he needed to say. "Let's go out back. Bring your coffee if you want. Orris has a wonderful garden." Any more talk along these lines needed to be done in the trailer, DeSpain decided. DeSpain swept his trailers for bugs and replaced them every so often, renovated them enough to pick up some profit. Broken-down trailers cluttered the landscape so badly DeSpain could get all he wanted for the hauling. Allen refilled his coffee cup and followed DeSpain out the back door.

This month's trailer sat on concrete blocks about five feet from the ground. A stack of old mill machinery packing boxes made the stairs. Allen climbed up the boxes to the trailer looking as if he would rather have crawled but the coffee cup got in his way; then he carefully put his weight onto the trailer floor. DeSpain watched the State Department man look around at the rubber soundproofing, then explained, "I rehab trailers from time to time. Soundproof so the neighbors don't complain about late-hour drilling and sawing."

"I'd have thought you would have your secure room away from home. Don't most people in your business try to keep the family out of it?"

"Orris would worry if I had a place out." Maybe Allen was a new-style federal revenuer, DeSpain thought, running a fancy variant sting operation with this alien. "So what do you want me to do for you, and how much protection will I get? I take it you don't want him gunned down."

"No. We'll protect you, but not for that." Allen put his coffee cup down. "We want to know why he's making liquor. Just like we want to know why one's breeding fish in Africa."

DeSpain smiled slightly, sure the man came stocked with too many stories of bib-overalled pickup truck drivers with semiautomatics in the gun racks. "How did the alien get his attention focused on me?"

"You threaten to inform on independent still men who wouldn't work for you."

"No, not me personally, but it has been done that way." DeSpain wondered if Bobby had gone to talking. "Look, why don't you tell the other aliens what Turkemaw is doing? And if they don't stop him, then you know who is doing what here."

"We don't know that their motivations are human. We won't know why."

"God, you need better spies. Shit, Turk knows us by name and occupation."

Henry Allen sighed. "I had no idea why he was so curious."

"You got him everyone's name, face, occupation?"

"Just eccentrics."

"How am I eccentric?"

"You're a trout-fishing moonshiner. I thought that was pretty funny. Like a radical lawyer living in Rocky Mount."

"So you set me up for him?" DeSpain wondered if people playing by their human rules would be able to deal with aliens. "How much do you know about them?"

"They have space travel and we don't. They know where we live and we don't know where they live. State and Defense consider both those things to be critical."

"Maybe we ought to belly-crawl to 'um and cut a deal.'

"Or get some of them to come here and educate us. Americans and Europeans did that for the Japanese."

"Allen, you've got to be able to tell me more than you're telling me. Yes, the man—alien—is taking over some of the local distillers' accounts, and yes, in the past we'd work over trade competitors in various ways. Mostly psychological, like threatening to turn them in to the law. But it was a decent business. Distillers I know never poisoned their buyers with lead salts. Shit, man, one distiller even tested for poisons."

"I notice you're not saying that was you."

"How do I know Turk isn't working for the feds in a tax grab?"

"I can offer you immunity if you testify against him, should we go that route. We need someone who understands the business and who can get close to him."

"Considering he drugged my memory out when I had my wife with me coming for a social visit, I don't think he exactly trusts me."

"You can find someone for us."

Bobby would be perfect, DeSpain thought. "I might be able to help you, but it's going to take some looking. I really don't have the connections I used to. Honest."

Henry Allen looked around the trailer, moving his head up and down, not just his eyes. He grinned when he saw DeSpain got his point. Yeah, nobody innocent would have a trailer rigged like this. DeSpain decided to get rid of this trailer and use his alternate secure room until this anti-alien deal had gone down.

5

Bobby Considers a Proposition Only a Trifle More Appealing

What DeSpain really wanted to do was to take Orris and the boy to the coast, take a charter out to the Gulf Stream, and kill a marlin. If only he were really rich, out of the mountains, with a accent nobody could trace, he could . . .

Do what? He had to tell Bobby to get close to the alien. But that might be dangerous if Bobby was so pissed about being bullied into work that he'd side with the alien.

"Orris, I'm going out."

"When will you be back?" she asked, her hands full of flowers she was arranging in a iron Japanese vase.

"By midnight. I'm taking the truck."

He drove to Bobby's after calling a garage to rescue his Volvo. Suit in a truck sure looks weird, he thought as he looked down at himself.

Bobby and his wife were sitting on the front porch snuggling their children, a little skinny girl against Bobby and the ailing baby boy sprawled in his wife's lap. Bobby said to his wife, "Think you better get the chaps inside." The little girl looked at DeSpain and ran. Bobby's wife lifted the boy up against her shoulder and stood up. She looked from Bobby to DeSpain, one hand cupped behind the boy's head.

DeSpain came up the porch steps and opened the door for her. He could barely hear her thank-you.

After she was inside, Bobby said, "So what brings you here, Mr. DeSpain?"

"I'm thinking that if you can help me out a little, then I might be willing to see you set up as an independent."

"You want me to go with your nephews and beat on somebody?"

"Bobby, just find me out some information."

"I'm not real good at being sneaky, Mr. DeSpain."

"Well, if you can do this for me, I'll see to it that you don't have to be devious anymore. Get close to the alien, offer him your liquor."

"That's not all."

"Well, I've got to consider what I want to know after you get close to him." DeSpain needed to know how much the alien intended to expand his operation. Maybe this wasn't a fuss, but if it was, and if the local law wouldn't cooperate at all, he could use Bobby to deliver a bomb.

"Shit, DeSpain, you wouldn't ask much."

"Are you afraid of the alien?"

"Sheriff talked about his helicopter and your car over the radio. Claim was, the alien's grapple brake cut loose and you just happened to be snagged. Dennis, maybe you're picking on something you ought not"

DeSpain's belly tightened, but he thought he was keeping his voice right when he said, "State Department is behind us checking."

Bobby said, "Put that way, I'll call on the space guy."

DeSpain said, "If he isn't in the phone book, then I can arrange for you to leave him E-mail." He got up, not quite sure that Bobby wouldn't side with the alien himself, but if it looked like it was going that way, he'd bring in his cousins again.

"Will you really leave me alone if I tell you about the alien?"

"Surely."

"Gonna look bad for you if you can't protect your own."

DeSpain didn't think of Bobby as his own.

When the Lawyer's Away

I asked in the recovery room if my operation was over, asked enough times that about the fifth time I was apologizing for asking. After I got that clear and was upstairs, I didn't feel like talking. Nurses came in offering painkillers. One was so nervous when I refused, I took the shot anyway. Stainless-steel staples ran every quarter inch from just below my navel to a finger span above the pubic bone.

I napped for a while, then woke up to see Marie sitting by my bed. She squirmed with all she had to tell me.

"Am I okay?" I asked. I had an oxygen gizmo poked into both nostrils and an intravenous needle holding my wrist rigid.

"It looked like a big gizzard," she told me, "only round."

"The doctor normally shows the organs only to the family." I've heard that only Southern doctors come out with the organs.

"But what I'm really here about is Bobby. He came by to see Berenice this morning. He's scared. DeSpain . . ."

"Uh. What about the biopsy?"

"I know you're not feeling quite up to working now, but Bobby wonders what it would take to get a court order to keep DeSpain from bothering him."

"What does DeSpain . . ." *Why did I come back here to practice,* I thought, *when I could have shared a practice in Charlottesville*? People would have let me recover in peace then. "Was my biopsy okay?"

"I don't know. They'd tell you first."

"Marie, I like you a lot and all but—"

"Well, maybe it can wait for a couple of days. DeSpain wants Bobby to check out the alien for him. Spy for him."

"I should be out in another three days. Tell them all to wait."

"Five days. The day of surgery counts as day zero."

I was too tired to suggest anything. Marie put a piece of ice in my mouth, then more, spooning ice into my mouth as if it were oatmeal. I threw up. Marie buzzed in a nurse to take care of the pan.

Argh. I don't know if I recovered faster from the worry or not, but after Marie left, I got up to use the toilet. The nurse rolled the IV with one hand and held me up with the other.

"Have you heard anything about the alien?" I asked.

She shook her head, but with nurses, one never can be sure whether the sign is for *no* or *you're not ready to get involved in that yet, honey.*

I slept after she gave me the pain shot, then woke up about four hours later, not particularly in pain, but really awake when the night nurse came in to take my blood pressure, temperature, and pulse.

"Need anything?" she asked.

I mumbled no and closed my eyes. I'd call my alien client tomorrow and advise him to stop doing anything that could get him arrested until I got better.

In the morning, I watched the IV needle keep coming and coming out of my hand as the nurse pulled. "That's why they taped you so good," she said as she covered the hole. As I reached for the phone to call Turk, I felt a dull ache at my wrist bones from the four-inch needle.

Turk's voice reminded me of how weak I still was. "This is your lawyer, Lilly Nelson. Don't mess with Bobby Vipperman. DeSpain's trying to get him to inform on you, but he doesn't want to do it."

"Thank you for the information," the alien said and hung up. I suddenly remembered the first time I'd seen him, how alien he seemed then. Over the phone, I forgot those stereo speaker ears.

Humans Getting Together

Bobby ignored me. Bobby was what we call a dumb-ass naive racist, so prevalent in Southwest Virginia they made DeSpain look good to me. "Berenice, that alien was right behind me, even when I was going ninety. I heard he knows everything in the county. I don't guess anyone could tell me how he came to know DeSpain wanted me to investigate him."

I asked, "Where were you?"

"I was driving around below Ferrum, thinking about spying on him, Marie. Berenice, maybe I should stand up for my own kind and help DeSpain deal with him."

Berenice said, "I'll get you some tea. Sit with Marie while I set up." Bobby sat off from me on the porch while Berenice made iced tea.

"You been seeing DeSpain, Marie?" he finally asked, raising his chin from where he'd been keeping it tucked.

"I'm not talking to DeSpain anymore," I said, flushing. "I told Lilly that DeSpain asked you to spy on Turk. I felt bad about disturbing her."

"But that Turk thing is her client. And you're keeping house for them." He sounded like that was the one thing about me made sense.

"I'm helping a friend, not working as a maid."

"I guess."

"Bobby, whatever all bad you want to say about Dennis, he talked to me like I was just another person."

He looked startled. "I'm just not used to talking to college people I didn't grow up with."

Maybe that was it, not racism at all, I wondered. But then Bobby looked away and tightened his face muscles. Maybe he didn't like to be talked down to by Dennis's ex-mistress, but I wasn't in the mood to credit him with a good motive.

Berenice came out with the iced tea. I went back for glasses and she filled them. Bobby almost said something to me, maybe telling me to help the poor old white lady, but he looked back at Berenice.

"All I ever wanted was to work honest," he said.

"All I ever wanted was to work smart and honest," I said.

"Marie, don't bait him."

Poor bastard looked so grateful at Berenice. I sat back and sipped my iced tea. Bobby said, "She's a bigot toward rednecks." My iced tea flew up my nose.

Berenice said, "You both know that Turk is making illegal liquor and drugs, both. Liquor is one thing, but drugs another."

"And we're all humans together," Bobby said.

"Maybe Dennis is playing Turk's role in the Urals?" Berenice said. "Getting ganged up on by the locals or cheating them. It isn't quite clear."

"What we gonna do now, in this country?"

I said, "Lilly warned Turk that Dennis wants you to get information on him."

Bobby set his glass down and stood up and paced. "Oh, Lordy, why'd she do that."

We women both looked at each other as if we'd realized that lawyer's messages that were sensible to a human might work different on alien brains. Berenice said, "I think maybe I ought to go see the alien."

"Lilly's due back day after tomorrow," I said.

"I'll go see him before then," Berenice said. She still had her driver's license, but I knew Lilly tried to keep her from driving. Said enough retired people clogged the roads.

"You . . . can you go with her?" Bobby said.

"He's selling liquor at The Door 18, so he might not mind a black woman much," I said.

Berenice said, "I've been rather bored lately for a woman who used to break bank windows."

"Why'd you do that?" Bobby asked.

"Banks represented imperial powers in the world," Berenice replied, her eyes defocusing as she recalled when she was young, blond, and an absolute stone radical. I had kin like that on Staten Island. We left them there even when Granddad was selling lots on our road to maybe common-law wives. Berenice said, "I've got to call Turk for a convenient time."

I rather hoped we couldn't go until after Lilly got back, but Berenice came back out to the porch before we finished our tea and said, "We can come right over now."

Bobby looked grateful. He finished his tea in two big swallows, then took off out of there.

I didn't feel really well, rather nauseated, but Berenice just grinned and handed me the keys to the old miniature Cadillac.

The car was rigged with electronic gadgets from a cellular phone to a radar detector to an old Toshiba laptop computer, everything absolutely dusty. I slid in and wiped the steering wheel off with the second tissue that popped out of the box. Berenice opened the laptop and pushed its jack into the cigarette lighter hole. "The batteries are dead," she said.

"What about the car batteries?" I asked.

"I've been recharging them every month. Some days I get in and just let it run in neutral. Pretty sad, huh."

"Bad for the air to idle a car," I said. Then I realized she must have driven the car here from the last place she'd been really free, not the old aunt needing a niece to take care of her.

"Had the tires changed last year. The old ones rotted through."

"Maybe we should wait until Lilly gets back?"

"She won't be fit for a deal like this for six weeks. And I'm so old, I won't scare him like a younger human."

So I turned the ignition, hoping that it wouldn't start. *This was worse than being a velveteen fool for a white bootlegger,* I thought as the engine cranked and ran with just a few spits at first. We reversed, then went down the driveway.

"Damn fine car. Small for a Caddy, though," Berenice said. She fished out a cable and seemed to be setting up a cellular phone connection to the laptop. I stopped watching when we drove through Rocky Mount, then looked at the rearview mirror to see if we were being followed. Berenice began pecking keys on the laptop. "Aha," she said, "Turk's having trouble expanding."

"That means he's going to be real testy?"

"The humans don't cooperate with him as much as they did when he first set up operations. I was more concerned with the human behavior than his."

"His we going to be looking at soon."

"Marie, he hasn't killed anyone, even when provoked."

"So far," I said.

"Marie, if you're going to be an old lady about this, I should have left you at home." She typed stiffly. I glanced at her fingers and saw how swollen the knuckles were. She paused in the keying in and said, "I hate being an old lady myself."

"What are you doing?"

"Checking Dennis's business volume," she said. "Bobby gave me some clues. I'm in through an aquarium store that handles illicit Asian arrowanas."

"Don't data hackers have to have fast reflexes?" I asked.

"No. An old lady who's methodical. Patient. Did I ever

tell you . . . no, now's not the time. In another case, there was this German who marched through most of the open data on Tymnet. Methodical, yeah, like a Methodist." I wondered if her brain had overloaded. She looked up and rubbed her eyes with her middle fingers, hands flat against her face. "I did think the Legion of Doom was terrible."

"Sorry, but I don't know what you're talking about."

"I was older then than Lilly is now." She hit two keys and pulled out the computer-to-phone cord. "Turk could home in on the signal from the phone."

"But he doesn't kill humans," I said.

"Just mucks with their memory, but age is doing that to me already."

"Not today."

"Adrenaline. I remember everything about protest marches. I even remember how testy you were with Bobby just minutes ago."

I wondered if any of the Vietnamese I knew would think she did them any favors, but didn't say more, just followed her directions into Patrick County, then back into Franklin on the dirt road that lead to Turks. When I saw the place, I kinda asked, "An alien in a ranch house?"

"He makes it look real alien," Berenice said.

The alien came out dressed in railroader's overalls, not farmer's: that is, the blue and white pinstriped ones, not the solid denim. No shirt, just naked leather skin. One of my aunts used to tell about a Philadelphia man back in the late seventies who'd come to homestead the hills dressed in such things. Turk made pinstripe overalls look more preposterous than I could imagine they could look even on doofus white hippie boy. Then, if you looked again, they looked sinister under that alien head, with only the eyes to look human. I wondered if the faceted ear domes were brittle.

"Hi, Turk," Berenice was saying.

"Ah." He paused, sniffed the air, and finished with

"Berenice, my lawyer's aunt. And"—another sniff from the wiggling slots—"the woman who visited The Door 18."

I'd heard he was half about omniscient, but he wasn't, then, old people and blacks he hadn't gotten files on. "Yes," I said, not wanting to explain that I was Dennis DeSpain's ex-lover and thanking Hugous for not mentioning my name. I remembered one of my great-grandmothers telling me how we always could use white bigotry, let them think us dumb, and sneak around back of the attitude. "I'm Berenice's nurse, Mary." I'd respond to Mary like it was my real name.

Berenice looked over at me curiously, then grinned. Turk waved a bare arm at us, motioning us in. The leather seemed stretchy, not wrinkled over the joints like human skin. He asked, "Does anyone know you're here?"

"Lilly," Berenice said, "and a couple of people in town."

Bare and sterile, the hall smelled of disinfectant, but Turk kept leading us into the kitchen, which smelled of alcohol and fruit. It was crammed full of dehydrators, moldy pots, retorts, scraps of stainless steel; the counters were cut up and burned in places. Turk looked at the mess and said, "Nobody comes to visit."

Berenice walked around the room, sniffing almost like Turk, her old nostrils in her long nose wobblingly flexible. She said, "I've come to talk about Bobby."

The alien froze. Then he said, "Can I get you something to drink?"

I shook my head. Berenice said, "Thank you. Water, no ice." She watched the water come out of the tap. "DeSpain attempted to blackmail Bobby into spying on you. Bobby came to us. He doesn't want to get involved."

"He came to you only after I caught him attempting to invade my property," Turk said.

I wanted to say something, but that might spoil my humble maid act. Berenice said, "Don't do anything. Let Lilly work it out when she's better."

"Bobby and Dennis DeSpain are illegal problems for me

to have. Not a lawyer's responsibility. Perhaps Lilly could help me with the State Department, as that is a legal problem I have."

Berenice looked like she wondered if her memory was still hyped. "State Department?"

"A man named Henry Allen."

"What do you want Lilly to do?"

"Get an injunction to stop him. I will take care of my illegal business rivals."

I hated myself for wanting to warn Dennis, but my hind brain threw me a flash of his little white-bread throat sweating, breath and blood bobbing through it. I'd never been just another one of his black mistresses.

"Don't do anything until Lilly gets back. You might not understand as much of human law and custom as you think."

"The State Department knows I'm making illegal liquors, but it does nothing."

"Human custom," Berenice said, "isn't particularly codified anywhere."

"I have human custom for my liquor," Turk said.

I said, "I think we'd better go."

Berenice suddenly looked old and forgetful again. I was about to ask if she knew where she was when she nodded.

As we drove home, she said, "Damn, sometimes," but didn't say more. Her eyes grew vague and trembled in her head. She opened the laptop, but just looked at it as if she'd known once what it could do.

"Took a lot out of you?"

She sighed.

After we got out of the car back at the house, she said, "I'd like to know more about their customs."

"Berenice, there's only so much you can do."

"I think if one thing happens, I can very well do another."

"What?"

"Marie, sometimes you have to defend your own, but who is my own?"

Sounded to me like the old cranial blood vessels were constricting. We went inside and saw the message light blinking on the answering machine.

It was Bobby. "Berenice, I can't let an old lady deal with all this."

I said, "What the fuck does he mean?"

Berenice said, "I hope he doesn't mean he's going to try to help DeSpain regardless."

The next message was from Lilly. "I called, but you aren't in. Turk called and asked if I could get an injunction against the State Department. He said it should be a civil liberties issue. Do you have any idea of what he's talking about?"

Berenice said, "Marie, wouldn't it be nice to have more tea?" She sounded like she was trying not to be the kind of woman supported all through her teenaged years by my great-aunts. A suggestion this was, not an order.

"I'd kinda prefer limeade myself," I said. "I've got some in the freezer."

Berenice said, "Sounds great to me."

"Aren't you going to call Lilly back?"

She reached for the phone as I went to the kitchen to make limeade. When I got back with the pitcher, she said, "We women are just going to sit. That's what Lilly suggested."

I poured her a glass first. "Berenice, that's best."

"I don't think it's best," she said, but I could see that her ankles were swelling.

"Want me to take off your shoes?"

She grimaced, but when I had her shoes off, she reached down stiffly and massaged her ankles. "Go talk to Dennis."

"I—"

"I don't mean you should offer your body in exchange for Bobby. Tell him to leave the alien alone."

"He wouldn't listen to me. It would hurt his gonads if his wife would put him on the phone."

"Chicks to the front," she said. I realized, after a moment of utter doubt as to her sanity, that the phrase came from radical times before women's lib.

"So far Turk hasn't hurt anyone."

"It doesn't look to me like he tried to leave people unbruised."

6

The Semi-Accidental Mess

Bobby was sweating as he told DeSpain what had happened to him, but DeSpain compared it to losing his Volvo to the alien's helicopter and to Henry Allen's memory lapses. After Bobby wound down, DeSpain said, "You must have done something stupid." Bobby looked guiltier than he should. "Tell him you're defecting from me. Just go right up and join him. Don't just nose around on his roads."

"He knows I'm working for you."

"I suspect he does, Bobby." DeSpain hid his anger, easy to do with such a sap. "How do you think he found out about it?"

"I asked Lilly and Berenice to help me."

"Lilly works for the Turk. You ought not have done that, using women. It's real easy, Bobby." DeSpain wasn't sure he cared now what happened to Bobby. "Just go up to the Turk and tell him you want to work for the most aggressive boss."

"Dennis. Mr. DeSpain."

"When I was twelve, I used to sneak out to where the revenuers lived and run a thing so their trunk lights would drain the batteries. I could fix them without ever touching the engine compartment or opening a car door."

"When I was that age, I was milking cows for Daddy."

"You would have been." DeSpain had brought a piece of rebar he'd filed almost through and patched with black wax. He broke the rebar across his knee.

Bobby said, "The old hippie woman was going to see the Turk. With the maid, you know the one you used to—"

"If an aged student agitator and a nigger bitch can see the Turk, then I don't see why you can't talk to him. I meant for you to do something straightforward, not sneak around his operation sites. Of course that made him suspicious."

Bobby's eyes flew sideways like he just thought of something, a lie or maybe a truth he didn't want to tell. The men sat so still that DeSpain heard Bobby's wife inside talking to her babies. Make the boy feel guilty, DeSpain decided, and he said, "You making it dangerous for Lilly and Berenice, dragging them into it."

Bobby didn't answer, but nodded slightly.

DeSpain said, "Bobby, I'll talk to you next week, then." He stood up and brushed off the back of his suit, then made sure he'd scattered the fake rebar wax crumbs. As he went back to his truck, he thought that he could play this several ways.

When he got back home, Henry Allen had posted him a note on Loose Trade. CONSIDER THAT THE SIXTEEN-INCH LIMIT ON THE SMITH HAS BEEN CHANGED JUST FOR YOU.

Other Loose Trade subscribers had left electronic giggles. DeSpain wondered for a second if Allen was mocking him, then decided to read the message as a license to kill the Turk.

He wasn't sure he could. Might be that the Turk would kill him, and maybe that was what the government wanted. And he wasn't sure that Allen's message had official standing. What was it about deniability? He almost typed *can't be just for me*, then backed up a few days to see what action there'd been earlier. He noticed a complaint from Luck Aquatics for messages they hadn't made and wondered why the hacker hadn't erased the charges. Some ecology freaks, he decided. Ecology, taxes—got so a man couldn't run an airconditioner without a federal permit.

Then he wondered if the message was from the real Henry Allen or if the Turk was luring him into an ambush. He reached for his phone and called the State Department. "Hi, I'm Dennis DeSpain in Franklin County and I want to talk to Henry Allen. I've talked to him before."

"Please hold." DeSpain waited, then the voice came back. "Mr. DeSpain, Henry Allen says you should proceed with caution. He wishes you well on your fishing trip."

"Is self-defense okay?"

Pause for music. "If it legally passes for self-defense."

"Before, I couldn't even defend myself?"

"I'm not privy to interpretations," the voice said. DeSpain hung up, pulled out his microfiche collection, and began going over old court cases beginning with Sidna Allen's trial in the Hillsboro Courthouse shootout. Yeah, DeSpain thought, if I'm understanding all this correctly, before the State Department decided not to protect the Turk, if I'd shot him, even in self-defense with him shooting at me first, I'd have pulled time like old Sidna for killing an officer of the court, even when the officers drew first.

Well, now DeSpain could defend himself against the Turk. He wasn't altogether thrilled.

* * *

Lilly's Attempted Convalescence

The doctor read me the biopsy report. Even though they hadn't found cancer in what they cut out, and even though the ovaries looked good for another five years, I ought to keep coming back every year for checkups, and, no they didn't get as high as my gallbladder, so I couldn't know what to expect there.

Berenice looked confused when I told her; not one of her better days, I thought. Marie, who'd brought her, said, "So, Berenice, you won't have to go to the nursing home any time soon."

Berenice smiled brightly and said, "Marie's been real good to me." Marie looked a trifle annoyed.

I sensed something, but didn't feel well enough to get into whatever hassle they'd had between them. I said, "Let's get me home. The hospital got their staples back."

I spent a day recovering in my own bed before I got a call from Turk regarding the State Department man, Henry Allen. I was lying down with a pillow against the incision, the phone on speaker mode. "I want to know if you can do anything to keep Henry Allen from encouraging Dennis DeSpain from trying to kill me."

"Can you prove it?"

"He left a message for DeSpain on Loose Trade, saying that the limit on trout sizes was canceled just for him."

I wondered if I could break my retainer contract due to Turk's being a Loose Trade subscriber. "Turk, you don't know what that trash means."

"DeSpain called the State Department for a clarification."

"Look, as your lawyer, I advise you that distilling liquor, much less adding drugs to it, is illegal. DeSpain keeps a low enough profile that while everyone knows what he does, nobody has ever proved he financed a raided still. And I wouldn't take Dennis as a client unless the court assigned me. Dennis can't sue you, you can't sue the State Department. Really, seriously, why ever you're making liquor, stop."

"I think this is an American Civil Liberties action, restraint of trade."

"It's tax evasion."

"It is the forcing of grain and fruit harvesters to sell decomposable products rather than add value by manipulation and set price by aging."

"Why don't you just . . ." I was about to tell him to give it away, but that wasn't his point. "Make Dennis an offer. Tell him you'll help him. After all, you think the law, not the business, is wrong."

"Is that legal advice?"

"No, it isn't legal advice. It's personal advice."

"DeSpain is hunting me. Can I kill his dogs if they attack me?"

I wondered what was going on here. "Please stay out of trouble for a couple of weeks until I've recovered from the surgery. Or perhaps you'd like to find another lawyer while I'm laid up?" Please.

"Do the human laws governing self-defense apply to me?"

"Turk, I'll get you an opinion on that." I guessed I ought to do that now. "I'll get back to you." I wished I could have told him no, but he could sue me for malpractice if he survived an attack.

Is this interplanetary protocol or just commonwealth rules? I wondered as I dialed Withold's office. "Can I speak to Withold?" I said to the secretary. "I need his opinion on a client's options."

"Commonwealth's attorney Withold Brunner."

"Withold, this is Lilly. I'm that alien Turk's lawyer. I just want to clarify a few things. Is Turk going to be legally treated as a human being under the laws of the commonwealth, or is there some sort of diplomatic immunity I should be aware of? Or how would he be treated if he acted against a human in self-defense?"

"Lilly, legally, he's human, subject to state and federal laws. State wanted us to be tolerant at first, but they've pulled out now. Didn't know you were representing bootleggers now."

"Thanks. I was intrigued by the alienness." I called Turk back and told him that he could defend himself. Never take another client on retainer this side of a corporation, I decided.

That afternoon Bobby Vipperman came by. Marie let him in and didn't offer anything to him. I lay on the couch half asleep, the surgery line feeling tense.

"Sorry to bother you, ma'am."

"What do you want, Bobby?"

"Just to talk."

"About what, Bobby."

He sighed like he was about to sing. Some of his people were singers in the poverty-stricken days when people needed aesthetic anesthesia against weather so coldly hostile it froze piss in bedside slop jars. Life then was so mean that boils quickly ran to blood poisoning and killed you at sixty. I took a closer look at him and saw that he'd pulled himself into a posture out of that old culture. That's why I'd thought of high lonesome singing. He was making himself into a little artwork fit for a ballad. I said, "I'm tired, Bobby. Can you stay where DeSpain can't find you for a few days until I can get a body mike for you? If he threatens you again and we've got a record of it—"

"It's all right," he said.

"Bobby, Turk can legally defend himself." God, if DeSpain didn't have him by the balls, I didn't know what was. I'd seen men who went to war or riot, then when war and riot ended, became demolition divers, drag racers, all to prove an image of masculinity women over twenty never were impressed with. I didn't understand this emotionally, no more than men understood women's haute couture combat dressing.

I almost asked Bobby to sing one of the old high lonesome songs to me, but by thirty I'd gone beyond where nostalgia crosses into sentimentality.

And I had to get sleep or I'd bitch out my aunt next stupid thing she remembered about the sixties. "Do as I say, Bobby." The other side of this was animal business, a subalpha sucking up to the dog who beat him.

He didn't answer me, just gave me a look like *what can a man expect from a pacifist liberal pinko woman*? and went on his way.

I began to wonder if I'd feel guilty over what seemed to be about to happen. No, I decided, testosterone rules.

Behind the house, I heard the Cadillac start. "Marie?"

Nobody but me was home. I went into my own bedroom and fell asleep against what I feared was going on. A pillow against my belly pushed my stitches back.

Collected Artifacts

"Marie, don't follow him directly there," Berenice told me. "Take 640 up to the parkway."

I said, "Have you noticed how redneck Lilly gets when she's tired?"

"She spent only seventeen years away, split into bits," Berenice said. "And all the mountain shit—it's like brain fungus. You think you've gotten completely modern when bam, you're listening to a string band play a ballad that you're about to reenact in real life. Is it that way for you and the blues culture sometimes?"

"I fucking hate it."

"Yeah, and I bet you've got at least one lowdown dress. Turn here, go up on the parkway and sneak down."

"You don't sound like a big-city radical woman now."

"Yeah."

"Bobby's hopeless. What are you planning to do, Berenice?"

"I want to see what happens."

I ran up 640 as fast as I could without rounding a curve at fifty-five and smashing some slow old boy. "I'm a chemical engineering student at Tech," I said.

"Meaning," Berenice said, "that all this—and DeSpain, too—is hopelessly out of context?"

I felt like three hundred years of rust was moving in on my stainless-steel lab equipment. "I've got to remember why I hate Hugous and The Door 18."

"Don't have to hate them."

"He's buying liquor from this Turk."

Berenice shut up then. I wondered a second if I wasn't on the wrong side, but drove on. Sometimes sides don't matter as much as being loyal.

No, Tech student, I told myself, that's an attitude that'll yank all your accomplishments right out from under you. "What's important, Berenice, being right or being loyal?"

"Sometimes you don't have the least fucking idea," she said. "I remember cops charging a late-night march on East 79th Street, seeing the fire-mouths, the ones who talked heavy trashing, lose it, seeing the Puerto Rican garage attendants grinning and waving. We cowered among Mercedes and Porsches while the garage guys closed the doors. Odd. We amused them, more than anything else, but those Puerto Ricans save our asses from a beating."

"Meaning?"

"Panic is disgraceful. I remember thinking that I'd rather get clubbed than to panic."

God, she was losing it. I hoped she'd know what she was doing when we got to the Turk's. Was I obeying her because she was a white woman, as dotty as she was? Had the bastards gotten that far into me?

The Turk was waiting for us at the house. He'd folded Bobby over one arm and his pinstripe overalls were bloody.

I stopped the car. Berenice said, "Reverse slowly."

I looked at her. Her face was immobile, her breathing shallow. Then I began backing. Something stalled the car out and the Turk came up and draped Bobby across the hood. "Good-bye," he told us. Berenice didn't look at him.

I started the car again, fearing that I'd flooded it. I couldn't look at Bobby laying across the hood, so I backed all the way out into Patrick County.

When we reached hardtop, Berenice and I lifted Bobby's body. It stretched. "He's got no spine," Berenice said. I pulled his shirt aside and saw the incision sewn back up. My heart lurched. *At least the alien has to cut to get at them,* I thought. We lugged Bobby's taffy body into the trunk and drove to call the Franklin County sheriff.

"The alien said it was self-defense," the sheriff said. "He has tapes to prove it, he says."

Faked? An alien who could stall your car out, we'd never know, I thought. We waited by the store for the ambulance.

"Berenice, we should have stopped him."

She shook her head, but I couldn't figure precisely what she meant.

When we got back to Lilly's house, the high wailing time had come. Bobby's wife, Sylvia, had her nails raking her face, screams coming out against Lilly and DeSpain. Her children in the car bawled to see their momma so upset, out of control.

She came at me with "his nigger bitch lover."

Berenice took her hands before she got me. I said, "I didn't put DeSpain up to anything."

"You cunt and a half." She might have been outraged, but not enough to be fighting an old woman. Berenice kept holding Sylvia's hands.

Dennis drove up then with Orris in a new car, a Saab. We nodded to each other and she smiled slightly, like *is he worth it to fight over*? Sylvia turned away from Berenice and screamed at Dennis, "You killed him, you coward bastard."

"I didn't tell him to attack the Turk," Dennis said. "Still, I'll take care of you."

Orris looked at Sylvia, then back at me, then straight ahead over the Saab's sloping hood. She reached over and cut the lights off while Dennis kept talking, "Bobby was a good man. He wanted to defend us against the alien."

"You bastard, you and your overeducated hillbilly wife and your nigger bitch and you killed him."

"Sylvia, I didn't want it to happen this way."

I looked back at Orris. She mouthed something at me. I jerked my head *what* and she said, "You'll find out."

Dennis stopped trying to soothe Sylvia and looked at Orris, who shrugged. She said, "Sylvia, we will take care of you. Why don't you call your minister and go home? Your children are scared to see you like this."

Sylvia looked at her children, who shrank back as if she were a stranger. "Oh, babies, I'm sorry your momma was so nasty-mouthed, but these people killed your daddy."

Berenice said, "I'm so sorry, Sylvia." She hugged Sylvia once, then stepped back. Lilly stared at DeSpain.

"Dennis," I said, "you ought go." And flinched to hear myself drop the infinitive marker *to* in front of Miss Orris.

"He going," Orris said. I didn't know if she was mocking me or dropping from stress into her own first tongue. We looked at each other again. I felt like we women had made a conspiracy against Dennis, but for doing what I wasn't sure.

Lilly said, "Sylvia, I can't drive yet, but I can ride with you to the emergency room. If you don't mind, Marie will take your car and the children back home."

Dennis started his car and was out of there. Sylvia said, "Can she sit with them until I get home?" She hadn't asked me, but I nodded. She looked exhausted now, face soppy with tears, wrinkles etching in heavier, a mill woman married to another mill hand. Half the income now, she'd drop down into welfare unless Dennis did take care of her. Racism was Sylvia's secret defense against knowing where in the social heap she was. I could play maid one night.

"Thanks, Marie," Lilly said, meaning more than Sylvia could understand.

The kids cried on the way home. I bathed them and rocked them. The sickly baby sucked on my arm as if he thought his mother had died and I could be recruited for the role if he tried hard enough.

Lilly and Sylvia pulled up after I got them to sleep. Sylvia looked drugged. Lilly said, "We've arranged for a forensic autopsy anyway. And we've been talking to the funeral home and her minister."

You're the Turk's lawyer, I thought.

Sylvia said, "Are my babies okay?"

"They're asleep," I said. "Please don't wake them."

"I want to see them."

She went in and put her hand on the boy's chest to see if he still breathed. We led her off to her own bed when she stumbled. "He's been sick," she said as Lilly and I undressed her.

"Do you want either of us to stay?" Lilly asked.

"I'm fine," Sylvia said. "My sister will be over in the morning. She's on third shift."

I wished we'd get out of here—the poverty made me feel guilty for being a college student, for having a schoolteacher mother. We went back to the living room with the framed photos of kin, weddings, and babies. Sylvia put her hands to her face and twitched her head. Lilly and I left.

"I guess she'll be all right," I said. "Dennis can't afford not to take care of her."

Lilly said, "Dennis will for a while. When people forget, he'll quit."

"How are you doing?"

"I'm going to sleep for the next twenty-four hours."

"You shouldn't let people bother you while you're like this."

"I told them to wait, didn't I?"

We drove home. Lilly winced as she got out of the car, bracing her hands against the doorframe. She reached for her surgical scar, but pulled her hands away as if remembering she couldn't touch it. I helped her with her shower to make sure she didn't fall, then gave her a pain pill and a sleeping pill. "Enough. You've got to get better first."

She pushed a pillow against her belly and said, "Should I let them all kill each other?"

"None of those trash are worth getting sick over. Go to sleep." I pulled the sheet over her.

As Lilly turned to her side and adjusted the pillow against her incision, I looked out her back bedroom window and stopped myself from exclaiming out loud, *Oh, shit*. The old compact Cadillac was gone. *You can't deal with this, Lilly,* I thought as I looked back at her in bed, eyes blinking in the dark, not quite asleep.

I went downstairs to call the sheriff, thinking about Bobby's body folded over his arm. No spine. I wondered if the Turk collected spines as trophies. Well, I thought, maybe Berenice was old enough to die. Old radical like her, she'd probably get a kick out of it and die biting and head-butting, too.

I said to the dispatcher, "Berenice Nelson, Lilly Nelson's

aunt, is out driving in a 1986 compact Cadillac. She's too old to be doing this."

"Does she have a valid driver's license?"

"Yes, she has her license but—"

"Has she been declared incompetent?"

"No. How long does she have to be missing before you do anything?"

"Twenty-four hours, unless her mental state was clouded or confused the last time you saw her."

"Well, actually, she threatened to deal with the alien, so doesn't that qualify as confused?"

Don't Take the Spine, That's Alien

DeSpain knew that he had to avenge Bobby's death if he was going to get his black accounts back. He put on the bulletproof vest with the false muscle lines, found the infrared goggles, then called his cousins. His cousins said they were busy, so he drove the truck into Rocky Mount and picked up a couple of guys at Jeb's Old War Parlor. "It'll be a good fight," DeSpain said. "I'll pay you five hundred each."

One man smiled and asked, "Where are your cousins?" But the others weren't listening. Three of them, two logging crew workers with less than twenty fingers between them, and a loudmouth fool DeSpain planned to put on point, nodded. They followed DeSpain out and climbed in back of the truck. "Any of you have a bike?" he asked them. Get them in first, he thought, then come in behind and shoot the fucker.

The mouthy one did, a huge overdone Harley. DeSpain said, "That's all right. I've got something lighter back at the house." They detoured back to pick up the moped the law made Dennis use after his liquor-running bust.

That would do. If the motor shorted out, DeSpain could pedal it. He gunned the truck to keep the guys in back from laughing and headed through the night toward the Turk's.

The guys in back yelled at each other and into the wind. DeSpain didn't care what they said. He was rather glad now that he wasn't using cousins. His left foot tapped against the bottom strip around the doorframe, then went to the clutch for the turn off 40. He'd thought about going around on the mountainside, but no, pass the sheep farm, then turn, turn again.

DeSpain stopped the truck. "Here, you take it down to the house," he told the fat mouthy one. "I'll follow right behind you. Road's rough. If the truck stalls out, then we'll have to walk in."

"We're going after the alien," one of the other men said softly.

"Damn straight," DeSpain said. "He killed Bobby Vipperman. Yanked out his spine."

"Bobby was no fighter," the fat mouthy man said.

Just like you, DeSpain thought, but he said, "Bobby was a bit soft or he'd"—no, can't say *or he'd have got himself out of the mill* because that's probably where kin of theirs worked—"have taken the Turk out."

"I see the Turk in town," the third man said softly. "He knows important people. State Department man was with him."

"The State Department told me the Turk's fair game now." The men DeSpain had hired squeezed in the cab together. The older logger drove. DeSpain started the moped, swearing praise for lithium batteries. If I can't get this alien, he might as well take me, DeSpain thought. He touched his 9-millemeter Beretta in his shoulder holster and the knife against his back. His spine, too sympathetic with Bobby Vipperman's spine, seemed to twist under the knife.

The truck stalled. The fat man got out and, screaming, ran back through the dark. The radio sudden cut on, induced into playing by the strong electric currents. Turk talked alien at them through the radio, obvious, terrible threats.

The two men still in the truck watched as DeSpain's moped stalled out. "Guess we get seven hundred fifty each," the younger logger said, scratching his nose with the stub of his index finger.

"Seems like it," DeSpain said. "You want more beer before we go in?"

"Not hardly," the man said, looking at the other man, who could have been his older brother. "You got two more pair of those night goggles? Are we beating or shooting?

"Defend yourselves however."

"Maybe we should talk a thousand," the older man said. "Seems like it's a bit more dangerous than poaching black walnut logs."

"Here," DeSpain said, fishing for his wallet, "I'll give you both three hundred each before, seven hundred after."

"Write us a note on it," the younger man said.

"The Turk knows we're here. We better get moving," DeSpain said.

"He'll wonder why we're sitting out here," the older man said, "and maybe come out of the house. Write us the note."

DeSpain wrote them a promise for seven hundred each after they talked to the Turk. Away from the house, that was where they ought to confront the alien. He thought, *next time, man or woman, alien or human, gets in my face, I'm going to kill 'em first offense.*

The two loggers let DeSpain pass them. He pedaled the moped up as far as he could go without actually seeing the house, then stopped and pulled down the night goggles. A ghost of infrared behind the trees. Too hot to get a good reading through these cheap goggles. He yelled, hoping those stereo speaker ears were keen enough to hear him, "Turk, we've got to talk."

"My lawyer's aunt warned me you were coming."

Shit on the old bat. "Don't believe what she told you. She's crazy."

"You and she are not in collaboration." The alien said it like he was reading voice stresses. DeSpain figured maybe stress analyzers came with the ears.

The two loggers stopped. "Come up to the house alone," the Turk called.

DeSpain whispered, "You won't get paid."

The older man said, "We've got enough."

"He'll kill you anyway," DeSpain said. "He can identify you through your voices."

"Don't believe Mr. DeSpain," the alien said.

"Hell, I'm one of you. He's alien. He's selling drugs. I just sell liquor."

"Dennis, this alien stops the truck, he tore out Bobby Vipperman's spine, he's buddies with Hugous at The Door 18, and you want all two of us to march on him?" The men stared at the gun in Dennis's hand.

He looked at it himself, then said, "Do what you want to. You'll have run off and left me."

They did. He thought about shooting them, but went on toward the Turk. Maybe we should work together, he thought, but I don't understand the motivations. Why here? Why liquor? Why with the blacks first? He said, "I'm not coming in your house where you can drug me."

"Fine. We'll come out with lights, action, cameras. I'll even have a human witness."

Berenice, Marie's friend, bitches both. DeSpain sweated under his bulletproof vest. The damn thing seemed glued to him by now, heavier than before, loaded with quarts of sweat. He put the Beretta in his front waistband, pointed to the left. Neither his spine nor his legs wanted him to walk forward, but he could force his body forward by thinking about how everyone would pick him apart if he couldn't deal with this alien. He wondered if news that an alien pushed him off his home territory would get back to Uralsk.

The Armenians were being difficult enough as was. Forward, get a look at the guy through the goggles if he's hotter than 75 degrees at the surface.

If he sees infrared, DeSpain realized, he'll know I've got a bulletproof vest on . . . damn, damn, damn.

"Mr. Dennis DeSpain, who served time for running liquor while drunk," the Turk said, as if identifying Dennis for all time with his previous lowest moment.

"Turk, who the State Department no longer protects," DeSpain said, watching the heat patch resolve into two figures, one Berenice, tiny, uniformly warm across the body, the other the Turk, large, with cold blotches over the head and torso. *I bet I could see him if I took the goggles off.*

"I can't see," Berenice said. "What are you doing?"

Bastard's lights flared infrared. DeSpain clawed the goggles away from his eyes, blinded from glare. He threw himself toward the bushes he'd seen before, pulled his gun, and tried to hear sounds, fire at sounds.

But speakers cut on, electric guitars being mutilated by band saws, microphones being run through hammer mills. "Mary and Jesus Chain," he thought someone shouted. A chitinous foot pinned his gun hand. He tried to kick, but the damn thing had such reflexes. The Turk had him by a leg. The foot against his hand squeezed its toes until he dropped the gun. Then the alien lifted DeSpain, still blinded, and tied his legs together. Another heave and he was dangling head down on what had to have been a hook. DeSpain wondered why the alien didn't just hook him through his Achilles tendons. Maybe Bobby's tendons hadn't held?

Then he heard a whuffled gunshot, a crack, and a second shot that went splat. The terrible sound stopped and he was just dangling blind there, wondering if the shots had been inside the electronic equipment or out. After a second DeSpain said, "I can't see."

"Figured you couldn't." It was Berenice. "I couldn't for an instant myself even though I'd closed my eyes. He didn't figure an old lady'd get him. The back of his neck cracked like a lobster."

"You warned him I was coming."

"Shit, Dennis, if I cut you loose, can you fall okay? If it was me up there, I'd break a hip coming down."

"Cut me loose."

"First, the Turk knew you'd come before I even told him. I told him so he'd let me get at his back." DeSpain fell onto the alien's body, which half grabbed at him. He scuttled away and tried to blink away the green blobs still blinding him. Berenice kept talking. "I couldn't know whether I could get through the skull and I didn't know where he had vital organs, so I went for his neck. One shot to crack him, the second to get the neuroconnectors."

DeSpain said, "Do you know where there's a phone in the house?"

"I'll drive you home. I don't want to explain the gun I used. Plastic. I used to have friends like that, smuggle them onto airplanes."

"I could say Henry Allen gave it to me."

"Dennis, I'll tell everyone you saved me. Let you keep your balls on with the other distributors and I won't have to explain this gun."

Marie Cleans Up

I got there too late to do anything, passed the alien dead next to a hook with cut ropes. Berenice and Dennis were walking up the steps to front door, both looking tired and sweaty.

"I killed him," Dennis said. "In self-defense." Berenice got the door open; maybe the alien had been so sure of himself that it wasn't locked. We went in the house and saw

Bobby's spine, cleaned white, curved like a fish over the mantel. Berenice said, "It looks rather handsome." Dennis shuddered. I thought it jangled between weirdly beautiful and grotesque—conceptual overload and exhaustion running my visual centers like the spine was an optical illusion.

Berenice found the phone and called the sheriff's department. I took the phone from her and told the dispatcher, "You shits couldn't investigate right away, could you?"

When the deputies arrived, they told Berenice to wipe the prints off the gun and help them destroy the tapes that were still rolling out in the yard where Turk had his meat hook. Dennis looked more guilty than I'd ever seen him.

"You mean you didn't save her. She saved you?"

"Damn tapes." I loved him then as hard as ever, nakedly happy to be alive, embarrassed for being saved by an old lady.

One of the deputies asked, "Where in the hell did she get a plastic pistol?"

The sheriff himself arrived in his business suit and after listening to a few people said to Berenice, "If you weren't as old as you are, we'd arrest you. Marie, take her home." They stripped Dennis of his bulletproof vest and his knife, and cuffed him.

"Take him straight to the hospital and call Dr. Tucker," Berenice said. "The lights blinded him. If you don't take care of him, he'll sue."

She never gets the keys again, I decided as I drove the Cadillac home. Berenice slumped over halfway home, asleep and drooling, looking a mess in early morning sun.

7

Aftermath for the Lawyer

Neither Marie nor Berenice woke me up when they got back. The first I heard about the second killing was at ten-thirty when Orris DeSpain called me to ask about filing separation papers.

"Marie was there again," she said, "and your aunt. Berenice killed Turk while Dennis dangled helpless. They brought out Bobby's spine and took it to the funeral home for burial."

But I'd told them all to wait. "What are you talking about?" I said. Why didn't they let me know what was going on? "Berenice?"

"Berenice. The alien turned his back on her and she killed him with a plastic explosives gun." Orris sounded as though she'd always known Berenice was dangerous.

I'd ask Marie. Berenice would lie. "Okay, Orris, but why are you filing separation papers?"

"I'm going for a law degree at George Washington University. It makes more sense than shooting Dennis or Marie.

What is this, some ballad with me as the villainess against the Nut Brown Maid?"

"Get another lawyer, Orris. I really don't want to hear about it." I figured she'd just called me to see what I'd known about the situation.

I got furious. Then my incision started throbbing, so I just lay back in bed, carefully bent so to relieve tension on that.

Berenice came in then and said, "I think we should tell you that your client Turkemaw is dead."

"Orris DeSpain told me. Damn you, I told all of you to wait."

Berenice sat down in a chair by my bed and looked at her hands, turning them this way and that. "If I'da been younger, I'da been in trouble. What if Turk's people don't understand? I could have been risking the planet."

"Wasn't it self-defense?"

"I killed him to save that Dennis DeSpain. Shit, was Dennis any better? Used the plastic gun. Never knew where that gun came from other than someone stole it. Never knew why I kept it, either."

I said, "Don't forget what he did to Bobby."

She said, "I'm confused about Bobby. Isn't he dead?"

Two days later, when I was trying to sleep in the afternoon, still using a pillow to hold the stitches in, a couple more aliens and a State Department man came by.

The other aliens were more alien than Turk. How, I wasn't sure, but as soon as I saw the other aliens, I knew Turk had been pushing his own limits the way he pushed Dennis DeSpain's. He hadn't been born or bred to be human, but he was crazy enough to fake it. These new aliens wore sashes and wristbands, not blue coveralls, and looked neater than Turk had looked. And they didn't look a bit like tourists.

"Was there a reason to kill Turkemaw?" the State Department guy asked. He wasn't the one I'd seen with Turk earlier.

Berenice said, "I'm sorry, but he was killing humans."

One of the aliens said, "We wondered," so flatly I decided they had rather globally wondered and sent us Turk to see how we'd react. A test. These aliens would never explain how the test worked. No right way, no wrong way, no blame.

"Is Dennis free then?" I asked.

"Your local law is holding him for the gun he couldn't use." The alien sounded vaguely confused, but then nobody arrested Berenice for her much-more-illegal gun, that CIA special that someone, probably an European leftist studying war in the Middle East, had stolen thirty years earlier, a talisman gun that had drifted around radical circles until Berenice stopped it when she returned to Rocky Mount.

The State Department man asked Berenice, "Do you remember who gave you that gun?"

"An old lady my age remember something like that?" Her eyes went vague, unfocused, then flickered toward me. Yes, I thought, absolutely, but nobody pushed for an answer. Both the State Department guy and the aliens stood for a few seconds looking at Berenice as though she were a monument, then left without saying good-bye.

After the door closed, Berenice said, "I'm sorry all this came at the time it did. I feel most guilty that I did enjoy it. Just a little, you understand. I hadn't been out like that in a long damn time."

I wished I wasn't getting the impression she'd done the right thing. And I pitied Turk, even if he were the alien equivalent of Dennis DeSpain. Someone trickier than he let him come. "Just don't get into more trouble until mid-August." I decided I'd have to take care of Bobby's kids—I'd been half responsible for him getting killed.

"I didn't mean to get you upset. And I didn't save Bobby, did I? All I got out of it was some more memories." She stopped as if checking that at least those memories moved from short-term to long-term memory. "I didn't think I could get more memories at my age. But poor Bobby."

Neither of us saved Bobby, old aunt. The warranty on my body has expired, even if the biopsy was negative, and here we are, later in life than we imagined when we were younger. In your radical days, did you ever expect to be so old? I thought I'd skip middle age myself, but no.

Yes, I was glad she showed Rocky Mount a bit of the old young Berenice who'd run radical in the streets.

Orris filed her separation papers with commonwealth's attorney Withold Brunner representing her. Everyone thought that bitchy of her, but she didn't betray any of Dennis's illegal business. But then Dennis rolled over when he heard who her lawyer was.

As Orris said she was going to do, she went to Georgetown University, but instead of returning to Rocky Mount or Roanoke as a lawyer, she became a State Department officer. When she was back once, trolling for gossip about Dennis and Marie, she said, "Henry Allen inspired me to do it."

"He seemed rather doofus to me," I said.

"Precisely. I knew I could do a better job."

Some time in the next year I sold the miniature Cadillac to make sure Berenice never again went adventuring and came home after signing the papers to incredible guilt. With the sale of her car or the death she'd caused or just aging in general, she never again was as clear or vigorous as the night she killed the alien. Sylvia, Bobby's widow, helped me with her. I felt odd, no possible children of my own, but with a sudden family that I had to support. I began taking bootleggers as clients.

Marie had married Dennis when the divorce was final. He told all his buddies he did it to strengthen his alliances with his black dealers. Rumor in the rougher bars and jukes had it Berenice had been about to shoot him next when Marie saved him. My bootlegger clients kept me informed as to various twists of the county's oral traditions.

When Marie got her chemical engineering degree a few years later, she applied for a legal distilling license for fuel-grade alcohol. They hired me to help them. We took it out in Marie's name because of Dennis's record.

Dennis saved Marie from becoming the officious techie I had imagined as her future when I first met her. Her white husband seemed to have made her wicked enough to be tolerant of human foibles—Berenice's senility, her outlaw cousins. With DeSpain with her, even trout fishing probably seemed erotic and slimy fun dirty. Whatever, years after Marie got her chemical engineering degree and her legal liquor license, you could suspect she still kept a shake-baby dress or two. I hoped she didn't think keeping a space for her outlaw side was a failing. I saw it as a sign of grace.

But poor Dennis. By the time he was forty, he was strictly legal.

We all met around Berenice's grave sometime after he'd turned forty-three. Marie wore a light purple velveteen dress that I knew wasn't disrespectful of the mourners of this particular dead.

Marie said, "Berenice said this color would make a white woman look yellow green. She said I ought to wear it a lot."

I said, "She refused to believe that you'd turn out to be just another dye-house chemist."

Marie looked at Dennis and said, "Is it so different?"

Dennis said, "We're doing better than that, Marie." He seemed embarrassed. He said, "Lilly, I'm sorry."

I knew he meant for Bobby, and just nodded. But then don't we middle-class Southerners always fail the rednecks who trust us? When Bobby was in high school, he asked his daddy's supervisor about getting in a support group for the college-bound. The supervisor earlier had said to the social worker organizing the group, "You damn fool, you're stealing my best future workers." And the supervisor told Bobby he'd be happier avoiding high-class anxieties and the college-bound support group was just a scam to give the social worker a job.

Funny, how I'd forgotten that until now.

The aliens neither invaded nor gave us FTL drive diagrams. Not while I was alive, at least.

Last time we heard about Orris, she was the American cultural attaché to Angola. *Time* magazine printed a photo of her driving a Land-Rover out of the embassy gates with the president's daughter. She was laughing.

The Tyrant That I Serve

O*h, Shelley, don't,* my mind squeals before I . . . Shelley, my sweet human mistress, switches on the kill-machine in my brain. Five times in eight days, I come up from the basement and begin hunting her through the walnut-paneled halls, down the chrome-railed lesser staircases, now across the atrium, my useless wings quivering, small bare feet, more human than the dog's they made me of, cold on the marble.

I claw at the buzz in my skull, but keep going, hands twitching, nose sniffing. I want this electric worm out of my brain—I don't hate Shelley. But I must try to kill her, and I hunt; and she runs, shrieks, giggles.

Each hunt comes back like a dream—a distorted house floats by, my foolish silk clothes flutter as I run, then I drop, creeping toward the twittering giggle. Then Shelley sees me and runs, shrieking.

I'm slower than she. Natural selection gives predators some advantage—speed, stealth—but, of course, I'm no *nat-*

ural predator. My two wings clap together as I race after her. On her belt, she has a small box, in the belt an antenna.

In my brain the receiver.

Chimera, fairy monster with useless wings, I came out of a crystal jar, the design of a young, rich girl who was seven when she ordered me, fourteen when she took delivery.

Humans must love to be terrified. Shelley hums, lures me to the huge main staircase with balustrades turned from oak logs; the matching ceiling drips wooden stalactites.

The lights go out. Caught on the stairs, impelled to chase her, I'm terrified of falling; and terror doesn't please me the way it does humans.

Shelley, please, don't turn up the rheostat.

I want even more to kill, beat the box before it cuts the brain-body connects at the last minute. Kill her so I can get some rest. Once she was gone for two weeks afterward, regrowing body parts. I didn't remember what I did to her.

So important to kill her, my brain hums, as I feel my way down the stairs with my toes, trembling in the dark.

When I reach the floor carpets, I sigh—no hideous wing-breaking tumble tonight. She's hidden in the draperies—I hear them rustle, then keep up my hearing, put my hands behind my small pointed ears. She breathes there, scared now.

Brain says, *run, kill.* She's powered up the signal. *Blood, oh, blood would taste good.* But in the dark, I can play off against the brain stimulation, so I go slowly, feeling ahead of me with blind probing fingers which touch open-pored wood, the big oak refectory table.

She'd had it moved; if I'd rushed her, I'd have broken ribs. Quietly I pad around it, going hand over hand. I smell wood, dust, Shelley, hear her breathing, *getting faster with the lungs now, hey, Shelley? Blood for my mouth, oh, blood.* My eyes have adapted for the dark; I see the lump in the drapes.

She switches the lights back on. Blinded, I rush her, grabbing her shoulder before I tumble, in a rage of pleasure. I try to squeeze the wings to my back as I go down.

Then blackness.

I woke up belly down on my kennel bed, fingers a bit sore, blood under the nails—maybe I killed her this time and we can take a break for a few weeks while she grows a new throat? They'd dumped me down in my hunting silks, not bothering to change me. I heard lion footpads, the click of hooves, and saw Hippogriff coming with a coffee cup for me.

Sleep, back to sleep to take me away from all this; but Hippogriff put the cup down and butted me with his beaked head, nudging me up, then checking with the little hands that grew from his chest, seeing if I'd been hurt.

"Hippogriff," I croaked. He maneuvered his bulk around in the small room, got the cup back in his hands without spilling it, and came up to me. As I sat up, I took the cup from him. "She dead? Badly hurt?"

The big head shook, *no*. I put my hand on his shoulder and pulled myself up, then checked in my little mirror for bruises. Not too bad, considering that I'd clipped her. Humans consider me beautiful and rave about my high cheekbones, expressive green eyes (I'm glad I've never seen them when I was hunting), and the chiseled nostrils. Myself, I think humans look coarse. So, to my own eyes, I looked normal, but dark under the eyes, a bruise on one cheekbone, jaw scraped as though I'd been dragged along the carpet.

Piss on her. I loved her. Why?

Hippogriff also brought me breakfast, awkwardly holding the tray. I took it from him before it tipped, and I gobbled down the breakfast—cold, already.

After I ate, I showered to work the stress-kinks out of my legs, arms, and wings. The feathers needed dressing, but Shelley liked to do that herself the morning after. One primary dangled, shaft broken almost in two—either I'd fallen on it when she brain-blasted me, or someone was careless when she, he, or it put me to bed. Or dragged me to it.

Hildegarde, the human maid with the big stunner tube for Hippogriff and the little one for me on her hips, came to complain about the hot water, my dawdling. "Breakfast, late," she snapped, certain that I really understood only a few words and those only as signals.

"Okay," I said, jerking on my pants, leaving chest and wings bare, slipping my feet into shoes; then, wings aquiver, I ran upstairs to serve Paul and Shelley breakfast.

"Ah, Ariban," Paul, Shelley's brother, said, "have a rough night?" Shelley didn't look at me. I noticed her stiff shoulder and the little electric healer wires curled around her neck. As I served her eggs, she cringed back, and I wanted to throw myself at her feet, beg like a dog for her forgiveness. If I had DNA for the tail, I'd wag it low, head down . . . *Shelley, oh Shelley, why can't we just be friends?* I missed the tail to wag.

"Maybe I should put a delay circuit in the box so he could kill you," Paul said to Shelley. "Then you'd have a few weeks to get the adrenaline out of your system."

My feathers rustled—fairy wings quiver at the least agitation.

"You disapprove of everything I do, Paul," Shelley said. "Quit putting pressure on me."

Paul looked back at me, and I shrugged my wings, hands full of the coffee tray.

Then speaking softly, as though I wouldn't hear if she whispered, Shelley said, "I want to take Ari on the roller coaster today. To show him how thrilling fear is."

"You use the chimera too much," Paul said. "But I've told you that. At least wait for him to calm down. After all, he tried to kill you last night."

"Not by my choice," I said, pouring coffee for Shelley, wanting to touch her.

"We know, Ariban," Paul said, "but . . ." He signaled to

me to hurry, then said to Shelley, "And I heard that you taught him to read, too. Shelley, get out more among people, real people."

My wings flicked again and I drew them up against my back, tightly. Paul gave one little tug as I poured coffee for him.

"Yes," Shelley said, "I'll take him on the roller coaster. A creature who gives scare thrills might be even more exquisite in his horror if he's experienced the Mighty Screaming Rails."

"Someone broke one of my feathers last night, Shelley."

"Oh, poor Ariban, Shelley will fix."

After I took the dirty dishes to Hildegarde, I met Shelley in the garden. She had the imping knife ready and the little irons to put inside the feather shafts, but she drew back slightly when she saw me coming at her. The cerebral cortex, the most human brain part, knew the hunt was over; but the ape-animal still feared me. Each morning after, she made herself re-dominate me.

I felt ashamed and dropped my wings and face as she took my elbow and sat me down between her feet. ''Oh, Shelley," I said, feeling lost as she stretched out each wing.

"You hate the compulsions, don't you? You remember more than you're supposed to."

"Yes," I said, feeling her tug at the damaged feather, then hold it steady, cutting the vane away just above the kink. While she trimmed the shaft and fitted it with an imping needle, I twisted to the side and flexed both wings several times, fanning us, working them before the one being imped was immobilized. She didn't look up.

"Ari," she said, holding the feather up with a drop of glue on the iron barb. Turning my back to her again, I relaxed the wing as she fitted the feather back in—shorter, but not by much, stronger with the tiny iron pin inside. She held the feather between her thumb and index finger and the wing with her other hand until the glue set.

"I wish it could be more of this," I said, pleased with her touch, "and less of that."

"I get bored. If I didn't work you, you'd get bored, too."

"I'd kill myself if it was all the other," I said.

"Perhaps I should send you back to the vet's for a suicide-inhibitor. Have them erase your reading skills, too."

I didn't say more, but lay down on my belly and spread my wings. "You little freak dog," Shelley said as she knelt over me, rubbing the complex knot of muscles around my arm-wing joints. Defenseless on my belly, I quivered, wings rustling the grass.

She loved that and sat more of her weight down on my back—carefully, because she's heavier than I am and all my muscles don't protect the spine. Tiny me, as small as could be made and yet still be dangerous—five feet of muscles, dragged down by those useless wings. Made male, to have as much muscle as possible on the frame, but sterile, like all chimeras.

I tried to pull my wings in, but she held them spread out—not much muscle there. "If I had a quilt," I said, "I could lie on my back without messing the feathers up, get warmer."

"Oh, Ariban, are you chilly?" She let one wing go and tickled under the other.

"Yes, I'm a bit cold," I answered cautiously.

"Since we're going to the roller coaster, I'll have to give you one of Daddy's coats to hide your wings. Don't want to offend the Muslims out there with an infidel dog."

Wing-binding. Sweet. A subtle torture, although I never complain. "Be careful," I said. She knew—the ape was pleased to see my fairy face wince.

"I love," she said, "to be scared."

"I know," I replied.

My wings—just cut them off, I thought as Hildegarde bound them down with stretchy knitted bands, carefully, so as not to permanently damage them. With them trapped down like that, I felt off-balance as I put on the human coat, fat monster fairy with a bruised cheek, scraped jaw, not completely hunchbacked.

Hildegarde patted me nervously. Impulsively, I hugged her around her middle. I'd never been out much, in daylight, outside the grounds, other than trips to the vet's for tanking—reprogramming in an iso-tank, watching kill holograms.

Hildegarde's hand dropped on the stunner. In five years, I'd never threatened her, but ordinary humans didn't like chimeras. I suspected from video holograms that they didn't like rich humans either, despite preserving the rich like national parks. And Paul paid Hildegarde.

Shelley called for me, and Hildegarde pushed me away from her, saying, "Ariban, don't touch. Go. Go to Shelley now."

"I want to say good-bye to Hippogriff," I called up to Shelley, nervous about that great outside of humans.

"Ari."

"Please, a minute."

Hippogriff was loose in the servants' hall when I went up and grabbed his chest hands. "Hipp, I'm going to a human amusement park. Out, you know."

He understood English—but oddly—and pushed me, trying to block me, keep me with him, but Hildegarde pulled out the big stunner, and Hippogriff let me pass. Shelley dropped the bars to keep Hippogriff from following me while opening the smaller basement door. He flicked his hands at me in the strange sign-language that only he and Paul knew.

Without any more words, we met her two bodyguards at the cars and got in an armored roadster that looked like an ordinary BMW from the outside. As we passed the gate, I turned around to look again at the outside of the house, so plain, like a block of ordinary buildings. None of the inside ornateness showed—*we don't share the visuals,* Shelley said once.

I wondered if she taped my wings down to spoil my appearance, to hide the visuals. Trying to get comfortable, I twisted around until I could lean on my side, not against the taped-down wing bones. Shelley smiled as I turned—humans are amused by strange things. I smiled back, not baring my teeth as we drove through the city, then toward a strange cleared ground partly covered with cars, the rest covered with whirling girder contraptions—the amusement park.

As though I were a child or her dwarf lover, Shelley held my hand as the bodyguards paid for the tickets. Humans, masses of them, swarmed around us, hopped on rides gaudy with lights and metal, enamel; and screamed, screamed as though chimera hunted them as the rides twisted on their metal joints. Shelley tugged me through the mob toward one huge thing that looked like a train track skewed across and through an unfinished building—girders in the air, immobile.

I trembled as though I'd done something wrong, imagined all the humans staring at me. "Exciting, isn't it?" Shelley said. "I'm out among people, like Paul wanted."

"No," I managed to answer, my tongue pulling free finally in my sticky mouth. I tried to relax—my wing muscles spasmed under the knitted bands. "Shelley, ride it by yourself."

"But we're doing it to show you how much fun it is. Your birthday, remember?"

Birthday? We didn't have birthdays, not chimeras. Purchase anniversary if you were a common chimera, stock. Delivery anniversary if custom. My wings ached. I thought, *let's get this over with. To hell with it and me.* I followed her through the turnstile and into the little car at the front of the small train. Seatbelts, lap bars. Shelley sat beside me and the two guards slid in behind.

Some God Militant, scourge of recombinant mock-men, tried to toss us into his blue sky. I screamed, pleading that I'd not ordered myself made. *Not me, I wasn't responsible.* Shelley screamed, too, raising her arms as if to be snatched from the car, like a God Militant worshiper, praying for the rapture, the great up-snatching to heaven of all real human beings.

Then the utter horror—upside down. Falling . . .

When I woke up, I found myself thrashing on a bench, pants wet, clotted with dung. A bodyguard peeled my fingers off Shelley's arm.

"I heard chimeras couldn't take it," Shelley said, "but I thought *you* were different."

"Unbind his wings," a man said from the crowd. I looked up at him and saw, beside the human who spoke, another delicate face, real like mine, not smeared and coarse like a human's. A free chimera? Only the Buddhists freed chimeras. The two came up and pulled the heavy coat off me while I sobbed.

"Get a blanket," one said.

I muttered about God Militant and true language, unreality, then slid more firmly into my body, and said, "Bathroom." The two from the crowd carried me into a men's room, where Shelley wasn't supposed to follow. One of her bodyguards came in, though, and jammed the door closed between us and the crowd.

While the human gently freed my wings, cutting the bands, I vomited into a toilet. The other chimera, a de-winged stock fairy, ran a basin full of hot water. I managed to pull myself up and went over to the basin, stripped. They washed me with paper towels, dried me, held me upright.

"Not all humans see chimeras as unreal," the human said. "Some think we all share a transcendental nature."

Buddhists, I realized, somewhat shocked—Zenbos were the bad guys on the video—but not surprised when he taped a small envelope under my armpit on the side opposite the bodyguard. "He needs a blanket—we have them in our car," the human told Shelley's bodyguard, handing him a parking stub and a key. As the bodyguard went out with their key, Shelley came in, her arm bleeding where my fingers had dug in. The human and chimera looked annoyed. I couldn't stop trembling, thinking of all the hostile humans who'd pounce when we opened the door, when we went out. Somehow the other chimera slipped out and brought back a first aid kit, coming back when the bodyguard did. The bodyguard gave the chimera the blanket.

The chimera whispered in my ear. "There's always a refuge if you're willing to work for it. Mind." He wrapped the blanket around me.

"I'm surprised," the human said to Shelley, "that the Society for Prevention of Cruelty to Animals doesn't crack down on you chimera owners for scaring your pets here."

The other chimera pulled one of my arms free and injected it with a drug that left me conscious, but unconcerned, limp. I smiled at him—Zenbos. The Buddhists say everything even a test-tube dog that looks human, is holy. He patted my shoulder, then looked up at the human, who came over and lifted me carefully.

"We'll carry him to your car," he told Shelley.

"Thank you so much, really. I didn't expect him to react this way." She opened her purse and the two guys took money as though giving first aid to terrified chimeras was their job. I felt a bit odd about that, with their envelope taped to my body, hypnotic Zenbo propaganda probably, full of subtle lies; but nothing mattered too much.

The drug wore out while I slept, and I began having nightmares: DNA, great chimera helixes I had to climb, while Shelley laughed from the top. A base rung broke and I tumbled. My scream . . . I tried to sit up, but lay paralyzed, half awake, half asleep.

Paul sat by my kennel bed. I finally floundered up, staring at him, wondering if I'd slept beyond breakfast.

"Breakfast?" I croaked, sounding as dumb as Hildegarde thought I was.

"Don't worry about breakfast yet. It's just a little beyond midnight. Buddhists taped this to you," he said, handing me the envelope. "Shelley's being such a bitch, perhaps going to a refuge would be a good idea for you."

"Why do you give this to me?" My hands trembled as I opened the envelope—already unsealed. On the paper were nine phone button diagrams, the push dial nine times,, with a graphic finger pressing different buttons on each diagram, and underneath, an arrow going from left to right—illiterates could dial the phone number, if they understood that the arrow pointed the number direction. And a Buddha and lotus in the corner—I'd seen them on fiction videos, those tricky Buddhists, sophisticals, stealing pets.

Hippogriff shambled up and lay down so he could put his big head against Paul's hip, and crooned, looking up at Paul, who scratched him idly around the feathered earholes. "Oh, Hippogriff," Paul said, "has little Ariban been happy lately, with his Sennatrix DNA-coil-segment brain?"

Hipp moved so Paul could see his hands and signaled. "He said," Paul relayed to me, "that once you asked how you could really make her stay dead."

"Sir?" I began to be frightened again.

"Shelley's got to grow up. And if you don't get her, she's going to get you." He spoke softly, "Terror's a life spice to humans, but . . ."

I sat up. "How can I get away, with these? What do the Buddhists really do with chimeras?" I jerked my wings.

"Poor Ariban, too intelligent for any situation," Paul said. He leaned back and lit a cigarette. "Shall I tell her you want to make her dead?" Hippogriff settled his bulk back down on the floor, also looking at me. "Call the refuge number," Paul said. "It has to be an act of your own free will, if I understand the matter correctly. They don't want aged pets dumped on them."

"Sir?" He was trying to get rid of me. I felt terribly tired, and slumped down on my side, wings behind, head propped up on an elbow.

"So suspicious," he said. "You're too intelligent for this."

"It's the only real home I've had. I love Shelley, if only she wouldn't . . ."

He interrupted me. "That roller coaster, I suppose, was lovely."

I quivered—the drug had completely worn out of my system—angry gods, terror. "No," I said. He sat down on the bed, rolled me to my belly, and rubbed between my wings, around the roots of them, and down my back.

"If you didn't have wings," he said, "you'd look like a lovely sulky boy, with those eyes."

I closed them. "Don't tell Shelley."

"Better dream about Buddhist monasteries."

In the morning, I served breakfast despite hunts, roller coasters, and strange Buddhist drugs. As I cooked omelettes beside the table and heated the plates, Paul told Shelley he'd take me to the vet's to have me tank-tested, in case the scare had blown my conditioning.

What free will does a creature with a brain worm have? Yet the Buddhist had been kind, and Paul wanted me to go. After breakfast, Shelley dressed me in a soft wool sweater with wing holes, gently working each wing through. My feathers were a bit ragged; but if I was going to be tanked, she'd dress them after I finished thrashing out imaginary murders in that dark warm brine.

The Buddhists would not have me tanked, I thought, *at least not that way.* Paul was going to set me free. Free? I kissed Shelley, held her.

"Oh, Ariban, you can't love me too much," she said. "I suspect you do need re-tanking."

Paul draped my wings with a loose overcoat and we got in his armored Jaguar. He drove us himself, without bodyguards. I looked out the windows; raining out there, streaks of water obscuring the view. I felt sleepy and didn't really want to go through with this. *If only Shelley would stop keying me up . . .*

"If you don't go, I'll really have you tanked." Paul took my chin in his hand, turned me to face him. "And if you hurt Shelley badly, there's a lethal needle for you." We stopped near a phone booth.

I walked through the rain with the number chart in my hand, feathers bruised by the wet overcoat, the wings writhing. *This is wrong,* I thought, but I remembered the roller coaster—the Buddhist man and the chimera knew pets didn't like those things, so Shelley must have known, too. *Okay,* I thought, opening the paper and pushing the numbers, first number, second number, third, fourth, fifth, sixth, seventh, eighth, ninth.

"Dharma Refuge," a voice said.

"I would like refuge," I said, suddenly feeling utterly lost. I looked back at the car, but Paul had opaqued the windows.

"Have you committed a crime, done anything that if you were human would be considered a crime? Have you taken more than the clothes on your back?"

"I'm a terror chimera, but I'm compelled to do that." *Maybe they'd turn me down because of that.* Rejected by a Dharma Refuge—I could go home—I couldn't figure out if the idea scared me or pleased me. I looked back at Paul's car, but the windows were still opaqued. Lethal needle. I could have been euthanized earlier, when I put Shelley in the recon tank for two weeks.

"Where are you? Are you calling from a pay phone?"

"Yes," I said, wings beating the glass walls of the booth. Cold, so cold and wet.

"Give me the number if you can read, landmarks if you can't. Are they searching for you now?"

"My owner's brother brought me to this booth."

"Are *you* sure you want to come to us?"

"Lethal needle," I said and began crying. Then I stifled the sobs and managed to say clearly, "Your people helped me when my owner took me on a roller coaster yesterday. She's used me five times in eight days. Humans make me nervous." I looked at the phone and said, "I'm at 43-456-8907, at the corner of 34th and Madeira." I'd betrayed Shelley; my heart twisted inside me as though it had been cut loose.

"Wait. We can't promise to take you in permanently, but we'll give you refuge and make a fuller investigation."

"I'll wait, please." If they had refused me, would Paul have let me back in the car? Refuge or re-tanking, nasty lying in dark salt water. I remembered too much of the last time, when I played through murder after murder, brainslammed, holograms of a dead Shelley floating in the dark. But I was cold in the glass phone booth, exposed—please, Paul, let me crawl back into the car. I thought about killing Shelley, the lethal needle. I shivered, then pulled the coat back over my wings. Wet coat, no help.

A cab finally pulled up, but stopped twenty feet back when the driver saw Paul's car. Paul drove off then, and two uniformed monks, saffron robes and tiny patchwork aprons, climbed out of the cab and came up to the booth.

"Do you seek refuge in the Dharma?"

"Yes," I said. Neither monk had helped me yesterday, but I was anxious to be out of the phone booth, to be among anything made of DNA, to be warm—physically, socially.

"Do you know your owner's address or have a tag?"

"Shelley Carteret. The address is . . ."

"Oh boy," one said to the other. Each took one of my arms and hurried me to the cab, stripped the wet clothes off, and gave me a couple of towels and string pants, hot tea from a thermos, as the cab took off.

As I shivered faintly, one asked, "Do you know much about how the Carterets are outside their house?"

"She only allowed fiction programs and channels on our videos," I replied. "Shelley let me see some God Militant shows, though."

"I saw you at a beach party on the news once," one of the monks said, "before I went to the Refuge myself. You looked more decorative then."

"Oh," I said, curling a towel around my back, threading it between my wings. "They've never shown the hunt, have they?"

"When you . . . no."

I blew stale air out of my lungs and sipped the tea as we rode through the wet streets in an anonymous fake cab with Shelley Carteret's escaped chimera in it—Sennatrix brain in tightening coils.

The Zenbo refuge was another rich house, older than the Carterets', that some rich human must have left to the Buddhists. We pulled up to the gate, entered only to come to a wall, a ninety-degree turn, and then through the last gate that led to the car elevator platform. The cab sank down to the parking garage, and the driver stopped in a row of about fifteen fake cabs. My rescuers motioned me toward another elevator cage which took us back to ground level. We walked under a covered pathway.

"We can take you to see the Roshi soon," one said. I kept looking through the rain at the tiny trees, expanses of gravel studded with lichen-crusted rock—my eyes running through a system of plants that made space expand and contract. Illusions. Like holos.

"Like Alice in Wonderland," I said out loud.

"What? Your owner read you that?"

"I can read." I remembered learning and began crying, *oh, Shelley. This is so nice,* I'd told her when I first understood what she was trying to teach me.

"Normal to have some regrets, but you mentioned something about a lethal needle?"

"When you see the Roshi," the other said, "kneel, then *listen* to him. Leave when he rings the bell."

The landscape expanded and contracted around me.

We took off our shoes as we entered a low wooden building, and walked on straw mats, past men and chimeras who barely glanced at me. My escorts bowed me into the presence of the Roshi.

Just another human American—somehow I'd almost expected an Oriental chimera, dragon, dog-lion, or at least a Japanese human with almost chimerical eyes. I knelt, bowed, and waited for him to speak.

"A terror chimera?" he said softly, smiling.

"Yes," I said, barely audible.

"We think if matter is complicated enough, it reflects mind—that all form is Mind. So we don't say that creatures from genetic mix-masters are less capable of transcendence than we whose parents complicated our DNA sexually. But we don't grant you equality with humans as you conceive us. We allow equality for all—rats, trees, chimeras, humans, mosquitoes that bite us all."

"I had a nightmare about DNA," I said, then remembered that I wasn't supposed to speak. He smiled at my confusion and embarrassment; and I smiled, nervously back, and raised my head.

"Don't smile too much, young angel creature; or you'll get raped." He sighed and looked beyond my head, eyes not focused on anything in particular. "If you want, we can amputate your wings. And whether you want or not, we may have to restructure your bone-muscle attachments so you're human-average in strength. The man with the cane is the Monjutor—he teaches you how to sit."

He rang a metal hand bell—I was dismissed. I scooted backwards on my hands and knees, remembering that one backs away from kings.

He laughed. "You're no longer a dog," he said.

My guides reappeared and showed me how to leave properly—quick standing bow, then go.

The bathroom was strange—showers or spray tubes to wash off with, then a couple of big cypress tubs to sit in, only for clean guys, human or chimera. My new escort, a human female, showed me where to put my clothes, handed me a towel, and stripped herself, breasts no odder than much of what was hung on chimeras.

"Are they functional?" she asked, staring at my groin.

"I'm sterile," I said, towel flipped off my shoulder, poised low.

She turned red from the buttock up. "Sorry. That wasn't . . . You have to get used to this place."

"I don't know what the trigger stimulus would be. I was a terror chimera," I said stiffly before I hopped in the coolest tub. We floated around each other. She sank down to her chin and watched me.

"You aren't the first terror chimera I've been in this tub with," she said. "Come on, relax. We'll have to get out soon enough."

"I'm scared of you," I finally admitted.

When we got out, she handed me a drier, some lengths of white cloth, another pair of string pants, and zoris with socks for them, with separate pockets for big toes.

"You'll hate the food," she said. "Most new carnivore-based chimeras do." Then she told me how to wear the length of cloth, threaded around between my wings and arms, before she dressed herself in an orange robe and took me down another hall.

"Since we don't have a clean-room class beginning right away," she said, "we're putting you on a non-clean line, just fitting hardware into cases—disc players this time."

"You don't make black boxes for chimera here?" Electronic things scared me—human business, control business.

"Of course not." A door swung open and I saw an assembly row—conveyor belts loaded with beige plastic shells and black stacks of wafer assemblies, speakers. The conveyors hissed softly on their rollers; otherwise the room was almost silent. The woman sat me down between a human male and another chimera, a tall, shaggy six feet of fur that thinned out enough on the face for the eyes to see through. He or she spoke perfectly, though, and told me to fit the assembly pins in the plastic case sockets. The big shaggy flipped two toggles; and the assemblies and plastic cases descended on their conveyors, hissing toward me.

I fitted my first assembly together, fingers trembling. Then the big shaggy slowed down the assembly conveyors and showed me where to put the assembled unit—on a faster conveyor that crossed below. I adjusted my chair so the conveyor that took assemblies away was at waist level.

"You'll do about four hours a day of this," the big shaggy said, speeding up the two conveyor belts that brought me parts, "unless you've got other talents."

"I was a terror chimera," I said, "but I can write, read."

The big shaggy looked down at me and snorted. The human to my left snickered. *Was,* I thought, *I said I was. Was.* Hugely relieved, I laughed back at my companions. If I faced nothing more than components coming at me, I could handle the refuge. The human looked at my wings and said carefully, "A lady's terror chimera?"

"Yes," I said, fitting my fourth stack into its shell and dropping it on the lower belt. "I *was* a lady's terror chimera."

"Any daughter of mine wanted a terror chimera like you, I'd have her psyched. Real problem bitch, I bet."

The Monjutor came and whacked the two on either side of me with a flexible bamboo cane. "Quiet," he said, "this is meditation, too."

Then the Monjutor looked curiously at my back, stick ready to crack, searching for an appropriate place to lay on.

The wings draped down to my hipbones, so he finally lightly whacked me across the back of my neck.

"They sent your medical charts," the Refuge's lawyer explained to me, "but Shelley filed a complaint against her brother and the Center the instant we sent the clothes back."

The Roshi sat near us as the lawyer told me Shelley had the right to see me in private after she was searched. I'd have to make a court appearance and swear that I found my role in her house morally offensive, that I sought refuge of my own free will. Paul would testify that she'd abused me.

"I had a Sennatrix chimera once," the Roshi said, "before. Like rolling a hundred-faceted die for the brain—some are most unusual. Many gametes to get one custom—they don't worry if the brain is more than needed for the form, the task. We promise to defend you, fellow-creature Ariban. And after you've had some training, we'll give you a tattoo."

"Will I belong to you, then, as I belonged to her?"

"No. It's a warning in case you did go back and were sold. Or if we're attacked and you're stolen. Zen-trained chimeras aren't as . . . reliable . . . predictable . . . as those who've never spent time with us."

"I already feel changed," I said, still nervous.

"Perhaps," he replied, "but your wing tips tremble."

The lawyer rose and said, "Be sure he's prepared for the court appearance. Judge Hickle is presiding—very pro–property rights."

"Keep a table between you and Carteret," the Monjutor told me as I opened the interview room door. Shelley stood inside, dressed formally, with gloves and a veiled hat, tears barely visible, glistening under the black lace.

I've hurt her, I thought, sitting down behind the table, leaning back into my wings to steady them. "Please sit down," I said to her.

"Paul sent you away."

"Yes, but I do hate what you make me do. You abuse me."

"As though you were a dangerous drug," she said, smiling slightly, sitting down finally. "I love you, and here you are, humiliating me, making a spectacle of us both. You shouldn't be ashamed of how I have fun with you—you can't help it."

"Oh, Shelley, why did you take me on the roller coaster?" My voice rose despite myself, questioning her. *Her.* She tossed back her veil to let fresh tears glitter at me, and I lowered my eyes.

"What do you do here?" she finally asked.

"I help make disc players, radios. I do sitting meditations. Work in the greenhouse some. Everyone seems friendly."

"No lovely clothes, just rags wrapped around you, uniformed novice." She'd stopped crying now, seemed frustrated.

I remembered the first week in her house, scared, fresh out of the tanks, then more horrified and ashamed after she set me hunting her, compulsion sizzling in my mind. When I woke up the next morning, she sat with me while I sobbed, stroking me, down in the kennel. I wasn't fully grown then, but still had almost the strength of a human male; I don't think she realized then that I could kill her if she didn't release the brain slam button in time. For a long time after that first hunt, she didn't use me, taught me to read, played with me.

Now, her hands twitching on the table, she watched me. I started to say, "I'll see you . . ." My voice broke, I struggled to finish, "in . . . court." Then I cried into my hands, trying to hide my tears.

"I'm glad," she said, "that you can cry, too. I've missed you so dreadfully."

"Shelley, go," I said. "Go."

She stepped around the table and stroked between my

wings. "Poor Ariban, so neglected these days." I arched my back for her, quivering.

"Time's up, Carteret," the Roshi said, walking into the room. "You've had your shot at him."

"Maybe he wants to go home?" she said, fingers rubbing where I usually itched.

The Roshi turned to me and said, "Ariban, she tried to smuggle this in." He laid my black box on the table.

"She . . . ee," I hissed, wings jerking, skin under the robes suddenly chilly. I turned and saw that her eyes seemed dead, empty. "May I leave, sir; I mean stay at the Center, get out of this room?"

"Carteret, you leave," he said. She put her hand around my neck and shook me slightly before turning to go. As soon as the door closed behind her, I looked back at the Roshi.

The Roshi took out an insulated wire, stripped one end, then the other. "Watch, Ari." He unscrewed a light bulb from a table lamp, then inserted the bare copper wire in beside the right-hand button, and pushed the other end of the wire into the socket. "Your box. What I just did generally ruins them."

"Don't test it," I said, sweating, panting slightly.

"If you have mental temptations, use mental resistance. Perhaps chimera should use physical resistance to physical compulsion, electricity against the electric brain worms. You could, of course, simply smash the control boxes. You never tried to find them when she wasn't using them, did you?"

"No. Shelley brought that, today?" I asked again.

"We'll use it as evidence in the hearing." He laid the box aside. "I wonder if you chimeras might not think yourselves around these compulsions, even if they are more forceful in your minds than our human desires are in ours."

I wanted to get away from the box. "That, sir, seems impossible."

"Strip down a wire yourself and push it inside the box beside the other button—do what I did."

I, trembling, almost cut the wire in two and was barely able to hold the wire steady enough to fit it down beside the button. Then, when I touched the other end against the copper strip in the light socket, I felt static, sparks frying those things inside the box. Suddenly relieved, I looked up at the Roshi, not so afraid of the box, and bowed to lay the box at his feet.

We grinned at each other; and then he cuffed me gently.

The food *was* lousy—vitaminized fat-glob, vegetables, and synthetic protein, with fish bones to keep the carnivores from going absolutely crazy. And pickles.

Informal hearing. While Shelley asked the court not to terminate ownership, the judge sat in his archaic robes, above the electronic field of lenses and terminals, staring at us—the Refuge's lawyers, me, and Paul—the anti-propertarians, the religious guys.

Behind the rails, the courtroom was full of humans who muttered between the judge's gavel blows. Our lawyers put Paul on the stand, to testify that I'd been abused. He offered to put Hippogriff up as a witness.

"Not a double-bonded chimera, not in my courtroom, Mr. Carteret," the judge said. "It seems you could have considered psychiatric consultation—sneaking your sister's chimera to the monastery seems excessive. Is the property in question capable of speaking?"

Property—I could etch chips, was learning to run a clean room, could read. The Refuge lawyers put their hands on my arms, squeezed gently, and pushed me up. I walked by a swiveling camera, its glass eye fixed on me, and went up before the bench, my wings quivering. A feather fell, drifted toward the floor—I resisted the urge to turn completely around and scoop it up. "Your honor," I said, "I can speak."

"Do you think you have any moral rights? Shelley Carteret designed you, the family paid for you. We do allow religious freedom, but I wonder if the refuge principle doesn't cater too much to sentimentalists. Chimeras owe us more than even womb-born meat animals," the judge said, towering over me in black.

"Sir, I hate what she had put in my brain."

"Why? We stop you from killing with a blast to the pleasure center a nanosecond before we cut motor control. If you're beaten, we take you away; but this is painless."

"I hate the compulsions. Sir, she tried to bring the black box into the Refuge."

Shelley spoke then, out of order, but the judge didn't hammer at her. "I was angry then," she said. "I love him and want him, but Paul took him away as if I had no rights in the matter." She reached toward me, stepped up close to me. "Oh, Ariban, I'd thought of making you something more than a terror chimera."

"Shelley," I said, my throat knotted, "I love you enough that hunting you is monstrous."

Our lawyers moved to put the final judgment date off, hoping, I suspected, to get another judge. This judge said, "The court wishes to honor both religious convictions and property rights, and will postpone final judgment if the owner is permitted to visit the chimera."

I rushed back, through the electronic media gear below the bench, camera swiveling with me, and sat down between the Dharma Refuge lawyers, leaning back against my wings, feeling the muscles jerk anyway, against the wood.

The media wanted interviews afterward, but the lawyers claimed monastic privacy and maneuvered me into a Refuge car before I could faint.

"I was tattooed today," I told Shelley when she came to visit, bringing with her a heater flask filled with eucalyptus water and towels.

"Your feathers are filthy," she said, opening the flask, pouring water on a towel. "And they haven't shaved your head yet. Maybe the Roshi likes you better with longer hair."

I loosened my robe and pulled it back, so she could see the blue lotus between my armpit and nipple, puffy flesh around it. She put her hand on it—for a minute, I thought she'd pinch—and said, "Perhaps I should have made you sexually responsive. But if I had, you'd be bedding some Buddhist. Male or female, you think?" She began stroking me, moving me around to get me between her feet.

"Shelley, a man here said if he had a daughter who ordered me as a horror chimera, he'd have her psyched."

"Well, here I am, being lectured by my chimera," she said as she began grooming my wings. "You are responsible now for making me very unhappy."

"What about Paul?" I asked.

"I can take care of Paul if you come back."

As she cleaned and massaged, around those knotted muscles and down the wings, I closed my eyes and hummed—getting from her about as much pleasure as I could take. She tickled me and I tickled her back, then she went back to work on my feathers.

"You stayed more than your court-allotted time," the Roshi said.

Shelley tugged me to my feet and said, "I made him beautiful for you, Simon-roshi. Ariban, Simon owned chimeras once, which he used in his own rich way, until all the publicity about his men and chimeras drove him to this monastery."

"I followed a chimera I loved," he said softly. I was shocked, remembering a man who caught me once so close that my extra-strong tendon-levered bones and muscles couldn't work. Suddenly afraid of both Shelley and the Roshi, afraid of human complexities, I said, "I don't understand human desires, the desire to be scared, to do sex."

Shelley caught me by a wing, then laid her hand on my pectoral muscle and touched her nose to mine, as we'd done when we were both younger. The Roshi groaned slightly.

"If I came back, would you promise never to use me in hunts again?" I asked, begging almost.

"She could promise you everything and do what she wanted," the Roshi said. "Ask her to join you here."

"Look at your Roshi carefully," Shelley said. "He . . ."

"I neither fight my desire nor make an approach," the Roshi said. "Your feelings, ethics, consciousness matter to me. But you have no standing, legal or moral, in her eyes."

"Oh, Shelley . . ." I didn't know how to get her to promise. I could imagine a compulsion only if I could yank it out of my skull, or act it out until my motor control was cut. But she and the Roshi had me spinning inside my skull—I felt most odd.

Mechanical compulsions, I told myself, trapped between them, *were different than ones the brain comes up with for itself.* "But I don't like any compulsions," I told them. "Not any."

For me, the work in the Refuge was wonderful, although many humans complained they could have done as well outside—the hours were only somewhat shorter than state corporation hours. But for me, when I changed filters with linen-gloved fingers, checked the valve doors to the clean room, my wings sprayed and draped to keep them from shedding, I was mastering electronics. When I ran a check on the ambient particulate matter, I thought of my attachment to all the humans and chimeras listening to music on our disc players.

And as I built the components, I realized that to be built of any DNA implied identity with all DNA-made creatures—chemicals had no original identity—no magic vitalism came from the womb, as no thingness came from phage-assisted insertions of DNA chains into repro cells. Chemicals were chemicals as chips were chips.

I tried to explain this to a new human, how wonderful mastery over technology was, as we both dressed after the bath. I was talking, damp after the bath, until the human, who'd only been with us a few days, screamed, "I came to escape that. And you, some high-tech, I never understood why you were too expensive to do dump labor. I couldn't buy brains . . ."

The human hit me, fist to chin. As I went down, he hit me again. I scrambled to the side—*if I hit him, I'll kill him—he doesn't understand.*

"Stop," the Monjutor said, laying the bamboo cane against the man's shoulders, calling for disciplinary monks.

"Too much, out there. In here, too," the man cried, kicking at me again. "I thought the Buddhists wouldn't let a chimera mock a man."

"I can't defend myself physically," I cried as the other humans and chimeras pulled the man back.

"You were showing off, novice," the Monjutor said as he laid the cane across my wings, not in a stroke, just pressing to get my attention. "Can't defend? Why not?"

"I'm very powerful—I could tear . . . t— . . ." I said, pulling my legs into lotus and trying breath-counting to calm myself.

"Then, if you didn't lose control, you could just stop him?" the Monjutor said, whacking at my hands with the cane until I grabbed it. "Like you stopped the cane now."

"Beast," the human cried from where the others held him. "Too expensive to do human, decent work. Pervert."

"We don't escape our culture," the Monjutor said, "we do other things with it." Then he hit me again when I let go of the stick. "Ariban, how powerful for your size are you? Could you lift this man off the ground?"

"Yes."

"Carry him into the Roshi's and explain what's happened?"

"If I had to, I could," I said, grabbing the cane as it came whistling toward my hands again. The new human thrashed his head from side to side.

"You have to."

When I came up to the man, I smelt his terror, felt his body heat, saw the sweat, fear in the eyeballs—old poor man with gray hair about to be assaulted by a chimera—and I ran, screaming. The Roshi and Monjutor found me and brought me into the audience hall.

I sat before them, quivering, sure they'd throw me out immediately for disobedience. "He was too terrified," I said.

"Where," the Roshi asked, "does a mechanical compulsion end and the brain begin? I don't ask to test you—but I wonder if you've let your ideas about that brain worm affect your mind."

"How could it not?" I said, scared still more, seeing the Roshi's eyes, remembering Shelley's and the new man's.

"Ariban, there's more to you than that electric thing in your head, just as there's more to me than who arouses my sexuality."

For at least a week, I had to sit meditating by the man who'd attacked me. And the Monjutor spent hours padding around us in his zori socks. Each time the man's eyes or mine shifted toward the other, *whack, whack*, for both of us. The bamboo stung, clattering against our robes. His and mine. I held my wings up. *Whack. Whack.*

Before we sat down again after the break on the third day, I tried to talk to the man. "I'm sorry, too, that I was born this way."

"Don't try to get me in trouble, you shit," he replied.

Whack. Whack. To both, equally.

We sat, trying terribly hard not to look at each other. I

tried not to notice his odor, the catches in his breathing—too much like a hunt.

Afterward, the Monjutor took me aside and said, "Don't try to talk to him. Worry about your reactions, if you must, but let him work on himself. He's been a slave to a machine as much as you have—fifteen years of watching one machine's numbers."

A few days later, Shelley came visiting, with feather combs, oils, and the heater flask. She hugged me carefully, arms under the wings, and said she missed me; but her heart wasn't wildly enthusiastic—beating slowly against my chest, breathing also under control. Then she turned me around and looked at my feathers.

"You're not pulling them, are you? They're messed up around the edges."

"No, that's where I hold them up when the Monjutor corrects me."

"They hit you?" she said, cleaning up where my fingers had messed up the feathers. "Ariban, the S.P.C.A. would step in if this wasn't a religious place."

"Do you see any bruises? Really it isn't a hard blow—just to stimulate acupuncture attention-medians."

I felt her fingers press into my back, touch here and there. "Red spots," she said. "Yes, and a bruise, two bruises. Ariban, I don't want to lose you. I've been thinking about ordering you a companion. Female, male, what would you like?"

"Female." Another of me, who'd understand everything. "Would you really make me a companion?"

"Tell me why you're getting hit, Ariban," she said, massaging feather oil into her hands.

"A human's afraid of me, hates me. They make us sit together and whack us if either turns toward the other in the least. It's not easy here," I said. "He was a machine tender, then took refuge here."

"Working people don't understand us," Shelley said as if we were both the same kind of creature.

"Shelley, he's scared of me. It's almost like a hunt, but I'm not in hunt mode. I hate that, anyway."

The feather comb jerked. I looked back at her and she broke a tiny smile across her stiff face. Before she left, she gave me a cashmere sweater, my old one, knitted with wing holes, full of kennel odors; and she kissed me as though I was a fully human male.

I took the sweater to my dorm and rubbed my face over it. If she'd only promised to destroy all my black boxes and never order another one, cripple the brain worm in my head . . .

Before I fell asleep, I thought, *if it didn't work out, I could always escape again. I'd remember the number.*

Perhaps, I thought, *I should go home. Home?* So strange that the Refuge, such a quiet, orderly place, could be so intense—so many minds whirling in thought voids, grabbing for quiet. And the Roshi and Monjutor pushing at me, using the terrified, angry human as a stick.

Shelley came again a week later, not asking me to come home with her. All she did was prattle on about Hippogriff, Paul, Hildegarde. When she left earlier than usual, I felt as though I'd been visited in prison.

After she left, I went to the factory, showered and put on the clean-room suit, then went in to supervise the machines etching chip-circuits, checking chips on the scanning scope. Proofing tiny circuits, even blown up a thousand times, against a template, got tedious—my eyes began to get blurry.

Whack.

"You bring dust in," I told the Monjutor.

"No," he said, "you left all the doors open." **Whack. Whack.**

Dust had filled the room, hit in by flying gas molecules.

I had to rescrub the room, trash the chips when the screen showed dust grains like boulders in the circuits. Suddenly the work was very tiresome, and I sympathized with the humans who complained about this meditation.

"The main duty of a Buddhist—sweep the garden, any size," the Monjutor said as he helped me decontaminate the room.

"Maybe I'm not a Buddhist," I said.

The human who hated me tried to beat me up again, in the meditation hall. As he hit me, I uncurled my legs and grabbed him, pulled him down. We both screamed hysterically, locked together, until the Monjutor and others reached us. Finally I let them peel us apart.

"He tried to kill me," the human kept saying. "The killer monster tried to get me."

"Go get a steel rod from construction," the Monjutor said. A monk scurried off. The human still screamed that I'd tried to kill him, but he became hoarser and hoarser. We finally waited in silence until the monk returned with a reinforcing rod.

The Monjutor tossed it to me. "Bend it."

"No," I said.

Whack. "He has no idea that if you'd wanted to kill him . . . bend it." The cane swished back, poised. I bent the rod. The humans all stared at me; the other chimeras wouldn't look toward me at all.

"I'm sorry," I said. "I didn't ask to be made like this." I didn't know I'd dropped the rod until it clanged on the floor.

"He didn't try to kill you," the Monjutor told the human, "so don't bother him anymore."

When I began to walk, almost blindly, to my dorm, the humans quickly got out of my way.

"His owner disappeared for a couple of weeks two years ago—guess he managed to nail her then," I heard one say.

"Then that's why he's such a wimp, he's afraid of his strength," another replied.

"Change me now," I begged the Roshi. "Cut my wings off—take the strength away."

"We can't yet. You'll have to be more patient with the court."

"Humans say I'm afraid of myself."

"You believe that? You restrained the man who attacked you without hurting him."

"For me, agitation has an unfortunate prior context—and human agitation makes me agitated."

"I think we haven't sent you hunting." He reached for his bell, but stopped. "But, we refuse to make a pet out of you either." He rang the bell then.

The Monjutor moved the man away from me in the meditation hall and shortened my sitting times; gave me more work in the clean room, alone, which made me feel isolated, more mind-aroused, and thrown back on my own resources. No one was as kind to me as Shelley then, when she came to visit, with scent vials and luxurious clothes for me that I couldn't use in the monastery. I wonder if she hoped to trap the Roshi in an indiscretion; but when I asked, she said not.

One day I took her into the garden; and she let me brush her hair and show her how we sat when we meditated, counting our breaths. "You could do that with me," she said. "What's so good about this place that you want to stay now?"

The Roshi walked up to us along the paths between raked gravel and boulders. "Ariban, you meet your guests in the visitors' room."

"I must go now, anyway, Ariban," Shelley said coolly. "Ariban, remember we always have a place for you at home."

Torn, I looked at them both, then went back to my room.

The clothes and scents were gone. When I asked, the Monjutor said, "Those things are not your life now."

"I'm confused," I told Shelley.

"This place," she said, watching me from her chair, removed from me, table between us, "has confused you. You're trying to break out of your nature. Ariban, do you think I could ever use you as a terror chimera again?"

"Shelley, don't confuse me, too." I'd been dependent on her for so long.

"I suspect many chimeras go mad trying to be human in these places. You look shabby, Ariban."

"They took away the clothes you'd brought."

"I promise, Ariban, if you'd just come home with me, everything will be all right. I miss you. You'll go mad here."

"I'm so alone."

"So come with me," she said, rising to leave.

"I have to tell the Roshi," I said. "I have to talk to him and the Monjutor."

"No, Ariban, come now or stay. I can barely stand to see you like this, in those robes, confused."

"The Roshi says doubt is necessary."

"He would."

I left with her, changing in the car to a sweater with wing holes and flannel pants. She dumped the monastery pants and robe in the gutter, and told her driver to take us home.

When we went down to the kennels, Hippogriff blocked my way, shifting from paw to hoof. Horse tail stiffly up, he shoved me back with his big eagle head and shook it from side to side. *No.*

I threw my arms around him and said, "Oh, Hippogriff, things will change now." He thrust me away and shook his head, then stared at me.

I looked back at Shelley and grinned, but she wasn't smiling a bit. "You're back now, chimera," she said, "where you belong. I'll have you re-tanked, clean that Buddhist crap out of you."

She left me in the basement with Hippogriff, too startled and too hurt to move, incapable of following her.

Before I could be re-tanked, I searched upstairs for black boxes when Shelley and Paul were out, and found one in a cabinet with a pickable lock. I smuggled the box to the basement, electrocuted all the mechanical compulsions in it, then put it back in the cabinet without arousing the suspicions of the house guard.

The next day, Hippogriff and I were in the garden, inside the great walls, when Paul came up with a black box on his belt. Terrified myself of Hippogriff's signal-induced rages, I backed away, then saw Shelley, with a stunner in her hand.

Hippogriff trotted a few jerky steps toward Paul, then the little breast hands fingered the air.

"They *do* teach them how to sabotage boxes in that hideous place," Shelley said.

"If your beast contaminates mine," Paul said, "I'll . . ."

Hippogriff wheeled, rushed up and hugged me, then nudged me onto his back. I bent down to unfasten the rampway gate and rode him down to the kennels, hearing the iron gates drop behind us.

Hippogriff showed me Hildegarde's liquor supply, and I opened a bottle for him and began guzzling quickly myself. After fifteen minutes, Paul came down with netmen. I wobbled to my feet and smiled at all of them, too drunk to function well under any compulsion, then sank gently to the floor. *Mechanical means.*

One of Hippogriff's breast hands pointed the middle finger. Hippogriff's eagle head looked down at the hand as though it had, much to his surprise, acted independently, while I giggled helplessly from the floor.

"Both of you will be tanked soon," Paul said. "Ariban, if you give Hippogriff any of your Buddhist ideas, your tanking will be most painful." He left the iron gates down when he went back upstairs.

But that night, before Paul could take me to be tanked, the brain worm woke me with its electric tickle. "No," I screamed, the hunting urge rising, "Shelley, you bitch."

Tear her throat open. I padded upstairs and found the top small door open—wide enough for me, not Hippogriff. Sniffing, I smelt her. "Please get out of my mind," I cried, hunting her, lethally hunting her. "You promised. Oh, damn bitch."

The house seemed empty except for the scent trail, the think mocking me in my own head. I lost my bearings when the kill urge hit especially hard.

Where does the mind begin, the Roshi seemed to ask from my memories, but I howled him away and searched the upper floor, caught the scent again, closer, so close that what tatters of rationality I had left wondered why she'd set up such a short hunt.

At the bottom of the great oak stairs. I rushed her, but she laughed and cut me down midstride. I beat my wings to try to keep my balance . . . tumbled . . . tumbled . . .

When I woke up, I knew I wasn't in my kennel bed, nor back at the Refuge. Vet's, I realized. Belly down on a vet's table with one wing in temporary traction, bone ends still grinding against each other. Sore from neck to hips. *Oh, the bitch,* I thought, biting the table pad.

"Well, I've tanked you before," the vet said. "One of those pseudo-talking ones."

"Can I be tanked like this?" I asked. The wing was numb, but I knew it had been broken in several places.

"Trying to pass for human in a Zenbo refuge? We'll tank that out of you. Why can't a woman keep her scare toys in peace?"

"Can I be tanked with my wing like this?" I asked again.

"You came in squalling that she did it deliberately. Tried to run away from her earlier. You want a Society for Prevention of Cruelty to Animals officer to take a complaint?"

"Trapped me on the stairs."

"You get hit with pleasure to bring you down, don't you? Hunting's built into your genes. After we improve your attitude, you won't complain." He bent over me and felt from the root of the wing up to the tip. "Smashed in a few places. You must have fallen on it."

"She'll kill me, eventually," I said. "Or Paul will."

"Can get you the S.P.C.A. rep. Make a complaint if you want."

"She didn't use the pleasure blast last night. Just cut me down. I want."

"Yeah, this first," he said as he injected me.

When the S.P.C.A. rep came, I fought the drug to talk to her. She asked me why I left the Refuge and I began crying, mumbling. "Too inhuman, too afraid." She looked at my back, touched my face, then put her recorder up and gently patted my shoulder on the less hurt side.

"We'll keep your case under observation," she said.

A nurse came in to keep me under sedation. I stared at the SPCA rep until my eyelids snapped shut.

The vet operated on the wing bones twice, putting in steel pins like giant imping needles while I lay paralyzed but awake on his operating table. Finally he put a support cast around my chest with metal struts in back to support the bound wing. When Shelley came to pick me up, she made an appointment for the conditioning tanks, whether my wing had completely healed or not. "Vigorous tanking," she said.

I wondered how much longer I'd live. The vet handed her an air injector with directions on sedation levels.

She made me lean on her as we walked out, each step jolting pain from my wing, as though a nerve had been pushed into a light socket. In the car, I leaned stiffly forward, uneasy to be near her.

I couldn't have hurt my wing and shoulder that badly in a fall, I realized. She'd tried to smash her broken toy.

Bodyguards took me down to the kennels where Hippogriff waited for me. My bed was in his stall—I lay down on it and he curled down beside me, lifted his head to nuzzle me gently with his beak.

For two weeks, I didn't see Shelley at all, not even when I walked in the big garden with Hippogriff. One of the bodyguards came down every four hours to shoot me down with sedatives. Then at the end of three weeks, she sent for me, looked at me, my splintered wing, and told the bodyguards to take me back to the vet, to take stunners in case I got violent. And they sedated me heavily. When we got to the vet's, they had to hold me up.

The wing drooped, but the bones seemed to be knitted. The vet disappeared for a while after checking my heart, then came back and told the bodyguards to take me home. The S.P.C.A. had put a hold on my retanking.

I suppose I was lucky he was an honest vet.

"Let's see," Shelley said, turning my still drugged body with her hands. "Yes, a certain raffish look, fallen angel."

I felt made of lead—face, hurt wings, all the body—although she turned me as if I was airy. "S.P.C.A.'s put a hold on my tanking," I said, lead-tongued, too.

"But," she said, "I can still use you. Yes, I can still use you."

She sent me to my own kennel room and had Hippogriff locked in his stall. The sedation stopped, suddenly, which left me tense and jittery. That night, as I lay awake, wing throbbing, I heard Hippogriff clack his beak softly, whistle.

Hippogriff's stall was locked, but Hipp clambered up the wall with his lion feet and thrust his breast hands out between the door bars. Something fell, glittering, back inside the bars. He lowered himself and felt around desperately, beak and hands scrabbling through the straw, then came back up, in one hand a knife, in the other a key. I took them.

Then he made a Buddhist hand sign, flurried his fingers. I shrugged in dismay, not knowing his sign language, and tried to unlock the stall door with the key. It didn't fit.

Then I felt, nauseously, the hunting urge. Hippogriff saw my face muscles tighten and whinnied in dismay, a strange sound to come from his eagle head.

Shelley, I'll really kill you this time, I thought as I stuck the knife in my belt and went upstairs in the dark. Working with purpose as well as compulsion, I broke the glass on their coin display and put a copper coin in the base of a lamp, screwed the bulb back in, and made sure the lamp would short out when Shelley reset the breaker switch.

I hunted better in semi-dark, and now the compulsion fed my natural rage—I glided with the compulsion, not resisting at all. When I passed Paul's desk, I found that Hippogriff's stolen key fit it. Noiselessly, I opened the desk and felt around. Money? Escape tools? Sliding drawer with a trick catch—there, I found a key ring, with two keys big enough for Hippogriff's lock. I cut off a piece of the drapes and tied the keys to my belt.

Then I went to kill Shelley, stalking over the carpets, smelling her hysterical breath, with wine on it.

The lights blazed for a second, then popped off. I waited despite a surge of compulsion, told my brain, *ah, this time*, as my eyes adjusted back to the dark. Then I moved slowly, avoiding the furniture.

I'd never *really* tried to kill her before.

She was near. I smelled her all over, strongest toward the library. A light bobbed there, and the kill compulsion washed over me.

I'll burn her—she'll stay dead this time.

The flashlight came back on. *She'll blind me with it.*

Then, back in my mind, I seemed to hear the Roshi, "Where does the mechanical end and the mind begin?"

Really, I thought angrily, *I do want to kill her.*

Trying to avoid the wavering light beam, I darted through the library door, bruising my hurt wing against the door frame. The pain calmed me some, but my wings writhed, and she obviously saw me. Stepping toward her, I pulled out the knife, expecting to be cut down by the skull-bound ecstasy, but she didn't move.

Where does the compulsion begin? Flashlight lens under her chin, Shelley's face looked like a skull as she waited. She was very drunk, sad.

My brain pushed my hands forward. The compulsion ends here. I cut the belt off her and stabbed the buttons over and over. A white flash flared in my mind, but not the usual ecstasy that collapsed my killing hunger.

"Shelley," I said sharply. I could hear her heart pound. And the compulsion to hurt her was still in my head, my mind, the machine—I didn't know.

She let me take the flashlight out of her hand. "I messed up the button," she said, "in case I chickened out at the last, but you can kill me now, can't you? Then Paul will kill you and we'll be dead together."

But no, part of my mind shouted to the killing urge. She was fighting the urge to run. I grabbed her arm and pulled her over to the drapes, slashed them—I'd tie her up. She wanted to die; I'd refuse her the satisfaction.

Hippogriff, I can escape on Hippogriff.

When she saw the twisted cords in my hands, she tried to scream, so I gagged her first. Then I tied her arms and legs together and kissed her on the forehead, above the frantic eyes, before I raced down to the basement, throwing the iron gates open.

Hippogriff's head jerked up and I said, "Got to get away."

He looked at me and made the sign with his hands, then

shook his head. The key fit his lock. After shuddering once, he came dancing nervously out of his stall.

As alarms began to ring, we went up to the front of the house and found a big window. When I turned my head aside, Hippogriff kicked it into a spray of glass, then I jumped on his back and he leaped. Another deeper siren cut in—Hippogriff's escape siren.

I clung to Hippogriff and pointed to the turns as he raced full out through the night streets. Nothing short of a full police squad could challenge him—horse body, head of an eagle, claws of a lion, the brains of a man—Hippogriff. Giddy, I clung to his back.

But the humans had surrounded the monastery before we got there. In front, nets and gunmen, electric flares dropping harsh light on them. Paul's Jag slewed to a stop behind the gunmen.

"Let's give . . ." I almost said *give up*, but Hippogriff threw his head back and screamed, charged them, speeding up the instant he saw the police. Desperately hanging on, I kept thinking, *we're going to get caught in a net, we're going to get killed . . .*

Lion paws slashing, hooves kicking, stomping humans he'd crippled, Hippogriff broke through the line and wheeled at the monastery door, almost crushing my leg into it. I slid off and the huge chimera walked stiffly forward, between me and the police, then went rigid, like a medieval statue.

We heard a helicopter, blades hitting the air like thick whips. A man with legs braced on either side of a side door pointed down a large gun—whale gun, elephant gun, hippogriff gun—and fired one round. Paul and Hippogriff both screamed; Paul ran toward Hippogriff as the monks inside opened the door behind me.

Hippogriff's intestines spilled on the street, but he still held his head and chest up with his lion paws. He signed with his chest hands, and I saw Paul's hand tremble, then sign back. Then Hippogriff shuddered, collapsed, the dark blood no longer pumping. The monks levered my arms from the doorjambs and pulled me completely inside.

I cried in someone's arms, human, chimera, I didn't know which or care, floating around in the cypress tub full of Buddhists trying to console me. When I stopped crying, they lifted me out of the tub, dressed me in monastery clothes, took me to the Roshi.

"The Carterets accuse you of stealing the Hippogriff," the Roshi told me. He sat on his dais, looking terribly sad. "We don't mind being used a little here, but the laws . . ."

"They lie. Hippogriff wanted to help me escape." I looked up at his eyes—two dull stones. Suddenly my stomach lurched—I felt shrunken and tiny. "Do you mean I have to go back to them? She'll kill me. Paul's already threatened me with a lethal needle if I hurt her." *Seduce him,* my mind suggested. I had no concept of seduction, just threw myself down in front of him, laid my head against his thighs, wings beating the air.

"You can't even think about it properly," he said. Then he smiled and stroked the damaged wing. "Obviously, you've been badly used. What did you do?"

"I planned to kill her. But I didn't. I stabbed the belt box. She wanted me to kill her."

"Sit." He meant in full lotus. "I trust you took the belt off before you stabbed it."

"Yes," I told him. "She held the flashlight with both hands, the dead-man switch jimmied, I think. Then I tied her up and unlocked Hippogriff's stall. He kicked out a window and brought me here."

"The big chimera thought Shelley was dead. Paul Carteret claims you lied to the hippogriff."

"I didn't." Since I came down conscious, walking, after being brain-roused to hunt, Hippogriff must have thought I'd gotten Shelley. "Oh," I said, suddenly realizing.

"And you destroyed a valuable coin, cut up draperies." He sat for a while.

I crumbled out of position—a tiny, helpless thing—and cried that he couldn't send me back. He poked me with the bell handle and said, "There's still the S.P.C.A."

"An animal," I cried. "So I'm just an animal then?"

"All of us are animals. Someday I suppose a silicon device will ask for refuge, but so far not."

"But they can't just put you away, legally, with a lethal needle?"

Until the S.P.C.A. officer arrived, I worked on an assembly line, worked numbly, ignoring those around me, the sympathy, the fear. The Roshi himself took me off the line; and I followed him to a reception area where the S.P.C.A. officer, a human woman, waited, the same one who'd taken my report earlier at the vet's.

"Hi," she said when I came in, "you look more alert today."

"I suppose," I said, "I've got more to be alert over."

"The wing, then, didn't heal properly? I'm supposed to put you in restraints," she said, sounding as if that was unfortunate.

"I killed the box, not the box's operator." Then I looked at the Roshi, eyes not at all, now, like brown stones. "Should I just go ahead and accept the restraints?" I asked him. Pound, restraints, like an old unwanted animal.

"Perhaps," he said, "you should consider how vindictive the Carterets might be, and how powerful that thing in your head could be."

The woman looked down thoughtfully—she'd be driving the car. Restraints, like an animal, yet they were letting me know ahead—I wasn't just thrown down under nets, stunned, shackled. I bowed to the Roshi and said, "Perhaps we all would feel better if nothing worse happened." Turning to the woman, I said, "I hope your restraints are comfortable."

"Perhaps Ariban could put them on, or help you?" the Roshi suggested.

Awkward fingers, hers and mine, rigged me with a harness that locked my arms down. Then she fixed my legs in chains so I couldn't raise the knees or take wide steps, and sat me down in a wheelchair.

"We'll clear the halls," the Roshi said, "so you won't be seen like this. I think you need a simpler refuge than can be found here, but if you do come back, you won't remember us watching you in chains."

"I suspect that's not likely," I said.

"But you'll always know how to learn," he said, dismissing me with the little bell.

As she rolled me through the halls to the garage elevator, I imagined I wore a costume, played a role—chimera in chains. We got in the car and drove into the big freight elevator. At the surface, the Monjutor swung the last gate open and bowed us out.

I saw Paul's Jaguar and hissed in my breath. "Paul," I said, tossing my head in his direction.

"Carterets," she said, "damn Carterets." She radioed for reinforcements as I began to feel rage, stimulation, tickle my brain. Paul's car swung into traffic behind us. "Remember," she said, "you beat that last night. You haven't been tanked for a while."

Yeah, why, then, were her knuckles white on the steering wheel? I leaned back hard against my sore wing, hoping the pain would numb the compulsion. Paul must have boosted the unit—burning, burning. Then I realized, said, "It isn't like the last time."

"Keep talking, Ariban," she said. "Describe it."

"I'm fantasizing about Shelley, like the tank holo, three-dimensional puppet. I don't have to move a muscle—it can be all in my mind." My arms suddenly stopped straining against the belt cuffs, and I slumped, as though my motor control was cut, but I could still talk. "Yeah," I said. "I can imagine I kill—I don't have to do it."

"Human minds," she said, relaxing her hands on the wheel, "are so complex they don't take signals quite like rats do. I imagine your brain is almost on the same order. You have to be conditioned to *believe* you have to react to the stimulus in a particular way."

"I don't have to *do* anything." I rushed a little mental Shelley through my mind—she shrieked, totally trapped. I killed her and made her get up, killed her again, and again. "Imagination . . ."

She didn't like getting up again, my fantasy Shelley. I wondered how the real Shelley I'd left tied on the floor liked getting up, not being killed. Drunkenly stumbling through the halls . . . I stood the imaginary Shelley up again, sulky in her blood, and I refused to be her killer, wiped away the blood, healed the wounds.

Some stimulus played deep in my mind—defocused, impotent. I looked back and saw Paul's car surge forward as though he wanted to ram us. Then he pulled up, parallel to us, and I saw Paul stare at me through the tinted glass, tears in his eyes. I arched my back, wiggled my fingers, then felt ashamed to mock him. The windows opaqued as the Jag passed us completely—the electric tickle in my brain going away with it.

I shook myself as best I could in my restraints and smiled over at the woman. She took one hand off the steering wheel and patted me gently.

"What did you mean, almost as complex a mind as a human's?" I asked the S.P.C.A. woman as she unlocked me from the cuffs.

"Well," she began to say. We were going into the pound building.

"Come on, you can't be one of those people who thinks

we just use language like elaborate parrots, signal and response?"

"Ariban," she said. The pound reception area was almost empty, just a couple of male humans, guards, and an old chimera, gnome, with an arm in a sling, sitting by a human guard, playing checkers.

"So I have to stay here tonight? Can I call you by a human name?"

"Nancy," she said. "I'm supposed to check you for weapons, see that you shower with miticide soap, and stay with you until you settle down. We've got the tranquilizers if you need them."

The trio of creatures talking over checkers and coffee looked at me and smiled. I went with Nancy back to the showers, and stood, shivering and covered with foul-smelling soap bubbles, while she checked me and my clothes for weapons. Then I rinsed in hotter water, and she wrapped me in a large towel, carefully draping it between my wings. As I dried off, she slumped down on a bench, long legs splayed out in front of her.

"You never owned a chimera, did you?" I asked shyly.

"Child," she said. "I was never a rich girl."

"What happens now?" I asked.

"We petition for resale. Paul Carteret already petitioned to have you killed as an uncontrollable chimera. I can testify against that. We'll win. We do have some of the rich on our side, some corporate district bosses."

"And I go back to being a terror chimera?"

She handed me coveralls and a shirt. "Maybe put the shirt on backwards, then if your wings get cold, we'll drape them with something." The coveralls had suspender snaps in front, low cut in back. "With that tattoo," she added, "no sensible person would use you as a terror chimera. And we won't arrange a sale with a screwball. We'll also hold permanent resale approval on you, too."

"Oh." I just stood there.

"Sleepy?"

"In a pound cage?" I asked back.

"This," she said, "used to be a human hospital. It isn't like what you heard about when you were growing up."

We walked back to where the old gnome chatted with the human guards as though they'd all been friends for a long time. "How could you have dealt with a chimera like Hippogriff?" I asked.

"You miss him, don't you?"

I began crying and sat down on a couch. She touched my cheek softly and said, "I'm sorry about him, too, but he did die knowing he'd gotten you back to the monastery."

"Maybe I gave him bad ideas?"

"Maybe you inspired him? He was free for a while—he could have surrendered you to the police. Do you drink coffee, tea? Or just water?"

"Lapsang souchong," I said, remembering when I'd steal it out of the human kitchen, and everyone knew because of the smoky smell.

"A tea?" she asked. When I nodded, she laughed. "Not so lush here, Mr. Ariban, I'm afraid. Would Silver Train do?"

"Yes," I said. As she heated the water and filled two cups, I thought, *a human serves me, how strange.*

As she handed me the cup, she asked, "And what can you do besides scare people?"

"Serve dinners, breakfasts, read, write. The Carterets had a great library."

She looked into her tea thoughtfully and pulled the tea bags out of both our cups, then said, "And what was the Dharma Refuge like?"

"Confusing. It seems peaceful until you actually get into the activities—very agitated inside the mind."

"So you chickened out?" She smiled to mellow the insult.

"I thought Shelley had changed. Or wanted to believe she'd changed."

"Sorry," Nancy said. "Grown humans don't, not often."

We'd been talking like two human beings, I realized suddenly, and I smiled at Nancy, then huffed out a little breath as I thought about what she said.

"Sleepy?" she asked again, taking the empty cups.

"You'll sit with me until I'm asleep?" I asked. She nodded. We went quietly into one of the small rooms where another chimera slept on the second twin bed. She just sat there until I was asleep.

The S.P.C.A. lawyers kept me out of the courtroom as they fought the Carteret lawyers. I think I was videotaped during interviews with Nancy—at least we went into mirrored rooms where she asked me questions I'd already discussed with her, about how I hated being a terror chimera, about how I'd been treated.

In her own video testimony, Shelley looked like a woman whose imagination, embodied in future DNA, was bound to graduate from terror to degradation. She'd sprayed her head with glass-bead-stranding lacquer. But the bubbled hairs looked hysterical. Her left eye was patched, a prompt reader or a medical patch feeding in drugs and calming visions. She seemed barely contained by sedation.

I thought, *the family would even expose her like this to get the court to take her self-destructive device.*

After the testimony, one day during the weeks while we waited for the judge to decide, Nancy told me, "Shelley's now in a European hospital where the media can't interfere with her."

"What happened?" I asked.

"Balustrades broke."

I wondered if Shelley'd done it with explosive worms.

After several quiet weeks at the pound, while I waited with other beaten chimeras, Nancy came in with the resale order.

A piece of paper—so much influence paper had on human minds. This thin slice of matted wood-fiber, with ink sprayed on it, saved me from a lethal injection.

Over tea, Nancy introduced me to the woman who was thinking of buying me, a middle-aged woman, but not too old, rich, who wore tweeds and white gloves.

"Could I please have my wings cut off if you buy me?"

"No," she said, that firm patron of the S.P.C.A., "then you'd just be another short man." She pulled out a pad, dictated to me, then had me add and divide figures on her calculator. After I had finished, she said, "We'll have that wing fixed, adjust the tendons, and deal with that worm in your brain, too."

I really didn't want to be owned, but society had no place for me—too expensive for a factory, compared with the price of humans.

Nancy smiled and said brightly, "The brain surgery alone will cost about a third of what she's paying for you."

I went under the anesthetic wondering if this was all a joke, and came to as my new owner smiled—tenderly, I suppose—down at me. I ached all over, especially around the wing and head.

My new owner, the heroine of her newscasts, took me out in public with her before training me to become her butler. After weeks of household accounts, I began to get restless. Rounds of tennis with rich women didn't wear me out enough. She treated me kindly, but as though I was a rescued dog. As her servant. I had free use of the phone to place household orders and relay news tips. So feeling bored one day, I called the Dharma Refuge and asked to speak to the Roshi.

"I'm not satisfied," I told him.

"That's life," he said and hung up.

Ice-gouged Lakes, Glacier-bound Times

Skinned, the creature looked like a man-sized water shrew—blockier head, longer proboscis. Then Litta saw its hands. Too much flesh was exposed to the cold. Despite black claws, as pointed as shark's teeth, the digits were long. Litta bent a thumb across the palm toward the other digits. *Opposable.*

"Litta, help me dissect. It's called scullada—another illegal alien import," the senior ecologist, George Mason, told her. "This one I fly-fished for, a giant fly with monofil cuffs instead of a hook."

"Rather peculiar thing to do," she said, wondering if the creature's brain filled the boxy skull.

"If I'd gone up officially, the Catskillers would have never guided me to tiger-stripers."

"You have the skin?" Litta asked.

"Here. Have a jacket made." He opened a freezer and pulled out the hide, folded twice.

Litta brushed ice crystals off the soft fur. "Like sable

crossed with tiger." Silver and black swirls—the fur seemed softer than cashmere.

"We'll have to exterminate them, so your jacket will be very valuable." He smiled slowly at her, his eyelids half drooping.

"Fingers aren't right for a glacier lakes animal. What if they're sapients?" she asked, sliding the frozen pelt to Mason, refusing it.

"The niche on any planet is too unstable for them to have evolved much," he said. "The Catskillers on Lake Albany claim this is a traditional northern game animal. But the Cheshee have sold some very similar furs—not Terran at all, wrong trace elements.

The Cheshee annoyed Litta—aliens like dinosaurs who traded technologies with the Mexicans and came wandering up to the summer glacier fronts like nuevo temperate tourists. Ancient and cold, they'd smuggled contraband before. No, she reminded herself, they weren't cold-blooded, just ironic, snide bastards. "The same DNA?" The scullada eyes also seemed more complex than a water creature needed.

"Yes. Come the next interstadial, or if the glaciers advance again, they'll be gone anyway."

"So we don't need to exterminate them, really. It's just us wishing we could boss the ice around. Could I study them on site before you send for Eco Control units?" She knew she'd spend this winter locked up in subways and dormicles, but maybe, come ice-out, she could escape the hordes of Mexican and African tourists come to see New York's art treasures, guarded against both ice and nuevo temps.

"What you after?" Mason asked her. "Embarrassing the Cheshee? Make them sapient killers?" The skull saw whined as Mason sliced a cap of bone off the creature's skinned head. He lifted the cap with hooks and peered at the brain. "It's a bit big."

"Do they all have such pelts?" she asked.

"Only a few males."

Finally the animal lay completely gutted on the soft plastic table, blood clotted in the table gutters, muscles cut from their tendons and pinned down. Mason photographed what he'd done, then cut away the muscles and photographed again.

Dark muscles, high hemoglobin, Litta thought, sitting on a lab stool, heels on the rungs, watching Mason cut out a lung. *How odd to be transported from planet to planet so sapients can have fun killing your relatives.*

"Dissect a hand, would you?" Mason asked. Litta got off her stool and pumped latex solutions into the veins and arteries.

After the latex hardened, she cut, and found the vascular heat shunts she'd expected to find in a subarctic animal, but the hands showed large secondary veins and arteries leading to the thumb and index finger, as though tactile sensitivity might be worth the risk of frostbite.

"They have odd eyes," Mason said. "Come directly from the top of the brain to the top of the head."

He detached the proboscis, a short trunk with bones and tendon attachments. The mouth and nasal passages were separate—no breathing through the mouth at all. A thin jaw, small grinding teeth. Litta wondered what they ate when she saw the teeth—both incisors and molars small and thick. Shellfish?

As Litta mopped the floor after the dissection, she thought, *Dead extraterrestrial animals dissected out looked as helpless dead as any Terran specimen.*

She went to the top floor for coffee and looked out over at the distant early ice glittering in the sunset. Litta thought briefly about the Croton Ice Wedge, the great fusion generators, the twenty-cent tax on her cup of coffee that went to fight the ice. But Manhattan had always been expensive. So expensive the lab couldn't afford the latest Mexican scanning array computers.

After Litta tossed her empty cup in the winter burner, she went to the basement and caught the lev-tube train down to her apartment by the city wall.

Inside, she turned on a holo of Mexico, where all the oaks were now, mule deer and high-rise apartments with balconies. Mexico, with the old continental shelves above water, growing oranges and corn. At least she'd gotten two years of study there, Cheshee and Mexicans both making her feel like an ice knocker chilling their Aztecoidal glow.

Finally she checked the emergency heat alarms and crawled into the bed-tube on the wall opposite the hologram. She went to sleep and dreamed about the size of that creature's skull.

The next morning Litta microtomed frozen chunks of brain tissue, then floated sections in Zamilla's solution. "They come to lures?" she asked Mason.

"Like a salmon fly, but with monofil hoops to catch the snout, a front paw. Haul you all over that water. What did he weigh, live weight? Two hundred and fifty pounds? About. Jumps some too . . . How does the brain look? Then the guide threw a rope around the snout, suffocated him."

"You'd think the first one that got away would warn the others."

"So they couldn't be *that* bright," Mason said. "The local headman got a law passed. Requires local guides and a five-hundred-dollar hunt tag."

Litta examined hundreds of one-cell-thick slices of scullada brain, a cell-by-cell examination of the structures of the brain. Then after she finished her studies with the light microscope, she coated frozen fracture sections with chromium oxide. The brain had decomposed between Lake Albany and Manhattan, enough for the dendrite structure to be blurred.

Litta looked at the photographs of the hands, calluses on

the fingertips, chipped places on the claws, and applied for a field study before the Ecology Control units began extermination.

"Stubborn as an iceknocker," Mason said, but he approved the study.

The Marcy Glacier and the Batten merged with transient ice over Lake Albany. Dead winter: all Manhattan switched to heat-producing work—manufacturing, sewage composting—all travel going through tunnels. The NYC-TV's test pattern was FIGHT D'ICE.

After the winter ice had broken up on the Hudson, Lita assembled her gear: cameras, tape recorders, foam-skin suits, vapor-permeable sleeping bag and tents, and a small lithium-powered stove.

A university plane bobbed on its floats, moored to oval granite and steel pilings under the 50th Street cliffs. Under the cliffs, farmers set muck crops in the glacial till, driving balloon-wheeled tractors with planter boxes, setting cold rice seedlings.

The city, built now of granite and steel-reinforced concrete, looked stubby compared with its outline in the twenty-first and twenty-second centuries. The spring crews were in the streets clearing away frost slabs. Behind the men cracking the frost slabs free, other men drove iron spikes in the frost scars and spread concrete.

"Lot of trouble to live here," a man helping load Litta's baggage said to her.

"Yeah? Just think of the last ice age—no fusion." Litta made sure they loaded her duffles where they wouldn't get punctured. Then she climbed in beside the pilot.

The plane swung out into the Hudson and began taxiing against the wind draining off the Adirondack Ice.

Litta saw the fishing village on the Catskill island, under a small mountain glacier whose winter path curved slightly around the village's concrete domes. "Eskimo and Catskiller blood down there," the pilot said, "real tough people."

As the plane taxied in, Litta saw three scullada bodies, all stripy furred, lying on the dock, one half skinned. The pilot opened his door and tossed a monkey's fist on a mooring line to an old man with blue eyes and dark skin standing on the dock.

The man on the dock handed the monkey's fist to a boy crouched at his feet. As the boy snubbed the mooring rope around a winch and pulled the plane close, Litta saw that the dead scullada eyes were closed, as if pinched shut. One's nose structure was torn almost off, but even that one's eyes were squeezed shut. An image of human bog burials, the far back Danish ones, came to her. *If they are sapient, they're as crazy as we were, coming out of the first ice with human sacrifices.*

"Here to study them?" the old man asked. Native and migrant genes had mixed in him—black hair with gray at the sides, blue eyes, but Asian eyelids like an Eskimo's. "Ya Charl Stonemarker, headman here. You Litta Serl?"

"Yes," she said. "You say scullada are a traditional game animal with your people?"

"Come down from North wi' us." He stood with folded arms, the eyes suddenly more Eskimo than Catskiller. "Make study, we take you out. But scudders don't like messing 'round their lodges. Split a guide's skull once when he got too curious, laid bone open with a rock."

Sea otters used rocks, she thought, but . . . "We need to know what the season should be on these creatures."

"Trophy coats scarce," the man said. "Trophy males, pointa honor to take." His language turned suddenly Standard. "We can manage this fishery ourselves."

"I need a boat, with a navi-comp, to take me up." Litta now wished she'd brought her boat and done her own surveys.

"We heard talk about getting the Eco Control people on

these creatures. Traditional game animal, offends us that you doubt it."

Mason talked too much. "How fresh are these?" she finally asked Stonemarker.

"Caught this morning."

"Can I take a skull now?" she asked.

"Brains and all?"

"Yes."

Stonemarker skinned the head and chopped through a cervical vertebra with an ax. Litta sawed open the skull and sliced the brain into preservative.

"Thanks," she said. Stonemarker knelt to finish skinning the body, then put something in the creature's mouth before he rolled the skinned corpse off the dock. It splashed and sank.

"We return the body," he said as Litta stared. "Scudders eat weird, give you gas."

"What if they're intelligent? You think you'd want to hunt them then?"

The old man stomped three times on the dock. A scullada trunk curled out of the water and whuffed at Litta. The scullada's body was just a vague darkness in the murky water. "If scudders don't mind us taking furs," Stonemarker said, "then what's it to you, city woman?"

The boat, a shallow-draft cruiser about thirty-five feet long, settled down to a steady fifteen knots, headed west over what had been the main channel of the Mohawk.

"Oughta set up on a rock island," one of two guides said to Litta, "then johnboat it to the scudder feeding grounds."

"Flies eat you if you don't have Tri-Acts," the other guide said. "They got to drinking Army Juice. Glacial outwash marshes real buggy."

"I'm prepared," she said. "Rock island sounds good."

"Done this kind of thing before, lone woman?" one

asked. "Feds overrode the local guide law for you, but you may regret it."

"With a wolf pack," she answered in full Standard, "I eventually got to pet the puppies. Just because I live in Manhattan . . ."

"Nothing against 'Hattan. Credit's good."

Alone, finally, on rock polished by the glacier's advance fifty years earlier, Litta sat on a camp stool, her lithium stove turn low to keep her coffee hot. The boat grew tiny, wake shining as the sun dropped toward the Batten Ice, invisible from here except for its reflection on the clouds. Patches of snow lay around her tent; lumps of ice floated in the water. She smeared on insect repellent, then turned the stove up to boil a food pouch. *Scullada, obviously alien, no predators except us?* She wondered what proteins varied to give humans gas.

The next day Litta explored the rock island. A tiny group of firs had found soil, rock broken down by lichen, in a cleft out of the wind. Across the island, willows and reeds grew in glacial till dropped by the sluggish current.

When Litta went down to get water, she saw two eyes floating just under the surface. Then a short nose tube came up, sputtered and arched toward her, sniffing. Litta went rigid. The nose tube quivered and then sank into the murky water.

Litta rose slowly and looked over the lake. She shook—the thrill, adrenaline jolt, of being alone with a free wild creature larger than a human. After looking over the misty water for V-ripples and bubbles, she slowly knelt back down and filled the pot.

An alien sports animal, similar to the wild boar and brown trout. So creatures with space-gate facilities, she mused, moved them from planet to planet, saving them from drought and glacier maximums. How intelligent did they have to be?

Funny, too, how obsessed we Northerners are with keeping Earth pure, as though we'd goofed ecologically and brought on the ice.

After breakfast, Litta loaded the johnboat with lunch, flares, and a radio. The boat, as she rowed, pushed aside the thin night ice. By midmorning she saw lodges in the distant marsh, much bigger than beaver lodges, towering over the cattails.

Now to probe their territorial boundaries. Litta shipped the oars and began poling, iron foot of the pole squishing into the mucky bottom.

No sign—no bubbles, no circular rise patterns, no dark forms in the water turbid with glacial till.

Then a splash. Two gray hands jerked the bow of the johnboat. Body humping convulsively, the scudder shoved the boat backward. The oars clattered against the thwarts, and the pole, caught in mud, snapped. Litta tumbled against the stern.

The scudder thrust the boat, many hard jerks, to deeper water. Then it swam around to the stern where Litta sat. It reared out of the water backwards so the eyes on top of the blocky head pointed at her, like a whale's spy hop, water quivering around its body as the invisible feet thrashed.

She said, "It's all right, scullada. I didn't come to steal your babies."

The creature blabbed flabby sounds from its trunk. Slowly it sank back into the water, then paused, eyes barely above the surface, breathing in and out rapidly through the up-curled snout.

Litta saw other scullada swimming toward them. The duffel with the hypo gun caught her eye, but she was afraid to shoot while the other scullada were out of range but closing in. *Maybe I ought to leave?* Gingerly she reached for the short spare paddle, not wanting to risk losing the long oars to the scullada, thinking, too, that the short oar might be less threatening. Slowly she turned the boat. The oncoming creatures halted, a ragged row of eyes and tube noses.

Litta eased the blades of the big oars back into the water, then began rowing, ready to stop the instant an oar touched flesh.

The sculladas stayed where they were. Litta sighted across the oarlocks to triangulate how far she was from the lodges. She rowed farther away and took out binoculars to watch the eyes and noses swirl away underwater. Then, trembling, she took out her note pad and jotted down her first observations.

By the time she got back to her island camp, her arms felt heavy, as though she'd been hand-turning compost. Weight machines didn't condition enough, she thought as she hauled the boat in and tied it before wading back through the icy water to get her duffels out. Encountering the scullada left her feeling dazed. "A pity Eco Control will want to kill them," she said out loud to the cold spruces growing in the cracked rock.

That night she heard sculladas calling around her island and a loon's laugh back.

The next day Litta rowed back toward the scullada colony. No sign of scullada. She took out her glasses and scanned the lodges.

Nothing. The boat rocked as she opened her duffels and looked for her wet suit and the rebreather. Carefully she poled closer, closer, sitting with her feet wedged against bottom thwarts and her back pressed against the edge of the seat. No scullada appeared, so she pushed the johnboat farther toward the lodges, seeing the canals between them.

Hogans, they're the size of hogans. She poled the boat through last year's cattails, blue glacier chunks. Beavers had built lodges against the larger scullada domes. The scullada colony was utterly silent except for the sounds of the pole thrusting into the mud. Even the beaver had gone.

Big logs in the house walls, and notched, not quite as neatly as human log cabins.

She poled the boat into a four-foot-wide canal, staring at the lodges, smelling the gas her pole stirred out of the muck. *No lodge entry from above water.* She tied the john-boat to a spruce log poking out from a lodge wall, pulled on her foam-skin diving suit, and strapped the rebreather to her back.

Then over the side in a mass of noisy bubbles, a waterproof flashlight in her hand. The water chilled her face, but she found the entrance and swam in very slowly.

Litta broke through the water surface and listened. Nothing except the water sloshing against the sides of the entrance tunnel. She raised her flashlight above water, turned it on, and saw a crawl ramp to her right.

Right angle turn out of the tunnel to the ramp, slows down invaders. She slithered up the ramp into a larger room built on two levels. Here she could crouch, almost erect, and scuttle around the lodge floor.

The place smelled of urine and dung. Cramped up under the ice all winter, even if they'd kept the tunnels open, some of the scullada would be too young, too weak to get out. Litta wondered if the scullada abandoned their winter quarters whether they were disturbed by invaders or not.

She almost poked through the wall for air, but noticed a hole in the roof in the upper level. The hole was over a depression, below floor level.

Litta looked closely at the stones around the depression, moved one, found a hand ax.

My God, they flake stone!

No batons, no core stones, just one chipped stone the size of a scullada palm, shaped like a giant scullada fingernail. Litta scrabbled through other rocks, but none of the others was shaped. For a second she wondered if the creatures had simply found an Indian stone ax; then she found a charred stick wedged between a log and the lodge wall—hidden, but not quite well enough. *They didn't want me to find artifacts.*

She raised her light toward the roof hole again and saw soot on the sides of the hole. *How in the hell do you make fire if you're an aquatic mammal?*

When she dove back through the entry hole, she found Charl Stonemarker sitting in a powerboat waiting for her.

"Do you know they're people?" she asked him.

He stared at her in her foam-skins so hard she grimaced. Then he cranked up his boat's motor. "Don't mess with them, city woman. Dying for the stripers is their life. We know to honor what helps us." He twisted the outboard's throttle, and the boat lurched, then rose on its stern as it sped away.

Litta sat by her lithium stove that night, hefting the stone. She radioed in to request more observation time.

As she put her radio back, she wished they'd worked up a code, wondered if Stonemarker listened. She put the stick and hand ax in a plastic bag and sealed it.

In the morning the sun burned a vague red through the haze as Litta went to the beach for water. She saw a scullada hauled up on the rocks. Its fur wasn't striped in broad swirls of silver and black, but before the creature wriggled backward into the lake, Litta saw traces of swirls in dark and light gray.

The creature turned around twice in the water and stared back at her. His snout curled out of the water and he tooted at her, then sank, eyes last, below visibility.

Litta set up a strobe camera where the scullada had hauled out of the lake.

Around midnight Litta heard a high scream, hit the spotlight, and raised her marking gun.

The scullada, blinded by the glare, screamed again, then lay its head down and whimpered. Litta felt a twinge of shame, but fired the red marking charge at the creature's back anyway. It cried out as the dye bladder hit, then went limp on the rocks.

After turning the light out of the creature's eyes, Litta loaded a trank cartridge and walked carefully toward the scullada. It reared back, stared at its hindquarters, and moaned through its nose tube..

Slowly she walked closer, saw the cock protruding from the genital slit. His eyes fixed on her face, the scullada reached back and dabbed his fingers against the marking paint, then sniffed his fingers.

"Only paint," she said. *He thought he was bleeding.* The bladder'd bruised him. "Well?"

The creature shivered, watching her. She went to her tent and got out large sugar crystals—most vegetarians and omnivores like sugar. He was gone when she got back, so she left the sugar near the water. In the morning, where the sugar had been, she found trimmed cattail roots and an ice-abraded Canadian coin.

Litta decided to check the lodges again, to see if the scullada had truly abandoned their little town.

The lodges were still empty. Litta dove into a lodge and began piecing together the slate shelves the sculladas overturned when they left.

She heard water splash, echoed in the entry chamber, then heard claws knock against stone. The male scullada with red paint on his rump slithered toward her. Litta kept her hands low and didn't look directly into the creature's eyes. He stopped.

I'll call him Sasha. She remembering another Sasha, a red howler monkey shivering in a freak Yucatan snowstorm on her first field trip. "Sasha," she said aloud, finally looking at him in the eye.

The creature bleated through his nose and bobbed his trunk.

As they stared at each other, Litta sat down very slowly

and held her knees to stop her shakes. She felt the way she did when she first met a Cheshee—that sense of conceptual kinship despite the alien's pebbly hide, awkwardly angled legs and arms, and eyes like calculating stones.

Sasha tore the stone shelves down again.

They don't want us to know they're intelligent. "I'm sorry I made you leave your nice house," she said. The scullada lay among the shelving rocks and moaned. *I'd rather be fellow sapients with him than a Cheshee.* She shined the flashlight over all the tumbled stones so much like Orkney Island neolithic human relics. "I'm gone now," she told Sasha; then she whistled to warn anyone else in the tunnel that she was coming out.

The pilot came back with Stonemarker, who seemed more alien than Sasha now. Both waded through the calf-deep water between the rocks and the pontoons, Stonemaker in oiled hide boots, the pilot in foam-skin leggings. "Come back," the pilot said. "This study's aggravating the locals."

"Sculladas are sapients," Litta said. "I've made contact with a male."

"He talking yet?" Stonemarker asked.

"No, but we've done silent trade on sugar." She told the pilot, "Drop me about twenty pounds more rock sugar and some chocolate."

"We have to take you out August first."

"It won't freeze up hard until September. Tell Mason. Take this stick and the stone with you."

Stonemarker looked at the bag and said, "My scudder pet, Skinhead, he don't approve of your scudder."

"I think they're as smart as men."

Stonemarker waded to the plane, then said, with New England twang and some Eskimo in his accent, "Men things got honor rights." (Or did he mean *rites*? Litta wondered.) "We and them do what we have to. Just like we always done."

She asked, "But is it really necessary?"

Stonemarker ignored her. The pilot unloaded Litta's supplies, then waded back to the plane himself. Litta, her boot against a pontoon, shoved them off. The engine cut on and the plane wheeled into the wind.

Sasha surfaced about fifty yards from the rocks and tilted his head to watch the plane leave. Then, as though the scullada was trying not to startle Litta, he paddled, hardly roiling the surface, to shore and hauled out around twenty feet from her.

Since their niche is so transitional, they sell themselves as game animals to be moved from planet to planet. And on some planets, creatures like Stonemarker know scullada are sapients, but hunt them anyway.

Bleating softly, Sasha looked directly at Litta; then as though he was exhausted, he sighed and wriggled over on his side to sun his belly.

Wonderful creature, Litta thought, wants to put *me* at ease. She stripped to panties and bra to get some sun herself. The scullada twisted his head to stare at her; then as she lay down on a warm patch of rock, he closed his eyes and muttered through his trunk, bubbling little sounds. Litta saw a bite on his hind flipper and noticed that the marking paint had been scrubbed half off. *Skinhead really does not approve.*

She fell asleep and dreamed of Yucatan, then jerked awake when Sasha trumpeted. Trunk curled down, he faced the water and bobbed up and down on his hands and hind flippers.

Another scullada trumpeted back from the water. While the sculladas screamed at each other, Litta ran to her tent and got the trank rifle. Sasha wiggled backwards. Litta exchanged the trank cartridge for a radio implant.

The other scullada, black and gray, exploded from the water, spray flying. As he bit Sasha's hand, Litta saw his hideous head, the scalp-pink scar tissue flushed almost crimson. She shot and placed the cartridge in his shoulder. Then she ran up to the two scullada, screaming, "No!"

The two scullada froze. Then the scarred scullada pulled his teeth out of Sasha's hand and slowly turned toward her. Sasha moaned and whistled through his trunk; the other one pressed around the radio capsule entry hole, staring at her. *Burn scars—oil-fire burns healed like that.* Even his trunk had been burned once, his hands. *Stonemarker's Skinhead.*

Litta slowly moved back and picked up her first-aid kit while the radio-tagged Skinhead shook himself and made a sound like lips flopping together.

Sasha hunched toward her awkwardly, his left hand bloody. Litta put her hand on his shoulder, wondering if he'd let her touch the hand. He closed his eyes and she knelt down and gently spread his fingers, cleaned the cuts, and sprayed on a micro-porous bandage.

The other scullada watched intently, but backed away when she finished with Sasha. Sasha whistled. Skinhead humped up slowly toward Litta, air hissing in and out of his trunk, then snatched the bandage spray from her hands before backing rapidly, hunch, hunch, toward the water. There he pried out the radio cartridge with a stone flake and called sharply to Sasha, who crept toward him.

Skinhead and Sasha slid into water, then five more sculladas spy-hopped from offshore, necks straight, backs arched, the eyes facing her from the tops of the skulls. One was silver and black. Slowly they sank down, trunks and eyes just breaking the surface as Sasha reached them.

The second gray-and-black-striped male swam close to Litta, and waited. She didn't move. Finally he began cruising, eyes out of the water, down the Mohawk channel, toward the monofilament nooses.

When Litta swept the radio antenna around the shore line to find the cartridge, the radio beeped faintly. The little transmitter beeps faded—the sculladas took the cartridge.

Litta loaded the boat and set up the telemetry antenna. A

fine rain began when she was about two miles from camp. Litta covered herself and the boat with a rain cape and continued to row, oar swishing wetly against the rain-cape edges, as she guided herself by the radio signals.

Finally, with binoculars, she spotted a scullada colony like a collapsed log cabin town in the rain. Litta pulled the rain cape back and raised the direction-finding antenna. The receiver beeped loudly.

Carefully she looked for scullada signs in the water with her binoculars, tilting them down slightly to keep the rain off the lenses. Then she dressed in foam-skins to go diving.

Litta set the mirrors on her facemask so she could see up and down. The water was clearer here than around the old lodges—not so much glacier rock flour. Swimming just above the muck, a small receiver in her ear, she followed the beeps toward the edge of the scullada village.

Beep . . . beep . . . Beep . . . BEEP . . . BEEP. The water was shallow here. She raised one of her mask mirrors barely above the water and saw Sasha tied to a pile of stones.

The tying seemed symbolic, plant fiber cords around his hind paddles, his hands free. The radio cartridge lay on a rock beside him. The sculladas had set out Sasha and the radio as a trap for Litta.

Glad of the rain and the oncoming darkness, she swam slowly back to her boat. This is *not* like working with naïve wolves, Litta thought as she set up a sonar alarm before lying down to sleep on an air mattress.

The sonar alarm woke her at first light—Sasha clung to the johnboat, reaching for the alarm box. Litta turned it off and touched Sasha. He grabbed her and tried to pull himself into the boat, making lip-flobbing sounds with his trunk.

Other scullada raised their trunks out of the water, still swimming rapidly toward the boat, eyes just above their ripples, talking in whistles and burbles.

"Oh, baby, what have you gotten us into?" she asked Sasha as she hauled his thrashing body into the boat.

He grabbed the oar handles, then let them go, pointing with his trunk at her hands.

"We wouldn't be fast enough." She watched the other scullada yell at Sasha. If the sculladas wanted her dead, she was dead. "Poor baby, those ropes bruised your feet. They must think you're a really naughty boy."

Wondering if these guys took bribes, Litta eased a piece of chocolate out of her duffel and offered it to one of the sculladas near the boat.

The scullada tasted the chocolate, then, with a low whistle that ended in a flabby nose-tube splat, tossed it to Sasha. He caught it and tucked it back in the duffel, awkwardly opening and closing the zipper with his clawed hands.

But to do that! Sasha either had watched her more than she'd known or knew how a zipper worked from one observation.

Another scullada spoke. Sasha shivered. Then the sculladas in the water began staring over Litta's head, to the southeast. Sasha patted Litta and plopped out of the boat.

Litta heard an airplane behind her, coming from the channel. At first she thought it was the university plane, but then she turned and saw it was red, not silver. Quietly the sculladas submerged. The plane dipped, then circled the lodges and came back, landing, taxiing across the lake.

Stonemarker, with a silver-and-black scullada prone on a rack beside him, drove the plane toward her. Litta stared into the man's impassive face as he heaved a rock at her johnboat. The gunwale split and Litta saw the scullada in the plane raise a smaller rock. The scullada's head was hairless, pink warty skin behind the eyes, and the trunk mangled. *Skinhead again.* She stared into his alien black eyes for what seemed like hours until the stone smashed her.

Half-light. Warm bodies. Stinking fur. Horrible headache. Litta rose up on an elbow and turned her head. A gray scullada and Sasha lay on either side of her. Light came in through holes in the lodge chinking. Finally Litta saw her duffels and canteen, brought in from the wrecked boat. She moved to get up, but her ears ached and she felt nauseous.

Dizzy when she tried to sit up further, Litta asked, "Water," the word echoing absurdly in the dimly lit chamber. She reached for her canteen. "Take it, fill," she said to Sasha, pantomiming the lake surface, filling the canteen.

Sasha moved to her in two nervous wiggles, sniffed inside the canteen, pointed to the water at the bottom of the ramp.

Litta nodded, then pantomimed drinking, pointing to her mouth. Sasha stared down the canteen's neck, then slithered down the passage and brought back a full canteen.

Litta drank from it, hoping scullada parasites didn't infect humans. The gray scullada slid down the ramp and came back with a trout. Giving the fish to Litta, the gray female make a sound with her trunk that Litta tried in vain to duplicate.

"I'm going to call you Mina," Litta said to the gray female. The trout thrashed and Litta dropped it. Sasha bit it behind the eyes, tore a hunk of flesh off the spine and gravely handed it to Litta. Suppressing a shudder, she ate it.

Mina pushed Litta back down against the beaver furs.

The scullada feed Litta raw trout, inner bark of spruce, and roasted cattail roots the first hazy week. By the second day, she realized she was close to being winter-stranded, but was too weak to swim out of the lodge. By now Stonemarker would have reported her dead, killed by scudders.

"I've got to get out," she said to Sasha. She found her diving skins, but Mina blocked the tunnel with her gray body. Litta realized she still hurt, shoulder, lungs congested, boat gone, too sick to walk out.

Both scullada looked concerned. Litta feared she'd die here, human bones to be found mingled with scullada bones after the Ecological Control poisoned the colony in the spring. Dangerous to man, that's how the scullada would look when Stonemarker reported her death. They were smart, but they couldn't have any concept of an Eco Control attack.

She lay back down on the beaver skin and cried. Through chinks in the lodge she saw four scullada digging cattail roots and harvesting cold rice. The terrain was like that around the lodges she'd checked. The sun sat and rose, sat and rose, while she began to recover.

One windy, cold day the scullada built a fire in her lodge and smoked beaver skins and dried grain in wicker baskets suspended from the ceiling poles. At sunset the fire was carefully put out, except for a small heap of buried coals. *These scullada are hiding.*

Sasha brought up more of Litta's gear from the lake bottom. She went through the muddy cold duffels and took out sealed food pouches, chocolate, foam skins, and batteries for the lamp. And she found a wet muddy cervical cap, cleaned it so she wouldn't bleed all over the lodge during her periods.

Mina brought her leaves to defecate on. Over the weeks, Litta watched the leaves turn gold, then brown before the scullada stopped bringing leaves and brought wet birch bark instead.

September, the ice is in. Maybe I can walk out when it freezes hard. I'm better. I think I'm better.

Sasha urged her to dive through the exit tunnel. She dressed in a double layer of foam-skins while he rolled to his side and twined his fingers together nervously. Then she slithered down the exit ramp, with him following.

The skins protected her from the water, but the air, when she broke through the thin ice, made her gasp. Snow whirled against her face, into her eyes.

Mina handed her a stone grubber and showed her how to

dig for roots in the marsh. She, walking, could reach inland plants they couldn't harvest from the canals.

The commensal beavers felled young trees, dragging them to the water, where the scullada gave them bits of Litta's chocolate and took the tree tips—spruce bark against scurvey. The beaver shied away from Litta, slapping tails against the water.

As the weather got colder, the scudders kept fires going through the night. The fire went out in the lodge once and Sasha gravely strung together milkweed cord on a limber stick to make a bow drill. He rolled to his side and whirled another stick with it to start birch punk burning. Mina taught Litta how to fray plant fibers and spin them on a hooked stick, winding the spun cord around the stick, then rolling it again along scudder body or human thigh.

Before the ice froze hard, a moose ambled out in the lake, dipping his large head down for water plants. The scullada whistled to each other, then dove under water, all disappearing except Sasha, who stayed by Litta. Then suddenly they surfaced, screaming and bugling through their trunks, throwing stones. The moose reared in the water as scudders grabbed its legs. Then it kicked back twice and began to swim away, head and shoulders breaking through the thin ice. It stopped as though snagged.

The moose screamed once, then rolled from side to side in the water. Finally, head limp, the moose only twitched as the scudders dragged it to shallow water. There they hacked it to the bones with flaked stone knives. Both the male and females pounded the meat with sticks over logs flattening it before drying it over the fires. Litta helped Mina pack the fat in birth-bark wrappers. *Will moose give them gas?*

Soon the beavers moved into the scullada lodge, sleeping by the fires like flat-tailed cats. The scullada spent a week frantically gathering more roots, then came inside and began drawing diagrams on the mud lodge floor, occasionally moving a beaver away from the firelight. Singing weirdly, they moved fish vertebrae on the diagrams.

Games. "We're both intelligent," she said sadly to Sasha, "but we're going to die if I don't get out this winter, stop the Eco Control." She put more sticks on the fire and watched him play.

Sasha and a visiting male finished one game; then Sasha dropped his eyes and drew another board. The visitor juggled the counter vertebrae, humming until Sasha finished.

As they played again, Litta analyzed the moves.

Sasha lost two games. He dove out through the exit tunnel and came back with arms full of roots and tree twigs as the other male smeared the crosshatches and circles of the game board back to plain mud.

Over the next week, she kept watching. More than one game, and males and females played each other, neither sex particularly superior. Mina and Sasha both lost some, won some, from both sexes, but never played each other. Losers did the chores.

When the scudders weren't playing their games, they sat chewing roots and strips of dried meat, constantly talking, whistling, and blubbering as they both inhaled and exhaled.

We're safe until ice-out. Litta decided to horde dried fish and beaver fat, to feed her on her trek for help. But scullada other than Mina and Sasha watched her, stole back the one cache she thought she'd hidden well enough.

One day Sasha brought Litta two pairs of her foam-skins, pantomimed that she should put both on.

They swam out, rising to breathe in chiseled spaces in the ice. Wind had stripped snow off the ice and the sun glowed through, fractured into rainbows that bounced on the water. Litta turned her face up, nose and mouth barely out of the water, breathed deeply in and out. Sasha was restless, ready to dive again, but Litta needed more air.

Back through a dark tunnel and up an entry ramp, Litta came face to face with a black-and-gray-striped male who held a stone lamp in mutilated hands. *Skinhead?* Her stomach spasmed; then she saw his scalp was normally furred. Broken, then set wrong, the scullada's hands twitched as he put down the lamp—Litta was one of his demons.

Sasha bleated and handed her a lump of maple sugar. Gravely Litta offered it to the crippled scullada, who took it awkwardly and touched his surprisingly dark tongue to it. "Ah," the striped male sighed as he lay the sugar aside, twisted one hand against the other as if trying to straighten the crooked bones.

The monofilament cuffs around the fly had not caught this scullada low enough on the wrists, Litta realized. So he'd pulled free and the others kept him alive. *Two black-and-silver survivors—Skinhead and this one.*

Sasha murmured to Litta. As she turned to leave, she suddenly realized that he'd conditioned her to respond at a reflex level to basic signals—*come, don't move.* He handed her a maple sugar lump now. She said, "Thank you," and broke off some for him. He whuffed.

One day, suddenly, Litta realized that she stank, that her hair was matted. Two beavers lay on their bellies by Litta, licking her hands from time to time. "I'm going mad," she announced to Sasha and Mina, who lay together on beaver pelts. "If I go mad, I can't get help."

Sasha's snout writhed up as he wiggled to Litta and touched her head with his hand. He tried to smooth her hair. "I'm insane," she said, sure he understood.

He lowered his nose and picked up a fish vertebra and made a noise she couldn't hope to duplicate. She held up one stone.

Sasha hooted gently, then stroked her hair again. She then said, "One," holding up one stone. He couldn't say *one, two, three*, but he recognized the words, holding up one, two, and three stones or vertebrae.

After they learned *one, two, and three*, Litta felt saner. She stroked Sasha's and felt hair coming off on her fingers. Under the shedding old hair was darker new hair. She turned on her lithium lamp. Black and silver gray coming in, very fine short hair.

Mina humped over, saw the new fur, and squalled.

Sasha shuddered, the shudders becoming body wiggles. He faced the wall, writhing. Mina, her trunk bobbing up and down, brushed the loose hair off and held him in her short arms. Then both scullada talked urgently, interrupting each other.

Litta began to cry, tiny tears as though she'd dried up under the ice.

"Manhattan's like an essential enzyme," Litta heard herself saying to Sasha weeks later. "We need it. We're going to kill the ice with iron dust, buy back the world." She reached for spruce bark, craving it now. "We have to keep our culture going." Sorry that they didn't understand, she picked bark fibers from her teeth. Mina pushed some sticks into the ground by the fire, let them sprout pale fantastic shoots which she'd eat like celery stalks. Litta gobbled them, fearing scurvy rotted her brain as much as the language-less time.

The water rose and the scullada, with rocks and sticks, banged air holes through the ice. The lodges began to drip, so fires were lit only at night during the warm spells.

The next night Sasha rolled on his side, shook her. He thrust her extra foam-skins at her, bleating. *Hurry, hurry.* As she was dressing, Mina lunged through the entryway and threw Litta down, covered her with beaver skins as another scullada came up the entryway.

Skinhead! As he stared at them and blinked scarred eyelids, Mina panted through her trunk. Skinhead wore a harness with a knife sheath. Slowly his pink head flushed dark and he spoke to Sasha, pulled out cords and measured Sasha, knotting the cords at the measures. *Skinhead brokers other scullada, sends them down to Stonemarker's camp.* Sasha lay quivering as Skinhead felt his fur, stuck his fingers down into it. Sasha's fur came up to Skinhead's palm. Skinhead gave a satisfied hoot.

Litta stared through a gap in the pelts. Then, fearing Skinhead would see the glitter of her eyes, she closed them and locked her muscles.

Skinhead ooched over the mud lodge floor, trunk sniffing. Litta heard him, almost on top of her. She opened her eyes into his horrible liquid black ones as he jerked out his knife and stabbed into the furs.

She twisted. Sasha heaved his body toward Skinhead as Mina jerked Litta away, hustling her down the exit ramp, through underwater brush that scratched Litta's face and snagged her foam-skins. Mina pushed her under an ice-embedded log. Litta surfaced in blackness and waited.

When the wet hand went over her mouth, she thrashed. But light—her lithum lamp in Sasha's hands. He wore Skinhead's harness pack, with Skinhead's knife on it, a faint pink in the water around him. He tugged her and turned out the lamp.

They swam under ice for miles. Litta's lungs strained even though Sasha let her rise to icy air bubbles when she needed, where there were air bubbles. Finally she saw a dark shadow on the ice. Sasha circled it, then swam to a creek mouth, where he chipped the ice open with the knife and hauled himself out. Lying flat on the ice, he lowered his arms to help Litta out.

It was another world on top of the ice—bright ice and snow, black rocks above the glaciers, willows and cedars dark against the snow, a huge blue sky full of hidden stars capping it all. And the wind hissed in her ears.

Both rolled in the snow quickly to dry off. His coat really is splendid, Litta thought, seeing the black and silver fur spring up as the snow and wind dried it. He looked up at her, as if wondering what to do next, then back at the hole in the ice. Making a moaning sound in his trunk, Sasha slid along the ice and snow toward where they'd seen the shadow from underwater. A black machine was frozen in the lake's surface, a trapper's amphibious ice cruiser.

Sasha lifted his snout at Litta, touched his fur, and looked one final time at the hole they'd come through, thirty yards behind them. Litta checked the batteries. Dead, but under the snow she found sails and an aluminum collapsing mast. Litta and Sasha chipped at the ice, rocked the craft. The ice holding it cracked and one pontoon tilted up.

"We have to get it up on the ice to travel," Litta said as if Sasha could understand. "It makes terrible time in float water."

Sasha heaved and the machine skidded forward a few feet, dangling half over water, half on ice. Litta crept forward on her belly, grabbed the bow rope, and hauled the cruiser onto firmer ice. Sasha watched, then helped her pull, claws shoving backward.

The cruiser's owner must have died in a winter blizzard—Litta found sleeping bags, food, and a navigator with dead batteries in the cabin. Using the knife, she chipped the outrigger and sail cleat free of ice, then stepped the mast, guyed it, and set the sail in the boom.

Sasha looked up at her from the ice, then reached for her. She grabbed his wrists and he clambered in, scrabbling against the cruiser's side with his clawed flippers.

Litta found a hand generator, cranked until she got a screen display on the navigator. Stonemarker and his pet scullada had tried to kill her, so she'd avoid the Catskills Archipelago. The nearest sizable town away from the Catskills was Pokeeps, down and across the old Hudson Channel. They sailed downwind. Then Litta headed the boat toward the Taconics when they came out of the Mohawk Channel.

For three days they sailed, floundering through the thawed patchs. Litta wondered if they'd get to Pokeeps before another blizzard and realized she couldn't have gotten out on foot. Sasha, head on the bow, hands gripping the rails, stared at the ice, the black trees, trembling occasionally. Litta worked the tiller and melted chunks of ice on a small stove with the white gas that remained on board.

Finally Litta turned the ice craft into a pleasure-boat marina at Pokeeps. A dockhand came out in the little crisp white canvas and fiberfill parkas that those people wore. Sasha trembled, muttered to himself, then almost tumbled down the cabin stairs, humping furiously away to hide. The dock attendant stared at Litta, and she knew then how smelly she'd be when she thawed, with matted hair and mad eyes. "Phone?" she asked, twitching at the sound of her own voice, disappointed when he didn't speak, just pointed to the marina store.

She went in, suddenly chilly despite the foam-skins, and asked again, "Phone?" The ice sailors, in pretty winter pastel foam-skins and nylon parkas, stared at her. "Spent the winter out there," she said, wishing someone would talk to her—almost as bad as being with scudders.

"Phone's there," the counterman finally said, pointing.

She tapped in the university credit code, then called Mason. "I'm not dead," she told him. "Call off the Eco Control. Have Stonemarker arrested, Skinhead. Skinhead's a scudder. He and Stonemarker tried to kill me." Her voice sounded croaky.

"Where are you? The Catskillers reported that the scullada killed you."

"No, ice cruiser at Pokeeps," she said. "Get us out before we're killed."

"Sapients? I killed one, you know."

"Damn, get me and Sasha out. Feel guilty later, okay? Let me tap credit for food. I'm starving. Mason, good to talk to you, very good."

"Phone credit's arranged. Who's Sasha?"

"Scudder friend. Saved my life. Taught me numbers."

She sat down at the counter and ate coleslaw, then bought a half gallon of slaw and two pounds of trout for Sasha, wondering if he'd eat it.

He came out of the cabin slowly, then shrugged several times as if trying to loosen his shoulders. Then he wiggled his proboscis tips over the cabbage. Litta patted him as he gobbled the fish and slaw, raking it in with both hands, not having to stop to breathe. A couple of the sailors watched. She felt nervous, as though humans were her natural enemies, too.

"Scudder?" one of the men asked.

"Yes," she said. "You can't kill them. Like killing people. Ice-lake people."

Sasha said the scudder word for *one*, and Litta held up one finger. Then two. *Tell them, Sasha, you little deformed space person.* She laughed. Hard to think of them as aliens, they were so primitive. Not like the Cheshee.

"Talks through his nose," she explained.

"Come in with him. Freezing out," the counterman said, having come to see what was going on.

"We found the cruiser on the ice," she said. "If you know the family, the human's dead. Don't think . . ." *Did Sasha kill the human to get the cruiser?*

Sasha didn't want to come in, but followed Litta, bleating nervously at the men, shuddering, whipping his trunk around.

"They're sending a chopper," the counterman told her. "Be here in about an hour, so you can shower, put on clean skins."

"Can't leave him," she said.

"We won't hurt him. Promise. Check yourself for frostbite. Here's ointment, fresh clothes."

Sasha hunched over to two men playing checkers and rolled upright in a corner to watch them. "He'll beat you if you teach him," Litta told them. Her voice seemed to echo; the other human voices clotted her ears.

In the shower she cried from exhaustion, from sheer funk, for dead and maimed scullada, for herself; then she combed her hair and put ointment on the various sores she'd gotten sitting all winter long. *Did Sasha do this to get me out or to save himself?* She dressed in fiberfill pants, a polypro undershirt, and a parka.

Sasha *was* playing checkers with the men when she went back. They'd helped him up onto two chairs set side by side so his head could droop down. He'd propped himself up on one elbow and moved checker pieces with his free hand.

"He plays like his life depends on it. Lost a game and seemed like he was going to fall apart," the man playing with him said.

She went up to Sasha, and he hugged her hard, his heart pounding under the beautiful fur.

"Chopper's coming," one of the men said.

Mason himself had come with the pilot.

"Sasha, show the man three."

The scullada held up three fingers, then picked up three checkers.

Mason looked gravely at the scullada. "I'm sorry if I killed a sapient," he said to Litta. "But it could be just conditioning. Did you learn more than numbers?"

"No. The phonemes are difficult," she said, feeling more complex thoughts flowing from a just-thawed portion of her brain. "I'm not even sure I could hear all of them."

"Sure you weren't signaling him? Unconsciously?"

"But he can play checkers."

"Well, let's sedate him for the trip to the city."

Mason got the needle in before Litta could protest or the scullada could slap the human's hands away.

The scullada fussed as the drug took effect, bobbing his trunk at both of them. As he began to go limp, he reached for Litta. She felt odd, almost guilty. Mason smoothed down the beautiful fur as they loaded the scullada onto a stretcher.

"Want anything out of the cruiser?" Mason asked Litta.

"No. Talk to me. God, that ice was cold." They climbed in the helicopter by the pilot, in front of Sasha's stretcher.

"Do the scullada travel much in the winter?"

"No, mostly they play games on graphs they draw on the lodge floors. They have fires, stored food. Sasha took me to see a crippled striper male once. Hands were broken, the snares didn't catch him under his thumbs . . . don't just surrender . . . so he tore free. Then there was Skinhead, Stonemarker's scullada buddy. Burnt, worthless skin."

"Easy, Litta."

"God, I can talk. Do you understand me?"

The helicopter pilot started the engine.

"You think striper males go out as ritual sacrifices?" Mason asked.

Litta looked back at Sasha, unconscious, brilliant in his new fur. "Yeah." She wondered what scullada legends, told from planet to planet, persuaded the black and gray males to die. Whatever, evolutionarily, the legends and the fur got them transplanted.

"Maybe this is the village atheist?" Mason said. "Or the coward?"

Litta felt her face grow hot.

"Ah, Litta, did isolation make you see more intelligence than is really there?"

When the helicopter landed, graduate bio students loaded Sasha's stretcher on an electric cart. Litta climbed in beside Sasha and held his hands. He began moaning through his trunk. Then he stared around him, wildly, body writhing.

Before Mason could sedate him again, he shuddered and closed his eyes tightly, breath whistling in and out his long nose, little pseudo fingers at the end of it twitching.

"Sasha," Litta said, stroking him. She almost felt the same shock, going from stone age to an electric world so quickly. *But is he intelligent, really intelligent?*

Eyes still closed tightly, he took one of her hands between his, trying to roll over on his side.

Mason prepared another injection, but Litta said, "Don't."

"If he behaves," Mason said, putting the charged syringe on a shelf under the stretcher.

Sasha hummed through his trunk and tried to sit up, but Litta was afraid to loosen the straps, suddenly seeing him as an animal. *Funny, he was like a person all the time in the lodge, but now that I'm back among humans, I'm nervous.* The scullada looked down at his fur, then pulled at it nervously as though he wished it would shed back to less lethal gray.

Technicians and postdocs X-rayed him. Litta felt him tremble, but he stayed where they put him throughout the series.

A technician prepared another syringe. "Dh'n't," Sasha said through his trunk. "Doon't." Three techs and Mason held him while the first tech injected him.

"He was trying to tell you not to," Litta said. "Language."

The technician who'd sedated him took tissue samples with a trocar and cannula and pushed a fiber-optic tube up the trunk to examine Sasha's vocal organs.

"Complex, really complex," the tech said.

They arranged a cool room for the scullada, with a swimming tank. Litta thought Sasha might want a hard foam pad near the water. So while the technicians went to get one, she sat with him, he still unconscious, bleeding slightly from a biopsy puncture over his sternum.

As Sasha regained consciousness, he beat his fists against

the gurney. Litta lowered it so he could get down to the floor. Weakly he crawled off and walked around, hands and feet curled sideways, looking and sniffing at the room.

"He'll eat soaked grain, roots, fish," Litta said. She felt weak and hungry, exhausted to the point of quivering.

"Come on yourself. We need to make sure you're okay," Mason said.

Poor Sasha, Little thought dizzily, *so small when I'm standing up.* When Mason took her arm, the scullada lunged, open-mouthed, at him.

"No," Mason said, sharply as though to a dog. Sasha rolled up to sit on his hindquarters, pushing one hand against the floor. He moaned through his nose, then dropped, grabbing Mason's pants leg with one hand and beating the floor with his other.

"Let me stay with him," Litta begged. "Bring me a bed in here. He knows me." Sasha watched her, still holding Mason's pants leg. Then Sasha reached up for Mason's belt and pulled the human down to his eye level, the great furry head cocked down so the eyes looked straight at Mason's. He whistled and made strange flabby sounds with his trunk, then shook Mason's belt and turned away, crawling across the floor toward the water tank. Then Sasha stopped, stared at the floor, and tried to scratch it with his index claw nail.

"They draw game maps on mud," Litta said.

"With their hands or with sticks?"

"Sticks," Litta said, remembering the challenge games the scudders played with each other in the lodge.

"I'll get pencils, paper," Mason said.

"Tomorrow. I'm tired, all of this."

"We'll get a bed for you, heated roomette inside this one," Mason said. "And steak and potatoes?"

"Wonderful," Litta said, positively zinging with exhaustion now. Sasha slid into the pool and swam in tight circles until Mason left. Then he came back out of the water and patted her ankles gently, rubbed his long nose against her legs.

"Hoo-kee?" he said.

Okay? "I doubt," she said to him, "you had any idea what you were getting into."

In the morning, Litta opened the roomette door and saw Sasha leaning against the waterbed frame, drawing with a pencil on paper, touching the graphite lines with his fingers. Mason and a Cheshee, leathery body wrapped in foam-skins, sat beside him.

She closed the door and dressed, then turned down the temperature controls and went out. "Doesn't leave a groove in the paper, does it, Sasha," she said.

"Ah, exchanged student, the Norte bitchy one?" The *b* sounded breathy, almost a *p*. Exo-linguist Carplel with the tattoo of a Terran rose between his eyes—Litta remembered him from Mexico. "You think these are intelligent enough to matter?" the Cheshee said with cold lizard slowness. "We tested, nonresponse. You . . ." He stopped and stared with unblinking eyes at Sasha.

Sasha drew ovals. Ovals, like ovals of monofilament, and hands. He felt the lines again, looked at them, then handed her the paper and pencil and sighed.

"Litta," Mason said, "if he was the village atheist, now he seems obsessed by their faith."

"Sapient?" Carplel asked, the rose between his eyes narrowing in wrinkles. "Import by us through a whirling black hole, but in that universe/space five sapient kinds hunted them. I tell you, we tested."

Sasha reached for the paper and pencil again and drew a scullada children's game board, one of the games he'd taught Litta. He slid it across the floor toward the Cheshee. Litta said, "He's challenging you, Carplel. That's a child's game among them."

"You also challenge, jealous. Don't you know Mexico affords us better than the glacier-stressed regions?"

"Let him teach me," Mason volunteered. Carplel turned his broad face toward Mason and blinked agreement.

The scullada slapped the floor and hooted when Mason sat down beside him. He tore up the game-board sheet and began again to draw double loops and roughly sketched hands, staring at his own hands from time to time as he drew. Then he handed the new drawing to Carplel.

"Oh, baby, no," Litta said, exhausted suddenly, despite a night's sleep.

Carplel pulled a photograph out of his Mexican cowhide briefcase. Gingerly, back joints and strut bones creaking, he bent down and showed Sasha the picture. Sasha stared at Carplel, at the photo, took it and strained it against his trunk. The trunk fingers writhed over the photo paper. Carplel said, "His lake. Wants to go back."

Litta cried, "He's not just an animal if he can read abstractions." Sasha dropped the photo.

"Apes can read pictures," Mason said, "but we don't give them sapient rights."

"Don't understand human reluctance to accept Cheshee animals when humans transport wild boars and brown trout over all Terra," Carplel said.

"Whether he's animal or sapient," Mason said, "he has to live his own life. Maybe they die when they reach this stage?"

"I saw two striped ones, the one who tried to kill me and another with healed mutilated hands in the colony," Litta said.

"We will try language contact protocols," the Cheshee said. "Then return to his lake."

Sasha drew monofilament cuffs and laid his wrists against them, his nose bent back to stroke his mouth. Litta decided she'd sedate Sasha, implant a radio-transmitter, if she could do it without either scullada or the men noticing.

* * *

When she went into to Sasha's pen to see if the transmitter stayed in place, Litta saw that his fur around the eyes was matted with oil. Her little radio box beeped. Like a child, he reached open-armed for her. She put the radio down and embraced him. "I'm going to catch you," she said, "if you have to be caught for the good of your species. I'm going to make you live."

He slipped slowly into the water, the fabulous coat dulled now, loose over the wasted body. She knew he wasn't eating and felt obscurely insulted, cheated.

The university helicopter airlifted Sasha to the scullada village and lowered him down. Litta watched from the air as he slithered off the stretcher into the water. Eyes above the surface, he began swimming steadily south.

The helicopter returned to the guides' port. "Come see this, bitch," a Catskiller called to her.

Litta followed, but stopped when she heard the wailing women. She knew. "Stonemarker's dead," one of the guides said. "He hanged himself rather than take a court disgrace."

Litta had a sudden vision of Stonemarker, the strange blue eyes in the almost Eskimo face-dangling from a rope. Nooses, pride, rites: she hated them all. She walked up to a man practicing casting on the dock and watched the big ten-foot rods whip through the air, the stiff monofilament leaders turn over, drop the huge flies and wrist nooses on the water.

Should I let Sasha die?

"We're gassed up again," her pilot said, ducking the giant feather lures that whistled by.

"He saved my life, that scullada, and now he's going to throw his away?"

"Cast for him yourself then, bitch, and keep him alive like a crippled old man," the fisherman said.

She got in the cockpit with the pilot and the men around

them backed off as the rotor blades began turning. "He's not old," Litta said before she realized she really didn't know. *Just my impression.* "Call Mason, get me money to buy Sasha from whoever catches him. I'll do anything he wants." An image of herself and Mason naked blew through her visual cortex.

The pilot made the call as they flew northwest. "Mason wants just to be your boss. He'll buy whoever catches him another scudder license."

The receiver began picking up the beeps from Sasha's radio implant. "There, that island," the pilot said.

"He's hauling out, with a bag."

They saw the scullada, tiny below them, creeping toward the firs.

"Closer," Litta said, "go closer."

"What's he doing?"

She saw Sasha dig through the bag. "Marking gun." For an instant Litta thought he'd shoot himself. At so close a range the bladder could do him considerable damage. But Sasha fired it on the rocks and rolled in the red dye. After five minutes, he touched his fur and then plunged back into the water.

The helicopter circled over him, flattening the tiny V of wake rippling behind his head. "He's not in shape for this," Litta said. He swam slower than the other scullada stripers she'd seen.

They saw the boat waiting for him, in the open water.

"Sasha, don't," she screamed. The whole planet seemed to wobble. "Go down, go down," she told the pilot. As the pilot came closer, the fisherman cast his fly. Sasha swam loops around it, as though he traced out giant cuffs around the smaller ones.

The helicopter landed on pontoons. Sasha looked over at it, then, without touching the fly, stuck one hand, then the other in the loops.

Both Sasha and the man tightened the cuffs, slowly drawing away from each other. Before Litta fumbled out of her seat belt and shoulder harness, the scullada took several deep breaths and sounded.

The pilot cut the engine. The only sounds were waves slapping against the boat and the pontoons and the reel clicking as Sasha sank.

Litta stared at the rod, bent and quivering, the line pointed straight down. *He's so thin.*

Then the rod bounced, the line went slack, and the man reeled in furiously. Sasha came leaping out of the water, twisting, his hands wrapped around the line above the cuffs. The *smack* when he hit the water coming down deafened Litta.

"Bid on your rod," the pilot said. "Buy you a new licence. That scudder seems weak."

As from a great distance, Litta heard Sasha bellow as he twisted up through the water again. He smashed into something floating in the water—a log, dirty ice. She realized he could die before he got the gaff noose around the snout. "You creep," she screamed at Sasha. "We saved each other."

Sasha stopped for a moment and stared at her. Then he sank. His eyes disappeared under swirls of agitated water.

The fisherman jerked the rod and then began to pump. Sasha's fingers splashed out of the water; he'd lost his grip on the line above the nooses. He faced the fisherman, sputtering when his trunk drifted below the surface.

The fisherman's guide maneuvered the boat closer to Sasha, who raised his black-and-gray-striped shoulders above the water, his trunk limp, floating on the water. The guide reached for it with the gaff noose, a loop of stout rope on the end of a pole . . .

"No!" Litta screamed. "Don't! Please."

The fisherman's guide pulled the rope tight around the alien's snout and turned him in the water. "Fur's messed up," he said to the fisherman.

Litta dove out of the cockpit and swam to the scullada, pulled the rope off, and began breathing in the cold snout. "Don't die. Not for some bitch's jacket. Don't . . ." An obstruction. "Wash out a gas line, ballpoint pen, something."

The fisherman's guide handed her a pipe stem.

She pushed it down past where the rope crushed Sasha's nose cartilage, and breathed into the nose tip, like a ragged clay tube against her lips. "I'll trach you," she said between breaths. "You've done your damn ritual. Live."

Another scullada swam up—the gray female, Mina—and freed Sasha's hands from the nooses, helped Litta hold him up, scolding him in scullada languages.

"I've got him breathing again. I'll pay for another hunt, a moose hunt, lions, anything," she said to the man who'd caught Sasha.

"All I want's a fur and he got some damn red stain."

"Litta, get out before you freeze," the pilot said.

"Help me get him out."

The guide pulled her out and took her to the helicopter. She tried to get back in the water, but the pilot held her and wrapped a thermal heat blanket around her. "We'll take him," he told her, "but you have to drink some coffee first."

Mina held Sasha up, her eyes jerking as the humans approached. Litta watched as the men rolled Sasha out of the water onto a stretcher and rowed him over to the helicopter. Mina cried from the water as the men put Sasha in the back of the cockpit.

Litta looked at him. His trunk was swelling; his right shoulder was dislocated. Mina called to him, but the tube kept him from being able to answer, the breath just whistling in and out in jerks. He waved his arms at her. "She's got to come, too," Litta said, beginning to shiver again.

Mina clung to the pontoon, moving away from the men as they tried to catch her, but surfacing and clinging to the pontoon, always looking toward Sasha. Then finally, trunk twisting, hands shaking, she reached for the ladder and tried to climb in.

"Mina," Litta said, stretching out her hands. The men touched Mina's flank. She didn't protest as they pushed her into the cockpit.

"New license, right?" the fisherman asked. "This his mate?"

"On a moose, damn you. These creatures are intelligent," Litta answered back. "He came back for her, not just the ritual."

As the helicopter took off, Mina eased herself upright and looked out the windows. Then Sasha, as painful as his shoulder must have been, pulled himself upright against Mina and stared out the window, neck curled down, trunk held in his left hand. Both of them looked out the window the whole flight; both were utterly silent except for the air whistling slightly in and out of their trunks. Litta touched each of them—light fingertip pats—as the helicopter approached Manhattan. Their heads looked almost painfully cocked as they tried to stare down at the city. Sasha moaned slightly and raised his head when the pressure against his wounded trunk became too painful.

Litta laughed. Sasha didn't *really* want to die. He needed to prove he wasn't a coward, get Mina, something of both. Mason would tell her she was anthropomorphizing, but she knew she was right.

Sasha rolled over slowly, onto his back and stared down. Holding his trunk in his hands, he looked at the gray blocks of city buildings, ice walls, the reactors, canals. Litta wondered what Sasha thought, the world turned upside down around him.

Sasha recovered from surgery in the cold room with Mina. Litta herself spent a few days in the infirmary. Carplel came in to tell her Sasha'd gotten through surgery.

"I am a bitch, but I saved them."

Carplel wrinkled his rose tattoo at her and said, "Only he and the female seem intelligent. Others we tested still play dumb."

"If we can prove they're intelligent, we won't hunt them anymore. Nobody would transport them to other planets. So they hide that."

"Perhaps they *are* intelligent. If they could earn further life for themselves in slow space, null acceleration. Space is like water."

I should have thought of that. "Until we work out what Sasha and Mina can do, I suppose they'll continue sending the tiger males off to be killed. That's why they've managed to survive in unstable niches. Other species move them around for sport."

"The Catskillers will it. Don't be bitter."

"I'll go see them now."

"Sasha?" Litta said softly. He looked up at her, leaning against the padded V-chair the students had built for him, a chewed-up corncob dangling from one hand. His nose was still tender, so he waved to her with his free hand. *A student must have taught him.* Mina looked up from a fish she was eating and said the simple forms of the scullada numbers, *bup, shree, p'hab.*

Litta held up one, two, three fingers. Mina shrugged slowly as if she wasn't quite sure what the human meant by shrugs, then pointed at Sasha, herself, and Litta. *Three of us here, right,* Litta thought. *All three alike.*

Mina hooted softly and wiggled up to pat Litta, who said, "Thanks." She took the scullada's head in her hands and look into Mina's eyes. "Maybe someday you can tell the others it's safe to talk to aliens."

The ice came slowly enough to allow humans in the North to escape—first Eskimos, Lapps, Siberians, then Russians and Canadians, Scandinavians—some through transformer gates to other planets, others to the south. After five hundred years of ice, the new loess lands in Burma and South China produced more than the American Midwest ever had. The sea sank, opening new croplands in Central and South America, cold pastures across reclaimed Beringia, grain and grasslands in the Sahara.

Each century, enough iron dust was shot up into orbit over Antarctica to keep the planet from freezing completely.

Manhattan taxed its citizens a 30 percent VAT for the great ice walls and for shuttleloads of iron dust.

Giant Flesh Holograms Keep My Baby's Eyes Warm

Judy Ridgley slouched in her bubble bag chair, picking at the algae-colored patch on it, trying to remember precisely how tall she'd had her chimera made. Someone knocked on the cube window. She rolled upright and looked at the monitor screen. *Cyril, by God,* she thought as she buzzed him in. His blond hair was greasy. Wire-rimmed glasses dropped down on his nose. Unsteadily raising one foot over the threshold, then touching the doorframe lightly as he brought the other leg inside, he entered.

She drew her vidcam, putting five layers of laminated glass between herself and him, watching Cyril shove his glasses back up with his middle finger. On the camera monitor, he was precisely miniaturized as she wanted the duplicate of him to be.

Cyril grabbed for the vidcam. "It's goddamn Judy Ridgley, camera for WPPA News. Shit, bitch, I lost four million rubles in that gambit. I'm off target, private citizen. Stop."

She rolled to her back, the chair bubbles creeping under her, camera glued to her face, knees up, feet crossed at the ankles, twisting her torso to keep the camera out of his hands, laughing now. "Poor Cyril . . . double poor, poor Cyril, lost it to the Cyrillic alphabet."

"Brain twisted, eh, Judy."

"No, no. But what about you?"

"Take that electronic mask off, stop being Lady Video," Cyril said, flipping through her digital stacks, loading something with a little hologram woman on the box. He stared at the movie briefly, said, "Piss on the bitch. She's got clothes on," then stepped across the tiny tube to Judy's refrigerator while she continued to watch him through the camera.

"Stay out of my beer," Judy said sternly, "You've had enough." She put the vidcam in its case. Her bare eyes looked like they'd been stripped of glasses—weak green, a permanent dent where the camera fit. Freckles almost blended with the rest of her skin except across the lower jaw, where they'd gotten some more sun. She got up off the quivering chair and took the beer away from Cyril with a sharp twist of her wrist. Her wrist strength stunned Cyril, but then wasn't her job basically lifting weights?

"You were my digital thing. I wanted to digitalize you all the time," she said.

"Digitalize," Cyril said, grabbing her by the shoulders. "Digitalize, like you digested me." A woman who lifted him out of life and into thousands of hologram sets.

"You were a madman, Cyril." July handed Cyril the beer as though she'd never taken it away from him. Then she giggled.

He asked, "Where are you planning to put this miniature me you've ordered?"

She pointed to the upper left corner of the room, said, "A tube bed'll fit."

"No camera now, just raw air between us." He lapped at her with his tongue. "You or your network set me up for the

Russians. Got me thinking I was a little American prince. Could do no, flat out no, wrong."

"When you're rich, you're public," she said, as if wondering if he hurt, to be suddenly not-rich after being digitalized for so long. "What happened to Alex?"

"Never trust a tomcat. He fled to the Buddhists before I could sell him. Beautiful little fucker, gold eyes, you remember. He wanted to talk to you once about Bach. But you, you were stuck behind your damn vidcam."

"I generally find the rich and their chimeras don't want more of me than they're forced to take. What kind of mind did you give him?"

"Stock. Stock bipedal cat. I'm not a bitch about losing him. I just didn't want to move into a cube right away, though. Lost the bond on him, too. He clawed a city cop who tried to stop him in front of the monastery." Cyril sat down and crossed his legs, staring at Judy through little sixties wire-rimmed glasses that suddenly dimmed, obscuring his eyes. "Still have these," he said, "to hide behind."

"Why did you come *here*?" Judy finally asked.

"Wanted to see what you were like without the camera, ba-bee." Cyril raised one corner of his mouth, then stared down at the beer can, shook it, and tossed it in the cruncher. "That's what going from a house to a cube's like, crunch. And you took out a license for my type. I want to see what you did with it. Thanks for the royalties, anyhow, too."

"I made a miniature of you. He's still in a growth tank. He really looks like you, except miniature."

"But animal DNA. Are *you* human DNA?" Cyril asked, leaning over his knees to study her face closely. He tweaked his fingers through her hair and said, "Too coarse to be anything but."

He's still pretty, Judy thought. *Wonder if the pretty's gonna rinse off in common tap water, wrinkle up like a smashed beer can?* "So the Russians took you? Ruble investments aren't protected. You knew that."

"I don't have to work, but I can't afford the house. I've been adjudicated a new private citizen." Suddenly Cyril's glasses cleared. He sighed, took them off, and rubbed the bridge of his nose. "You cheered me on, yelling behind that camera."

"You're not rich anymore, so now you can care what I think or feel," she said as she bent over the camera case, a strip of skin showing on her back as her top rode up. She put the camera in front of her face. "I can't sell you anymore, so I'm buying you."

He stared at the lens, then touched it, smudged it with his fingers, greasy with nose oil.

She said, "Stop!"

"God, did I hurt your baby?" Cyril said.

She bent over the camera, cleaning the smudged lens. "I'm responsible for this, you know. I *do* have a job."

"When do you take delivery on me? My chimera."

Judy froze, one hand moving the lens tissue in a compulsive circle. "He's more like my idea of you than you are, if they built him right. I was maybe somewhat fascinated by you when you were rich."

"Custom chimera . . . megabucks . . . Judy, you've taken bribes to ignore something."

"Someone put a bequest on me to make me public rich, but the network helped me dispel it, except for the chimera. I'm still private. I wanted to be a chimera designer when I was younger, but I wasn't smart enough with computers and lab techniques."

"Shit," Cyril said. "I want to see him. My double." Bitterly he added, "Little me. Sex slave?"

"I'll take you with me when I pick him up. Monday. I'd like to compare him with the real you."

"Or me with the real him?"

"Something like that. Maybe you can learn from each other."

"Or you're taunting me."

"I don't think I'd be capable of doing that, Cyril. I like you enough to have duplicated you."

"Would you have me instead?"

"It's not sexual. And besides, you know you're not still rich."

Monday was one of those days when the rundown machines bothered Cyril—a new wave of rust and minor breakdowns as though metal caught viruses. Unoiled screeches nagged him as he took public transportation to Judy's house. Damn bitch, maneuvered her way out of a bequest with money enough for a chimera of him. He flipped the switch in his pocket that dimmed his glasses and leaned back against the graffiti-covered plastic seat. *She'll probably bring the camera with her, her dildo eye.*

Judy was waiting at her stop, hair blowing in the wind the trolley made. Cyril thought that without the camera in front of them, her eyes looked as though she'd been floating dead in a puddle for years. The trolley was crowded, so she couldn't sit beside him, but rather pushed in and held on to a pole with her underwater eyes closed. Then a guy in paint-stained coveralls got off and she sat down.

Are we going to take a chimera home on public transportation? The bitch has no idea. He remembered his cat-man's disdain and nervousness when he was around ordinary humans, too fastidious for their coarse faces and odors. Yet Alex abandoned him for a Zen refuge when the going got tough. Chimeras were unfaithful beasts.

"We'll take a taxi back," she shouted across the car.

He sank down in the seat, wondering if anyone recognized them. *I used to be rich; she used to digitalize me constantly.* But he knew the people on the trolley would never recognize her—she stayed behind her camera always. Could anyone recognize him without the antique Rolex, the chimera, the Hebrides tweeds?

He remembered Alex's green eyes and the little tucked-in

lip corners when the beast smiled, just before breaking bond on the policeman. *I must have been crazy to have bought him with claws.*

He grimaced, his hand clenched on his glasses dimmer. One of the passengers murmured to another, not faintly enough, "He is the one who lost forty million dollars to the Russians. I thought he'd committed suicide."

"Nah, it's all fake. They aren't any richer than we are."

It wasn't fake. He remembered the thick-faced men coming to his mahogany and old velvet room in the Metropole. *Gospodin, we are so sorry*—kak zhall. And a Slavic equivalent of Judy, emotionally blind behind her camera, filmed him as he realized he'd lost it. *How did I let myself take those risks?* he wondered, closing his eyes and leaning back against the vibrating metal car wall. He wondered how many Americans had been hoaxed into believe the new New Economic Program was right around the corner. Now nothing. On the level of a news girl. At least Judy didn't follow him to Moscow. That's when he should have dodged the deal, but he hadn't thought of her as a person with enough feelings to have avoided seeing his fall. She wasn't so careful of his feelings if she'd gone on to duplicate him after his deals collapsed. News bitch, that's what she was. Just a fluke she wasn't in Moscow.

He'd drunk a week's ration of beer last night, listening to each can crumple in the crusher before he popped open the next one.

Judy said, "Next stop."

He opened his eyes and looked at the bleak exteriors of what he knew to be elaborate houses. *Real woods and stone, hand-laid plaster, not this dull metal and plastic crap.* If Alex hadn't stolen himself away, blown his bond . . .

Judy was standing, ready to leave. Wearily Cyril stood up, looking at her face. She looked like a sexed-up rat, he thought. He realized he was almost thinking of the chimera as a son. *Not a son, more like a giant flesh hologram.* The feeling of loss—wasn't that over what he'd lost? He *couldn't* be identifying with dog meat shaped to her idea of him.

When the trolley stopped, he stumbled into Judy getting off. She looked at him and said, "God, do you look hung over. You should have taken something for it."

"I wanted to feel rotten."

"I think I shouldn't have let you come."

"Why did you let me come?" He followed her into an expensive vet's. *Damn her, how did she arrange this? She had to have . . . the bond alone.*

"I wanted to see how well . . . Okay, Cyril, I feel somewhat responsible. I know I'm not, but since you asked to see him. A bit of me doesn't feel quite right."

The lights inside the vet's office were nicer than the sun, and his headache subsided. The receptionist stared at him and said, "You're the model, then."

"I bet he has a dharma phone number memorized already," Cyril said, slumping down on a chair. *Damn gel-chair, why can't they use inner springs?*

"Chimeras who've been exposed to outside influences and aren't allowed to associate with new chimeras," the receptionist said in a prissy little voice. "Judy, Maxine will take you in."

"Cyril can come with me."

"I'd leave him out of it, but it's your chimera," the receptionist replied as woman in coveralls entered.

"Poor little bastard," Cyril said, following Judy and Maxine through leather-covered swinging doors into a hall carpeted ceiling, walls, and floor with red shag. "Lady's terror chimera."

"Not at all," Maxine said. "Judy's having him trained with her digitals of you. He's been taking training holos in the stim tank. He's quite a conversationalist."

"Not to be confused with conversation piece," Cyril said. "Judy, you don't know the real me."

"The person I digitalized for seven years will do," she replied, eyes and mouth tight. "After all, I helped created you, too."

"You going to buy him little miniature planes and Ferraris?"

"He'll have those in digitals. I can't afford the reals." Judy looked back at Cyril, seemingly confused by this, as the aide opened the door to a cell-like room soundproofed with gray acoustical cones, like the inside of a giant cardboard egg carton. In the center of the room was the coffin-shaped tank, all matt black. Cyril touched it—the surface was gritty, cool. Wires and clear hoses entered it at the top, where the head should be, was.

Demon mechanical womb. Cyril shuddered as Maxine turned a valve at the bottom of the tank. As the warm Epsom salt solution drained away, she turned off the holos and opened a hatch.

Cyril felt queasy as a naked, wet miniature of him, eyes obscured with hologram goggles, crawled out of the tank hatch, dripping salt solution.

The creature took off his goggles and said, looking at Cyril, "You're who I'm supposed to be." He handed the holo goggles to Maxine. "Thanks, I take it this is when I leave." The little miniature winked at Judy.

A cocksure son of a bitch. Is that how she saw me?

"But I'm smaller," the creature continued. "Why?"

"Her place is small," Cyril said, "so you had to be miniaturized. What are they calling you?"

"St. Cyr. So she wants to tuck me under her bed?"

Judy quickly wrapped a towel around St. Cyr's waist. Cyril found a plastic stool and sat down. The chimera smiled a wicked little smile and said, "So that's why I have to wear glasses. *He* wears glasses. Judy, you didn't ask for weak eyes."

"Don't you want to know anything about the world out there?" Cyril asked. "Not much that you remember has been real. How are you going to be me without real-time Ferraris?"

For an instant, his miniature self looked confused. St. Cyr put a hand against the indoctrination tank, gripping the towel firmly in the other. He didn't look at either Judy or Cyril, but stared at Maxine, who said brightly, "Now, Cyr, do you want to walk around?"

Me? They used my pattern on cat DNA for this? "The streets are dangerous for unprotected chimeras," Cyril said harshly.

The little chimera asked, "How would they know I was a chimera? I look just like you, but smaller. And why are the streets dangerous for unprotected chimeras?"

He's anxious now, and seems more . . . human. "Perhaps they will think you're just a poor human who couldn't afford restructuring. A human midget."

St. Cyr said, "Arggh, to be not just born poor but built poor as well." But then he laughed, like the old Cyril jumping into danger.

Judy had forgotten his clothes, so St. Cyr dressed in a drab vet uniform that reminded Cyril hauntingly of the uniform novice Buddhists wore. "Let's walk a bit in the garden," Maxine said brightly. "We never walk our clients in the street."

They only seem sophisticated when they first come out of the tanks. Hypno-learning, holograms, and language tapes played day after day as they float in growth and conditioning tanks. But he is like me, not the slick surface, but. . . . She caught something she can't possibly understand.

As they walked to the vet's garden, the little chimera stared up at Cyril as though Cyril had been ugly. "What does happen outside?" he asked.

Cyril felt guilty for complicating the creature's life so quickly. "Poor, working, whatever, nonrich people associate chimeras with privileges they don't generally have."

"Judy, are you rich, then?"

Cyril said, "Someone tried to make her rich. She dodged."

"What is rich?"

So naïve, really. Cyril realized that the chimera's idea of the world was no more complicated than Judy's, at best, or more likely, than an edited version of her digitals. "Rich have public position and money to support it, generally from appointment or risk-capital ventures. They're public figures. They live for the rest of us. I used to be rich," Cyril said, "but I lost it."

"Cyril, you were such a cynic," Judy said, as though he were dead and hadn't just seconds earlier been cynical in what Cyril thought was a lively way. "But the cynicism didn't stop you from being naïve, too."

St. Cyr said, "I have no interest in being naïve." He looked at Judy and the aide.

Cyril felt sorry for the chimera, but being near him made him dizzy, as though he was talking to himself in a distorting mirror. "Don't worry. She'll probably get a bigger cube. She's media-wise." *What does that mean? She makes most of it up.*

The chimera grinned a wicked-little-boy grin. "She's a fool over me."

"Don't bet on it." No, she was a fool over me, Cyril thought. Or perhaps I was a fool over the image she made of me.

"I've seen even the outtakes, the digital visuals that didn't make the news stories."

"No way you've seen everything I've done. I lived for thirty-four years." Have been living, Cyril amended in his mind.

Judy didn't know if she preferred St. Cyr to Cyril as he'd been. Of course he was vastly better than Cyril after he'd collapsed, first hating the poor life, positively vicious about cubes. Now, even more disconcertingly, but perhaps because minor investments protected him from work, he stopped seeming ultimately degraded. But then her chimera wasn't quite as camera-docile as his human original. Just as Judy had framed St. Cyr interestingly, he said something to startle her. "Cyril talked to Alex at the refuge the other day," St. Cyr said, his little shades opaqueing into mirrors, throwing the camera lens back at Judy. "I talked to Cyril today. He still visits his cat."

Judy knew Cyril had given St. Cyr the Refuge phone number. "Are you happy here? We could get a bigger cube."

The chimera curled up around her legs and bopped refraction rainbows through his glasses, then said, "It's better than a novice cell. Of course I could be relieved to believe that all life is illusion, not just mine."

She reached down and stroked his hair, thinking about how he got behind her lenses as no one else ever had. *My beautiful . . . Maybe Cyril himself, if given a chance . . .* No, this was safer, she realized. She plucked off his glasses and tried them on, pushing the earpieces out a bit. She mirrored them backwards, staring into both her own eyes and St. Cyr's. "You're such a character, but don't tease me about going to a Refuge or I may take us both to one."

"Cyril's a boring drunk. Why did you make me in his image?" He took the glasses back and bent the frame gently back into shape before staring up at her.

"He didn't seem to drink so much when he had money. He wasn't boring at all then."

The chimera turned away from her but settled down against her knees. "How much of him am I?"

"Physically, pretty close, don't you think?"

"Yeah, but—"

"Mentally, we tried, but we were running transforms on cat DNA with modified cerebral development genes."

"Did you see me before they re-formed the face and body?"

"I could only afford fifteen zygote tries."

"So, really, I'm just sculpted and indoctrinated to be like him. Mentally, inside, perhaps I'm not him at all. Perhaps there's something real to me?"

Judy decided that she'd have to have St. Cyr re-tanked soon, have those Cyril holograms and digitals replayed often into his dubious mind. Expensive little chimera. "Maybe you shouldn't answer the phone when I'm not here."

"Do the rich copy each other in chimeras often?"

Judy tried to remember, remembered. Sexual obsession cases, most of them. And a few bequests got turned into flesh, the chimeras hidden off in a middle-class block. *Hey, maybe there's a story there?* "Does he ask you about where you sleep?"

"Yeah, but I don't think the question is just about sleeping."

Judy looked up to the carbon-fiber tube bed she'd had installed up in the corner, as though St. Cyr climbed a rope ladder into a giant telephoto lens each night, Cyril in camera.

St. Cyr said, "He's worried about sex, isn't he? But no, you want me to babble on about my formula one racing car. The one I imagine I drove."

"You're so small," Judy said, feeling slightly nauseated, "that it's like you're far away, bright and rich, even when you're in here with me."

"I want you to tell me a story for a change." St. Cyr climbed the rope ladder into the carbon-fiber tube and wiggled in. He looked down at her and flashed rainbows off his glasses before pulling his head completely in. She heard him sigh and then the click of earpieces being folded up against the glasses frames.

"Would digitals bother you?" she asked.

"Why can't you tell me with your voice? Cyril said the Church Militant was going to be demonstrating outside the Zen monastery when some rich—"

"I don't want to talk about Zen monasteries."

"It's going to be on Channel 7, if you want to miss it," St. Cyr replied. "Why is the only alternative to my being owned so obnoxious?"

"What do you mean?"

"Buddhists. All life is an illusion, not just mine. I'd have to join them or stay with you. Or hide, but I don't want to hide. If all life is just an illusion, then this is less work than the monastery. And just as illusionary."

"How did you find this out?"

"I called a lawyer to see what my rights were. It will be on your bill. You ought to tune your phone to just your voice if you want to make sure I don't run up your phone charges."

"Do I have to do that?"

"Judy, I would if I were you. I've been duped to think I need certain things. I might get this crazed fascination with emeralds some day. You'd have to sell me."

"Thanks for the warning." Judy was relieved that the Buddhists didn't tempt St. Cyr, but then she'd had him modified that way. "Good night, St. Cyr." She listened to him turn restlessly in the tube, then the rustling stopped and he sighed once and yawned, popping his jaw open. As he began breathing regularly, she plugged in her earphones and put on hologoggles, the mirrors bouncing visions of an archaic Amazon river basin around her eyes.

When she slept, she dreamed of St. Cyr as a jaguar.

The changes in her phone billing system cost her more money than she'd expected, but when she saw St. Cyr's bill, she realized he'd found out more than just his legal right to Dharma Refuge. He'd known he could be sold if she couldn't pay her bills.

"Why can't I see him?" Cyril asked. He and Judy had met for lunch in a museum park. "Why won't your phone let me speak to him?"

"Why is it so important to you? He's just a chimera," Judy said. "I'm just a camera."

"The rich love their chimeras."

"Oh, sure. That's why you get them to terrify you, fuck. Well, I love having St. Cyr around the cube as company. I don't particularly think of him as you that much anymore, or even as a chimera. If anything, you're becoming more like him."

Cyril realized he was becoming obsessed by the chimera, that it was irrational. But there is was. He should walk away now, but he didn't. "I'm beginning to realize there was nothing to fear in the cubes."

Judy stared at him as though he'd given his mind away. "Don't you have a job yet?" Judy asked.

"I'm still living off the house sale."

"If you invested that . . ."

"I don't really give a damn," he said. "I'll go on workfare. Join a monastery. Let me see or talk to St. Cyr when I want to; don't be such a bitch."

"Take him to a monastery?"

"No, even though Alex is happy enough there."

"St. Cyr isn't really you. Conditioning and surgery mostly."

"He's like me. I feel it. We're both adjusting to the real world after too many fantasies we lived for other people." Cyril decided that he'd talked too much; that if he said more, Judy would be afraid he'd steal St. Cyr. "I'm a bit catty myself."

"I've got you an invitation to the network New Year's Eve party. Everyone's bringing their chimeras. I've finally been invited and they've asked you to come with us. It's private. Everyone's curious. I don't know if you want to tell them that cube life isn't so bad."

She had no idea, he realized, of what some chimeras meant to their owners, but if he could see St. Cyr, then fine. "I'd appreciate that. You don't seem interested in me now that I'm not rich, you know." But now her bosses were curious about him. Cyril wondered if he'd feel more poor among them. Lately he didn't feel different than himself, just depressed that he couldn't go where he wanted, but then his past seemed more and more unreal. "It's odd being poor. I haven't really changed."

"You're drunk a lot now. I have St. Cyr."

I knew them when, Cyril thought, darkening his glasses reflexively. He'd been at this house before—Judy must realize that—sat with Alex beside the phalaenopsis, cascades of white saucer-sized flowers. Amusing Cyril on digitals double time, a diversion—perhaps that was all he'd been, even to his rich friends. He took digital time so they didn't have to serve. What is this? Cyril asked himself. Normally I'm not so bitter.

The gardeners had grouped orchids on the wire racks by the fountain again, a puffy mound of green broad leaves with flowers rolling off pendulant stems. Among them was a cattlenopsis, purple cattleya blooms on a phalaenopsis stem. *Even the orchids are chimerical.* He wandered by the wire-based mounds and saw Judy with St. Cyr. Judy looked bare-faced without her camera.

Cyril knew the man talking with St. Cyr in precisely the same tones he'd used when he'd talked to Cyril, admiration and condescension. Funny, I didn't identify the tones when I was him, Cyril thought, then stood wondering if St. Cyr had replaced him. No, Cyril had been a popular media figure. St. Cyr's story intrigued a different class.

Not late enough to be fashionable, but I wanted to see if I could take it.

"Cyril, I thought you'd died," a brittle network wife in antique hippie clothes said.

"No, I went private."

"The Camera's chimera is just like you. Isn't it droll for

her to have a custom chimera? Like diamonds with gym clothes. We did her a favor to dispel the bequest."

"Sure. Droll."

"I'm sorry, Cyril."

"I like the orchids. Always have."

"They're making chimera odontoglossum with better heat resistance, but we just haven't had time to—"

"There's something cool about phales."

The woman pushed wisps of hair back under her silk headband and looked at Cyril as though he'd said something anti-party. *How welcome am I, really?* "Is it too bad," she asked softly, "living in a cube? I think I would die."

How many times has her face been rebuilt? he wondered to himself before he answered, "Not too bad. The state people have offered counseling. Alex wants me to join him in a monastery, but I got enough from the house sale to live on for a while. So I'm in the cubes, but not of them. My neighbors . . ." She didn't want to hear that, or anything about the neighbors, he realized as her face twitched slightly and her eyes shifted focus.

She said, as if confessing a vice, "Some of my younger friends think the workpeople might be . . . exciting?"

Cyril said, "They think we're exciting. My neighbors also wonder how I lived through my fall." *What was this we?* he thought. *I'm privately poor now.*

"Well, I guess you let the Camera get to you. Cameras are less human than chimeras, I think."

"You're right. Judy looks sluggish without her camera. But isn't my little double cute?"

"Oh, Cyril." She moved back and stared at him as if not sure whether he was joking or not. "All chimeras are cute. All Cameras look like albino slugs without their machines in front of their faces. We invited her for his sake. He needs to be in a proper setting. I don't understand why she doesn't sell him to someone who'd be more appreciative."

"Shall I get you a drink?"

"No, I'm fine. You might see if the Camera wants one. I've never seen one drunk."

Well, I am dismissed, Cyril thought as he went toward the bar. Something utterly gorgeous poured the drinks, red mink hair down to her hips, the utterly perfect tipped-up nose, and green eyes fringed with black and red eyelashes. Cyril was suddenly nervous, not knowing if the creature was an augmented human daughter or a sex chimea. "Scotch and water, please," he asked, trying to keep his tones noncommittal. He decided that they wouldn't have their daughter out serving drinks. *God, in the past, I'd have realized that immediately.* In the cubes, everyone assumed both the rich and their chimeras are artificial; he was beginning to believe them. *Thoughts corrode, that's what happens when the money goes.* He felt worse here than he'd felt in weeks, more degraded. *If I was home,* he thought, then stopped to examine the implication that *home* was his present one-room apartment, with the neighbors who worked on an assembly line and spent all their money going to parrot shows.

The female chimera bared fangs as she bent toward him. She sniffed his breath and said, "Point 02. Don't drive away."

"Where did you learn to tend bar?" Cyril decided to ask. Man's terror chimera?

"It's one of my secondary attributes," she said in the sly tones of a chimera who knows humans aren't always smarter than chimeras.

"What kind of party are they planning?"

"They're going to turn me and some others loose later tonight. Perhaps we'll catch each other, *trabaher*."

Worker. "I'm not a worker, but I'm not rich now either. I feel like just a person, no attributes."

She smiled at him. "Sometimes I feel like that, too—human." Odd way she said *human*, as though meaning she felt human sometimes, not just addressing him as the human, but Cyril couldn't prove she meant it that way, either. "I saw a miniature of you, I think. Cat-stock?"

"Yes."

"Is there really any difference between us, or is it something we've been told? After all, *human* DNA is restructured." She smiled again.

"Look, I could have kept my house if my damn cat hadn't run off to a refuge."

"Your miniature is a lot more witty than you are. You were rich then, but I wouldn't have thought a Camera would idolize her public drama man."

Oh, chimera bitch, can't you see what she did to me? Cyril took his drink and began looking for Judy, who'd been a fool, he thought, to bring St. Cyr here.

He saw men, or humanoids, mounted on large horse-form chimeras, holding lances tipped with ribbons and banners, the lances wiggling as the large chimeras jostled their riders. *I used to be able to tell instantly—chimera or man.*

Then he saw himself—rather St. Cyr—swung through the air in a real man's arms. Before Cyril could reach them, the man dropped St. Cyr on a fox-horse. The fox-horse turned its head back and seemed to be talking to St. Cyr. Cyril recognized the man. The man changed chimeras frequently. Two years earlier, his chimera before this one stomped his chest flat, but the man had a spare heart.

"Be careful, St. Cyr," Cyril cried, pushing through the laughing crowd of humans. Judy stood beside the fox-horse, looking almost transparent, out of place, neither chimera nor rich. She took Cyril's hand and squeezed briefly, then dropped it, blinking her eyes.

The fox-horse looked at Cyril and asked, "Are you the larger model?"

"No, I licensed my structure. I was famous once."

"And you didn't commit suicide or go to a monastery when you lost it?" the chimera asked, its fox mouth and tongue writhing to make the human sounds.

"Cyril's nice," St. Cyr said from the creature's back.

"But, like your nonrich owner, he doesn't belong here. You belong with us, not with them. You're what he was."

Judy turned an ugly mottled red as the fox-horse spoke.

"You and I are free. No implants, no compulsions, no brain worms, no fame, no jobs, St. Cyr," the fox-horse said. "St. Cyr, we can do anything we want to." The trimmed hooves, with gold chains around each fetlock, began drumming the ground. "I could run if they'd get out of my way."

"Can't you just run over them," St. Cyr cried, "if they don't get out of our way?"

"You're right. I don't have to be nice, but let's begin mellow. You two humans with the flowered hats, please step aside," the fox-horse said. The humans did. The fox-horse jumped, almost throwing St. Cyr, then bolted for a riding ring. "First, some pre-hunt training."

"Judy!" Cyril cried. The fox-horse jumped over the riding ring fence. St. Cyr laughed.

Judy said, "I should have had controls put in, everyone tells me."

"Surely you have insurance on him?" the fox-horse's owner said. "Besides the bond?"

"He's all that's left on a bequest," Judy said.

"Well, then," the man said, eyes on his own creature, "they're beautiful together. Why not sell him to me?"

"No," Judy said before Cyril could say anything. "I need his company."

The fox-horse was gavotting in the ring, snapping its teeth each time it leaped. Still laughing, St. Cyr dropped the reins and gripped the creature's fur.

Was I really that mad? Cyril wondered. Then he remembered challenging some almost cybernetic German skier to mixed Nordic events. *But this side of brain destruction, I'd have been reconstructed. As long as I had money, death wouldn't take.*

No one was looking at Cyril now. His miniature had all the attention—giggling on a fox-horse.

Judy came up to him and put her hand against his chest. "I'm just a camera." Her tawny eyelashes flicked nervously. "I'm droll, just not as droll as St. Cyr. Perhaps I should sell him?"

An image flashed through Cyril's mind: his old cat chimera ringing a bell and chanting, "Repent, repent." "I don't really understand why Alex left. I'd have made sure he was happy with his new owner. Don't they seem happy to you?"

"They're going to have a grand hunt later. Three years ago, I managed to sneak shots of the gathering of the prey. My boss sent some prehistoric reconstruct after me, something with a very primitive crusher jaw. Crushed the holograms, the tape, but missed the camera."

"Archaic hyenas were popular about three years ago. It's a capital W Wild Hunt. Sometimes even humans die. I want to get Cyr—St. Cyr out before the madness begins."

"St. Cyr doesn't have a brain worm, a compeller. He can slip away."

Cyril remembered more about the fox-horse's owner, about settling up over a woman's miniature rhinoceros. "The fox-horse plans to take him to the hunt."

"Then help me get St. Cyr off that damn fox-horse."

"If you let me see him more often." Cyril felt almost as if he had money and parts to spare for a second.

"Damn you, Cyril." She suddenly looked more like a real human and less like something almost chimerical stripped of protective covering. Tiny eyes squinched up, and a huge crack of a wrinkle between her eyes. Blood-swollen capillaries under the freckles gave her skin a mottled blush.

Horns sounded. A man ran backward from a zombie chimera. As the zombie ran, flesh hanging ragged on huge bones bobbed and swayed like misplaced breasts. The chimera, awkward as a walking corpse, stumbled.

The human stopped to laugh. Finger pressed against a

transmitter button on his belt, rigged to drop the chimera if he took his finger away. Electric brain worms coiled around the zombie chimera's motor center.

Judy said, "So that's why some rich activities are off-limits. I didn't know about this side of your life."

"Humans crave as much excitement as they can afford." *Your life, meaning all the rich*, Cyril realized. He smiled down at her, feeling almost as though he were performing for her again. "Just push through slowly. If anyone hands you a box, release the button. Or does your insurance cover chimera damage?"

A long-haired young girl in a white muslin dress tried to hand Judy a box, but Judy lashed out, shoving the box against the girl's velvet belt.

"I'm not part of this," Judy said. "My insurance—"

"You have a chimera," the girl said. She seemed almost stunned, as if no *human* had ever threatened her before.

St. Cyr, still on the fox-horse, grimaced as the zombie chimera shrieked and collapsed, clay-colored fingers brushing a man's face, fake rotten flesh flopping across its belly. Cyril nodded slightly to St. Cyr, meaning *come away*. But when St. Cyr tried to get off, the fox-horse nipped his leg and giggled.

Judy darted past Cyril and went under the ring rail.

"Why should you have a chimera?" the fox-horse asked her. His voice was deep, rumbling out of the big head and chest, as if he'd spoken with a falsetto voice earlier. "We think we'll keep him. We can buy him, dead or alive."

"Let me off," St. Cyr said quietly. "I'm not having as much fun now."

"But I am having more fun. Five-seven-nine-oh-eighteen hundred," the fox-horse chanted, "will see you free in the lotus land."

"Shut him up," some yelled from the crowd.

"I don't have implants. And the little fake man dropped

the reins." The fox-horse winked at Judy, then charged, slamming her with his shoulder.

"Rheinholt," the fox-horse's owner screamed. "Don't kill her."

Judy smelt fox breath in her face and a hoof on her ankle. St. Cyr gasped.

"Rheinholt," his owner said. "Lethal needle."

"Oh, you're bluffing again," the fox-horse said, but he reared away from Judy, almost throwing St. Cyr, and said, "Why, I haven't done anything yet. I'd like to kill you, too, but I've heard you have a couple of brains in stock. Is there an S.P.C.A. officer in the house? And it was the *old* Dharma Refuge number anyway." He crept up toward Judy while talking and dabbed his head down to bite her camera finger.

"I want off," St. Cyr said. "You're being cruel."

The fox-horse turned his head and stared at St. Cyr for a long moment, then said, "But I was made to be cruel."

St. Cyr kicked off the stirrups and bent his knees, his heels up by the stirrup buckles. As the red chimera wheeled and bucked, Cyril ran under the rail himself and grabbed St. Cyr off the fox-horse. "Throw dirt at it!" he yelled to Judy. "In its eyes."

"*He, his* eyes. I'm a male," the fox-horse said, teeth bared, nose tucked down as he stared at Judy. She bent down, scooped up sawdust. "Stupid human. Sawdust is too light to travel far if thrown." Judy froze, leaning on her knuckles, bleeding through dust on her hands.

The fox-horse's owner said, "Oh, stop, Rheinholt. We shouldn't hassle the help."

"And her blood is bitter." Rheinholt lowered his head to wipe his mouth against a fetlock and his owner darted in to grab the reins. Rheinholt sighed. "I do know the real Dharma Refuge number. But they don't have room to play."

"We're going," Cyril told Judy and St. Cyr. "Private parties get very chaotic. And neither of us has insurance that covers chimera damage."

As they walked toward the car gate, Ct. Cyr pointed at the zombie chimera, who raised his head off his hands and stared dumbly at them all. The beautiful vampire chimera was wiping off his dangling bit of flesh. St. Cyr stared. "You can see up close," he said to Cyril, "that it's healthy flesh, not real rot."

"Keep moving," Cyril said. He hated to see chimera made that way, so ugly they couldn't be used as daily servants.

"I'm not like the other chimeras," St. Cyr said. "Don't sell me to those people."

"No, I just realized you are a chimera," Judy said. "Even though I didn't have a brain worm installed, you're still warped just the same."

"It's not my fault you fed me your bullshit fantasy holograms. I was very unprepared for being a chimera."

"I didn't think of you as a chimera."

"What if you die? I'll be sold just like a chimera."

"Stop," Cyril said, wanting to slam both of them together, several times, hard. "Judy, say good-bye to our hosts, your bosses, I believe, while St. Cyr and I call a cab."

"Fuck all of you," St. Cyr said. "I don't know what's real. Literally." St. Cyr touched his glasses into deepest dark. From under the wire rim, a tear, rimed with dust, rolled down his cheek. "I thought I remembered parties."

Cyril stared at the tiny distorted image of himself on the dark lenses and knew St. Cyr stared back.

Judy came back, face muscles like tiny wires under papery skin, the freckles floating like splotches of crud. "Said I did better on the other side of the camera, obviously. But perhaps now I would be 'reduced' in my work."

The cab pulled up. "Dark windows, please," Cyril asked.

"The little one a chimera? He's crying. You hurt him? They have feelings, you know."

Cyril suspected they had a Buddhist cab. The Dharma centers stripped calls from the taxi lines and sent out counterfeit cabs. The cabdriver laughed when Cyril didn't answer.

"I'm not a chimera like the others," St. Cyril said, almost touching his glasses frame to push the glasses higher on his nose. His index finger quivered and dropped. Cyril noticed that St. Cyr had neat little nails and wondered if Judy groomed him or if St. Cyr took care of himself.

"No," the cabdriver said. "You don't have to be owned?"

St. Cyr stared at the framed license, not the man, then said, "What is the alternative? Judy, do you have to own me?"

"I ordered you to be made."

"Do you have a phone in this car?" Cyril decided to ask. "My old chimera took refuge, but I'm allowed to visit."

"No, Cyril," Judy said. "Bad idea."

"Alex is a delightful animal."

"I don't want to be a chimera. All the things I think I remember about my life before you picked me up, Judy—they're all synthetic, right?"

Judy stared out the window, didn't say anything, just watched the streets roll by as though they were some digital production she had to edit. Finally she said, "Do what you want, Cyril."

"There's a refuge," the cabdriver told St. Cyr, almost as if man-to-man. "All you have to do is ask."

"Reality, I demand reality. Fuck unreal Buddhist bullshit, holograms in the eyes, fake . . ." St. Cyr kicked out convulsively at the driver's seat, twice, and began screaming, raw broken screams like some unknown code.

The cabdriver pulled up to the curb, pulled hypodermic case out of the glove compartment. St. Cyr's scream blotted up all other noise. He handed a disposable injector set to Cyril, who grabbed St. Cyr's arm. The cabbie came around to Cyril's door to help, stretched St. Cyr's arm out while Cyril injected the drug. The cabbie tapped the syringe when the plunger was halfway down. Cyril stopped and withdrew the needle.

St. Cyr gasped and stopped screaming. Cyril pulled the dark shades off and saw eyes with hugely dilated pupils, focused on nothing. Then the eyes seemed to be watching something vastly distant, wobbling in the sockets gently. Cyril looked at Judy. She had her eyes tightly closed, tear beaded up around the lashes.

"Is he crazy?" she finally asked.

"I don't know," St. Cyr answered. "Cyril, is Judy crazy or are you? I don't always want to be reflecting." He sweated as if speaking had been a great effort.

"Take us to 1234 Nagagochi," Cyril said, remembering the vet's address.

"I didn't know it would be like this," Judy said, finally opening her eyes.

St. Cyr turned slowly and recoiled away from her, leaning up against Cyril. "Is *this* real?" he asked quietly.

As the cab merged back in the traffic, the cabdriver said, "It doesn't matter." St. Cyr didn't say anything more, but occasionally Cyril felt the little chimera's ribs jerk.

Judy said, "Should I sell him to someone who can take care of him better?"

St. Cyr groaned.

Cyril said, "He doesn't want to go to a Refuge." They both helped St. Cyr out of the car after the cab stopped at the vet's.

"Memory shock," Cyril said to the receptionist.

Two aides came out for St. Cyr. "Wait out here," the receptionist told Judy. "It's best."

"A cabbie gave us something," Cyril said, handing over the vial.

The receptionist looked at the syringe, raised one eyebrow, and spoke into an intercom: "Zenbo standard tension juice. Say about five mils." She looked up at Judy and Cyril and asked, "Want him to go to a Refuge?"

"He started screaming when the cabbie suggested it," Judy said.

"Was he around other chimeras today?"

"Yes," Judy said. She sat down in a chair, pulling at her pants above the knee, picking at the threads.

Cyril sat down beside her. "Do you think this would make a good video?" he asked, somewhat surprised at the sarcasm in his voice.

She lurched back in her chair, eyes closed, then said, "Probably. Did you look for cameras?"

"No."

Grinning, she opened her eyes. "Meta-realism, a Camera caught on camera." The grin twisted into a grimace.

The vet came out and said, "He's sedated enough from the Zen juice. How do you want him re-tanked?"

"How much is it going to cost?" Judy asked.

"Around five hundred to six hundred new-ones."

"I could help," Cyril said.

The vet looked closely at him and sighed rather harshly. "Or you could take him home, see if he calms down. If not, turn him over to the S.P.C.A. for resale."

"I can't afford to keep him truly artificial," Judy said. "What bothers him the most?"

"He has some delusions about needing to be his real self," the vet said. "The Buddhists could help him realize there is no real self."

Cyril suddenly felt very possessive of St. Cyr, as though he was a human DNA sexual recombinant, a real son. "Let him come stay with me, Judy."

"No, I'll take a vacation and spend more time with him."

"Judy, I have more time to spare than you," Cyril said.

"Cyril, he's my chimera."

Two aides, each gripping an elbow, lead St. Cyr out. He blinked, small between them, with eyes that seemed surprised to see anything. "I thought," he said haltingly. "I remembered things that really happened."

"Before we picked you up here last time, your memories were almost all synthetic," Cyril said.

"Maybe the party was synthetic?" St. Cyr asked. "It wasn't that different from what I remembered, but from a chimera's point of view. Then I got on the fox-horse."

"Maybe—" Judy started to say.

"Isn't what really happens important?" St. Cyr asked. The aides tightened their grips, and one put a hand on his shoulder. "If I can't count on my memories being real, I can't learn from them."

"I planned to take care of you," Judy said.

"Why install memories at all?" St. Cyr asked.

Judy said, "Your memories are decorative."

St. Cyr looked at the aides holding him and said to them, "I don't like my situation at all, but I won't fuss physically now."

"Okay, St. Cyr," one of them said, dropping his hold on St. Cyr's elbow. The other one looked at the first, turned St. Cyr's left elbow loose, but kept his hands close, tense.

"Let's go home now," Judy said.

"I've got to talk more to Cyril. I want to know what I really am supposed to be. Your camera missed some of the most important parts."

"We can begin in the cab," Cyril said, catching the receptionist's eye. She nodded and dialed on a secured line.

Cyril, dizzy from beer and tea, was shocked when he opened the door the next Wednesday afternoon and saw his little miniature standing there. St. Cyr had taken a tremendous chance, walking the street alone, unescorted through mobs of workers, as though he were human.

"Why didn't you ask me to come there?" Cyril asked.

St. Cyr didn't answer until he'd looked Cyril's cube over. Cyril wondered if the chimera could see that it was bigger than Judy's, what with the mess. St. Cyr sat down on Cyril's bed and replied, "I picked Judy's lock. Would you have done that?"

"I don't know—but you could have been mobbed on the street."

"I wasn't. Some humans are this short. And I didn't wear the glasses."

Cyril realized that without the shades St. Cyr looked less like a caricature of him. *Would I,* he wondered drunkenly, *looked less like a caricature of myself bare-eyed?* "So did you leave a note telling her where you'll be?"

"You live here and don't work?"

"It's called a small untouchable trust fund. My great-aunt left it to me. She must have had her doubts. Did you leave Judy a note?"

"Why couldn't I have real memories?"

"Shit, St. Cyr, I'm drunk. Don't ask me questions like that."

"I've got to get away from her some or I'll kill her."

"I found her a little distasteful sometimes, but nothing like that."

"Cyril, I *never* get out of there. And she's setting up holos in my sleeping tube. Bootleg brain feed—everything about tanking except the tank itself. She can get the drugs easily enough."

"Oh." Cyril stumbled to the toilet and pissed, almost curious as to what Judy would do to the chimera with holograms and memory confusers. *Con . . . fusers, yeah.* "That means she's desperate."

"Don't you care? I thought I'd grown up with you, lived all those years at your right shoulder."

"Two years in the growth tank. Have to play something in, or the brain wouldn't develop right."

"No, it was more like fifteen." St. Cyr sounded hysterical. He stood rigidly in the doorway.

"Two. I know because I remember when I was notified that someone was making my type. Fifteen's an illusion."

"How long will I live?"

"About thirty-five to forty years." Cyril's drunk tongue blooped that off; something in his personality not quite as drunk as the rest of him recoiled, and he felt dimly ashamed.

St. Cyr's eyes seemed to wobble.

"But you have as much adult life as most humans," Cyril said, trying to reassure St. Cyr.

"All fake. I can't trust my memories, so I have to be a chimera. Thirty-seven, thirty-eight years of living up to some you she actually . . . created . . . the image of."

"She likes making images."

"Thirty-seven years. I can't stand being with her that long."

"I thought you'd be upset that it was so short." Cyril did notice that St. Cyr took the upper figure as his life span.

"And how do you even know how real any of your memories are?"

Cyril felt as if his own memories were kaleidoscoping, a tiny brother clone always at his shoulder, observing the lens always pointed at his head. "She needs you. She's desperate. If I weren't so drunk, I'd help you think of a way to make use of that."

"She needs me?" St. Cyr seemed to have never thought of this.

Cyril decided his chimera variation was as self-centered as he'd been. "Yes, she needed me as a rich man. She needs you as my replacement, and you could make something of it."

"Give me some advice? Surely you have ideas about being needed."

"Fresh out, St. Cyr, my son. I'm planning to go with my neighbors to a car race this evening, maybe catch some wrestling, watch some rich people. Folks love me because I can explain what's really going on."

"Really. Then how come the Russians took you?"

"St. Cyr, you're just a little miniature me—nyah, nyah, nyah. Don't you want a beer?"

St. Cyr said, "So here I am in a world with no acceptable alternatives. And I come to my role model and he offers me alcohol."

"It makes me as depressed and bitter as I'm supposed to be. Otherwise, I'm sure I'd just be quite boringly normal."

"Have you considered a 12-step treatment program?" St. Cyr asked.

"I don't take advice from imagined creatures."

"I can imagine you need my advice," St. Cyr said. "So you think she's desperate? And all I have to do is entertain her?" He put on Cyril's glasses and bopped reflections at him. Cyril turned his head away from his drunken image in the glasses. Perhaps he merely needed to shave. Cyril decided that he didn't want to see either Judy or St. Cyr for a while.

A few weeks later, Judy called and asked, "Is he with you?"

"No," Cyril said. "He came over on the fourteenth, but I haven't seen him since. Walked through the humans."

"I tried to recondition him at home . . ." Judy's voice faltered. "He picked the synthesizer and made his own tapes. He faked taking the pills."

"Turn him over to the S.P.C.A."

"But he's been so nice otherwise, telling me stories. I thought . . . I only just found out what he'd done. I've got to find him now. He's been gone since yesterday. I thought the Buddhists had to turn over chimera novice's clothes to their owners within twenty-four hours."

"Well, I didn't expect him to go to the Buddhists. Maybe he thinks he can pass for human?"

"But his memories aren't functional. He doesn't know anything real beyond four months ago." She shut up then; Cyril didn't say anything for a while.

Then he asked, "Do you really give a damn?"

"Yes. I never had any children. He's been inventively witty lately. Stuff I've never heard from you. It wasn't you I needed, but my idea of you."

Cyril interrupted her. "He's not a real child." He wondered if she wanted St. Cyr to be helpless, dependent on her. *I myself became her image of me, forgetting that she was making me a story, that I had to crash.*

"He's a bit too strong for me to wrestle down and inject. Cyril, the SPCA said they could take him, but they didn't think they could place him. He looks too ordinary. They could use him for shelter maintenance, since he can't figure or read."

"Why didn't you let them, then?"

"Cyril, look at what happened to you once you weren't rich. You've turned into a boring drunk."

And that's more interesting than I'd be without the alcohol, Cyril thought. "He isn't me."

Cyril heard metallic snapping sounds. He visualized her sitting beside her camera case, index finger and thumb pulling a fastening loop up. She snapped the catch open and shut until Cyril wanted to reach through the phone and grab her hand, make her stop. Finally she said, "I was going to keep him on holograms and Memoratin most of the time, so he'd think in the evenings that he was still rich and had just come to visit."

"Judy, don't tell the cops he's missing. You could forfeit your bond."

"Okay."

I don't really have to get involved, Cyril thought as he hung up. *I'm hardly the same person who licensed his type.* He slumped forward and rolled to his feet, then stepped across his cube to check the beer.

Cyril saw a program on the flat-tube later, where St. Cyr—him, obviously him—played a chimera who had passed for human. He quickly called Judy, "It's him, on the PS station. I tuned in late, don't know if it's fiction or program."

On the screen, St. Cyr finished up his day, assuring one battered old bipedal lion that the SPCA had found something better for him than a lethal needle. Before St. Cyr went through the building's front door, he smiled and darkened his mirror shades as if smiling for Judy and Cyril. Then he went out. Cyril recognized the street five blocks up from where he lived. The camera moved back and followed St. Cyr as he waited for a streetcar, his mirrored glasses reflecting nothing of the camera crew that must be right in front of him. He hopped up onto the streetcar when it stopped.

He's coming my way, Cyril realized. *But they might have filmed this earlier.* He heard Judy laughing through the phone.

St. Cyr pulled out today's paper. Then after reading the front page, or seeming to, he stopped at Cyril's house and went to Cyril's apartment. "It's not real. I'm private," Cyril said to the phoned Judy.

A man playing Cyril came out and said, "Without money, I'm just a boring drunk. Without alcohol, I'm just another poor guy."

"Have you considered trying to work your way back up?" St. Cyr said.

"First, a 12-step program," the man who couldn't be Cyril said. Judy was laughing hysterically through the phone. She said, "He just came home now. Lot of the scenes were synthesized. I'm pissed that he didn't let me in on it."

St. Cyr went home to an empty cube and crawled into his carbon-fiber tube. He began to play holograms. The flatscreen went between and around the actors as if the hologram scene was real.

Judy said, "He learned how to do one thing."

"What?" Cyril was still expecting a knock on his door, Judy behind the camera. He was too drunk, he realized, to make sense of what St. Cyr had done.

"He makes up his own life now."

Farming in Virginia

Su'ranchingal's scales stepped down the human sun wave frequencies. Heat. His brain sizzled until he hallucinated humans turning into *zr'as.* Already they had thin hornlike sheets on their toes and fingers as if nature, beginning at the extremities, was working scales over them. Two million years from now, they'd have scaled hands; then a million years later . . .

It's not just the heat, it's the *ti'if,* Su'ranchingal thought, the drug the ship machine used to sedate him and Hu'rekhi, the other ship specimen. The humans kept feeding it to him.

But Hu'rekhi had stopped, pulled the pills out of her throat sac with her double-pointed tongue. She drank isopropyl alcohol, the skin under her scales turgid from it. Hu'rekhi hated everyone. Being locked with Hu'rekhi in the research labs reminded Su'ranchingal of the way humans kept birds and fish in small arenas, no choice of mates, no escape from constant bickering. Being housed with Hu'rekhi in Virginia was more tolerable, more two birds who hated each other sharing a three-hundred-square-meter aviary.

Yesterday the human Culpepper told him they were going to send him and Hu'rekhi back to the descendants of the *zr'a*. But I'm so harmless and addicted, Su'ranchingal thought, and Hu'rekhi's a drunk. I grow the human's food. I'm useful. And the *zr'as* sent us away. Hu'rekhi thought that going back was more than stupid. She hated the *zr'as*.

Visions of glass hot-towers with another sun going through them, and *zr'as* walking always at a distance, through the tubes connecting the hot-towers, among the vats and sleeping ledges.

If I don't cool off, I'll die, Su'ranchingal realized. He checked to see if his human neighbors were watching, then frothed on his belly, tongue lashing out gobs of cooling saliva. His genitals felt heavier than usual. He touched a tingle into them. Then he leaned down and tasted the sour dirt he'd hoed, with the iron in it.

Su'ranchingal saw the tracks—cloven hooves: deer, huge herbivores—and wondered if the locals down at the store would tell him what cured gardens of deer.

C'yanginthu, w'yanamthi, th'yamgi—now just alien sounds—murmured through his head, meanings vaguely smeared between Spanyol and Amerish. Su'ranchingal hugged his toes, suddenly a child again, with another child, chilled, sleeping five years away, tended by a machine with speech cones murmering Spanyol and Amerish at them both, warping and drugging their baby brains.

I'm still too hot, Su'ranchingal thought as he walked out toward the faucet with the coiled hose attached. He turned on the water and sprayed himself. Humans preferred that he did that rather than use his own froth. *Ohna'a*, the alien word rose in his mind, "rain on the grass."

He raised the scales over his belly and lungs while he played the hose against the blood-gorged skin. When he was almost dizzy, he thrilled a pitch too high for the humans.

The neighbor's cat slouched across the garden to see if Su'ranchingal would feed it. Up in a hanging basket on the porch, Su'ranchingal kept a carton of cat snacks he suspected were addictive to cats. High-order sapients tended to addict their underlings with something.

"Mee-ow," the cat went in its funny little voice, meaning, *I like you, but don't tease*, according to the program Su'ranchingal had seen on the television. Not language, signal. Not sophont, but sapient.

"Would you eat a deer if it was finely minced?" Su'ranchingal asked the cat. He fed the cat a lump of the cat snack and rubbed its flesh over the skull behind the ears. "Is it legal to kill a deer for eating in your garden?"

The cat could eat a whole deer, frozen and thawed in chunks. His house had a freezer—it had been explained as though the house was capable of ownership, he thought at first. *The house has a freezer. I have a deer problem.*

Can Hu'rekhi and I have children?

The human scientists had been very interested in that. They told Su'ranchingal he was male genetically and Hu'rekhi female. Gave them pronouns, genders: he, she, male, female. Su'ranchingal had heard nothing about matings when young in the creche.

Creche was the word the humans gave it.

Have. Gave. Possessive mammals sparsely coated with almost invisible hair except on some arms and legs, male chests, and major joint inner surfaces. They smelled each other but weren't aware of doing it. Su'ranchingal wondered if he and Hu'rekhi did things to each other that they weren't aware of.

"Me-ow," went the cat again, breaking through his mind thoughts and images.

"Ah, cat," he said, giving it another morsel, "do people plan to send you back to your original home, too?"

He had to put on overalls before he went looking for Hu'rekhi, who was probably drinking too much again with human males. Hu'rehki . . . Thinking about Hu'rehki made him terribly anxious, suddenly.

The human intelligence agent Culpepper had always come to the store about three minutes after Su'ranchingal—that human tracked his every move. *A boring job for poor Culpepper,* Su'ranchingal decided as he fastened his overall suspenders and slipped on foot covers to keep them free of road tar, watching mismatched creatures from space. As he was walking by the old Morgan place, Su'ranchingal wondered why Culpepper and Josephine Vann, Hu'rekhi's watcher, didn't share the house with Hu'rekhi and him.

And Su'ranchingal was jealous of Hu'rekhi with the human men. *Jealous—possessive. I'm mentally humanized,* he thought as he walked down the hot asphalt and rock that keep brush from blocking people and cars. He wondered again why he and Hu'rekhi were sent here, why the humans wanted to send them back.

Vann was at the store instead of Culpepper when Su'ranchingal got there. She came up to him, eyes wobbling in their sockets, avoiding his own eyes as he bought a Dr Pepper.

Su'ranchingal said, "I thought you watched Hu'rekhi. Where's Culpepper?"

Her eye muscles went rigid. Finally eye to eye, she said, "Culpepper went to Washington to brief the new man."

Secretly thrilled that Vann finally gave him eye contact, Su'ranchingal asked, "New human watcher for me?"

"Yes," she said. "Culpepper asked to be taken off your case when the results on Hu'rekhi came in. He'd believed you."

"Culpepper told me yesterday you wanted to send Hu'rekhi and me into space."

"Where is Hu'rekhi?"

"Drinking isopropyl with your ethanol-drinking men. If I had not been a creche baby, I think I would be lonelier." Hu'rekhi was strange company—and the local humans were aloof, with flabby eyelids that blinked so slowly you saw the flesh go up and down. Vann looked away now, eyes twisted back slightly to look at him again. Suddenly he missed the days when Hu'rekhi and he had landed into a midst of questioning, touching humans, patchy hair concealed under white clothes. Then they'd acted as though he were important, so he had thought so, too. But he knew now he'd just been novel.

"We will send you back," Vann said, "even if we never find Hu'rekhi."

"There is no back in spacetime," Su'ranchingal said.

She sighed. "You're sure you don't know where Hu'rekhi is?"

"I haven't see Hu'rekhi since you checked her blood and excretory crystals," Su'ranchingal told Vann.

"Her hormones changed. We think she's pregnant."

"We have no idea of how to raise our reproductions."

"Say children, it's less weird," Vann suggested.

Su'ranchingal thought *children* was for humans as *fawn* was for deer, but since he and Hu'rekhi had been treated as honorary humans, then *children* made sense. Up until yesterday, when Culpepper told him about the plans to return him to the *zr'as*, he thought he was an honorary human. "*Children, child* for young language users, then?"

Jo Vann said, "Better not to have *any* children. They'd be so isolated growing up. And any matings would be genetically dangerous."

"We'd have to reproduce heavily for fifty generations to threaten your biomass," Su'ranchingal said. He felt, in waves, alternately close to the humans and distant from them, as if alternating pulses of caffeine cleared the *ti'if* from his head, then washed more from his digestive web to his brains. He tried to pinpoint which pulse left him feeling close, the clearing one or the muzzy one. "We don't have enough genetic material. Within a few generations, we'd be clones of each other from inbreeding, as your cheetahs were before gene splicing." His back tongue flap twitched the *ng* toward a *zr'a* phoneme, but the woman's face went cold—if cold was a rigid adjective, as cold water went rigid itself into ice.

"Gene splicing?" Vann said.

Su'ranchingal realized he'd said too much about gene splicing and yet knew so little about it. "I don't remember giving Hu'rekhi genetic material."

"Maybe you fuck in your sleep?"

"And sleepwalk to the other side of the house? Pretty obscure sex," Su'ranchingal slurred, back flap instead of front trying to make the *t* sounds. Su'ranchingal, fighting the *ti'if* as best he could, "I am anxious more than usual, now that Culpepper is gone. Why is your posture so stiff?"

She said, "You make us nervous."

"How can I force you to be nervous? I'm so helpless I have sex I can't remember with a female who hates me," Su'ranchingal said, "But I can grow you lettuce, make you a crop, not nervous. Are the *zr'as* still . . . are you still getting radio signals?"

"Still sending."

"You can't possibly know that. They are two hundred light-years away." The whole confusion of whens and wheres hit Su'ranchingal like more ti'if. "I've been most of my waking life here." His eyes felt dusty, so he rolled them back into his head a few times before remembering humans loathed seeing his eye moistening. *Well, they blink their flabby eyelids disgustingly slow.*

"But you didn't evolve here," Vann said as if that mattered.

"You evolved in Africa—why are you here?" Su'ranchingal asked. "You don't send cats back to the Libyan Desert. You don't—"

"It's the planet we evolved on."

"Your people tried to terraform Venus."

"Our solar system, then, when that becomes habitable."

Su'ranchingal remembered how drugged the *zr'as* had kept him in space, ungrowing, perpetually chilled. "Are you going to send me alone?"

"You are worried about her, aren't you? We want to terminate the pregnancy. We're not going to be inhumane about this. We don't think alcohol or *ti'if* could be good for genetic material. You'd probably spawn monsters."

"In-humane?"

"Cruel."

Something vaguely reptilian—archaic shock instincts—screech of scale or fingernail on slate, a zr'a *vowel we can't use.* Su'ranchingal felt too numb. "You should have scales, thin fast eyelids."

She shuddered faintly, the same muscle recoil vibrations he'd seen in others who braced against a flight reaction. "I'm sorry I feel the way I do. You are a very social creature, aren't you?"

"Humanized. Not with Hu'rekhi."

"You do seem a bit shocked. Hu'rekhi lost, probably pregnant, and your flight back coming up." She bought him a another Dr Pepper. "But we'd appreciate a little more honesty, not the farming pseudo-yokel shtick."

"I don't remember . . ." He took the bottle from her and up-ended it, tongue flaps directing the fluid to his digestive web. "I remember space." He looked at her evasive eyes. "It was extremely inhumane."

"Your people were the cruel ones."

"I don't remember doing sex with Hu'rekhi. I used to hear about times when sexual tissue was swollen." He remembered touching his genitals in the garden, feeling them tingle. Vann's eyes swiveled down. Su'ranchingal's fingers twitched around his waist—where humans had their nonfunctional navels.

"It must be cleaner than our fucking," Vann said when he drew his fingers up toward his mouth. "Your sex isn't between piss and shit."

"But it's unimportant if I did it without noticing." Su'ranchingal felt very strange. "Can someone help me with a deer that interferes with my vegetable-growing duties?" He stared to wobble and added, "I don't think I can take another Dr Pepper."

Vann stared at the clerk, who switched the cash-register screen on and off; then they both looked at Su'ranchingal and hissed breath around their teeth.

The next morning a message chip arrived, a chip for an obsolete computer. Su'ranchingal finally found one with mud daubers' nests on it in the basement. The loading port had been sealed with plastic that now shredded to his touch while the disturbed wasps vainly tried to sting him through his scales, eyesheaths, and thicker-than-human skin. He cleaned it, brought it upstairs, and plugged it into the house circuits—the receptacles still took the same plugs—then nervously turned the computer on. *Uk ka, a self-boot*, tongue flaps alternating. He looked at the package the chip arrived in and found a brittle yellow paper with odd-shaped alphabetics on it—"Call up vis.inf once you get the c prompt."

Nervously he typed in VIS.INF and the return key; he'd seen visual of these archaic Terran computers in the archives, but working on one by hand was strange.

Pixtels. He strained to make out the image, to read it as a three-dimensional visual of a woman, and wondered how the *zr'as* originally learned to decipher this code of colored dots. Finally he worked on the focus and contrast to make the image more appropriate to his brain's visual centers. And the woman was talking:

> My name was Alice Maxwell. I arranged for friends to deliver these tapes to you to assure you that some humans are your allies. I'm dead now, but I lived long enough to hear the first signals.

Su'ranchingal froze the picture and looked at the woman, trying to imagine why a dying human would want to tell him this. *What had she been? And why am I only now getting this message tape?* He started the image and the sound moving again.

> Did you first decide to send to us because of our radio signals, TV signals? Or those nuclear blasts? Will you help us? I didn't find out when I was alive, and now I'll never know.

He waited while the woman on the tape drank a glass of water, throat muscles working, but no lump bobbing up and down as in the male humans. She seemed sick; she was dead many years now. Then she said, "You have friends among us. I started an organization. This is their contact with you."

Random light hashes bounced on the screen. Su'ranchingal knew the message was really for another kind of alien and turned the computer off, pulled the chip and destroyed it, his digestive web burning itself slightly.

Culpepper came walking out of the deer's path into the garden while Su'ranchingal was wrestling with the Rototiller. "You aren't my watcher anymore," Su'ranchingal said to the human. "You resigned."

"Do you want to go back?"

"I grew up in Annapolis. I don't understand when my original language speaks to me. And if I went to the planet I was born on, I would be an alien all over again. And there is no way back in time to where I was. My immune system is not as evolved as the germs on that planet now."

"But no one would be afraid of you."

"That's stupid," Su'ranchingal said. "Why should humans fear me? I'm a drugged addict. Do you fear me?"

"No, I don't fear you. But when Hu'rekhi turned up pregnant, I thought you'd lied to me. But now I think I know what you are."

"I don't remember inseminating her."

"You're the experimental chimp, not the guys who sent you. You could inseminate while you were asleep."

"Or drugged," Su'ranchingal said primly.

"There are people who want to help you. You're still a sapient, but I suspect it would go better for you if you stayed with us."

"Sophont, linguist. And you want me to go back to those people who called me . . . made me . . ." A concept lurked in alien sounds that he had almost forgotten—*sr'arrXch*, not of full quality/dignity. His bottom tongue flap spasmed with the stop that the humans lettered X. "They took away what you would call my dignity."

"Dignity? That's important to you? I don't believe we've ever discussed that. Bizarre, considering. I wonder if the people we think may try to help would be so interested if they knew you weren't the inventor of your ship."

He is still a watcher, Su'ranchingal realized, hearing Culpepper's voice shift tones and cadences, seeing the human's body stiffened as though he'd sighted a deer or a space-going chimpanzee. Su'ranchingal said, "A word, *sr'arrXch.* I didn't be brought up to it, but when I first arrived, you gave it to me." He realized the idiomatic thing to have said was *didn't get brought up to it*, human possession again: *getting, having, holding*.

"All you want to do is stay here?"

Su'ranchingal imitated with his rounded shoulder blades a human shrug and looked like he was drawing his head into his body. When he realized Culpepper looked perplexed, he said, "I like to trick plants in a garden."

"Hu'rekhi escaped."

"Escaped? To where?"

"Someone helped her out before we could a—"

Before humans could abort her babies, Su'ranchingal realized.

Culpepper said, "Help us find her before she gets hurt."

"We were not close friends." Human talk, *close* metaphorized as if two mental lives brushed up against each other, closely. "We were thrown together without testing."

"You got her pregnant."

"We must have a truly occult sex life," Su'ranchingal said. "Did you sent me the old lady's visu-chip?"

"What visu-chip?"

"Laser erratics, not a message, just the picture of an old woman." Su'ranchingal felt hot and pulled the hose from the reel and sprayed under his belly scales, the tiny erectile muscles aching like a thousand pins from both cold and tension. He wondered if he'd really fooled Culpepper or if the human tested him.

Culpepper leaned away from the water as if wetness could damage him. "Su'ranchingal, give me the visu-chip. If you still have it."

The possessive human language seemed to melt in Su'ranchingal's mind, oozing over all the images of his past stored there. "Culpepper, I've never been socially normal—I was raised to send me here. I want to be socially normal for my own kind, but now that's impossible. Return for me is degrading." He was angry that Culpepper had believed humans rather than him about his closeness to Hu'rekhi. To disgust the human, Su'ranchingal frothed on his belly, lashing out at himself with his tongue. Now, an instant after he hated Culpepper, he hated himself for being so inhuman. At the corner of his vision, he saw Culpepper go back to his car and sit down in it, talking into a microphone.

"You missing a friend?" an old man whispered to Su'ranchingal while the new watcher, Baxter, paid the clerk, who began bantering about the new visual chips dispenser that let you program endings, mix actors who'd never shared realtime.

"No," Su'ranchingal said.

"A friend," the old man said fiercely. "You know, like a mate?"

"Hu'rekhi?"

"We . . ."

Baxter, as he walked by them to the chip machine, stared at the old man. He programmed a chip with fast jabs of an old message spike, saying, "Su'ranchingal, you know you're a chip character?"

"Message," the old man whispered, shoving a scrap of plastic at Su'ranchingal. *Lose him.*

Baxter popped recorder contacts onto his eyeballs and stared at Su'ranchingal, then at the old man, then at a girl walking back from the toilet.

The old man stiffened. Su'ranchingal saw him force limpness into each muscle, waves of human muscle bunching, then mentally pressed loose.

"I'm not brave like Hu'rekhi," Su'ranchingal said to everyone in the store. Memories Su'ranchingal had repressed, of human horror films, jagged through his vision centers so hard they blurred the air world beyond his eyes. "I don't want to see my own kind ever again. Under the circumstances."

The old man stayed put, his muscles twitching gently under his thin wrinkled skin, his eyes unfocused but occasionally flicking toward Baxter, never quite engaging in eye-to-eye contact with the watcher. Su'ranchingal stared, fascinated, at the man. Then he realized the man was scared. He said, "Baxter, we must go."

Baxter paid for the drinks and the chip and said, "Let's go, then."

The clerk handed Su'ranchingal the bag. Su'ranchingal felt the cold bottles through the bag, the four-inch-square case housing the tiny movie chip. He felt very small himself—deer bit away his bean pods and no human would help him stop them. He touched his dewlaps with the bottles, cooling the blood surging there.

The old man disappeared. Baxter looked around as though he'd left something behind, then popped off his lenses—finger squeezes to either side of each lens and a moist suck of lens released from eyeball. Su'ranchingal remembered an array of other lenses in a tube, pointed at his eyes—somewhere, on Earth, on *Za'aga*—while he was pinned down with drugs or straps, he didn't remember now. Baxter dropped the lenses in a case and they walked out of the store.

"Do the lenses record?" Su'ranchingal asked.

"You betcha," Baxter said. "You've been approached. We'd like you to cooperate with them."

"No."

"Pretend."

"I don't understand pretending. My mind . . ."

"Relax and just do what I say, Ranch, boy."

Ranch? Unsure as to whether he'd been insulted or not, Su'ranchingal's head jerked back and his head scales flared. He stopped walking. Baxter took his elbow and pulled. *I'm just a specimen. I can take insults as well as examinations.* "So you want to call me Ranch?"

"We all call you Ranch."

"Oh. What do you call Hu'rekhi?"

"The Wreck."

"And she's missing, presumed pregnant, and not dead?"

"Yeah. We never thought . . ." Su'ranchingal could almost feel the man's thoughts creep around his speech centers, down to the vocal instruments . . . *never thought a pregnant alien could get away, and with ideas about gene recombination.* A cheetah walked through Su'ranchingal's visual centers, overlaid on what he was perceiving of Baxter's face, a guy who wanted to expell him and Hu'rekhi from this planet. He wondered if he would ever stop hallucinating or if what he saw was normal.

"What do you want me to do?"

"A man approaches you—go with him. I'll get lost. Try your best to lose me."

Su'ranchingal and Baxter watched a holographic movie of Su'ranchingal and a small woman in a white lab coat. Su'ranchingal's tiny image plotted the force lines of a ramscoop on a computer screen the width and height of a man's thumbnail. "But I don't know anything about ramscoops," Su'ranchingal said.

"You'd cooperate with your return?"

"I'm helpless," Su'ranchingal said, pouring himself another *ti'if*-spiked Dr Pepper. His visual focus wavered. "You'll send me to strangers, just like the *zr'a* did."

"Go down to the store tomorrow and see if anyone approaches you again. Then lose me. Go with them. Maybe we'll let you stay."

A roadfuser was moving slowly down the left half of State Road 696 by the store, the road surface hot and smooth behind it, too hot to walk on, so Su'ranchingal walked through blue chicory blooms the state bush hog would slice down after the roadfuser did its work. Three guys sat on a short length of sidewalk that ran thigh high above the street, talking about the inches in the rain gauge—archaic, Su'ranchingal thought, since the rain gauges were now electronic, the raindrops themselves measured for velocity and volume as they fell. They hushed when he came within three feet of them as though he couldn't have heard them before.

"Good morning," Su'ranchingal said.

"Um," one answered, then another murmured, "Munnin."

After he passed, the talk shifted to how some kid buried automatic plow guide stobs either side of a hardtop road and the tractor just sliced the hell out of the road until the chisel popped. Su'ranchingal wondered if humans always changed their conversations when he passed, tried to remember other occasions. They shifted topics as though his ears polluted the gist of the earlier sound.

A small boy sitting on the back of an old-fashioned driven tractor, behind the Plexiglas cab on an air conditioner hump, hissed like a cat at Su'ranchingal, who felt ashamed, as though he had frightened the boy deliberately.

The boy hissed again. Su'ranchingal remembered that humans, unlike cats, rarely hissed in fright. He went up to the tractor.

"Follow me and get up in the cab from their blind side." The boy nodded at the men sitting on the sidewalk. "Cab's rigged to show false image in the glass, looks real. I'll take you to see some people who want to meet you."

"Hu'rekhi?"

"Sho-o-sh." The boy swung off the air conditioner apparatus behind the cab, climbed in the tractor cab, closed the door and turned into a man who started the tractor. Su'ranchingal wondered if the cab windows played a distortion of the boy driving it or a hologram utterly unrelated to what was happening inside the cab. *Will what shows in the glass when I'm in the cab be human enough to fool Baxter?* He wished he could live the rest of his life behind such glass if it would make him look human.

Su'ranchingal walked around the store to the back, then raced for the tractor, flung open the right-hand-side door and jumped in. The window appeared tinted with tiny flecks of various colors that squirmed in the thick glass.

The boy handed Su'ranchingal a note: TAKE OFF YOUR CLOTHES.

Su'ranchingal was relieved to be out of his overalls, but wondered how the boy would react to seeing his belly, his excretion glands along his groin. The boy grabbed the overalls, swerved the tractor in front of the roadfuser, threw out the overalls, and swerved back. The roadfuser ran over the clothes with a spurt of greasy smoke. A fan blew the ashes aside. The roadfuser, sensing an irregularity, backed up and remelted the road.

The boy giggled, then said, "We didn't know until yesterday that the fuser was going to be working, but it sure took care of any fed gear in your stuff."

Su'ranchingal pried up a scale and scratched out an aspirin-sized capsule. "This too."

"Damn." The boy swerved in front of the fuser again and tossed the capsule out. "The feds got my voice."

"Have your voice? What do people see when they look in at your tractor windows?" *Remember they're possessive.*

"Bastards got voice prints on me now, damn. Oh, they see two guys in a drive tractor. We'll cruise around for a couple hours."

"Out in the open. What if Baxter searches the tractor?"

"They'll expect you to try a long fast run out of the area. And we're not running, you know, just plowing a field or two. No place *in* the tractor to hide something as big as you, and the visual stuff playing the window ain't a loop. From out there, we're two grown men plowing."

"I want a suit of this glass."

"The Wreck's around. Spacer freaks helping her."

"Are you a saucer freak?" Su'ranchingal knew that some humans felt he and Hu'rekhi were gods who'd reveal themselves only to true believers. Obviously, these people were insane.

"Not religious saucer freaks, okay. We're spacer freaks. Jesus, they have my voice." The boy, face crumpled by rigorously contracted muscles, turned the tractor up into a field and lowered gang plows into the soil. He muttered again, "My voice."

About five o'clock, the boy drove the tractor back through the village and down a dirt road, the tractor bumping on ruts, Su'ranchingal feeling oddly soothed as though the computer glass transformed him into a real human on both sides of the graphics. The planet was kind, rocking them both. The boy didn't say anything, just pulled at Su'ranchingal until he climbed out of the cab and followed the boy into a pine forest with scrub oaks and mountain laurel mixed in. The boy walked up to an oak tree with the sprawling limbs of a former pasture tree, stunted pines around it, and took a pocket knife out of his pants pocket. Carefully he pried out an irregular chunk of bark. Su'ranchingal looked over the boy's head and saw a handprint pad. The boy turned the pad twice, then put his left hand on it.

Su'ranchingal almost asked out loud, *What happens next?* But the boy laid a sweaty finger on Su'ranchingal's rigid lips. Su'ranchingal knew the sign for *quiet* and wiped the boy's sweat away.

They continued to walk through the woods, tall brush between the pines. Brambles scratched at Su'ranchingal, and he was so tense in the ears he heard the longer thorns screech against his scales, his heart pounding blood through all eight chambers, air hissing through his lungs and bones.

The boy dropped to the ground when they saw the cabin and slithered up to an old stump. The stump flipped to the side, revealing a tunnel, and the boy motioned for Su'ranchingal to crawl in.

"But it's dark there."

The boy hissed at him; Su'ranchingal went down into the hole, squeezing his closed eyes with all his ocular muscles to make light from nerve pressure. His fingers began to figure out this space, so he switched to an imagination of it well lit, then suddenly the boy was against his back and the whole visualization jumped beyond Su'ranchingal's body space . . .

. . . and turned yellow. Su'ranchingal opened his eyes, saw that the boy had turned on a light, and rolled his eyes to moisten them. The boy made a funny sound in his throat as though his back tongue flap had spasmed on a stop. But humans didn't have back tongue flaps, just a tiny protrusion that hung down from the far back of the throat.

"Sorry," Su'ranchingal said. His eyes had gotten dried out by the air conditioning in the tractor cab.

The boy patted Su'ranchingal's shoulder as if to say eyeballs rolled into the head didn't bother him too much, then pushed more firmly to urge Su'ranchingal on down the tunnel. They followed a string of bare light bulbs wired along the ceiling. The tunnel was made of metal, iron and zinc tastes in the air. Underfoot was a wooden walk suspended about a foot off the rounded floor. Water trickled down under the walk, leaking from seams in the metal walls.

They went for twenty minutes underground, the tunnel sloping gradually up. The boy stopped at a barrier and opened another lock box and laid his hand on the palmplate, then stuck one eye against a rubber eyepiece. The barrier slide to the left with a greasy hiss.

"Who paid for this?" Su'ranchingal gasped, the *d* flipping down to the throat flap, strangling all resemblance to a human phoneme. Behind the door he saw a wrinkled skin woman, another young boy, and a grown human male with collapsed skin folds around the mouth and eyes, wrinkles. Su'ranchingal remembered that humans wrinkled with age.

The boy pointed to his vocal cord structure and moaned.

"Recorded your voice, Tommy?" the woman asked.

Tommy nodded vigorously. They all ran through a short broad stretch of tunnel, then climbed up into the kitchen.

Hu'rekhi sat in a chair, one leg bent, her ankle on the top of her thigh, but away from her distended belly. Su'ranchingal stared at the belly, skin white stretched between scales that seemed to float loosely over rigid internal organs. Distended, but not hugely as pregnant as the female humans got. Hu'rekhi said, "I'm pregnant, you asshole. They tried to abort me, but—"

Su'ranchingal interrupted her. "But what are we going to eat?"

"I smuggled out yeast. Bet you don't have any *ti'if.*"

"Ti'if?" Su'ranchingal wondered why he felt hot.

"They addicted you to it, remember."

"You have some, then?"

"No. If it's a bad withdrawal, you're fucked."

The older woman came in and said, "We've got to do surgery on Tommy's voice."

"Didn't you get that transmitter out from under your ventral plate?" Hu'rekhi said, massaging the distended skin between her own scales.

"He said they got his voice before we threw it under a road steamer."

"Melter?"

"Yes, that." Su'ranchingal realized he didn't want an entire lifetime with Hu'rekhi. He didn't like her that much. "Will we stay here? Together?"

She flushed red between her scales. "How do we raise my babies? What kind of education?"

Su'ranchingal suspected their children would be sociologically human, as he was almost human, with his mind crystallized in Amerish. "I don't know. Did you ask the human scientists?"

"I have no nipples."

"Nipples, oh, yes. Perhaps their digestive systems will be more mature at birth."

"I don't have *any* idea." Hu'rekhi sounded hysterical. "I will have three babies, so the humans told me. It must hurt when they come out."

"Biologically, it would be inefficient if birth killed you for only three young."

"You idiot. What do we do?"

* * *

He withdrew from *ti'if*, hurting like a whipped child, wondering if he'd go mad before his nerves resheathed themselves.

Two months later, Su'ranchingal was with Hu'rekhi when she sighed and the skin stretched around her scales twitched as if she was trying to raise them. Su'ranchingal, almost revolted, watched her belly squirm more as the young inside it moved. He thought he could understand why the humans want to send the two of them back, away, out. Three at a time plus parental care was K plus Y reproductive strategy. Hu'rekhi finally tilted the scales on the sides of her swollen belly up and *humphed* like a human at him. "Su'ranchingal, we don't get along, do we?"

"No."

"Have you ever considered that the humans preferred that we not be a team? Two isolates are not as scary as a mated pair."

Su'ranchingal remembered how Culpepper had encouraged him to speak badly of Hu'rekhi, how the men got Hu'rekhi drunk on the isopropyls. "But we didn't have to like each other to breed. It was unconscious. The *zr'as* knew that."

"Yeah." She rolled her eyes back into her head convulsively, little strands of eye muscles visible at the bottom of her eyes when they rolled all the way up.

One of the space freaks came in and watched Hu'rekhi without looking away. The freak was a male, tall for a human, with black hair and brown and white eyes, white bordering the variable eye color as with all humans. He called, "Mary," and a woman came in with warm olive oil and began massaging Hu'rekhi's skin between the scales, pouring oil on her slightly haired human hands, then rubbing around Hu'rekhi's belly.

Hu'rekhi said, "My genitals need to be stretched."

A vague image rose in Su'ranchingal's visual center: *zr'a*

hands loosening a belly sphincter, then one of the older *zr'as* laughing and moving him out of the room. "Yes," he said. *I'll have to do it for her.* His throat seemed heavy—something in it gave way and he felt thick matter rise, gulped and saw Hu'rekhi gulp at almost the same time. *One to two babies, one parent nurses; three babies, two parents feed.* "Hu'rekhi?" he said in human question tones—there seemed to be vague memories of a ritual for this, but that was fractured into only partial visuals and feelings, memories of electronic media, focus lost by a child who didn't understand what he witnessed.

Hu'rekhi's eyes fluttered back and up again—he felt her distress. "We'll never do it right," she said. Su'ranchingal bent his head and took the oil from the human woman, began massaging Hu'rekhi's belly, touched her sphincter gently with an oiled finger. When the Terran oil didn't seem to burn, he began working to loosen the sphincter muscle ring. "You're an idiot," Hu'rekhi told him, her eyes still rolled back blindly in her head, "but we have to try. If things go badly, get help."

"They'd send us out to space."

"I'd rather not die."

Digging his finger into Hu'rekhi's belly hole seemed right; being sent to the humans seemed right; everything seems right to Su'ranchingal now. *Earth aches for our biomasses.* He wondered vaguely if he'd been drugged. *No drugs now, it's just really right.* The humans left them alone as he worked on Hu'rekhi, and that was perfect.

"Personalities," Hu'rekhi mumbled, "don't matter now."

Su'ranchingal felt air tremble from speech apparatus to auditory organs, but her meaning seemed to coil out of his own brain. "I hope these humans will like lots of us." He drew the first fist-sized baby from her and thick matter rose to his tongue, which curled into a tube. The baby drank.

Projectile Weapons

His green Coeshee cloak hanging limply around him in Earth's gravity, the young alien, Chastain, leaned back in his library chair so his basketwoven spine—the curved processes of bone and cartilage—took the gravity instead of his long delicate legs. *Accelerating into the UCal Library System,* he thought, *no, this tugging always is gravity,* as he worked the keyboard with travel-stiffened toes.

After several false name-character combinations, he found out how the library listed Onosaki and called up his thousand-year-old digital—*humans must be as fascinated by their guns as I am,* Chastain thought as he began to watch again, in a clearer copy, the Gunmaster movie once caught by Coeshee receivers in space. All through space, he'd dreamed of Earth, its wildness.

The Zen gunmaster, just as Chastain remembered, stood on an Okinawan beach, with wild water crying for him—the man with eyelids bent in the corners . . .

Sar, the senior male in the Coeshee exchange group, had

told Chastain many times that the digital was fiction, but when Chastain left the Coeshee transport, dazzled by Earth's sunlight, he'd bumped into a human with a gun. Fictions, Chastain decided, weren't utterly spun from nothing. Now, he sped the movie up to the end. The Gunmaster on the screen raised a black iron weapon. Again, the electric robots cut him down with lasers. Chastain's circulation system went into acceleration mode as he watched the blood, red as his own, pump out of the man.

And, on the screen, water jumped madly.

Suddenly, Chastain wanted to see that ocean—uncontained water stretched from Asia to California, oxidized stars, glittering with smelly sodium chloride like planet sweat. His button nose, rough as a dog's, quivered.

Earth wasn't like a giant hollow Coeshee home structure with its meticulously balanced ecology—it was a wild place, with gangsters. Chastain was sure of that. And he could do things on a planet he'd die doing at home.

Bending his long alien fingers in the gun gesture he'd seen on other Earth digitals, Chastain pursed his stiff thin lips and went *"pow!"* Then he called up a transportation map and dressed in human clothes, with his feet locked in walking shoes with pads, damp and sticky, under his toe arches.

Since his huge eyes were too sensitive to stand direct sunlight, Chastain dabbed flesh glue between his eyes and behind his ears so his glasses (which got dark when too much light hit them) would stay up. Contacts, which he would have preferred, made his eyes itch.

Feeling sticky, glue between his eyes, feet sweating in walking shoes, Chastain looked at his reflection in a mirror and tried to twist his lips into a human smile. His whiskers, like a seal's, bobbed instead.

Then Chastain went out and stared at the clouds—glowing from several hundred square miles of tower lights, furry—his own huge black universe invisible beyond them.

Humans live in an absolute accident, wild air, wild rocks. Why are they so carefree about it?

Sar came back from the library earlier than Chastain, thinking about the Aztecs, wondering what the humans would think of his reading—he knew, despite the assurances that Coeshee privacy would be respected, that humans tracked his every move. He switched on the sleeping room light and saw the two water beds filled with other Coeshee, all except for Chastain. *If the Spanish accounts were true, then the Aztecs were insane monsters who deserved to be conquered; but humans are so odd, so horrible.* He always wondered if humans helped with the Coeshee plagues to show Coeshee what terrible biological powers the humans, otherwise primitive, could have.

If I could find out, in their biological labs, what they might be preparing for Coeshee, Sar thought as he took off the human clothes he'd worn to the library. He felt as though the humans teased him—this room so obviously full of surveillance equipment—so obvious he didn't need to open his kit to check—but his Population Control Officer's instincts tugged at him—*they're teasing you*—as though they were more teases than the simple ones. He took off his Coeshee briefs and went into the little recycling and cleaning room.

Bending over the recycling pot, he noticed a grid of electric-eye beams just above the water and grew very angry, then very cold. *Like lab animals . . . That's why none of us were invited to Thomas Leech's party. The project director doesn't celebrate his grant in the company of his lab animals.*

Sar went back to his kit and painted the one-way mirrors with opaquing screen. Then he took out the small sensitive meters and found every microphone and rewired each one to play Coeshee breathing, his own heavy breathing now as he struggled through the gravity, climbing up into each room corner.

Then he went back into the cleaning and recycling room

and shoved his fist a few times through the toilet's electric-eye beams before he ripped the entire apparatus out. Then, in the privacy the humans had promised, he stepped into the shower and washed all over. Carefully, Sar cleaned his genitals and then, satisfied that the humans couldn't complain of the musk, retracted his penis into its sheath again. He turned off the water and plugged his hair drier into the adapter the humans gave him. *Perhaps they have a device in that,* he thought, but he was too tired to do more than dry his body and head hair, keeping the hot air away from his sensitive whiskers. Then he put on fresh briefs and went to wiggle into the Coeshee piled in the water beds. *I've got to keep my ears open for a morning wake-up call—our sleep habits are so disturbed,* he thought just as he was about to close his ears.

When the phone rang, Sar heard a bell in the middle of his dream about the asteroid mining, when he broke his arm. The bell insisted—he started up, disoriented, wondering why they still accelerated. Then he recognized the tugging—gravity. Looking around, he saw the phone and wondered if he'd set off alarms when he disconnected the monitors that made him feel like a lab animal. He moved gently off the bed so he wouldn't disturb the other Coeshee and answered the phone. The human clock showed a strange hour—too early, Sar thought, for the wake call. Alarms.

As soon as Sar recognized the voice asking his name, he went right in. "We were told that we would be an exchange team, not laboratory experimental animals. So I disconnected your equipment and screened the one-way mirrors, realizing that some mistake had been made."

"Is that what being a Population Control Officer means, to disconnect the equipment we need for our studies? We study humans like we had hoped to study Coeshee, to make for better understanding among our people." Sar could hear Leech sigh with frustration. "But I didn't call about that," Leech continued. "Chastain left the campus about three-thirty after checking BART—that's our tube transport system—routes."

Sar decided humans became weirder each time he'd met them and asked, "What can happen to him in your dark?" Humans acted superior because they'd helped the Coeshee. That biological information only arrived 200 years after the worst of the plague. By that time, Coeshee immune systems were adapting, but the humans gave them something new to worry about—humans. The human bio data allowed some near-light-speed travelers to come back despite unadapted immune systems. *But now we're supposed to share life space with them.*

"I thought you needed to keep track of your people here," Leech said.

"Dismantling all your misplaced lab animal equipment was very tiring. I prefer to sleep. If trouble, let me know. Is your planet more dangerous than our home structures?"

Sar suspected the humans had not tamed all of their kind, but then Chastain knew how to handle himself with predators.

The humans had warned the Coeshee that the B tube transports were more dangerous than the A trains—more thieves—so Chastain bought a B card and went down into the station. The BART station made Chastain feel at home, humming electric coils for moving trains, contained air (but too thick, always too thick with useless nitrogen), good light—no monster blue glow-tube skies. He twitched his whiskers, leaned back against a pillar, and watched. Just like any tube transport the train pulled into the station . . . and sank, unlike Coeshee tube trains, on the coasting rails just before the doors opened. Chastain hopped in, the train doors hissed shut, and he worried for a minute about acceleration on top of gravity. The train gave a little hop. *They have to lift it all the time against gravity,* Chastain thought, marveling at how much more electricity these human trains would use. The forward speed increased smoothly, so Chastain pushed his bristles forward and looked around.

Most of the females painted their lips in sexual-arousal imitation—Chastain wondered how the males stood it, then sniffed and realized the females and most of the males masked their pheromones. "God," he heard a female say, "he isn't much bigger than a man—taller but skinny—but he's got plum-sized eyes. Look, he just wiggled his beard stubs like a cat."

He wagged his chin at her—her own eyes became larger. "Where's somebody with him?" she asked her male companion.

"They understand Amerish," the woman's male said.

"Yes," Chastain agreed. Then he closed his ears, the muscles falling with a moist clink in all the gravity, to avoid hearing more human jabber, but he kept staring around at all the rubbery faces which looked so exotic in a tube transport that could have been in a home structure. Humans bent face muscles to send out mood signs—Chastain was fascinated but still slightly queasy.

Then a trio of human adolescents, a female and two males, padded into the car, moving like digital outlaws. Chastain liked them instantly. They held their faces rigid and they made all the other passengers very uneasy, just as he'd made humans uneasy. Chastain sniffed, smelled human anxiety sweat, so he opened his ears. They terrorized the other passengers; he'd only made the humans uneasy.

The female wore clothes so tight her muscles showed through the shiny black fabric, and the others also wore tight black pants. Chastain looked back at the girl, with ragged black hair and strange skin, for a human: not pale, not brown. She'd painted around her eyes and wore a thick leather belt with a huge two-tongued buckle.

She stared back at him, lips twisted in a not-smile. Chastain didn't mean to challenge her, so he dropped his eyes slightly, looked at her hands and saw she chewed her nails, like a caged beast which bites its flesh. The two males, blunt-faced, bulky creatures, stood on either side of her.

Any Coeshee, Chastain knew, as wild as these humans would die of it. Blood pounding in his head, he was not quite convinced of this situation's reality. They looked at the space on the bench around him, wanting to sit but uneasy. Chastain reached out a hand toward them.

"You an alien." The girl announced this flatly.

"Yes," Chastain said, wanting to be utterly melodramatic, like his digital heroes. "Thieves, you will show me your ocean. We can't hold oceans in a space colony."

The males sat down hard on either side of Chastain as the car collectively hissed in its breath. The girl sat down by the biggest one, leaned over her companion's knees, and asked, "You space monsters got coin, credit chips?"

"I don't speak much odd Amerish, just UCal Standard, some digital."

"Money, you with money? We'll take you to the ocean for coin."

Chastain pulled out his wallet pouch and showed them the little bit of human money he did have. The three looked at each other dubiously, about to leave, when a BART patrol approached. Chastain loved seeing tense men with guns—*very proto-digital*, he decided, wiggling his chin with glee. One patrolman came forward while the three others stood back.

"Alien?"

"Yes," Chastain said, happily agitated. The girl giggled.

"Papers on all four you?"

Chastain handed his wallet pouch to the officer. The humans sitting beside him pulled out various tattered IDs.

"Chastain, isn't that a human name?"

"Digital idol in your history. Shows reached us when I was a child. Took a human name to fit in better. I love humans—the wild planet life."

"Bad company for an alien guest, Chastain Coeshee. I suggest you come with us to a safer car."

"Oh, no. I have permission to travel California without a population control officer's permission." Chastain didn't want to leave his companions, so totally fascinating, and he wanted to impress them into staying with him. "Can you dare give me an order?" he asked as thuggishly as he could.

"Your companions might be dangerous. Do *you* understand that?"

"They know the way to the ocean, I am sure."

"I should make you come with us. You're just a kid."

"Bad idea," Chastain hissed, coiling into a Japanese fighter position.

The girl spoke then, "Hey, patroller, we bruise the spacie, be monster interplanetary incident. There's no hired-law could get us out of cage then."

"And hiding an alien would be difficult," the patrolman pointed out. "Chastain, I suggest you see the ocean at Seal Rock—well-patrolled area, even at night. And don't pay your guides here more than ten dollars each."

"Coeshee," Chastain said, "are forced by space life to be very nonviolent, but extraordinary good hiders."

Just then the train reached a transfer station, and the human girl said, "Hey, pat, we take the alien to the ocean all right. *Buen* public relations."

The three took Chastain by his arms and led him quickly out of the car, away from the officers.

"Population control officers?" Chastain asked.

"You got an alien law team tracking your ass moves, Chastain?" the smaller male said as he leaned against Chastain, who was happy for the touch. Chastain felt his wallet pouch being lifted, and thought *a playlift, not so skillful.* They ran down the concourse together and he bumped the male who'd lifted his wallet and took it back. Since the male didn't seem to notice, Chastain bumped him again and took his wallet, too, just for fun. *What a game to play in gravity, where all the little weights add up,* Chastain thought, hoping his toes weren't breaking from the running.

He tossed the human's wallet to the girl and stopped to lean against a pillar and pant for breath.

"This gravity!"

The humans froze. "You popped in the head, spacie," the girl finally said.

The male whose wallet Chastain lifted took Chastain's arm firmly. "Come on, spacie, we'll show you the ocean, right under . . ."

"We're wasting the night," the larger male said.

The girl held up her hand to the males. "Wait a minute. Could you lift wallets for us, like you did Ro's?"

"Yes," Chastain said. "Show me the ocean. I'll steal for you." He bumped lightly against each of the three in turn. The girl wrapped her arms around his skinny body. She was thin, too, and felt almost like another Coeshee, but smelled oily.

The girl squeezed lightly. "You'll do for us, Chastain."

Chastain was utterly touched.

"I'm Meg," the girl said, "and the guy whose wallet you lifted is Ro. The big man's Heyzus, spelled like you wanta."

Finally, the train doors opened, and they tumbled into the train like rolling, playing ferrets. The girl sat down beside Chastain and carefully felt the spines in his back—high-tensile bone.

"Very protective against abrupt space acceleration," he explained, "but it isn't worth a damn in gravity." She giggled.

When the train came out of the tube and stopped, Chastain and the humans got out and walked by many twenty-story apartment towers near the ocean. As they walked, arm in arm, toward low-lying clouds, Chastain smelled salt and rot—dead plants and animals, decaying, wasting.

Suddenly, Chastain saw the ocean. His shoulder fur went on end under his human clothes—and he tiptoed toward it, ready to jump back.

How, he wondered as they crossed the sand and stopped by the ocean's foamy edge, *could something so immense hide behind a city?*

Wild alien water rippled, collapsed, cut down by gravity. Loose gray-green water slopped against his shoes as he bent to touch the foam bubbles. The ocean was a bit hideous, as though water had escaped and gone crazy, running all the way from Japan where Onosaki made the Gunmaster digital a thousand years earlier.

No change in the ocean, Chastain realized, *or always constant change that cancels itself out.* He sensed there was a visual order to the waves, but it wasn't exact.

Finally, eyes almost in shock, he turned to his companions and noticed for the first time how grubby they were, how improbably bored. *And now I'm standing in a three-dimensional fantasy. I'm obligated to steal for them.* "You are very lucky to have such things around your city, I think," Chastain told them.

"Well," Meg said, "you kinda did the night for us."

On the way back, on a really crowded train, Chastain found that no humans would let him close enough to lift wallet pouches. But he made a handy distraction for the human thief team, so they weren't too upset.

The four sat down on a bench near the UCal Station and sorted what they'd got. Meg began to throw away the credit chips, and explained to Chastain that to get coin from them required proper biologicals, like the right live hands.

"Computer-operated?" Chastain asked. When she nodded, he said, "It's not a matter of faking the first-level code switches, but faking the okay-got-the-right-inputs, inside the computer more. I think I could help you. Computer crime is the main Coeshee outlaw activity."

"They whack you for that, even more than what you'd get lifting in the trains," Meg said, fingering the credit chips.

" 'Cause they don't catch the really good ones that often," Ro added.

"I'll do it for you," Chastain said. For a moment he remembered how dislocated he'd felt on the beach, but then he tumbled softly against Meg and tried to hold his gaze to her—her human touch-by-look, not challenge eyes at all. Then he tumbled softly against the males and went out into the glaring Terran day. His glasses obligingly darkened.

As Chastain entered the campus, he realized how exhausted he was and decided to go to the sleep room.

Sar was waiting for him in the hall. Firmly the senior alien gripped Chastain's elbows. "Humans," Sar said, eyes pinning Chastain, "don't really like much unescorted travel."

"Oh," Chastain said, wondering if the human population control officers on the train had reported him to Sar.

"Hard for you among their young, in your studies?"

Chastain realized Sar had heard nothing about the night and tried to twist his elbows out of Sar's hands. "Not so hard. Thomas Leech and his scholars are not typical."

"Third time I've been among humans. They've become less friendly each time. If this planet has secrets, it is not your job to discover them or blunder into them. Tell me where you go when you leave irregularly." Sar squeezed, then dropped Chastain's elbows.

Sar asked the human who was trying to study him to take him and another Coeshee to see the ocean before he talked to Thomas Leech.

Vertigo—no, gravity—tugged at his feet. His very eye muscles seemed unbalanced, sore at the top where they balanced against gravity. The ocean squirmed to infinity, air blown into water, water into air, contaminated, hideous. He looked at the other Coeshee, who stared at the ocean as if half fascinated.

Sar felt vaguely as though he had something to hide from Leech but couldn't analyze it, which increased the ocean's hideousness. Then he went back to the University and up to Leech's office. Leech made him wait, and Sar knew waiting was the same for humans as it was for Coeshee—being made to wait. When Leech's assistant finally told him Leech could see him, Sar stalked in and stood over Leech, staring down at him.

"You seem upset, if I read your signals correctly," Leech said, waving Sar toward a seat.

"Chastain. His attitude toward me is bad."

"The BART patrol reported to us that he rode into the city with bad people, scutters, on the B train. We told him about the B train."

"So your digitals are based on something real in your planet life. What do they do bad?"

Leech said, "Steal wallets."

Sar relaxed. "We do that all the time—a social-release tease. Minor—like a traffic law here, if you keep the wallet pouch. Humans hate that? Any touching you hate. You're a cold people."

Thomas Leech looked away from Sar, out his window to the bricked yards between the towers. "We aren't Coeshee. We're uneasy about you as it is. He'll give your people a bad name."

"Uneasy about us? But I've seen you become more and more uneasy about us the closer we approach. One of your people had to steal a plague cure for us. Was he a bad human, to try to help us, 'aliens'?" Sar put snarling quotes around the last word.

"We did that centuries ago. Now we're exchanging people with you."

"Not centuries for me. My flights to meet humans folded me into the future."

"I admit we were intimidated. Then, if you didn't have recombinant machines . . . you don't realize how intimidating you seemed at first. We have a species dread of other species attacking us."

"Don't be obtuse—we also have this dread. And Chastain is not a commensal predator who eats the old and crazy, thus being used to recycle . . ." *Why did this human make me want to defend Chastain?* Sar wondered, uneasily remembering Chastain's love of guns, his choice of Terran digitals. "And we have no room for random wildness in a space-colony structure."

"Yeah, and why'd he get close to tube scutters?"

"We consider humans to be the same as Coeshee. Perhaps that's an artifact of radio contact for so many centuries."

"We didn't know you were space creatures until the first video protocols. We thought you were like us, at the same stage."

"And so didn't tell us what you knew and we didn't."

"But we helped you. People who knew the Coeshee well helped you."

"And some didn't."

"I know that was thirty years, twenty years ago, something like that, for you. But for me, that happened centuries back. Now I have a twenty-million-dollar contract to study you and your fellows. And scutters are a problem for us—uneducated thieves. I'm embarrassed by them."

"Educate them. We couldn't have such waste in our structures." Sar looked around, wishing he'd stayed in the human space station, among humans who were beginning to evolve away from their wild planet origins. Here in Leech's office, Sar saw more typically lush human interior patterns—sprawls of textures that blurred functions, fake wild tactile things, glass plants. *To make up for their lack of touching, perhaps.* Sar stared with horrified fascination at a fake animal made of fiber, cloth, then thought, *I must get my mind back on the problem with Chastain.* "Planets are very strange."

"Your people originated on one. Life doesn't start anywhere else."

"We left planets. Our commensals eliminate our non-thinking ones. But you humans have no controls. Perhaps that's why you are so distant—you could murder each other at whim."

"I didn't take this job to cuddle up to some seven-foot spider monkey," Leech said.

They both stared at each other, then dropped eyes. Sar felt sad, embarrassed—all he wanted to know was whether humans planned to hurt Coeshee as they hurt each other in the past. He quieted himself down and said, "You, as senior human male to us, must held me with Chastain. I know nothing of wild sapients."

Leech said, "We should both discuss this when we're calmer."

Sar quivered, then agreed.

Meg, Ro, and Heyzus lifted wallets from citizens who backed off as Chastain stomped through the train, rowing his whiskers through the air and counting in Coeshee.

The BART patrol that finally surrounded the humans wouldn't have brought Chastain in, except one patrolman heard his holster snap open. He looked down—his pistol was gone. Then he saw Chastain rubbing his whiskers against the barrel, sniffing the cartridges. The little scutters being chained giggled.

As much as Chastain loved upsetting standoffish humans, he decided not to push his scene further when all the other guns came out, pointed at him. He carefully shrugged and gave the gun back to the man he took it from, holding it by the barrel like surrendering digital outlaws do. When the man grabbed him, he screeched.

BART passengers began screaming, pushing for the end doors. Meg and her friends heaved against their restraints while Chastain swung off the handholds trying to kick the officer. He misjudged the gravity and deceleration and sprawled on the floor as the train stopped. The angry officer piled on top of him.

These are aliens! Chastain thought as he flailed, truly panicked, while the BART patrol cuffed him, hand and foot. The man who'd almost lost his gun to Chastain reached down and ripped off Chastain's sunglasses, pulling off glue and skin. *Vicious!*

The patrol called for back-up before moving their prisoners off the train at a patrol station. Some passengers booed and threw trash, but most were work commuters who went from hysterics to eyes riding rigidly forward.

Chastain, outraged by the human fear sweat (after they'd chained him) and rough behavior, refused to speak Amerish, cursing the patrol in Coeshee snarls. They grabbed him with their stinking hands, puffed armpit stink at him, and took his knife.

Chastain had never been without his knife in public, where the predators might be. "Protect me," he said to the patrolmen in Amerish before he realized humans could be the predators themselves, on this planet.

"He does understand us," someone said from behind a desk. "Don't put him in a cell. You weren't even supposed to bring him in."

"He's an asshole. Stole my gun. Lucky we didn't blow his alien fat eyeballs out."

"Pinhole-eyed planet crawler," Chastain snarled back.

"Hold it, Chastain," the man behind the desk said, holding his palm flat at Chastain. Then, to the patrolman, he said, "His Berkeley people are coming for him. His alien boss says he's immature."

"Hell, immature. I say he's about sixteen. We ought to charge him."

"No," the man behind the desk said.

Chastain's whiskers relaxed, although he was still scared to be without his knife, obviously waiting for discipline. "I watch many time your patrols in the BART. Isn't your control supported by the general population?"

"You should have been taught better than to . . ." the man whose gun Chastain had held sputtered.

"Check, clean him up if he's bleeding," the man behind the desk said. "I guess, he's got something like diplomatic immunity."

"By now we'd all be dead in my colony," Chastain said,

calming down more. "Predators eat out-of-control quarrelers."

"Whip his ass like we do diplomats' kids." The man whose gun Chastain lifted would never be friendly, Chastain realized. He hauled Chastain to his feet and spun him around. "Hey, Jack," he cried triumphantly to the man behind the desk. "We did get him a bit. He's bleeding back of the ears."

Chastain felt behind his right ear, then smelled blood on his fingers. He shuddered. Then he realized how awful he felt. His toes felt cramped and sprained in the shoes, so when the man dropped him back on the bench, he leaned over and took them off, wiggling and snapping his toes. *No stress fractures,* he sighed with relief.

"Unreal," Jack behind the desk breathed. Chastain glared at him. Crazy planet people, grabbing him in a transport tube, subjecting the tube to stresses by throwing people around, braking the train suddenly. Attracting predators. No, he realized, just humans—no predators. Humans were too mean to have predators.

"You about to keep yourself quiet?" Jack asked as he came over from behind the desk. He squatted down in front of Chastain. "I'm Captain Jack Ortega. You're a long way from home, aren't you, Chastain? That trip here must have taken you away from your people at an early age?"

Chastain shuddered and refused to talk, staring away from Ortega. *This man is more upsetting nice,* he thought. Ortega continued softly, "Tell me why you helped the scutters, Chastain."

Chastain hissed.

Ortega leaned back and pulled out a cigarette, refusing to be scared. After he lit up, he slitted his eyes at Chastain, who slumped in his handcuffs on the bench. Ortega gently blew smoke at Chastain, who flared his neck hair and stared rudely at Ortega.

"Look, Chastain," Ortega said calmly. "You must be

someone's kid among your people to be one of the first on Earth. You wanna get in big trouble with Earth people, you run with those scutters. But don't be stupid. You'll give your species a bad reputation. Most people are nervous enough about you as it is."

"Are you nervous about me?" Chastain said, hoping Ortega would say he was. Ortega shook his head. "What's their bail, man?" Chastain said with his best digital sneer. "I'm gonna spring them outa this joint."

"Shit," a little antique alien scutter," Ortega said, standing up and walking back to his desk, with his hands in the air. The officers all laughed.

Thomas Leech had gotten a University auto and drove Sar across the bay to the BART police office. Leech, cold and hostile, led him through a maze of human buildings and corridors to a dirty room where Chastain sat in chains.

In chains—Sar had never seen a Coeshee in chains: medical restraints for the badly space-injured, but not in chains. He could feel his bristles jut forward and quiver, the muscles in his eyes jump. Sar felt almost as fiercely upset as fierce, but he wasn't surprised to see Chastain roll into a defensive ball.

Three BART officers had to pry Chastain's arms up to get the cuffs and leg irons off. He stayed in his defensive posture, each leg or arm snapping back against his belly as the humans released it. Sar walked up to Chastain and kicked him lightly at the bast of the spine. *How you embarrass us,* he thought.

"I'm Captain Jack Ortega," a human said. "Are you the Coeshee law?" Sar looked tensely at this human, whom he'd seen laughing and walking away from Chastain when he and Leech entered.

"And are you the human population control officer? Why had no one told me of this earlier?"

"Yes," Ortega said, smiling slightly. "We were trying to

handle this diplomatically, but . . ." Sar sniffed for the human fear scent—thick here, but not from this man."

"What happened?" Sar asked, hoping that perhaps he'd reached a reasonable human. He looked coldly back at Leech. "I'm a little lost on your planet, and your academics *like* studying my lostness, counting my . . . pacing behaviors. Perhaps you, as a fellow officer, can tell me what to do with Chastain when he thinks he is a human-type thief?"

Ortega grinned and said, "He worked with scutters by distracting BART passengers while the scutters picked pockets. And we think he broke bank chip codes for them, because that bunch never had so much money before."

"I explained that you do not like these money-pouch tricks. He swore he was not doing that." *Not precisely and physically himself doing that,* Sar realized—Chastain hadn't lied. "Could someone load him in the University car?" Two officers took Chastain away, wrestling with his tightly curled body.

"Then, today, he lifted an officer's pistol when we were arresting his scutters," Ortega said. "If he wasn't an alien, the other we'd just warn him about."

"Projectile weapons? And you actually shoot these weapons?" Sar had seen digitals and worked out some of the ballistics on a Coeshee computer. They would be almost random killing machines.

"Yes; what do *you* use to control your population?"

"Not projectiles, without gravity to trap them. Like humans shooting in an underwater boat, a submarine." Sar looked around the patrol station, noticing all the guns. "Many wild humans?"

Ortega nodded.

"Please tell me personally if you sight him again with those people." Sar handed Ortega a card, then took it back to write his University phone's number on it. "I think you will remember when you can't read the writing who gave it to you."

Ortega nodded again, then smiled. "But we find it somewhat difficult to tell your people apart." His grin broadened, and he added hastily, "At a distance." A human joke Sar didn't understand. Chastain was the lightest.

"*Any* Coeshee with scutters, call me."

"I'd like to get together with you sometime and compare notes. I've been reading about you guys all my life. Maybe we can find out new things from aliens, Coeshee. What's your major crime among your people?"

"Electronic theft. Confrontational crimes are too dangerous." Sar rose to leave, then added, "If your wild humans use much electric surveillance, I can tell you much about shutting it down."

When Sar got in Leech's auto, he looked in the back seat. Chastain curled back up again. Sar told Leech, "When we get back to Berkeley, you will arrange a soundproof room, with a call button, and no secret cameras. I do not wish to embarrass Chastain too much more." Sar looked in the rear-view mirror and tilted it so he could see Chastain. Chastain quivered.

Sar stood as close to Thomas Leech as the human would allow and looked down at Chastain curled on the soundproof room's padded floor. "I should have asked Ortega how he would have handled this," Sar said.

"Chastain isn't human. You're free to do what you'd usually do as long as the other Coeshee tell us it was the usual punishment in your colony structures."

"This is not in the least unusual. And gravity changes all the rules." Sar's voice faded and he whispered, "This planet excites him too much, I think." He sat down and took his shoes off. Neatly laying them aside, he stood, slowly, then gave Chastain a nudge with bare long toes.

Leech tensed, expecting Chastain to leap up fighting, but Chastain just pulled himself tighter. "Could you bring us beers when I finish with him?" Sar asked. He handed Leech his knife.

After the door closed, Chastain looked up at Sar and uncurled. Sar asked in Coeshee, "Why, Chastain?"

Chastain shrugged as the humans did, which infuriated Sar. He tapped Chastain again with his toes. Chastain slowly stood—the two Coeshee stared at each other. *Be tough,* Chastain thought in Amerish.

"Child, your home-leaving in childhood was not natural, but you must listen to me," Sar said, hoping to heal the social break without a beating, but calling up his own fighting experience just in case.

Chastain opened his mouth so Sar could hear the ear muscles click shut. Sar trembled, closed his own ears; then, screaming, lashed out at Chastain, thinking in Coeshee, *how this planet acceleration complicates this.*

Chastain hit Sar back, fists doubled up, which astonished Sar so much that Chastain landed several blows. *Juveniles don't attack seniors,* Sar thought as he attacked back vigorously, horrified not only that Chastain contested the discipline, but as his own anger, the pattern of his anger at humans, at Chastain, then furious that Chastain dared make him so angry.

Finally Chastain dropped into a bruised tight coil. Sar, panting, rang for Thomas Leech.

When the human opened the door, Sar said, "Have him taken to the sleeping room." Chastain moaned a little. Leech stood dumbfounded with two beers in his hands. Sar took one as Leech called for graduate assistants to take Chastain away. They entered the room, stared at Sar, then remembered Coeshee manners and dropped their eyes before taking Chastain away.

"Is he hurt?" Leech asked.

Sar sighed and sipped the beer, then looked slantingly at Leech. The human was too nervous. He wondered if the human officer, Ortega, would be so nervous. "I doubt badly. He fought back. I simply went until he fell down. The gravity friction holding the feet made the blows harder to gauge."

Sar wanted to get out of the punishment room now. "Your office? We need to discuss this, without being defensive."

He's afraid of me, terrified now, Sar thought as Leech briefly touched his shoulder, then flinched, as they went toward the elevator. They both got in, Leech facing rigidly forward. Sar turned his face toward the wall, slumped against it, and felt hideously lonely, almost unable to face other Coeshee. "How can I make you believe such things as Chastain did are not things we do in our home structure?"

"Such things as Chastain did?" Leech turned and sighed as Sar looked down at the floor. When they were in Leech's office, Sar put both his hands on Leech's desk and cried. He slung his head sideways to clear the tears, but some drooled into his whiskers, trapped in the gravity, irritating his skin. Leech put a box of tissues on his desk and pushed it at Sar, who took one and wiped his face before speaking.

"You humans are brutally distant. We are not monsters."

Leech moved toward Sar, then held back, asking, "How distant?"

"Precisely like that. Do I smell bad—I wash—or do I remind you of predators? Am I so strange-fleshed and -toed that you can't come near me?"

"We don't . . ."

"Not even in the tube trains when they're crowded—always space around us. You are kinder to cats, dogs. Surely . . ."

"Listen, Sar, I don't touch other humans, not males, at least, the way we see Coeshee touch each other. But some humans touch more than do the dominant cultures on this continent."

"Then let us go there, or back to the human space-colony structure, before Chastain goes utterly mad."

Sar felt the human's fingers crawl like nervous animals onto his forearm, stop, quiver. Leech said, "We'll have a staff meeting about this."

"Not good hair?" Sar asked. He laughed horribly, a cutting imitation of a human laugh. "And tell me, now, about other problems a young digital-crazy Coeshee can get into, with your gravity and crazy un-built planet."

"Your hair feels vaguely like a rat terrier's hair. We had no idea he'd run with scutters."

Leech, Sar thought, *makes it sound as though Chastain has terribly poor taste. Rat-terrier hair might be an insult, probably is an insult.* "We had no idea," Sar said, mocking Leech, "that your night tubes were so dangerous even for human males with guns that they are patrolled by groups."

"Did you start your contact by telling us about the beasts you let pick off your sick and aged, predators I suspect you could eliminate if you wanted?"

"If you were Coeshee, I would ask you to also come with me to a soundproof room. No wonder humans prey on each other—no natural predators, no balance. I saw your humans in space fight once—no discreetness or shame, wide out in the open."

"So you picked up some human fighting tricks to use on Chastain," Leech said. Sar could see him think about the $20 million in grant credit and force himself to stroke Sar's shoulder, which bristled under his human clothes.

Sar slowed his breathing, apologized, and bumped his body slowly against Leech, saying, "Too upset for arguments tonight. Perhaps the real error is that we expect to be like members of the same species." He rubbed his knuckles where he'd bruised them against Chastain, then added, "Thank you for the beer. We have a similar drink. Could I have my knife? I'll take the other beer to Chastain."

Leech shivered slightly as he turned the knife handle toward the skinny alien hand. Sar didn't say anything about that, but walked out stiffly, planning how he would listen in on the meeting. Then he would hide his officer's kit, wait until he could find the way to check the humans' possible war plans. *I'm letting him bother me too much,* Sar thought, *but perhaps that's what the humans want.*

* * *

Sar found it ridiculously easy to listen to Leech's meeting—he simply put a tiny microphone in the telephone and then called from his room as the meeting began. He decided not to tape it.

"Look, if I thought it would save the situation," Leech said, "I'd ask one of you to go to bed with Sar. Or Chastain. Whichever needs it the most. Sar says Chastain is going crazy because we are not really physical with them—too cold, distant."

"I get along fine with mine." Sar recognized the voice, a graduate student. "Think of them as similar to the working classes—they lean on you. It's all right. Doesn't mean they utterly love you or want sex with you. Watch them walk together—always little bumps."

Genna, Leech's assistant, said, "Coeshee or working classes walk bumping each other?"

Sar wished he hadn't done this. The Coeshee who worked with the graduate student really thought they had an honest partner. The graduate student said, "Both. That's my point. You see humans bumping down in the Barrier."

Sar heard a hiss of nylon against nylon—Genna, crossing her legs like human scissors. "Aliens as ethnics," she said. "I feel so much more relieved about Chastain now. We know his place—behind the Barrier."

The humans laughed. Sar put his teeth against his lower lip and hissed, headphone against his ear. This was worse than he'd imagined, he decided. *They underestimate Coeshee. How can they do that? We've been living in space stations for 40,000 of their years.*

When the laugh faded, Leech said, "About Chastain. I think we should get him linked with undergraduates who'd be willing to tolerate the same physical contact he got from the scutters. You see the police slide here—they're practically plastered together. Scholarship students, perhaps, would be so physical, entertain him."

"Several senators," Genna said coolly, "suggest the aliens should be studied in space, where they can be contained."

"Officially, they are here to study us, so that might be awkward. Sar suggested a more physical country, but I'd hate to see twenty million go to Mombasa, or Djakarta."

The graduate student who got along with his aliens said, "Sar just about put Chastain in the hospital, then came up and brought him a beer."

"My beer," Leech interjected. "Remember how alien they are. I'll work to contain the senatorial objections to our studies here."

"Maybe there's more wrong here than we know. I mean Sar really beat the piss out of Chastain and then seemed very upset about doing it," the grad student persisted.

"Psychotic Coeshee," Genna said. "How charming."

Sar heard the chairs being moved and realized the meeting was over. Softly, as though they might hear him, he hung the phone up, and sat dazed, sorting all the information out. *They underestimate us,* he thought again, *but that might be better than the other. But they seem so afraid of us.*

Later, Sar got the microphone out of the phone in the conference room, and dropped it under a BART train as it settled on the glide rails.

"Your stupid students couldn't keep Chastain away from the scutters," Sar said, pacing Leech as they hurried to Leech's office. "Officer Ortega called me. They tried to stop Chastain and his scutters, but they disappeared into the Barrier Flats. Ortega said his men don't patrol the Flats. You and your wild humans."

Leech unlocked his door quickly, acting as though he thought Sar would hit him at any moment. "I had no idea he'd left until you told me. Did Ortega tip the media?"

Sar felt his whiskers flare, and he stamped his feet. "I have never allowed myself to be so angry. You underestimated Chastain. This is hideous for all of us."

Genna brought in the undergraduates. "We took him to the beach at night—he said he wanted to see the moon on the ocean," one said. "We lost him in the fog."

"That's not all," the other added. "He made a model gun down in the lab. He's great at tech work, tooled it right up from rough schematics."

Agitation in public is lethal, the old Coeshee maxim, popped into Sar's head. He stood, bristled forward, on the sides of his feet, with his hands jammed in his Earth-style pockets, trying desperately to be calm. Finally, he turned to Leech and stared him down, a full huge stare, with the yellowiris muscles quivering. Then Sar looked at the hopeless young humans. "Lost him in the fog? Can't you smell?"

"Not like you can," Thomas Leech reminded him. "Is he likely to be dangerous? This would be terrible publicity for your people."

"And it will ruin your studies of us here. If he had never left a colony structure, perhaps he would never have gone so wild." Sar was sure of that—Chastain went wild for reasons that made Sar uneasy: the planet life affected him too. He looked slantwise at the young humans, trembling little humans. "A gun, or a model, not working, of a gun?"

"It had everything," one young human breathed. "Even a little gadget to make bullets."

"Check your chemistry department to see what Chastain got from there," Sar said. Leech put his arm around Sar's shoulders, but Sar went rigid and stared at Leech again. "You can make your population control officers go into the Barrier Flats?"

"Would he use that gun?" Genna asked.

"He has been fascinated by Earth gangsters, projectile weapons, even before we left the colonies." Sar coughed. "Such powerful images you send us—wild land, wild humans."

"Will you need a gun?" Leech asked.

"The officer Ortega, who called me. He seems . . ." Sar

paused, pulled his hands out of his pockets and rotated them to look at the tendons bunched up on the backs, the faint bruises from the day he'd beaten Chastain. "A human with a gun. He seems kind, concerned." Sar shook both hands vigorously and sat down firmly in Leech's office. "I'll wait while you arrange that."

"Can't you track him from where they lost him yourself?"

"Not easy in the city. And probably too late for that."

Leech sighed and reached for his phone.

At the border of the Bolinas Preserve, the Greater Bay Urban Area stopped—abruptly—as though all sorts of glass and pastel metal towers had been shaved away to let a new wilderness of black sage and manzanita grow back. *Like nothing, except the ocean, I've ever seen before,* Chastain thought when the scutters showed it to him. He saw redwoods and eucalyptus valley groves under the spiny hills—vegetation gone wild. The only coherent structure was the tiny silver line of a tube train that crossed the Bolinas Preserve headed north.

The three human thieves lay on their bellies while Chastain crawled forward in his sunglasses through the dirt, new gun heavy in his shoulder holster, going to look at the surveillance equipment around the Preserve perimeter.

Meg whispered to Chastain, "Can you get us through the electric stuff?"

"Why can't we take the tube out?"

"They record all legal visitors. You need a permit. It's the Preserve. Lot of people so rich and mean they get themselves duplicated over and over—don't want nobody but themselves to have their money. Space returnees, real rich directors setting up the world outside by modem—real un-BART tube, real un-street. Lots of coin, rubies and other juice rocks," the girl muttered, "in simple-seeming antique houses."

"Past-worship? Like the people in our colony structures

who keep giant flasks of real Coeshee soil?" Chastain asked.

"Credit-chippy past-worship."

"Yeah," Heyzus said. "Chastain, you gotta deal reason into that gun thing of yours. Shooting for stuff is real dubious. Show the gun to bully only if the clones start something. But don't fire it."

Chastain rolled to his side, took the gun out—polished like a ball bearing—and bared his teeth, imitating a human smile.

"Boy," Heyzus continued, "thrill got to be split from business. You up-money little . . . you do for *us*, Chastain, and keep the digital shit out. No twists. We get you top brain buzz after."

Meg crept up and took the gun and slipped it back in the holster. "Take off your shirt, Chastain, and put it over the gun. You mess the gun up in all this dust. Especially when we tunnel."

That night they tunneled under the security barrier, bracing their hole with tubes. Chastain rigged up a randomized replay of the normal ground movements into the seismic detector. They dragged themselves and packs through before collapsing the tubes. Chastain crawled belly-down to another scanner to splice in more false readouts.

"If they do catch us," Ro said, "they turn us over to the rest of the world's patroller's to get bone-stomped. But all the check stuff on the out rim. You rich, you don't answer to no BART patrol."

"I know about bone-stomped," Chastain said.

But why are we crawling into this nightmare, Chastain thought. All intelligence-shaped structures had gone, lost in the fog and brush-covered hills. *The wild zone, the wild zone*—as though cosmic rays cut patterns into jumbles. Rocks without symmetry, huge trees left to rot. *Planet life made my people desperate for mind, to escape into structures.* Humans, Chastain decided, tricked him here—these humans, the first man who was so desperate to meet the

Coeshee he stole plans for gene splicers for them. Chastain remembered now that the first man who met the Coeshee had a house in Bolinas. "Bolinas—a clone with a house in Bolinas. I've heard about him."

"Yeah," Meg replied softly. "Space-timers get lots of coin for little fancy escape houses—your bank regrinds the credit for a thousand years."

"A house on wooden legs, a 150-year-old Japanese farm house always. They made me come here." Chastain shivered as the fog wisps eddied around them, nervous about his companions now, but dreading being abandoned here, in the wild land.

"Tonight," Meg said, "we'll get as far from the border and as high as we can on the mountain, then spend the day hidden."

Gravity held Chastain by his belly as he crawled with toes and fingers across the pungent brush. "Sar can track by smell."

The humans froze. Heyzus and Ro looked around, but didn't see anything. Chastain, slowly climbing through the gravity to his feet, sniffed the wind. He smelt the city in the wind and calmed down a bit. No trace of Sar—or any other Coeshee.

In the morning, Chastain watched gravity and wind play with strange orange and black insects. He found out from Heyzus that they were monarch butterflies. While millions of the insects drifted over, he held his knees tight to his chest and craved steel geodesic struts and panels to hold off the wildness. He nuzzled his pistol, feeling its hard sleekness with his whiskers, smelling the tangy gunpowder and iron. He'd made, he decided, a more beautiful gun than the pistol he'd almost stolen from the BART patrol.

The humans crawled out of their clothes and lay down in their sleeping bags as the sun rose. Chastain did the same, shading his face with his clothes.

When he woke again, Chastain felt pain from sun blisters

on his arms. *The fusion source is out of control,* he thought in a panic. He opened his eyes and the mad planet jumble hurt them.

"I want to find the space clone's house," Chastain said, feeling angry and totally disoriented as he glued his glasses back on.

"If you can jack through their computer guards," Meg answered.

Later that night, Chastain's hand-sized screen flashed a small map of the space clone's area. "He collects Japanese things. Are they valuable?"

"Chastain, they see you, they get all us," Heyzus said.

"Japanese things—if you find the right people, if they're real good. Hard to figure—some real juice things are ugly. Better take gold stuff, real juice rocks. And get straight on what we're here to do, steal, with you jacking around the electric fences," Meg said.

"And not," said Heyzus, "for you to play digital with your homemade gun."

Chastain tried his human smile on them.

They climbed up the mesa in the dark toward the house. The four circled it at a distance and came up behind it, Chastain sniffing for dogs, for anything not human. All listened for voices and watched for lights.

A rabbit darted out from under their feet. Chastain quivered and pulled out the gun, but Meg touched him and whispered. "It was nothing."

Chastain kept the gun out.

After they reached the house, Ro and Heyzus burned a hole through the floor with a laser torch. *If clones feared thieves,* Chastain thought, *building with wood was stupid. Humans are stupid, primitive,* he decided, watching Ro hold the wood while Heyzus burnt out a circle. Ro wiggled his fingers and slowly lowered the wood disc.

Chastain climbed into the house quickly, using toes and

fingers, one hand wrapped around the gun, with the three humans following him through the hole. *Fear sweat, burnt wood*—the smells excited Chastain. Some woods were jewels in the station. His gun hand trembled.

From the front of the house, a male human called, "We know you are in the house and outnumber us. Just take the jewel box in the bedroom and we'll give you twenty minutes lead time before we call in the report."

Chastain began stalking the voice, so familiar from the historical reels. Meg tried to get the gun away from Chastain, but she stepped back when he shifted the barrel toward her. Chastain pushed by her and kept creeping up toward the man—made from the first human who'd touched a Coeshee. Had the humans or they begun the centuries of radio contact which led to the first meeting? Some Coeshee thought it was the humans; others disagreed. Chastain decided humans forced their radio into the Coeshee structures—humans brought him here.

The man and woman stood in the middle of the room, the man forward, poised on the balls of his feet. Chastain stopped, legs spread, gun pointed at them, barrel wagging irregularly from one to the other. At that instant, Chastain didn't know what he believed, then he thought his mind cleared again.

The man looked at his altar niche with the holograms of the first human/Coeshee meeting, then back at the young Coeshee gunman standing in front of him. Chastain lowered the gun to his waist, still pointing it forward, and moved the safety lever off, chambered a round and raised the gun back level with his eyes. The man said softly, "Small universe."

Chastain aimed at the man. The woman moved slightly, but the man signaled her with a very tiny hand gesture and asked Chastain calmly, "Did my ancestor make a mistake then?"

Chastain's whiskers flattened against his head. The

woman wet her lips and looked at the humans coming up behind Chastain.

"Can you speak English?" the man continued. In almost incomprehensible Coeshee, he added, *"We friends."*

"I'm a thief," Chastain said in Amerish.

"And you've brought scutters along. Why me? What has been happening out there to alien/human relations?" The man laughed dryly.

"No, you are the aliens. Your planet makes me wild. Attacks me with crazy rocks, gravity, digital dreams."

"Could the humans say something?" the man asked.

"Pretend this never happened. Didn't know how nuts he was," Meg said, glancing briefly at carved stones in the altar niche, the cups on the low pine table.

"Does he know how to use the gun?" the man asked.

"Stop!" Chastain cried.

"He made it," Meg replied.

Chastain wondered if he was really doing this thing. He said, "Your planet is just a dream, a hard dream." His gun hand sagged.

The man nodded when the woman looked down at her fingers. Before the thieves could react, she leaped away from them, slashing through the paper and lath partitions, tearing the shoji screen, and dodged away into the night.

Chastain spun, fired wildly at her as she escaped, then turned to the tormenting man, took aim as best as he could with his hands trembling, and shot, wounding the man in the forearm, knocking him down. While Chastain held the gun on the man, the human thieves bolted. The man sobbed and caught his breath.

"Strange," Chastain said panting.

The man slowly sat up on the floor, holding his wounded arm tightly. Chastain fidgeted, wanting for obscure reasons to see the man act more hurt, to plead. But the man said, "You might be crazy." He spoke very slowly. "Without a frame of reference?"

"I have a gun," Chastain said. Gunpowder stench burnt in Chastain's nostrils. Stunned that a shot man could still talk so calmly, he backed out of the room, staring at the human as though the wounded man was very dangerous.

When he got to the hole in the floor, he called the humans. The gunpowder stench kept him from tracking them—and they wouldn't answer.

Chastain heard helicopter blades cutting the air in the distance and ran. When he got back up the mountain, all that the humans had left him was his sleeping bag. He dug his second box of bullets out of it, pulled the magazine out of the handle, and put new bullets in for the ones he'd shot. Then he crawled up against a rock and quivered, pressing his chin against the gun handle.

Nervously, Sar approached the wounded man in the hospital bed, knowing Chastain shot him—knowing the man's ancestor had tried to help the Coeshee. Bending deeply, trying not to scare the man more, Sar touched the man's hand with his forehead. *It would be terrible if this one flinched. Other humans were willing to let us die.* Sar forgave the ancestor his compulsion to physically meet Coeshee as the man nodded. Sar knelt on the floor with lowered eyes and said, "I am Sar, a Coeshee population control officer. I knew those who touched your ancestor. Chastain has been very evil. I am terribly sorry."

The man sighed and turned Sar's chin up with his uninjured hand. "So some are good, some crazy—like us. He seemed insane to me."

"Can he control his gun?"

The man looked ruefully at his bandaged arm. "Control as in aim? If he meant only to hit my arm, then well. Control—the gun seemed to control him. You'll say he's an aberration then? You're not all gun nuts?"

"Yes, he's out of pattern, not Coeshee. But this planet life makes our rules loose in our heads. I will insist now that the others, other Coeshee, stay in structures—it is the wildness of all your life here."

Leech came in, with a portable phone. "Sar, Ortega's on the line again."

Sar spoke his name and listened to Ortega. Then he turned to the clone man and asked, "Did he have three humans with him when he invaded your home?"

"Yes. A woman and two men."

"The BART patrol picked them up. They abandoned Chastain in the Preserve. Mr. Leech, you can take me to the Station House."

When Sar and Leech arrived, Ortega was leaning back in a chair, watching the three scutters. Sar smelt fear, which intensified when he came in. *Dirty, uneducated, scared—wild humans,* he thought.

"No more bond for you guys," Ortega said.

"We never told him to craft a shooter," Meg said.

"He made us. Forced us with the gun. We were gonna tell you where to find him," Ro said.

"We had a terrible time getting out of the Preserve," Heyzus added.

"Where, then, is he?" Ortega asked.

"We dumped him when he weirded out with the shooter," Meg replied.

"We know that," Ortega said. "In the Preserve. But . . . where, in the Preserve. Deal down time. Where'd you hide the first day?"

"We trying to cooperate, patroller," Heyzus said.

"Cage lock could rust on you. Breaking and entering, first into the Preserve, then into a house. Accessories to shooting."

"Chastain made us, with the shooter. He had the shooter, weird . . ." Meg stopped talking and glared at Sar, who smelt great fear despite the face gesture. "His pat, who beat him up?"

"She asked if you were a legal force over Chastain?" Ortega translated with a smile.

"Yes," Sar answered, hearing for the first time how alien his voice sounded.

"Your boy's gone crazy. You drove him crazy. Bet you're all crazy."

Sar's whiskers jerked up, back. "Mr. Ortega, we must find him fast. Being alone, abandoned, is bad for any Coeshee."

"Where?" Ortega asked Meg, "or would you rather talk to this alien pat?" Ortega pushed the girl against Sar.

Her muscles jerked when she touched Sar, who realized Chastain must have seemed very insane. *Must we be monsters to them, they to us?* Sar reached to touch her gently.

As the girl cringed away from Sar, Ortega continued, "It's not like puffing the pats on a friend, not like that. You tell us—none of your fellow scutters will mind a bit. Chastain spoils hunting on the Outside Line, in the Preserve, now, doesn't he? Isn't he more video than real, like a rich dump kid running with you for brain twist?" Ortega winked at Sar, who realized this was an interrogation game. He wiggled his chin back and tried to sound threatening—the opinion of these didn't matter.

"You will tell us. Or I will have to talk to you alone. In a soundproof room. Did Chastain tell you about the soundproof room?" Sar thought a second about beating many humans up, one after another, and trembled.

"Up on Tam," Meg said hastily. "On the east side."

Sar brushed her head thankfully with the side of his hand, wondering why humans varied so wildly. She flinched. "Not trying, now, to scare you, but thanking you," Sar said, trying to make his voice sound more human. She blew her cheeks out and sweated more fear stench. "Where," Sar asked more gently, looking at Ortega slantwise, "on a map?"

Ortega grunted with satisfaction and pulled a topographic printout. The girl sullenly pointed. Sar took her chin and shook it gently. "Be pleased," he told her. Then Ortega motioned for the officers to take the scutters away.

Sar looked at Ortega and said, "Strange to be an object of terror."

"Not all of us are like that. Some of us are really curious about you." Ortega put his arm around Sar's chest and squeezed. "We've got a job to do. I heard you can scent-track. Shall we get ready to search?"

"Yes," Sar said. As they waited for the search jeeps to be loaded, Sar and Ortega walked around the police facility, which seemed more complicated to Sar than need be to control sentiments. "You want to be issued a pistol, or are you armed, Sar?" Ortega asked.

"I should see how to shoot one," Sar replied, wiping sweat from his hands. His feet were sore: the prospect of walking across hills and broken rock—the Preserve as Ortega described it—appalled him.

When Ortega took him down to the shooting practice area, Sar felt all the humans watch. *So odd, their expressions. They wonder about me, my own control of a gun.*

Ortega explained the gun to him. "This is a .357 Magnum—very old design, but we'd rather not have something out that could get stolen in the field that we couldn't trace. Someone steals this, we can trace the bullets. If they've got the gun, we've got them."

Sar took the heavy metal lump, machined to hold fire, thinking, *yes, there is a fascination. I feel like I'm taking my own sanity into my hands.*

Ortega put ear protectors on Sar as best he could, then signaled him to shoot. Sar lifted the gun and sighted down the barrel at the small patch on the target alley wall.

Tremendous power! Head echoing, nose blocked by the smell, Sar, as though half in a digital, watched his hands lower the gun. Then, defying gravity, he raised his gun, closed his ears, fired again and again, until the cartridges were spent. *Yes, we could defend ourselves against humans.*

Then he shook the tensions out of his muscles and handed the pistol to Ortega. "I have never shot before," Sar said quietly.

"You did great for a first-time shooter," Ortega replied, clapping Sar on the back. Sar looked at all the humans—none seemed particularly afraid of him. His hands sweated profusely. Sar wiped them, then clapped Ortega back for reassurance.

"If you are used to them," he told Ortega, "then better for you to carry it. We may need to kill Chastain."

"We'll try to get him with a sedative dart or an electric stunner. I'll show you how that works, because you may be able to talk yourself into range."

"If he is permanently mad, he is dead with us."

Chastain spent the rest of the night staring at his gun, wishing it, the only mind-made object in the creaking might, was large enough to crawl into. He decided, as the hideous sun rose up over the chaotic landscape, that he was beyond being in the digital he'd seen—he was in the events that lay behind them—an isolated social creature. He would try to get to the tube train he'd seen in the distance earlier—*like the long extended barrel of the gun,* some random wave in his mind added.

Although he knew what he did next was from another movie, another kind of digital, he fired three shots, waited, fired three more, then reloaded his gun and stuffed extra cartridges in his briefs' pockets before leaving where the scutters had camped with him.

"It's electric," Ortega said to Sar as they got in the jeep, "so it shouldn't interfere with your nose." Sar sniffed a few times, smelt ozone and rubber, but not too much, nodded, then climbed in to drive with Ortega through the Preserve. "Daybreak, we heard shots, signal shots."

Sar, holding the roll bar and seat braces with toes and

hands, trying not to brace so hard his bones would crack as the jeep lurched across the chaparral, said, tensely, "He has more than a gun full of bullets, despite the bullets the scutters had with them."

"Two of your medics are with the backup people. They think Chastain sounds nuts."

"No, he no longer fits the Coeshee pattern."

"We'll try to catch him without hurting him. I hope you're not upset . . . but I almost enjoy manhunts."

"I think he is not a man," Sar said, but he felt something strange rising in him, as he'd felt with the gun—chase excitement. His hands and feet sweated heavily now as his nose captured strange animal scents, the distant city and ocean tang. *Out of our past, hunting,* he thought, *and were quarrels always thrashed out in soundproof rooms?*

The crazy landscape lurched around—mottled rocks, thorn trees, land that pitched them all around the jeep: wild land. Sar shuddered, trying to ride the jeep rhythm like a tube car, but the seat caught him randomly. The sky glowed the worst blue he'd seen yet; then Ortega turned the jeep into a fog bank and stopped to let Sar smell the air more carefully. "They think he was about here sometime in the night," Ortega said.

As Sar checked the wind direction, noticing how scents traveled in it, he visualized shooting Chastain with a .357 Magnum—cutting his muscle control to let the crazy gravity drop him. He shook his head at Ortega—no trace of Chastain here—and climbed back in the jeep. Ortega drove up the mountain.

Suddenly Sar felt awful-Chastain dying over and over in his mind. "Stop," he told Ortega.

"See something?" Ortega asked as he hit the brakes. Sar bent out of the jeep and vomited—huge heaves that hurt stomach muscles. Then he straightened up; Ortega handed him a tissue and the canteen. "Sar, we can get dogs to find him." The human squeezed his arm.

Sar wiped his mouth and pulled his body upright. Sighing deeply and sipping the water, he shook his head, then said, "No. Coeshee may not kill, but we are tough."

"Sar, I have to ask you a question. It may hurt. Can I ask?"

Sar almost signaled Coeshee affirmative, but remembered to nod. He grew chilled.

"Do Coeshee kill Coeshee? I don't want the diplomatic answer; I want the operational answer. I don't care if you've got magic rays that zap would-be killers. Could a Coeshee kill a Coeshee?"

Sar looked at his vomit and said softly, "Yes."

"So, I've got to watch your back."

Sar sighed deeply and then again, tension-relieving sighs. He drank some water and handed the canteen to Ortega, who drank without wiping of the spout.

Ortega looked at him, shrugged, and tucked the canteen up under the dashboard again. As he started the jeep, he said, lightly, "Some guys get butterflies in the stomach before a raid, like you just did, throw up. It's not unusual."

"This is alien, utterly alien."

In silence, they drove into the wind, quartering across Mount Tamalpais. Sar caught a distant scent—gunpowder, a Coeshee—and tightened his hand on Ortega's thigh. "Where are the medical Coeshee?"

Ortega picked up the radio to check and looked at Sar. "Point to it, Sar."

"Has to be Chastain, the gunpowder." Sar pointed and Ortega turned the jeep toward the scent trace, sniffing the air a little himself, driving the jeep slowly through the chaparral, talking into the radio softly. "We're bringing people from Mendocino—in helicopters. They're off . . . now. They'll fly behind the Coast Range, then come in."

"Still far, in that direction," Sar said, "maybe double the distance to the mountain top."

"Let's get over the top. We might stop him. Hang on."

Sar flattened his whiskers and rolled his eyes at the human as the jeep bucked up the serpentine ridges. After skidding a few feet down a fire road, Ortega pulled the jeep back to a rolling crawl, while Sar shook himself and sniffed. "Chastain, closer, but moving. And much salt smell."

"If we drove him up to the cliff, what do you think he'd do?"

Sar didn't answer—couldn't answer.

"I mean would he jump?" Ortega drove one-handed, talking more into the radio while Sar tried to think of what Chastain might do. Then Ortega hung the radio back on the dash and said—sadly, it seemed to Sar—"Feds say whatever you want to do with him is okay with them, and with your people. The feds, in fact, say you have to handle it. I think they think you're setting us up for some kind of incident. So, now, tell me what to do next, Sar."

Humans! Sar knew what the federal humans said upset Ortega. "Ortega, use Earth law on him. I don't know how to use the capture stick, the guns."

"Feds say they want to see if Coeshee can control their own."

Sar felt hot and confused as the jeep crawled after Chastain's scent. Humans preyed on humans, but they asked him to deal with Chastain, who wanted to be a predator as if the planet pulled something very old out of him—a 40,000-year-old rotten relic of a hunting passion. And it tugged Sar the same way. He touched Ortega for reassurance, and the human reached over and squeezed his shoulder. *Planet feet, always struggling against gravity, always ready to struggle.*

Below them was the Outside Line tube, sitting on curved pylons. Chastain was running for it—they both saw him, running and stumbling through the gravity. Ortega slowed the jeep even more and it rolled across the hill like a walking animal. "He hasn't actually killed anyone," Ortega said. "The clone probably won't press charges if you ship him off

Earth fast. They've got detention facilities at our Moon base—people there probably little more relaxed about Coeshee than our Earth prisoners and guards would be."

"That tube looks so strange in this wildness." Sar thought of himself shooting Chastain again, red blood hanging in the air—no, falling through the gravity. Chastain should be dead, but what would it do to him if he killed Chastain himself?

"I'm going to rush him before he gets to the towers—wouldn't want him climbing up to the juice." Ortega gunned the jeep. "Heard you just about put him in the hospital after we picked him up with scutters. I'm calling for backups. We need shields to approach him. Gonna drive him under the tube, out to the point."

"We don't control by shooting: we dominate—push into curled posture, surrender posture. He fought back. Hard."

Chastain stopped for an instant under the tube, by one of the pylons. He gave a tremendous cry that Sar and Ortega heard, then ran on. Sar and Ortega looked at each other. They drove up to the pylon cautiously, slowly, in case Chastain had hidden behind it.

Sar could hear the helicopters even though he couldn't see them—behind a ridge. Ortega got out of the jeep and held Sar's shoulders for a moment, trying, Sar realized, to stop them from trembling. He hadn't realized how much he trembled until he felt his flesh in Ortega's hands. "Think," Ortega said, "about how scared he is. Most of the time, in police work, it's just shots fired to scare. Or someone freaks. Crazy people generally are terrible shots." Ortega climbed back in the jeep, said, "We'll go up just a little before we wait for the helicopters."

Quickly helicopters came up from behind the mountain and flew along beside the jeep, washing it with their prop blasts as the police team pushed Chastain out onto a point. He stumbled even more now.

When they had surrounded the point, Ortega stopped the jeep out of pistol range. Sar looked at the line of helicopters hovering with nets over the hills, bouncing up and down in their own turbulence, glittering like monster insects. He looked at Chastain, so tiny out there, one of his own, with all these humans after him. *So much, so many helicopters to get one Coeshee who has only hurt a human.*

An officer handed Ortega and Sar graphite shields with radios. Then Ortega asked for a stun stick, like the one Sar had practiced with at the police station. "Remember, fifteen feet's all it shoots. Try to get in closer. It tucks in here—you can stick it out the gun port."

Each shield was about six feet high, three wide, with a gun slot to the right of the head and tiny peepholes set at human-eye distance. Sar turned his around and saw white abraded scars on the outside. "Used shields? Shots just fired to scare?" he said to Ortega, fingering the scars. If he stumbled, if the shield broke, if a bullet pierced the shield through one of the abraded spots, Chastain could kill him. Sar hadn't considered that earlier—he, not Chastain, could die.

"Well, ah . . . yeah. Budget problems," Ortega replied. Sar watched to see how Ortega put his hands on the crosspieces. The shield didn't fit Coeshee body structure; the peepholes were too close together; but Sar held the shield as best he could and went forward, crouched, sidling beside Ortega, who grinned at him.

Chastain stood back from the cliff edge, stripped to his shorts and a shirt worn over his shoulders like a Coeshee cloak, gun hand lowered. As the two graphite shields came bobbing through the brush toward him, he raised his pistol slowly, utterly exhausted.

Sar looked at Chastain through the gun slit, feeling lost in this situation. Ortega braced his shield against a rock and asked Sar, "Need to glass him?" Sar brought his shield up to Ortega's and took the binoculars. Spreading the eyepieces, he saw Chastain in a circle of light, like the targets he'd shot when he tried the gun. *Transfigured, that's what the human words means.* Chastain looked as though some ocean light shone through his eyes as he looked over Sar's line of sight. Sar knew Chastain was watching the helicopters. Skin peeled on Chastain's hands and forehead, and he looked at the shield periodically, squeezing his whiskers tight and looking more terrified then. But then he would look up at the helicopters again and his eyes . . .

This is too much attention for him, Sar thought primly, almost jealously. "Strange," Sar whispered, handing the glasses back to Ortega. Ortega began to grin, but stopped, watching Sar's face. Then, as Ortega raised the glasses to look at Chastain himself, Sar said, "The glasses make him naked to us."

"If he were a human boy, I'd say he'd be looking forward to surrendering now. But the helicopters don't scare him a bit, do they?"

"We've got to take him alive," Sar said.

"Yes," Ortega said.

"We can't let him crystallize all this attention with his death."

Ortega lowered the glasses and stared at Sar, who tensed though he knew the human wasn't challenging him. Ortega squeezed Sar's upper arm gently. "Feels like the same kind of muscles we've got in there," the human said as he fluttered his fingers against Sar's muscles. "Both you flesh and blood like all us."

"There is very much different—the spine, the face nerves, the genitals." Then Sar motioned for the glasses again and watched Chastain, standing wild in the crazy blowing air, in a little round screen of magnified light. "Maybe you humans can help save him?" He picked up the shield and said to Ortega, "I'll go forward, try to talk to him." Ortega took the glasses. Both officers looked at the ground, calculating, before Sar crept toward Chastain, who swung the gun toward the advancing shield.

When Sar got close enough, he said in Coeshee, *"Rejoin pattern, Chastain, and we'll send you off Earth before you truly kill, have madness ruin your mind. The human medicine may help you, too."*

"Sar?" Chastain's voice floated to him as faint, almost as much inside Sar's mind, as a memory voice.

"Yes, will you rejoin Coeshee?"

"Not to die like some old passive baby!" Chastain fired at the shield. Sar felt and saw impact dimples. Then the gun clicked.

"Rush him, Sar, he's out of ammo," Ortega said through the radio. Chastain bent down and pulled a frame out of the gun's handle. Sar hesitated, then pulled the stun stick out of the shield and tried to run. The shield nearly tripped him, so he threw it aside. He heard Ortega yell, "You stupid!" as Chastain slapped the frame back into the gun handle and raised the gun.

Sar looked into the darkness, inside the gun barrel—Death—and wondered why Chastain thought any excitement was worth that. Chastain said, "They told me about the stunners," and backed away.

Sar, feeling almost hypnotized, stepped toward him.

"If I get you down," Chastain said, "they'll have to kill me."

To do this for the humans, Sar thought, moving by tiny delicate steps toward Chastain. His feet ached—the stunner was heavy. As Sar began to raise the stunner, Chastain lifted the gun and squeezed. One click, the second time a bullet explosion. Sar threw the stunner as something monstrous grabbed his shoulder. He thought he heard another gun go off.

Gravity, Sar's mind screamed as he fell, a heavy burning in his shoulder. He smelt blood and gunpowder as his hands and toes scrabbled against the dirt and brush. He closed his eyes tight and screamed—he thought he remembered seeing the top of Chastain's head come off.

"Sar," Ortega said, grabbing him and rolling him onto his back.

Sar opened his eyes, feeling a terrible weight in his shoulder, as though a whole being's mass had been wadded up and pushed into his shoulder. He looked at the blood spreading over his shoulder, then at Ortega, who helped lift him onto a stretcher. "Death?" Sar asked.

"Sar, you'll be okay," Ortega said as he arranged Sar's legs on the stretcher. As they waited for a Coeshee medic, Sar stroked Ortega and the other humans with his hands and toes. Ortega put his hand on Sar's belly and rubbed gently. Sar clutched convulsively when the medic probed the wound.

"He'll be okay, won't he?" Ortega asked.

"Yes," the medic said, easing a needle into Sar's forearm. *"You will not be killed,"* he told Sar in Coeshee. *"Lal will rebuild your shoulder bones."* Sar knew there were no commensal predators on Earth but still felt deeply comforted.

Ortega patted his belly again. Sar looked at him and sighed, "Was I stupid?" When Ortega didn't answer, Sar wiggled his chin at the human.

"Yes," Ortega said, "you don't charge an armed anything without gun clothes or a shield."

"But I was too clumsy for your shield. Chastain?"

"Sar," Ortega said slowly, quivering beside the stretcher. Sar knew that fantastic image of Chastain's skull pieces flying through the air was true. "Chastain is dead. I shot him. He would have killed you. You were my partner. That's what I thought."

Sar looked at the Coeshee medic, then said, "Odd." *None of the others knows how to take this killing. I'm the only one who understands why Chastain wanted to die . . . center of attention . . . better Ortega than a strange human. I know Ortega didn't want to.* Sar felt his attention being cut by the drug and said, in Coeshee since his Amerish was escaping now, *"Tell them to do with Chastain's body what they do with those of other, human, gun people."*

The drug dropped him into unconsciousness as he was reaching to touch Ortega's face, which was wet with tears.

Essay: Aliens and the Artificial Other

I can't read alien invasion books without subverting them. The aliens with their borrowed technologies who collapse into allegiance with us despite their stolen hyperdrives must be us. Why would they be somewhat dumb two-trunked baby elephants if they weren't Republicans like Jesse Helms and Strom Thurmond?

Alien stories are never the highest level of the field, some of the men say. I wonder if they are obsolete because women write them better.

But strictly speaking, few of these stories are realistic. We won't be just contacting or contacted by alien intelligences. We'll be getting partial to whole alien biotypes. If we're lucky, we'll be Eurasiafrica contacting NorthandSouth America.

Something is signifying something about us as a species here that we make a metaphor of this. If life in space exists, we'd better hope we don't get contacted by a hundred-member federation of tens of thousands of planets exchanging genetic material and competing for ecological niches for a million years. The worst invasion case, biotope contamination, provides us with the fewest stories: Disch's *The Genocides* comes to mind. More commonly, we go out and inflict our planet fatally on another single planet. If we consider that on this planet, invasions from one continent to another more decimate than exterminate, these stories seem the guilty side of "and in six weeks we knew the secret of their star drive and repulsed them with great fervor."

But when *we* invade alien cultures, we never find ourselves so overwhelmed. Few of us, male or female, write the story where the space colonists land in the equivalent of New York or Berlin during World War II. We always land on tropic islands or deserts the size of planets and we are always either a bad influence on the ecology or just what the planet needs. Or they're systems about ten to a thousand times more informationally dense than we are, *but we quickly become equal partners*. Occasionally, our one puny ship whips all of theirs and precipitates political revolution in their culture. Aliens never attempt to use humans in their intraspecific quarrels the way the Mexican Indians thought they could use the Spanish in their quarrels with the Aztecs. Humans unite against the aliens.

Most animals have their worst quarrels with their conspecifics. When my cats fight, I might be what they scrap over, but my wishes aren't taken seriously. In most fish tanks, the aliens are killed, ignored, or allowed to pick off the parasites. They're spawn predators, food, null water space, or cleaner wrasses. What would be the s.f.nal equivalent of an invasion of cleaner wrasse? We wouldn't need to dominate them at all.

C. S. Lewis, in *Out of the Silent Planet*, speculated that perhaps our attachment to our animals expresses our longing for a world of the intelligent others who aren't part of our intraspecific squabbles—the way my cat and dog could care less about what happens in SFWA. That seems to me to be as appropriate for aliens as Anglo-American invaders or disguised Zen Buddhists. Cats have about as much need for a dominance relationship with us as I suspect the hyperdrive invaders would. Of course, if they knew what we did to their kittens, they'd probably arrange to exterminate us.

We have turned each other into our own aliens. Nations, cultures, tribes, hippies—it's easy to see culture as aesthetic. When I was in Cherokee, North Carolina, I found that people there resented being asked if they were Cherokee. "I'm going to go to Asheville," one woman said, "and grab people on the street and ask them if they're white." What a pity you've lost your culture, the white would-be Indian would say, and then miss the sports story in the *One Feather* where a man offered free dental checkups if another basketball team would throw games to his team. I considered that it was even possible that the story was planted as a Cherokee joke to confound the sociologists and anthropologists who probably outnumber as subscribers the newspaper's Cherokee readers. Whites are politely not consoled for the loss of their true culture. "We're all assimilated to White Appalachian Culture," they say. Suddenly one realizes the men are the hysterical decorative ones and the women are the Cherokees' norm. No, they don't know their clans, but yes, they're still very matriarchal. I commented to someone that half the Cherokee men have mustaches, while all the local whites have full beards or are clean shaven. When I came back in a few weeks, the museum director, with a freshly bared upper lip, grinned at me.

White Appalachian culture has a niche for the armed woman.

Who assimilated whom?

I begin buying makeup, playing with it. A woman biologist friend comments that what makeup does is create an artificial sense of sexual interest. Knowing that, I can't put on eyeliner. A Cherokee man, phenotypically a redheaded Irishman, complains that the new tribal chief in Oklahoma is a woman named Mankiller. I tell him about my grandmother who was never allowed to drive. Sexual alienation of this degree is terrible whichever sex is turned into the hysterical decorative one. Mustaches indicate masculinity and white blood. Lipstick signifies I'm hot. We refuse to look at our messages that closely.

Perhaps we dread the aliens because they will see us the way we see our animals. "You pick your orifices when you're nervous," they tell us.

They invade our sense of ourselves as definitive, even us artificial ones: the Cherokee man with leggings and the white girlfriend and me with my red dress that makes me seem so much friendlier than I did in my black suit with the velveteen collar—the suit that makes me look like a woman in the security business when I was in a gun store. In an Appalachian gun store. In a county with lots of Indian grandmothers.

Then we ask the alien, "What precisely does the display of erected face hair mean?"

But aliens are only metaphors, the man complains. He's an engineer who believes he'll be immortalized as a computer program.

Is consciousness in the information or in the structure? The male engineer, wishing to believe in the information, creates aliens who talk like white boys in fuzzy suits. If structure determines information and consciousness, then alien bodies make different consciousness. The fish who can't verbalize can still have a sense of self. There's a point where the learning switched from being obviously conditioned reflexes, same for the pupil of my eye as for my African butterfly fish, to being much quicker, as in the spiny-finned bony fishes. The African butterfly fish, hardwired to eat only from the surface, took a year to learn not to mess with the big female. The nice male cichlid learned to run after one really bad experience with another fish, obviously recognized as an individual female who'd lured him into an ambush, abandoned him, then chased him herself.

These guys not only learned to eat alien food like cichlid kibble, they learned what a food container implied in less than a conditioned reflex amount of time. But since we can't get to that sense of self as completely transferable information, have we proved that it doesn't exist or that we can't communicate partially with food containers and wiggles against the barrier glass?

Is self the data or the structure or the interaction between them both? The looseness of the chemical bonds that makes growth and change possible makes us fragile. Do we have identity hard-wired in to make up for the biochemical fragility of life in general?

If self-consciousness and some rudimentary sense of individual others exist in birds and the most intelligent fish, then identity can't depend on language-ordered data. The alien intelligences may not follow us to the Chomskian deep structure of what is human in message exchange.

But we seem to crave cognitive dissonance to the point of inventing artificial mystery. We're lonely for the others in their alien biotopes. As humans, we imagined the aliens first in the farthest Terran lands. They had faces in their bellies, one foot large enough to use as an umbrella. Trees grew sheep that gave wool. The roc carried grown cattle in its talons; the phoenix burned. Now, having found that most Terran mammals look rather like rats, and that primitive Ethiopians can turn into loud Israelis in four years, we look to the stars for our equals who aren't our conspecifics. A projection, perhaps?

If the dilemma my female fish faced—whether to make a family with the nice willing fish or the tough but less willing one—is not unfamiliar to human women looking for mates but is a problem that independently evolved in birds, cichlids, and mammals, then *are* we going to find real language-using aliens who are intelligent but not like us?

Perhaps intelligence rose to identify problems more specifically. The dwarf gourami who learns to spit out of the tank when hungry may display only a shaped behavior, but the African butterfly fish has no alternate feeding strategies to chose from. Then individuality has the evolutional niche of countering intelligence in other individuals. If the ratchet converges even in different forms, we might end up arguing over Bach with tentacled Ph.D.s

On to the ultimate question: What if self-awareness is hard-wired and containable in the cerebral difference between the butterfly fish and the biparental care cichlid, with my poor gourami spitting to get food whether I'm in the room or not somewhere between the two? If that's true, and if someday we find a way to constantly replicate brain cells, to have some sort of physical immortality of the body, will "I" be myself after the relevant cells turn into the next generation of the self-consciousness generator?

In the science fiction story, the female asks lots of questions. It's the function of the hysterical decorative one to need definition and limits on the individuality. Leggings and a mustache.

We of the genus that includes humans and chimpanzees turn whole groups of conspecifics into artificial individuals, troop against troop. Our enemies are fry predators—baby killers—and must be slaughtered, not just dominated as loser conspecifics. Humans seem to be the only one who further turn conspecifics into aliens: the Cherokees, the Yanomamo, the primitive cultures that must be preserved as though they were endangered species. Otherwise, why do they seem to have lost their culture when they operate computers? Did we turn into an extension of Chinese culture when we borrowed the spinning wheel, the magnetic compass, and the horse collar? (Perhaps this is the real secret of Western culture—it is really the convergence of Oriental and North African.)

Sometimes we turn ourselves into the aliens, wearing primitive clothes and wire-rimmed glasses, MBAs growing ginseng and playing dulcimers.

I asked my woman biologist friend if dog DNA configured into human DNA would be human or dog. She said, "You wouldn't start with dog DNA, you'd use nucleotides, and of course it would be human." If nucleotides weren't quite an exact map of the human genome . . . Can you patent artificially configured DNA in a human pattern?

(But some humans are subhuman killers who play kickball with our babies' heads or rip them out of their incubators, and we demand an unconditional surrender.)

If it's got the human structure in its genes, my biologist friend who's a woman says it's human. But then there are these tricky legal definitions, these metaphors, those eighteenth-century fractions of a real man. We need something to remind us that humanity, too, is a limiting construct, a metaphor.

Conservatives who believe that human nature never changes read Shakespeare as a guide to the way things should be. *I* read Shakespeare because his people, to me, are alien humans, not incomprehensible, but . . .

Technology makes the human as well as vice versa, for a woman whose odds of dying in childbirth are better than fifty-fifty doesn't have the same interest in independence that a woman with her own car and birth control prescription might have.

I said to my woman biologist friend, re a quarrel, "The only woman who was as vehement as the men grows chin hairs." Me, I aliened myself so we could laugh a bit easier.

She laughed. "So do I."

We depilate our upper lips and thin our brows to draw an artificial line between male and female. The aliens are on the outside of our operating metaphors for who we are. We want our identity to be independent of the body acquiring information and the terribly fragile relationship between brain and environment.

But no.